IDLE
Sins of the Fathers
Book 4

ARELL RIVERS

IDLE

Book 4 in the **SINS OF THE FATHERS** series

ARELL RIVERS

Editing:

Theresa Leigh, Velvetfire Press

Trenda Lundin, www.facebook.com/ItsYourStoryContentEditing

Nancy Smay, www.evidentink.com

Proofreading:

Angel Nyx, www.facebook.com/ProfreadingBayouQueen

Roxanne Blouin

Cover design:

Dar Albert, Wicked Smart Designs, www.wickedsmartdesigns.com

Blurb:

Jennifer, Romance Rehab, www.RomanceRehab.com

 Created with Vellum

"To be idle is a short road to death and to be diligent is a way of life; foolish people are idle, wise people are diligent." ~ *Dwight Goddard, translating a Buddhist quote*

Paige

I wave at the hostess and breeze into the restaurant. Theo told me we were meeting at our "usual spot," so I pass through the main dining room and make my way into the back section that's set up to look like an old railway car. Sliding the pocket door open, I slip into the room and am shocked to realize I'm the first one to arrive.

Pulling out my cell, I double-check the time. Should've stayed home and played today's Wordle, since I'm a full five minutes early. I tap my finger on my bottom lip, then drop my phone onto the table and wander around the room. The fake pull-down beds are a nice touch, although the oversized handles are way out of proportion.

Perhaps if I'm seated, a server will stop by and bring a bread-basket or something? I grab the back of an overstuffed chair and sit facing the doorway so I can see when someone enters.

Several people pass by, but no sign of my brother and his fiancée, or Xander and his. They foisted this meeting on me, telling me their friend needs help I'm perfectly suited to give, and now they're late? Even though they couched it as I was doing them a favor, I think it's more they want *me* to become what they consider to be a "contributing member of society." I huff. I'm happy with my life, thank you very much.

A tall guy with sandy brown hair stops outside the door. He has a perfect Roman nose and is wearing a suit, beneath which I can tell he's well built but not with the oversized bulkiness from a gym. He pulls out his phone and checks it, looks at the sign on the wall, and then directly at me. Bless everything holy. This man has the most unusually colored eyes I've ever gotten lost in. I'm drawn to explore their khaki depths when his gaze drops to the phone again, and his hand slides the door open.

I straighten my spine, deciding to remain in my seat, although I don the practiced smile that reels in most men. He enters the room, his head at a tilt. "Paige?"

He knows my name? *Who is this specimen? He looks like a man who knows how to make a girl sing. And by "girl," I mean me. And I don't mean sing either.* I rise. "Yes." He should be at my side in three, two—

The mystery man inclines his head to the right. "We're meeting your family in the next room over."

I can't help it. Everything inside me flags. Why does this god have to be the dolt my brother and "cousin" want me to meet about a stupid Renovation TV show? More importantly, strike one for his not crossing the room to me.

"Oh." With dragging feet, I follow him out of our "usual spot" and into a larger space. At least this guy has a nice ass. I stifle a snort. Jerk didn't even have the manners to allow me to enter the room first. Strike two.

Theo jumps up. "Paige! Jesse! I see you've met."

"Yeah, she was sitting next door. Thanks for texting me her picture—that's how I knew who she was."

Kudos to my wonderful brother. *Not.* He comes over and gives me an embrace as if we hadn't seen each other in weeks rather than a couple of days. But he's a good guy. He's let me crash at his place when I reach my limit with Mum and Father. Not to mention he filled out my college applications for me when I was otherwise occupied with my high school friends. I relent and return his big hug. But I do whisper in his ear, "Should've given me the correct room."

He squeezes me. "Sorry, Little Bit."

Dumb nickname. Although, truth be told, I do like to graze. A little bit of this, a little bit of that . . . I step back and stare into his chocolate brown eyes, slightly darker than mine. "Forgiven. Mostly."

Hugs are shared all around. Amelia, Theo's fiancée, and Madison, Xander's fiancée, are super sweet, even though they share a baffling hard-nosed work ethic. Xander, my oldest "cousin" is the final person to approach me. Given our ten-year age difference, we've never been too close, but recent events with our fathers have brought us together. His dad and Father are best friends who started VOW³ Media ages ago, plus Xander's uncle Ward. Since the FBI arrested all three of them at the Tinsel and Tatas Gala last winter, we've all been riding a hellish rollercoaster. Despite the circumstances, I've enjoyed getting to know my cousin.

Who messes up my pixie cut. "How are things going, Little Bit?"

I fix my hair and cross my arms, pretending to be annoyed at his use of my brother's nickname for me. "Why can't the family drop that pet name?" I skewer Theo with my gaze. "It's all your fault."

He throws his head back and laughs. I'm still jarred by how open and happy he is, thanks to Amelia's influence. "You're stuck with it, I'm afraid."

"Dare I ask?" Jesse wades into the conversation. I'd almost forgotten he was here. I glance over to him. *Almost.*

"No." I respond, causing the two dummies to chuckle.

Madison enters the breach. "Why don't we all take our seats? Paige, you're here," she points to one chair. "And Jesse, you can sit next to her."

Oh joy. At least he can help me into my seat. Not a chance in hell my brother or cousin would. I walk over to the spot Madison indicated and stand behind the chair. Jesse walks around me and pulls his own back and sits. *Seriously?* He failed the easiest items on my checklist in record time. Well, it's not really a checklist, but that's what my "cousin" Chloe—one of Uncle Ward's daughters—dubbed my preconditions for someone to achieve boyfriend status with me, and I never bothered to rename her term. Besides, I'm not here looking for a date anyway.

With a huff, I pull my chair out and plop into it. If memory serves, *he* is the one my family wants me to help—hence today's meeting. Good luck with that.

Unaware of my internal ire, Xander starts the conversation. "Madison and I got a text from Jesse, which led us to set up this dinner. Jesse's looking for an interior designer to join forces with him for a new Renovation TV competition show. Since you already flipped a house in Brooklyn and have been looking for a fresh project, we automatically thought of you, Paige."

As I expected, they want me to get a job—like them. I don't need my brother and cousin meddling in my life. I'm an independent twenty-three-year-old. *Who lives with her parents.* Jesse drops his napkin on the floor and leans over to pick it up. My eyes roll. How much fun would it be to spend any amount of time with this good-looking Neanderthal anyway? Zero.

Back upright, Jesse takes a sip of his water. "Yes, that's true Xander." He looks around the table, his gaze finally landing on me. "I saw a post on their website that they're casting a brand new show to take place right here on the High Line. The pay's solid." His long index finger taps his glass. "Apparently, they've purchased an apartment building in need of renovation, which is what the show will feature. The teams—five of them—will be housed in an apartment there, which the network's already fixed up, like a lot of reality shows do."

Can this get any less enticing? This guy's actually suggesting that I move into some rinky-dink apartment on the *West Side* to live and work with him and a bunch of other strangers? Not my jam.

"It sounds very exciting to me," Madison chimes in. "I know you've been looking for a new place to flip for a while now, Paige. This opportunity is right up your alley." Her blue eyes pierce my soul. For some reason, out of everyone, Xander's fiancée has always unnerved me most. Maybe because she's so skilled at reading people.

I lick my lips. "Well, I—" I reach for my water goblet.

Jesse dives in. "Of course, simply agreeing to apply with me doesn't mean we'll be selected for the show. They have an interview process outlined on the website, which includes a request for photos of your work."

Is this a challenge? "I do have plenty of pictures of the house I flipped." I rub my hands on my napkin.

"And I can help you put together a great package," Madison oh-so helpfully adds. She started a PR firm about five years ago, at which Xander's been named partner.

"They'd be crazy not to accept you. A banker," Amelia points to Jesse. *He's a banker? What is he doing trying to get on a renovation show?* Amelia's finger moves to me. "And a Hansen. The other contestants don't stand a chance."

I better put an end to this farce. "I'm not sure I want to be on television. I mean, with everything going on with our fathers . . ."

"That's the reason you have to apply," Xander jumps into the pregnant pause. "We need to clean up our name, and this would be great press." Madison turns her head, her scar catching my attention for a fleeting moment, and places her hand on Xander's arm.

Xander's comment stops me cold. Could I save the family? What a novel concept. The server enters with our drinks and the first course. I'm sure Theo placed our drink orders—the only variable the restaurant allows—when he made the reservation. It pays to be members here.

Jesse picks up his fork. "I didn't order this, but it looks fantastic." Theo fills him in about the benefits of membership.

As I nibble on my kale and pear salad, Madison asks Jesse, "How are things going at Handmade by JD?"

Next to me, Jesse's Adam's apple bobs with his swallow. Damn. Why does such a jerk have such a masculine movement? I sigh into my napkin. "Good. I love working with my hands—"

Although he keeps on talking, now I'm focused on his hands. Which seem to be larger than normal. His fingers are long and tapered to perfection. I'm awash in thinking about how they could strum my body, if only he were a gentleman and not such a caveman. Maybe he'd be the first . . .

Spearing a kale leaf, I tune back into the conversation. "So it's time for me to make a decision." Not interested in his life story, or even continuing with the farce of a TV show, I keep my head down and finish my plate. The guys talk sports while the women dive headfirst into wedding planning.

"And Halle said we need to choose a band once we get the location set," Amelia says.

When the two seem stumped, I hop in. "Have you thought about reaching out to TLR? I met their drummer, Dwight, at a club a few months ago, and he was cool."

"I don't think I want a big name playing at our wedding," Madison replies.

"Agreed," Amelia replies.

Shrugging, I sip the remnants of my Mexican mule, the tequila giving me the strength to suffer through the rest of this meal. Halle, Xander's sister, is only one year older than me, but you'd think she was closer to twenty years my senior. That girl's had it going on ever since we were playing on the swings in Central Park. She's always been "in charge." If you needed someone to write your term paper, she could whip out a list of about ten people to choose from—and take her cut before turning over the name. No wonder she's grown up to be a high-powered wedding planner who has celebrities and musicians on her roster.

The main entrées are served—pasta primavera with spicy rice balls. This place never disappoints. While the others talk amongst themselves, Jesse leans over and murmurs, "Tell me the truth. Does trying out for the show interest you at all?"

My eyebrow raises. Seems Cro Magnon Boy is more astute than I gave him credit for. I give Theo and Xander a quick glance, but they're too involved with their meals, and their fiancées, to pay attention to us.

Still bristling over my brother and cousin's interference plus Jesse's lack of manners, I'm about to tell him to pound sand when what Xander said makes a forceful reappearance. I've always been the one the family saves—the reverse could be interesting. Although overwhelming. "I'm not sure."

"What would change your mind?"

He stares at me, the amber ring encircling his khaki-colored eyes giving me pause. "I need to think about this. I mean, with Father's notoriety, I'm not sure if I'd be a positive or a negative to your application. I certainly don't want to be the person everyone loves to hate on the show."

"I see your point. How about considering this as an opportunity to turn the tide for the Hansen and Turner names? You could show the world you're not your fathers."

How can such an unmannered man be so insightful? Last week when Chloe and I talked, she was in a tizzy over her lack of interviews. She's the only student in her graduating class who hasn't scored at least one interview, and we both believe it's because of the status of VOW-cubed.

Might I be able to change this? Seems an uphill battle. "I'll think about it. When do you need my decision?"

He twirls the pasta around his fork. "Can you let me know, either way, by the end of the week?"

Three days. Reasonable enough. "Yeah."

"Good." His hand lands on his tulip-shaped pint glass filled with Guinness. "And please consider saying yes. You're my last hope, and I need this exposure."

No pressure at all. I trace my finger over the lip of the copper mug. "Friday."

He wipes his hands on his napkin. "I think you'll enjoy the experience if we're selected for the show. Both Xander and Theo talk highly of your skills with your house flip."

Now he's laying it on way too thick. Sure, both of them came to see the house once I had finished it about eighteen months ago. But they didn't come during construction, nor did they sit with me while I argued with myself for two hours about the size of the towel racks. Forget about the days spent trying to decide on the right tile for the kitchen backsplash. This Renovation TV show will only highlight how pretty everything looks at the end of the day. How about figuring out how to re-route the electrical or deciding on what pattern to use for the window coverings?

"I'll get back to you."

Jesse pulls out his phone. "Let's exchange numbers. This way we won't have to keep involving your brother or Xander any further."

Makes sense if I were inclined to do the show with him. I doubt I will but recite my contact info anyway, after which I drop my fork. This entire dinner has taken far too much out of me.

"Who's up for dessert?" At Madison's cheery question, I sink back into my seat. When will this meal end?

2

Jesse

Dinner finished about thirty minutes ago, and I continue to chat with my business school buddy, Xander, and his cousin, Theo, while the ladies huddle on the other side of the room. Xander and I became fast friends during our first year in biz school, and he's always been supportive of my ideas. Although I've helped him too. A certain evening with too much bourbon comes to mind, causing me to suppress a grin.

I nudge him in the ribs. "How's the Madison Welch PR Agency treating you, Xander?"

"Great. Did you see we were named a 'mover and shaker' by *NY Magazine*?"

"I think someone sent me the article." I laugh. "Make that two someones." Both he and his fiancée texted me the link the second it came out. And I don't blame them—they've been working hard for this accolade.

Xander's eyes stray across the room, then swing back to me. "So tell me, what are you going to say to the bank when you and Paige are selected for the show?"

I love his positivity, although his cousin's been giving standoffish vibes all night. Even if she agrees to apply with me, it doesn't mean we'll be chosen. She would be an excellent addition to the cast, however, given her name and . . . looks. She's the tomboy ultimate fantasy. I can picture her poster now, with her wearing a toolbelt and nothing else. I gulp. *I'm talking with her brother and cousin.* "Not sure. Taping will take about six weeks, so I'll have to ask for a leave of absence, I guess."

Theo asks, "How much vacation time do you get? Can't you use that up?"

"I only get four weeks."

He snaps his fingers. "What about a FMLA leave? To provide aid to your elderly mother who needs hip replacement and you're her only option?"

I shake my head at his creativity. "I can tell you're an author." I raise my index finger. "My mother isn't elderly, and she'd have your hide if she heard you talking like that." A second finger is added to the mix. "If such a thing were to happen, I'm pretty sure Homer would be the one helping her. He is married to her, after all."

It's close, but Theo manages to swallow his drink. "Homer?"

"And Marge." I started calling my parents by these names after Diana—

Theo shakes my hand. "You win. That's a lot better than 'Mum' and 'Father' like I use."

"Or boring Mom and Dad like me," Xander remarks.

Once our chuckles die down, I say, "I guess if the network picks us—if we even apply—then I'll figure out what I'm going to say to the bank." I pray I also won't have to deal with a promotion my boss's hinted about as well.

They murmur their agreement. "I bet Paige'll agree. I hope so, anyway. She needs some direction, and this sounds like a great opportunity." Theo puts his massive paw on my shoulder. "But remember, Little Bit is my sister. My *little* sister."

Seems all grown up to me.

On my opposite side, Xander's hand clamps onto my other shoulder. "And she's my cousin. No monkey business with her, got it?"

I raise my hands, dislodging theirs from my person. "No fly

zone. Message received." I can't help but allow my gaze to slip across the room, where I drink in the forbidden fruit.

My musings are interrupted when texts ping on everyone's cell except mine. One by one, they check their phones. Then the cursing begins.

"Shit."

"Damn."

"Oh crap."

"Shoot."

"Fuck."

I look around the room wondering what happened for a full minute before Xander catches my puzzled expression. "The VOW-cubed partners' motion to dismiss was denied."

I process his statement. "Which means the case is proceeding?" All heads bob. "Well, that sucks."

Theo and Xander exchange glances. Their fiancées approach and give them hugs. From across the room, Paige announces, "I better get home to deal with the fall out." The rest of her family murmurs their agreement.

She walks to her chair to retrieve her purse and I intercept her. Despite this bad news, I need to reinforce the deadline. If she turns me down like all the rest, I'll never raise my woodworking from hobby to business—and be stuck living out Diana's life forever. "Please let me know your decision by Friday, okay?"

Her distracted reply doesn't give me much hope. "Yeah. Sure."

They all leave, and I collapse into a chair. Given Paige's lack-luster response, my chances of applying to the network seem to be sinking faster than the S&P 500 in a bear market. I haven't found the guts to tell my parents I want to leave banking and become a carpenter. My Etsy shop has gained some traction, but the proceeds from a few orders a week won't pay the rent in New York City. I'll come clean to them if she agrees.

Or if we're selected for the show.

A pretty server comes into the room carrying a tray. "Oh, I have dessert. Will the rest of your party be returning?"

"No. There was a family emergency."

She gives me a once over. "I have six strawberry shortcakes here. What should I do with them?"

She's not asking about dessert. Standing, I raise my hands as if in surrender. "Sorry. Please send them back to the kitchen and I'll take care of the check." At least my job allows for me to pay such unexpected expenses without any problem. A fact Homer touts.

A disappointed expression crosses her features. "The Hansens and Turners are members here, so no check. Are you sure I can't interest you in even some whipped cream?" She picks up a spoon and drags it through a dessert.

With everything going on, a hook up isn't on my radar tonight. "Thanks, but I should be leaving."

My entire walk home is consumed with worries. What if Paige says no? Is there anyone left I haven't asked? How about if Paige agrees, but Renovation TV turns us down? Where will I be?

Right back at the bank.

My shoulders droop as I trudge the remaining five blocks to my apartment. I pass the nondescript doors on the outside and stop at the row of mailboxes and retrieve my mail. All junk, except for a letter thanking me for my latest donation to Mothers Against Drunk Driving. I take their letter with me as I ride the elevator to the tenth floor, wipe my feet on my welcome mat that says, "Sawdust is Man Glitter," and open my door.

I toss the letter into a file to be dealt with by my accountant and enter the bedroom to change out of my business suit. Now in a pair of worn jeans and a long-sleeved T-shirt, I return to the living room, stop in front of the bookcase, and pick up the framed photo of my family. It was taken fourteen years ago—half a lifetime ago. I trace my sister's beaming face, recalling we took this the day she was accepted into Fordham. Good times. I consider calling my parents but I'm not ready to get into this with them until it's real.

Only one person outside of my NYC circle knows about my desire to work with my hands. He'll give me valuable advice, considering he's never let me down before.

Picking up my phone, I call my high school woodshop teacher. "Jesse, how are you doing? How's the big city treating you?"

"It's good, Mr. Hooper." Even though he's asked me to use his first name, Marcus, I can't bring myself to do it. He's given up trying.

"And Handmade by JD? I checked your website, and you added another side table. Looks great."

"Thank you. I wasn't sure about the drawers but decided to go with one versus two. Thought if I divided them, it would be too shallow to be of use."

"Smart thinking." He coughs.

He can't get sick. "Everything okay over there? Do I need to take you to a doctor?"

"No. This will pass. A gift from Covid."

He coughs a few more times, and I make a mental note to reach out to him again in a week to ensure the cough's gone. "If you say so."

Clearing his throat, he asks, "What brought on this call? Fancy any design tips?"

I wish. "Nah, I'm good on that front. I heard about a new remodeling competition show on TV and I've asked everyone I know to apply with me, but they turned me down. Just met with my last possibility. She said she'll get back to me by the end of the week."

"She'll come through for you, have no fear. Your work deserves to be out in the world."

His positivity is what I needed. "I hope you're right."

"Without a doubt. It's always darkest before the dawn."

Gotta love his clichés. "So you say."

"Keep your chin up."

We hang up. I send a prayer out to the universe that Mr. Hooper was right, and Paige will agree to be my partner. And, of course, that Renovation TV will pick our application. Which Madison and Xander will prepare for us, so it'll be kickass. *We'll be picked*. No other way around it.

By the hearth, my whittling paraphernalia calls out to me. Instead of designing a new bedframe to go with the side table, I choose a more relaxing pastime. One Mr. Hooper taught me back in high school. Picking up a block of wood and my knife, I decide to create a swan in homage to Paige, whose long neck reminded me of one.

Not to mention her easy smile, pert nose, and seductive eyes. Xander and Theo didn't say I couldn't look. No matter. Homer's drilled into my very being that career comes before pleasure.

I place my knife on the wood, all the while my mind lingering on the gorgeous tomboy who holds my future in her hands.

She'll say yes. *She has to*.

3

Paige

As I wait for the elevator to bring me up to the apartment, my gut churns. I bet Mum and Father will need a mediator following the judge's ruling. The cab's door opens and I'm greeted with the sound of glass breaking, accompanied by yelling. Things progressed faster than I imagined.

Straightening my shoulders, I enter the solarium and take in the scene. Shards adorn the floor in three different places. My parents stand across the room from each other, arms crossed, faces red. Both of their heads turn toward me.

"Paige," Mum yells. "Did you hear the news?"

Seems like a safe question to answer. "I did." My eyes stray to Father. "Got it over a Google Alert. Why didn't you text me?" His fist slams down on the desk. *Shit*. He probably took my question as an accusation. I rush to add, "Not that you had to reach out to tell me."

"So happy to hear I didn't need your permission," he sneers.

"Don't use that tone of voice on our daughter."

Great. Mum's jumped into the brouhaha I caused. Better try to smooth this over. "The judge denied your motion to dismiss, so what happens next?" Wish I knew more about the law. Well, not really.

The thought of going to law school makes my stomach revolt—way too much work. "Do you have to give a deposition?"

"I'm sure I will at some point."

"You should volunteer," Mum interjects. "Go first. Everyone knows that the first person to give evidence wins."

"This isn't a game, Ivy. There's a lot more to it than Jeeves in the kitchen with a candlestick."

His reference to one of my favorite games, Clue, would put a smile on my face under usual circumstances, but this is anything but normal. Mom picks up another vase, which I try to divert her from throwing. "Well, this will give you more chances to prove to the government how wrong they are. I don't know what they're looking for, but all you have to do is show them you're on the up and up, and the case will go away."

Mum lowers the vase to the table. One crisis averted.

Father replies, "Oh, to be that naïve. We did that in the motion to dismiss. The judge denied it, and his order made clear he's on the government's side. It doesn't matter what we say, he's going to rule for the prosecution. And if they find out about—" His lips clamp shut.

Mum raises the vase again. "Find out what, Ogden?"

"Fuck. Maybe I should turn myself in. That way I won't be subjected to this type of inquisition all the time. Prison might be preferable."

The vase hurls through the air.

Closing my eyes, I back out of the solarium. I'm of no use here. I slink into my bedroom and shut the door. Lock it for good measure.

Planting my ass onto my bed, I try to ignore the screaming coming from down the hall. Punctuated with more glass breaking. Things have never reached this level.

Turning on my speakers, I drown them out with some TLR. My brother and cousin may not want them to play at their double wedding, but that doesn't mean I can't enjoy their music. I hum along with "Let Me Give You A Sweet." When Trent Washington-

Hunte stops singing, I turn the speakers down and am rewarded with silence.

Blissful quiet.

Now that I can think again, I want to talk about what happened today with someone who would understand. Who wasn't in attendance at the luncheon. Picking up my cell and a lollipop, I Face-Time Chloe.

She picks up, looking more bedraggled than me. Guess it's bad on her end, too. "Hey, I'd ask how you're doing, but your face says it all."

"Yeah." She plucks at her sorority shirt. "Daddy went off the deep end when the motion to dismiss was denied."

Her father, "Uncle" Ward, is business partners at VOW-cubed with Father and Uncle Vince, Xander's dad. "So did mine. He and Mum were going at it when I got here. I tried to smooth things over, but only managed to make them worse."

She rubs her nose. "Daddy didn't yell or anything, but I could tell he was freaking out on the inside."

Which is better? I'm not sure.

She continues "What can we do to help? Law school takes three years, and their case will be long over by then. I wish I could think of something." She plucks her shirt again. "Can't even get an interview, but I want to be useful."

Here my cousin is trying to get her life in order and find a job, only to be stymied by her last name. Wanting to try to help, I say, "I'm sure Uncle Ward wouldn't want you to throw your life away trying to help him. He's hired the best attorneys. They'll all be free soon." I hope.

"From your mouth." She slurps something through a straw, probably her ubiquitous root beer. That girl must have it running through her veins. "I find it weird, though, that their motion to dismiss was denied. I thought this was all a big mistake, but now I'm wondering whether Mommy's been right about Daddy all along."

If this is true, our fathers are up to their necks in illegal activities and will spend many years in jail. I don't want that for our families, no matter how uncaring our fathers have been. To be fair, Chloe's dad treats her more like a sibling, an equal. Much nicer than how Father rules our family, IMHO. "Since we don't know the answer, let's move on, shall we?"

More slurping. "Sounds good. So, still no job interviews for me and graduation's a week away." She sighs.

"I feel you." I gesticulate with my lollipop stick. "Have you considered applying under a pseudonym? That might work."

"Yeah, but if I get the job, I'd have to come clean with all the paperwork. I know this because my degree *is* in human resources."

I stand and walk over to the window, moving the curtain aside. All the lights in Central Park are aglow, making it look magical. "How about getting a quickie marriage so you'll have a different last name? You must know some guy who could help you out." I allow the gauzy curtain to flutter into place.

She giggles. "Now this is an idea I haven't considered."

I snap my fingers. "Now that your problem's solved, how about helping me fix mine?" She covers her mouth to hide her ongoing giggles, and I continue, "I hate it in this house. Mum and Father are one half step away from coming to blows. When I came home today, at least three different vases were broken on the floor. They've been screaming about the motion to dismiss being denied. It was awful."

"That sucks." She brings her straw to her mouth and takes another sip. "Why don't you stay with Theo until this dies down?"

"I was at his and Amelia's last week. Honestly, I'd rather take my chances around here than have to be around those two for more than a night. Love my big brother and all, but a single gal can only take so much, am I right?"

"Oh, I hear you. The last thing on my mind is finding someone to date."

"Amen, sister." Jesse's offer replays in my mind, so I decide to share it with Chloe. Before I speak, I take another suck on my lollipop. "A weird offer landed in my lap today, though, that could take me out of the apartment for like six weeks."

"Oh? Do tell!"

"Theo and Xander's friend wants to apply to be on a new Renovation TV show. It's one of those home remodeling competition shows."

"I love them. It's so cool seeing how the designers come up with completely different ideas for the same spaces."

I pace around my bedroom. "I guess it could be cool." I sigh. "Their friend needs an interior designer for the team. I don't know. I'm not really a designer. I'm a house flipper."

"Too bad the show isn't about flipping."

"Right? I'd be all over that."

"Still, did you say this show would take you out of your house for six whole weeks? No parents, and no engaged couples?"

I take another lick of my lollipop, then point toward the door. "That's true. It would provide me a safe haven for over a month and a half. But if we're kicked off sooner, I'd lose the sanctuary."

"There's a simple answer. Don't lose." She punctuates her statement by putting her lips around the straw.

Her idea does have some merit. I could solve my housing problem for a few blessed weeks of quiet. "I don't know."

"Think about it. I'd like for one of us to be gainfully employed." She shakes her hand, and the sound of ice cubes banging on the inside of her cup comes through the screen. "Do I know this friend?"

I picture the gorgeous *banker* with the amazing eyes. Plus a bod I'm sure he knows how to handle in all the right ways. "No. I only met him tonight." *Neanderthal.*

Her mouth flies open. "Wait a minute. Him?"

"He went to business school with Xander and now fancies himself a carpenter."

"A carpenter, huh? Bet he's good with his hands."

I pull my best imitation of Halle trying to corral a bridezilla. "He has to be like thirty. Ancient." At least seven years older than me.

She waves her hand, the mug swirling in the air. "That's nothing. My guess is he ticks all the boxes off your famed checklist."

"Your name, not mine." She winks at me, to which I return with a frown. While he is sort of hot, he failed the easiest three items within minutes. Nope. Totally not boyfriend material.

She takes another sip. "Well, I've gone through all my soda, so this is my cue to hang up. Consider what I've said. This show could be your temporary way out of the hell you're living through."

I nod. "You make a good point." I sit on the bed. "You should consider a fake marriage, too. A new—legal—last name could take you far."

Chloe runs her fingers through her hair. "I don't know. I think I'd rather be you than me. At least your solution involves you getting national exposure on television for a good reason rather than what we're getting now."

I force my lips upward. "We'll make it through this. We always do."

After we hang up, I flop onto my back. Should I take Jesse up on his offer? Putting Chloe's comments about how skilled his hands are aside—*not that I ever considered the same*—it would get me out of this awful house for a while. I flinch when another glass breaks.

Maybe this isn't such a bad idea after all.

4

Paige

I rip the top sheet off my desk calendar. Friday. The day I promised I'd let Jesse know if I'm willing to be his partner.

I've spent the better part of the past couple of days trying to make up my mind. From a housing perspective, it makes total sense for me to do this. Yet I'm still unsure. Seems to me the show will entail lots of hard work, which is the only four-letter word I abhor.

The intercom rings. Because Luna left about ten minutes ago to run to the store, I've been put on door duty. Lucky me. Leaving the kitchen, I answer the buzzer and am told Father's lawyer is here. Allowing him up, I go into the solarium and tell Father.

"Andrew Laughlin is coming up."

Father straightens to his full height and strides to the foyer. With nothing else to do, I trail in his wake. When the elevator door dings, a distinguished grey-haired man with a briefcase steps out of the cab. We all shake hands, then Father ushers us into the living room.

The attorney looks from Father to me then opens his briefcase. "Normally, I wouldn't share any information with anyone but you, Ogden, but I'll make an exception in this case. Especially since it involves Paige as well."

My chest tightens. Why would Father's legal troubles involve me?

With those ominous words, we sit down. Mr. Laughlin opens his briefcase on his lap and holds out a stapled document to Father. "I'm sorry to be the bearer of bad news, but the government has made a motion to freeze all of the assets owned by the partners of VOW-cubed."

Father jumps to his feet and rips the papers out of his attorney's hand. "You have to be fucking kidding me. How could you have let this happen?" His growl ricochets off every corner of the living room. No, the entire apartment.

Why did the lawyer want me here? I sink back into the cushions, trying to make myself invisible.

"Now what?" Mum appears from the bedroom wing. Rising, Mr. Laughlin repeats his statement and Mum snatches the papers from Father. "What does this mean?" With every word, her tone gets higher and higher. I remain transfixed, wondering the same exact thing.

"Let's all calm down so we can discuss this." Mr. Laughlin motions toward the multiple seating options.

Instead of following his lawyer's advice, Father grabs the paperwork out of Mum's hands and stalks over to the windows. I'm positive he doesn't see Central Park.

Mr. Laughlin purses his lips, but then sits after Mum takes her chair. "This means," he begins, making eye contact with Mum and then me.

Again, *why me?*

"It means the government is seeking to freeze the combined assets of you and your two partners as possibly tainted. They're claiming everything was received as proceeds of a crime. You would no longer be able to access your business equipment, vehicles, rental properties, business or personal bank accounts, investment accounts—"

When he gets to the part about our personal bank accounts, Father spins on his heel. "Stop them." With measured steps, he approaches the attorney and I push deeper into the cushion, thankful for not having chosen the leather sectional. "File an objection. Do whatever it is you *do*, but make this stop."

The attorney licks his lips. "I understand, Ogden. The office is already drafting one. We'll definitely ask to keep access to this home, one vehicle, and a certain portion of your accounts."

For the first time since Mr. Laughlin got here, I inhale a full breath. This will be okay.

Father's expression takes on a calculating air, one I've seen many times in the past when he's crafting a new idea. "This objection better outperform your motion to dismiss," his growl is lower and more menacing than before.

Without reacting to his client's tone, Mr. Laughlin nods. "I have a couple more things I need to tell you about the prosecution's motion. They've also sought to freeze your home, inheritances, and assets owned by your spouses."

As he's been ticking off the items, Mum's red face turns purple. She jumps out of her chair. "Excuse me. 'Assets owned by your spouse'?" She points to herself. "Me?"

While Mum carries on, I focus on the item he said prior to that. *Inheritances*. Does this mean our trust funds? I'm still two years away from getting mine, Chloe and Gabrielle are three. Hell, even Halle still has a year to go, as does my older brother Ryder.

Wading into a gap in the heated conversation, I lean forward. "My trust fund?"

The grey-haired gentleman turns sad eyes toward me. "I'm afraid so."

I exhale and fall into the cushions. While not much, I was banking on my million dollars to be a safety net. Now it might be gone. As will *everything*, thanks to whatever Father and my uncles have been up to. *Allegedly*. I clamp my mouth closed.

"We're going to fight this motion with all we have," Mr. Laughlin says. "At the moment, I suggest you sit tight and make a list of any assets the government cannot claim as being 'tainted.'" He focuses on Mum. "Like anything you might have brought into the marriage, Ivy."

For me, the list is short. Everything I have is because of Father, even the proceeds from my one and only house flip, since he both found and funded the original purchase. However, at my eldest brother's insistence, I did set up a separate limited liability company and ran all monies through it. I explain this to the attorney.

"Because you paid your father back for his loan from the proceeds of your flip, this business account should be excluded from this request. Good job, Paige."

I nod. A fraction of the tension his arrival brought seeps from my bones. I keep my thoughts to myself, as my parents appear as if they're on the verge of starting another world war. Against whom, I'm not sure.

Reading the room, the attorney says he'll be in touch and walks to the elevator. After the doors close, I rail, "Great job, Father. Now the whole family gets to lose out right along with you."

"What an ungrateful brat you are," he snarls. "I think it's rich that the only one of my children still living at home is complaining about possibly losing her trust fund. Guess I would too if I had no ability to live on my own."

His words cut deep. I leap to my feet and, without saying another word, I speed walk to my bedroom. Flinging the door shut, I bang my hip against it. And again. And once more.

Father's a jerk. An egomaniac. An asshole.

My body stills. *How am I going to survive without my trust fund?*

Four of us already passed twenty-five and got their money. They have to share with the remaining five. They just have to. It's not my fault I was born later in the lineup. If I received mine and others didn't, I would give them part of my trust fund. Assuming I still had some left from the paltry amount, that is. A million doesn't go far nowadays.

Let me see . . . my brother Theo received his three years ago and bought his apartment. Even with his new career as an author, he's presumably house poor. Xander's the same with a much nicer apartment and only recently becoming partner with Madison at their PR firm.

My eldest brother, Dr. Kiefer, is probably the only one of us who has cash, considering he's a plastic surgeon. But he got out of med school and started his practice last year, creating his client base from friends of our parents'. No. He won't be able to help me either.

The only other person to have received his trust fund is Xander's younger brother Sebastian, otherwise known as Chef Bash. He's made a name for himself apart from the family on the YouTube world. He must have the capacity to lend me a few bucks.

I'm reaching for my phone to get my request in when I remember the twins, Halle, and Ryder all won't receive their trust funds either. I'm pretty sure Sebastian can't float all of us money. My empty hand falls to my side.

This sucks. Fucking Father.

What am I going to do?

Peeling myself off the door, I cross the room. "Alexa, turn on the television." I sink onto the upholstered bench at the end of my bed and wonder whether Alexa soon will be a thing of the past. Not to mention a TV.

For some reason, the last channel I was on was NewsTime, as that's what pops up. My former Aunt Yvette, Uncle Ward's ex-wife, is being interviewed. I open my mouth to change the station but slam it shut when she utters, "I'm going to host a blowout gradua-tion party for my twins since their father's under indictment and his assets are being frozen. As are those of his scumbag partners."

So much is wrong with her statement, but my focus lands on my "cousins," her kids, Chloe and Gabrielle. My vision flashes and it's all I can do to stop myself from screaming. This cannot be happening!

I. Need. Out.

Jesse's offer reemerges from the dustbin of my brain. It doesn't matter that he's a Neanderthal, he *is* offering me the opportunity to flee the nest. Away from my bullheaded Father. Not to mention my bitchy Mum. Plus, didn't he point out something like the cast would be paid?

I can do this. Hell, I am a twenty-three-year-old woman and already have flipped a house. Without further contemplation, I pick up my phone and text Jesse, relieved we exchanged contact information.

Meet me in an hour at Vinnie's Place on Seventieth and Fifth.

Without waiting a beat, I press send. Bouncing my cell against my thigh, I await his reply. He'll say yes. He has to—he needs me. As expected, his response is in the affirmative.

I'll prove to Father I don't need him or his dumb money.

Grabbing a lightweight sweater out of my oversized walk-in closet, complete with an island and a window, I swing open my bedroom door and proceed with singular focus toward the front door. Rather, the elevator.

"Where do you think you're going?"

Mum's question attempts to stop my feet from moving, but fails. After pressing the call button, I cross my arms over my chest and face my parents. "Out."

My one-word response is not well received, judging from my parents' sour expressions. Tough. This is my life.

"Young lady, you live in our house, so we deserve to know where you are going." Father's voice booms.

Chloe was right. I have literally no other choice but to accept Jesse's offer, no matter how repugnant. "I'm meeting someone." Thankfully, the elevator pings and the cab opens. I don't spare a glance backward as I step inside and jam the button for the lobby. Repeatedly.

On the descent, the impact of my hasty actions sinks in. While I'm not excited to spend time with Jesse and his barbaric ways, they're preferable to sharing a roof with my parents even one more night. I raise my chin. I will get through this like I always have—with my head held high. Success will follow.

Instead of calling our vehicle concierge, I choose to walk to the restaurant. About five blocks in, I realize my folly. Despite their good looks, my shoes were not built for walking. With a sigh, I pull out my cell phone and call Jimmy. Our vehicle concierge answers on the second ring, as usual, and tells me my car will be here in five minutes.

"Thanks, Jimmy. I really appreciate it."

While I return my phone to my purse, I consider whether Jimmy will be out of a job soon, considering he maintains and keeps tabs on our cars and drivers. This sucks. I've never really thought about all the people on our payroll before, but now it seems like the list is growing. We have our maid Luna, Jimmy and the drivers, and all of the caretakers for our various houses. I'm sure there are many more I'm forgetting. For the millionth time, I wonder what Father and my uncles have been doing all these years.

A limo pulls up. The driver tips his cap toward me before exiting the vehicle and opening the door. Sliding in, I offer a quick thanks then relax against the black leather interior. This vehicle is equipped with a full bar, TV, and can seat up to ten people. How much longer will this be at my beck and call?

Needing to shut down the crazy tumult of my thoughts, I instruct Google to turn on my "happy" playlist and groove to the upbeat tunes. Soon, we pull up to Vinnie's. "Here you are, Miss Paige."

Sliding out of the limo, I do an impulsive thing and kiss the driver on his cheek. "Thanks." Without lingering, I cross the sidewalk and enter the darkened space.

At the hostess stand, Shelby greets me. "Hi there, Paige. Great to see you."

I force a smile I don't feel—I'm the "bubbly one" according to media reports. "You too. Do you have my table available?"

Shelby consults her book, her nose ring moving on a wince. She looks up at me, "Sorry. Both of your tables are taken tonight. But we do have a nice spot for two in the corner."

Seems like everything is falling apart today. I hide my grimace. "I scheduled this meeting last minute, so I'll take it. Thanks."

I follow her to the sad little table shoved into the corner and pretend it's my new favorite place in the entire restaurant. *Which it might be, if the government has its way.* With this grim reminder of the reason for agreeing to meet with Jesse, I choose the seat facing the doorway so I will be prepared when he arrives. Checking my cell, I realize I'm two minutes early. *Better stop making a habit of this.*

At the top of the hour, a sandy brown head enters the restaurant. Jesse interacts with Shelby, then turns in my direction. *I won't be swayed by those consuming khaki eyes.*

Sporting a knowing smile, Shelby leads Jesse toward me. If only she knew his exterior may say "sexy man," but his interior is all nerdy cave dweller. "Your date is here, Paige."

I shoot her a dirty look—to which she licks her lips—then transfer my gaze to Jesse. "Take a seat."

"Thanks."

After Shelby gives Jesse another once over, she leaves. Oblivious, his overly large hand lands on the back of the chair and pulls it backward, allowing his well-proportioned butt to sit across from me.

Shunting my wayward thoughts aside, I decide to play nice. "I know this was short notice."

"I hope you have some good news to tell me." He picks up the napkin and places it onto his lap, pretending to have some manners. I remember our lunch from the other day and know the truth.

Mirroring his action, I lift the fork and remove my own napkin, rubbing my suddenly clammy hands against it before dropping it to my lap. "Well, I do still have some questions."

"I understand. Shoot."

To buy time, I play with the stem of my water goblet. "What do you know about this new television show? It's a competition, correct?"

"Yes, it is a competition program where every team is going to be given the same exact room in similar apartments to renovate. The judges then come in and judge each room, with the loser being eliminated."

Our server pours the sparkling water I ordered prior to Jesse's arrival and asks for our drink orders. He leaves to get my Mexican mule and Jesse's Guinness while I process the theme of the show. "I've never seen a show set in an apartment building rather than individual homes before."

"Me neither. They'll have all of New York City to show off in addition to the remodeling. I don't know, they may request that we purchase items only available here, like something from a special design store on the Upper East."

A couple of my favorite shops flit into my mind. "Guess it depends on who pays the advertising money."

His fingers fiddle with the silverware on the table. I try to ignore how masculine they are. "It's always about money." His face contorts, as does mine, but I'm sure we have very different reasons.

Our drinks are dropped off and we place our orders, both of us choosing items off the appetizer menu. Something the restaurant can do fast, which will allow us to get out of here quicker than picking tile for a backsplash. No point in prolonging this agony.

A table filled with women take their seats next to us, each one of them ogling my date. Date? No Neanderthals need apply. Possible business partner. *Get your head on straight, Paige.*

Swallowing my first taste of the refreshing mule, I ask, "Can you please explain more about what would be required of us during this competition?"

"As best I understand, we will be given directions about how to complete a room in the most general sort of terms. It will be up to us to decide how we want to move forward. I'm not sure if there will be extra carpenters at our disposal or available props like paint and furniture. The website doesn't say." He ends his description with a swig of beer.

"Essentially what you're saying is I'll come up with a design idea and you'll execute the items inside it like furniture, a fireplace mantel, shelving, that sort of thing. I will be responsible for the overall look and feel of the room. Do I have that right?"

"I think so." He lifts his beer. "Although, I would expect to have some input into design as well."

This arrangement is along the lines of what I did when I flipped the house in Brooklyn. Then I was able to access professional interior designers and got their feedback on my designs. No matter what, my flip was successful, so I'm sure I can deal with this little competition. I fiddle with the handle of my drink.

"How many other people did you ask to be your partner before you landed on me?"

His sexy eyes—which are taking on a greener hue from the walls that are a shade of evergreen—meet and hold mine. *I wonder what secrets they hide?* After indulging in a prolonged sip of his Guinness, he replies, "I did ask around. It's a tough sell, given that it's a busy time of year. I, myself, am trying to figure out how to make this work with my job if, in fact, we are selected by Renovation TV."

That's one worry I don't have. Score one for the unemployed! Remembering our meeting today with Mr. Laughlin, my joy is short lived. Deciding to deflect attention, I ask, "You work for a bank, right?"

"Yes." he sits taller. "It's a respectable job, a reliable one," he shrugs. "I'm hoping this television show will give exposure to my company—Handmade by JD—and allow me to explore working in carpentry, but banking is a solid career."

"Never said it wasn't." His vehement defense of working at a bank gives me pause. What is he hiding?

Our appetizers are brought to the table, and I dig into the stuffed mushroom caps. I get these every time I come to Vinnie's, as the crab and crème fraîche add a level of sophistication to an otherwise pedestrian dish. For his part, Jesse picks up one of his ten ribs and dunks it into the barbeque sauce.

The women at the next table all stare at him eating with his hands. When he sucks his thumb into his mouth, they giggle. Scowling at them, I point my fork at him. "You should use your knife."

His eyebrows reach his hairline. "Too hard with the bones. They're delicious. Want a bite?"

Not really, especially as he's holding out an entire rib. *Barbarian.* But maybe I should, to show those women he doesn't match his wrapping.

Perhaps it's the devil on my shoulder, or the green-eyed monster lurking behind me, but I lean forward, open my mouth, and bite into the rib he's offering. Ripping the meat off the bone, I pull away and chew the succulent morsel. Sauce dribbling down my cheek leaves a wet trail that causes me to retrieve my napkin and wipe. Only when I glance at Jesse do I realize he's returning his napkin to his own lap. I bet the women across the way are swooning at such a perceived intimate gesture.

Swallowing the rib meat, I admit, "That's delish."

He holds his appetizer in front of me again. "Want another bite?"

Yes. Shaking my head, I reply—more for my sanity than any other reason, "No. I'm good." I spear one of my mushroom caps and hold it up. "Want to try mine?"

His perfect nose scrunches. "Not a big mushroom fan. Enjoy."

Stop flirting. I focus on cleaning my little plate, mulling over the question of whether I want to be on this show. It fulfills my number one priority of getting out of the house. I shift in my seat.

I follow his tongue as he licks his fingers. "I can try to answer any of your questions."

The fact he's able to read my mind does weird things to my stomach. And not because of the new food I put into it. "Do you have any photos of your work that I can check out? A website maybe?"

He nods. "Sure do. Thanks to your soon-to-be cousin-in-law, Madison." Grinning, he produces his phone and taps on the screen, then passes it over to me.

Not knowing what to expect, I look down at the website and my breath stutters. His work is beautiful. With a capital B. He offers inventive tables, chairs, bookcases, and even a bed. But not any old tables and chairs and bookcases and beds, no. These are works of art, with flourishes and special cuts that make them pop. I swipe through his site.

"Your work is fantastic." The words are out of my mouth before I can censor them.

"Thanks. I'm proud of my pieces." He chuckles. "Not bad for a banker, right?"

"Certainly not." I can't imagine him stuck behind a desk doing whatever he does in banking when he's this talented.

"Okay. Your turn. Can I see some photos of the house you flipped?"

After seeing all his furniture, my singular flip seems . . . paltry. My chin juts upward. My house did sell for a profit—my only nest egg now, if the government wins its motion. "Sure thing." I pull up the photo gallery and pass him my cell, fiddling with my silverware while he swipes through the pictures.

He returns my phone. "You did a gorgeous job. I love the backsplash you picked for the kitchen, and the creative use of space in the small powder room. I never would have thought of that."

I sit taller. The powder room was my crowning achievement. Wanting to elevate his work, I reply, "It's nothing like creating bookshelves from pieces of wood."

"Each complements the other. Can you imagine a bookcase without anything on it? No, carpentry and interior design truly do go together."

His goal is to find a partner to win this television show, while I'm only looking to relocate. Goal? I've never had a need for one. "I don't know about this, Jesse. I'm not sure we'd make a good team."

His head tilts to the side. "What do you mean? I think our skills would work well together."

How can I explain this? Instead of answering him, I ask my own question. "How long have you been doing carpentry? Not as a business, but as a hobby."

"I got hooked during a class in high school. My professional life has been spent in banking, though." His arm reaches forward, and his palm lands, upright, on the table. "I think we would make a good team."

I stare at his open hand, knowing he wants me to take it. Giggles from across the way confirm that any one of them would be delighted to be in my position. *He's your ticket away from your parents.* Six weeks out of the house and possibly assist my brother's friend realize his dream.

Screwing my eyes shut, I allow my hand to fall on top of his. His warm palm tightens around mine, giving me a sense of security and belonging I've never felt. Shocked at the depth of the touch, I pull away and grab my napkin.

His eyes widen. Without saying another word, he takes his own napkin and wipes his hands.

Let the games begin.

5

Jesse

Dimitri stops by my cubicle. "Hey, do you have a moment to talk?"

Coming from my boss, this is a rhetorical question. "Of course."

We enter the conference room where Dimitri offers me a chair, then perches on the table beside me. "We've been talking, and we really like your performance in compliance, Jesse."

Who's this "we"? "Thanks."

Dimitri's leg swings. "We've also been reviewing the organizational chart, and decided to make a few changes to the department."

Oh crap. Please don't let this be about the rumored promotion. I clasp my hands.

Unaware of my agitation, Dimitri continues, "We would like you to lead a new team in handling ultra-high net worth clients as our newest executive director." His broad smile communicates I should be excited about this opportunity he's laying at my feet.

It's been a week since I submitted the application that Madison and Xander created for Paige and me, and haven't heard anything. The Renovation TV website says decisions are being made shortly, whatever that means. How long can I hold Dimitri off?

I place my forearm on the table. "This sounds very exciting, Dimitri. What's your time frame?"

"We're thinking it'll take about sixty days to get this project underway." His eyes gleam at me, so I force my expression to exude positivity.

At least he didn't say next week. The way things move around here, two months might as well be six, or even a year. I can fend him off for the length of time it takes to shoot the Renovation TV show, assuming we're selected. *God, I hope we're selected.*

"I'm flattered to be thought of for this new position."

"To be honest"—Dimitri leans in as if conspiring with me— "This has been in the works for a long time. It's been hard keeping this a secret, and we're excited to begin the project. Your name was the only one we considered."

Wonderful. "I don't know what to say."

For a brief moment, I allow myself to wonder what my sister Diana would feel about this promotion. My job, the bank, was supposed to be her wheelhouse. No need to wonder what Homer would think, however. As the chief compliance officer at a rival bank, I'm under no illusions as to his take.

Not knowing what to do next, I extend my hand and we shake. The time-honored way of showing appreciation within the business community. Standing, I retrace my steps to my cubicle.

With no expectations, I open my personal email for the third time today and almost miss the message. *Holy shit!* My pulse gallops. I close my eyes for a brief moment, then click on the email. And hold my breath.

Dear Mr. Dimon and Miss Hansen,

Thank you so much for applying to be on NYC Views. Over one thousand applications were made for the five spots we have available.

My heart stutters, and my limbs feel as if they've gained fifty pounds. I tried. *We* tried. Even Madison and Xander's best work couldn't pull this off. Guess I'm looking forward to a promotion at the bank.

I'm about to close the email when the words, "We are excited," catch my attention. What are they excited about? I return to the email:

After considerable discussion and review of all the applications, we are excited to extend an offer to you to be in the cast. We believe your skills, positivity, and the chemistry between the two of you in your demo will capture the minds and hearts of our viewing audience.

If you are still interested in being on NYC Views, please reply to this email and we will give you information about the show as well as our taping schedule. We really hope you accept our offer and await your response.

Yours sincerely,
Quinn Walker, director

I reread the email several times, confirming our application was accepted. When I'm convinced it was, I pick up my phone and call the only person who still has the power to end this. On the third ring, she answers.

"Paige. We got in!"

"What? Is this Jesse?"

In a flurry of words, I reply, "Yes. It's me. Jesse. I got an email from Renovation TV and we're in. They want us for *NYC Views*!" I forward the message to her. Not able to contain my excitement any longer, I cross the office toward the exit sign.

"Are you serious?" Her voice betrays no sign of enthusiasm. *Yet.*

"Deadly. I just forwarded you the email from a Quinn Walker."

"Let me check." As I leave the building, she mumbles, "Got the email—you're right."

"I know!" On the sidewalk, the smile I've been restraining all day emerges. It's the one Dimitri would have preferred to have received from me, but it's reserved for this amazing opportunity. For what feels like the first time in my life, *my* dream is coming true.

"Have you responded to Quinn yet?"

Even though Paige can't see me, I shake my head. "No. I wanted to check in with you first." I take a few steps. "You're still in, right?"

She sighs. "You have no idea. Tell this Quinn person we accept."

"With pleasure."

After we hang up, I click on the email icon and type our reply. After pressing "send," a sense of lightness overtakes over my body. This is my make or break moment. My big chance to get out of banking to do what I love.

I stop in front of the iconic St. Patrick's Basilica. This Neo-Gothic church with twin spires always takes my breath away. I allow myself a minute to duck inside where I'm once again captivated by the soaring ceilings and gorgeous stained-glass windows. Despite it being a Tuesday, several groups of tourists—interspersed with parishioners praying—sit in the simply made pews. While I'm not a particularly religious man, ever since Diana was taken too soon, I accept the solace these hallowed walls provide.

I walk around the altar, taking in the ornate carvings and soaring pipes for the organ surrounding me. It's in these quiet moments I sense Diana's presence as if she were walking next to me, grabbing my hand like she used to when we were kids. This sensation calms me. I channel her upbeat positivity while pondering how to tell my parents about this opportunity.

A notification of an incoming email dings, so I slide into an empty pew and pull out my cell. It's from Quinn. She's excited we accepted and asks that we report next Monday to a New York City apartment—providing an address. I close my eyes. This is all happening so fast, yet I've waited my entire life for this moment.

After leaving a twenty in the donation box, I return to the bustling outside world where people race along the sidewalks and cars honk. I have two unsavory tasks ahead, but waiting won't make either better. I text Homer:

Can I swing by tonight?

While awaiting his response, I walk back to the bank and stand outside Dimitri's office. I force myself to rap on the doorframe and he waves me in. On legs as weak as a stripped screw, I enter the room and do a controlled slide into his guest chair. Managing to swallow after three attempts, I begin, "I want to reiterate how humbled I am by the bank's confidence in me." I rub my clammy palms on my thighs.

"We really like your work ethic, and how you get along with your colleagues. You do a great job here."

His kind words are not making this any easier. But I have to do this. *For me.* "I appreciate that. However," my hands move to rubbing together instead of on my legs. "After our meeting, I received a different opportunity that I would like to pursue. It's a very short gig outside of the banking industry. I'd need to take a leave of absence for a maximum of six weeks starting next Monday. Once it's over, I have every intention of returning back here." *Unless I win.* "I don't know how this affects my promotion."

Pushing away from his desk, he wears a frown that rivals a trader's when the market tanks. "This 'different opportunity,'"—his fingers frame an air quote motion—"truly has nothing to do with the bank?"

My palm goes across my heart. "I swear."

He rests his forearms on the desk and leans forward. "What will you be doing?"

Knowing he'll find out sooner or later, I suck in oxygen and reply, "I was selected to be on a Renovation TV show."

His face first registers shock, followed by his cheeks puffing as he tries to hold back laughter. "Is this something your girlfriend put you up to?"

Many things are wrong with his assumption. First, I don't have a girlfriend. Second, this is my dream, no matter how crazy it might seem. Third, I practically had to beg everyone I could think of to be my partner on the show. A vision of Paige flits through my mind, with her adorable pixie hairstyle, lanky frame, and her light chocolatey brown eyes that remind me of creamy milk chocolate. Sexy tomboy.

I close my eyelids for a moment and the image disappears. "No, this was my idea." He doesn't need to know about my furniture business, or my decade-plus long love affair with carpentry.

He rolls a pen on his desk. "Will you be behind the camera, or in front of it?"

I cross my arms across my chest. "I'm going to participate in a competition-type show."

His eyes narrow. "Do you have any say over your wardrobe? If so, you can wear some of the bank's logoed shirts, use our mugs and pens." He tosses me his pen, which I catch. "Free advertising never hurts."

Leave it to my boss to figure out a way to benefit himself. Rather, his employer. *Our employer.* Who knows how this will turn out? "I'll see what I can do."

"I'll have to discuss this with the higher-ups, but if you're able to worm our name onto the show, I think the bank will be more than agreeable."

I stand, realizing this is my best chance to exit. "Thanks. We'll keep each other posted, right?"

His response is a salute.

Returning to my cubby, I shoot off an email to Quinn asking about wardrobe issues, then set about getting my tasks in order for someone else to take over. As I'm working on a transition memo, she replies that the wardrobe and props departments have final say over everything that ends up on screen, but they would consult with me. I forward her message to Dimitri as a show of good faith. If my dream comes true, I'll never return here working for him.

One down, one more to go. While I'm packing up for the day, Homer texts me back to meet them at their favorite Italian restaurant for dinner. Instead of returning home, I trek across town and slip into the booth. At least we're in a public space, so they can't make too big of a scene.

As expected, Homer's more than thrilled with my promotion. The chief compliance officer in him practically crows at my being named executive director at only twenty-eight. I dip my focaccia into the olive oil but leave it on my plate. "I do have one other opportunity I need to share with you."

"This is an evening for great news!" Marge tips her red wine glass toward me.

Here goes nothing. "I also was chosen for a new television program on Renovation TV. It's a competition-type show where the contestants renovate an apartment on the High Line."

Marge uses her fork to point. "Here? This High Line?"

"Yes."

Silence. No one moves, eats, swallows.

I sit up. "I already told the bank I need leave of absence." I pause. "They agreed so long as I can promote their logoed products."

Homer's knife clatters onto the floor. "They agreed?"

"Yes."

"Then get this blue collar whim out of your system. When you come back, you'll be ready to assume your promotion at the bank where you belong."

The server brings him a new utensil. While not a ringing endorsement, it's as good as I expected. Our conversation turns toward their upcoming trip to Washington, D.C., where Homer's speaking at a banking conference.

———

The time from our acceptance to the show's pre-taping flies by. At seven in the morning, I place another bank T-shirt into my luggage. With one final check around my apartment, I lock up and get into the waiting town car that will bring me to the High Line building and the start of what I hope to be my new life.

As per the instructions, I enter the main lobby and wheel my suitcase to the lounge area beside the reception desk. Four other people sit on the art deco sofas fidgeting with their cell phones. Donning a smile, I address the group, "Hi everyone. I'm Jesse Dimon. Are you all here for *NYC Views*?"

Four heads nod. A girl with shocking pink hair says, "I'm Marion," She hooks her finger toward the diminutive woman sitting next to her. "This is my sister, Peyton." She offers a shy wave.

Next to them, a good-looking guy dressed in perfectly pressed linen pants says, "I'm Robbie. This here is my boyfriend, Frank." I shake all four hands.

Choosing a spot on an empty loveseat, I add, "My partner's Paige, an interior designer—she should be here soon. We live here in New York. How about you guys?"

Frank replies, "We're in Miami. Robbie's a fantastic interior designer, and I can hold my own with a miter saw."

Marion chews on her gum for a minute, then adds, "We're originally from Oklahoma, but escaped to LA the first chance we got and started our house-flipping business. We don't have set roles for it, though. We both do it all."

Impressive. "Cool."

Another couple approaches our group, holding hands. "Hi! Can you believe the day has finally come? We're so excited!" Our murmurs of assent do not match this woman's level of enthusiasm, but this fact doesn't put this chirpy woman off. "I'm Nancy, and this is my boyfriend Dan. Has anyone from Renovation TV been here?"

Robbie answers for all of us. "Not yet."

"I'm sure someone will be by here soon. Probably that Quinn person. Did you all get emails from her?"

I can tell this chatty woman is going to drive me bonkers, so I pull out my cell and pretend to have received a text. Which I should have by now. From Paige. *Where the hell is she?* As if on cue, Paige's message arrives to tell me she's fifteen minutes away. Fifteen more minutes of Nancy? Oh joy.

I focus on the men in the group. Robbie and Frank appear as enthralled—using the term loosely—as I am with the newest arrivals. The sisters are engaging her, and my guess is the boyfriend Dan has no choice but to be part of that conversation. I direct my next comment to the two men. "I've never been to Miami before. What's it like?"

Robbie rubs the top of his bald head. "For starters, it's nothing like here. We have sun almost all the time, and music plays in the streets more often than not."

Frank joins in. "The vibe here is different, but good. You know?"

I consider his statement. "It's alive in its own unique way, for sure."

Robbie snaps his fingers. "Alive. Perfect descriptor of New York City."

My attention is drawn to a new couple walking through the doors. She has long blonde hair and is dressed to the nines, her clothes draped perfectly over her shapely body. He, on the other hand, carries a Stetson and wears ripped jeans, a wife beater, and cowboy boots on his feet. But for their matching Tumi luggage, I wouldn't believe they were together.

Her southern drawl is like a caress. "Are y'all with the show?"

I force myself to remain in my seat, although all I want to do is hop up and offer it to her. "Yes. We're waiting for someone from the network to show up." Plus my truant partner.

I'm rewarded with a wide smile from the bombshell. "Thank you." She approaches and points to the empty spot next to me. "Is this seat available?"

Interesting she didn't stay with her Tumi twin. Considering Xander and Theo made it very clear to me that Paige was off-limits, I welcome this new beauty. "Sure is."

She glances toward the cowboy and settles in next to me. For his part, the grubby cowboy sits in the empty loveseat opposite. Near chatty Nancy. I lean over to the blonde and extend my hand. "I'm Jesse."

She slides her palm over mine and shakes. No sparks fly like they did with Paige in Vinny's, but she's a no-fly zone. "Mary Ellen."

As she gets settled, I ask, "I'm from the New York, New Jersey area. How about you?"

"Dallas."

Not long ago, I spent a week there meeting with one of the bank branches. "I was there recently. Gorgeous town. Big."

She laughs, the sound pinging down my spine but not in a good way. More akin to horses neighing. Well, I guess everyone has their own flaws. "Yes, we do everything big." Her eyes bounce from my face to my crotch, and back up to my eyes.

Forward. And not hard on the eyes.

Across the way, her partner makes a big stink out of introducing himself. By the time "Bo" reaches me, I've learned he's the third-generation carpenter in his family and rides rodeo on the side. Yee haw.

When Bo approaches me, I stand and shake his hand. Dude is about my height, with dark brown hair rather than my lighter color.

"Nice to meet you, Jesse. Do you do carpentry or are you the interior designer of your group?" He looks around. "And who is your partner?"

Deciding to take his questions in order, I reply "I'm the carpenter. My partner is Paige, and she should be here in about five minutes."

"I reckon." He glances at his partner sitting next to me, then turns on his boot-covered heel, and returns to his seat.

I repeat his phrase—what the heck does that even mean?

Mary Ellen mutters, "Asshole."

"But he's your partner."

"Don't remind me."

All conversation ceases when the door opens again and the whirlwind known as Paige Hansen enters the building wheeling a matching set of Louis Vuitton luggage. Her brown eyes light up when she spots me, a smile dancing about her mouth for a brief second until she realizes I didn't save her a seat. She glances around the group, zeroing in on the only available space on the loveseat next to Bo. A pang of guilt bounces through my body. Paige is, after all, my partner for the show and I don't need to rile her up before action is even called. Too late now.

With a huff, Paige plops herself down by Bo. Narrowing her eyes at me, she deliberately turns her entire body toward the cowboy. "I'm Paige. Judging from your arms and"—she picks up his hand, running her slender fingers over his—"hands, I can tell you're the carpenter of your team," she purrs.

I roll my eyes at my partner and focus my attention on the lovely woman sitting to my right. "So, how did you get paired up with him?" I tilt my head across the room.

"We were married."

I cross my left ankle over my right knee, trying to hide my shock. "Oh. For how long?"

"Three years. Can you believe it?" She studies her ex and my partner, their heads tilting close to each other. "Other than amazing sex, we had nothing in common."

That's a vision I didn't need. Stomach churning at Paige and *Bo* chatting it up across the room, I force my gaze to the beauty next to me. "Honestly, you two seem very different."

She smiles, her face transforming into something breathtaking. Easy to see what Bo saw in her. "I'll take that as a compliment."

A woman with long, brown hair about the same shade as Paige's approaches our group. *Wonder what Paige would look like with long hair? Nah. She's perfect the way she is.* The new addition removes her sunglasses and holds up a sign. *Welcome to NYC Views!*

Everyone clamors to their feet and claps as she introduces herself as Quinn Walker, the director for the show. She will be with us every step from now until a winner is crowned. "I can tell you've already started to get to know each other. That's great. Why don't you grab your bags, and we'll go up to the apartment that you'll be calling home for the next five weeks, or as long as you're on *NYC Views*," she smiles.

Rolling wheels against the granite floor provide the soundtrack as we move to the elevator bank. I approach Paige. "Hey, sorry I wasn't able to save you a seat out there."

"No worries! I enjoyed getting to know Bo."

The way she says his name, as if he were some long-lost piece of art deco that will complete the entire room, makes me want to vomit. But I don't let my disgust show. I'm here to work my ass off, win this competition, and put the banking world behind me. Whoever Paige wants to spend her time with is of no concern to me. Xander and Theo pounded this into my brain.

Paige and I enter the same elevator cab and ride up to the twenty-fifth floor in silence. When the door opens, we're in the foyer of an apartment. I've heard of apartments where the elevator does this but have never experienced it before. It's disorienting.

I turn to Paige. "This is really swanky. I've always wanted an apartment where the elevator opens into it. Very cool."

Page shrugs. "It's like the set-up for my parents' apartment, only smaller."

My shoulders sag. Of course Ogden Hansen's family would live in such luxury. I mumble, "Bet their view is of Central Park too."

"It is."

My eyes slam shut as I absorb her flippant response. No, not flippant, rather matter of fact. *Remember our differences.*

We're spared having to talk further when Quinn grabs everyone's attention. Standing in the middle of the living room, she says, "Welcome to your new home! For the next six weeks, you all will live in what we've dubbed the ViewPad. We renovated this apartment specially for you, with some special upgrades."

She looks at each one of us as she continues. "Cameras and microphones are in every room except the bathrooms and patio. Please keep in mind your every move will be documented and could potentially be used during an episode of *NYC Views*. Don't let this overwhelm you or prevent you from having normal conversations with your partner and others on the show, though. We want to provide our viewers with a complete picture of how each team operates, not only when they're working."

Way to start things off with a bang. I vow not to share anything I wouldn't want the whole world to know, because apparently, they might. Since Diana's death, I've become adept at keeping my lips shut.

Quinn continues, "This is the living room, and over there are the kitchen and dining room." She points toward the quartz and stainless steel renovated kitchen, complete with ten bar stools around a massive island with a waterfall edge. I presume the dining room is tucked behind. "Bring your luggage and follow me for the rest of your apartment tour. We'll start in the bedrooms."

We walk down a hallway where two doors parallel each other. "On this side"—Quinn points to the right—"is the women's dormitory, and that side is the men's. Go on in and check out your new digs. I'll be waiting right here once you've claimed your beds."

I follow Robbie and Frank into the men's bedroom, where three sets of bunk beds and six small dressers greet us. Robbie perks up. "I'm on the top."

"You know," Frank replies. "Why should anything be different just because we're going to be sleeping with four additional men?"

Their repartee makes us all laugh, and the ice is broken. We spend the next ten minutes claiming our bunks—I select a lower one in the corner farthest away from the window, in the hope that the city's noise won't be as jarring. Dan chooses the lower bunk across the way from me.

I'm opening a dresser drawer near my bed when Bo does a three-sixty in the center of the room. "Who's going to get lucky and have me sleep on top of them?" His southern twang makes his question seem that much more absurd.

Dan and I exchange glances and focus on unpacking our suitcases rather than responding to the annoying Bo. "Don't all volunteer at once."

Realizing he's not getting a response, he sighs and slaps his hands on his thighs. "Eeny, meeny, miney, mo. You win!"

Afraid to look, but knowing there's no excuse not to, I force my attention to the cowboy. Who's pointing at me. *Crap.*

Bo wheels his Tumi luggage over to me. "No other man can claim the privilege of having me sleep above them." He glances at Frank and Robbie. "No offense, guys."

"None taken," Robbie replies.

Bo claps. "There. It's settled. I'll try not to make too much noise for you, okay Daisy?"

At his use of such a pejorative nickname, I bring myself up to my full height. Eyes equal with the cowboy, I warn, "Name's Jesse. Use it."

Playing it off as if he was only joking, he shoves the back of my shoulder. "Lighten up there, Daisy. Only joshin' 'ya."

This guy is going to be a fucking pain in the ass. Knowing better than to engage with the jerk, I bend down and finish unpacking, trying to keep his sighs and grunts out of my Zen. I'm not here to make friends. I'm only here to win this competition and get my own show.

And prove to my parents that this is a solid career path, not some flight of fancy.

6

Paige

I look around the bedroom that's been assigned to the women of
NYC Views. The walls are painted a khaki color, which immediately brings Jesse's eyes to mind. Shaking my head to rid such
fanciful thoughts from my mind, I admire the design on the curtains
while taking in the three bunk beds set around the room. Bunk
beds? I've never slept in one of those, but it might be fun to be on
the top.

I roll my Louis Vuitton across the room and stop in front of a
bunk bed by the window. Placing my hand on the top bunk, I
announce, "I'll take this one."

The other women nod at me while scoping out their sleeping
arrangements. The sisters choose a bunk closest to the bathroom,
while Nancy goes to the bottom bunk of the beds across from me.
Which leaves the blonde that was chatting up Jesse in the lobby.

She's pretty, I guess, in a plasticky sort of way. Never cared for
the bottled shade she uses on her hair, but that's her choice.
Assuming she'll take the top bunk of Nancy's bed, I wheel one of
my bags to the dresser and unzip it.

"May I take this bottom bunk?" A breathy, southern drawl seeps
into my bones.

Dropping my bras back into the suitcase, I force my lips to tick upward and take my time turning toward the woman who asked me the question. I wave. "Knock yourself out."

"Bless your heart."

I pick up my favorite sexy black thong and mutter under my breath, "Bless this."

My new bunkmate wheels her luggage next to mine. "Paige, right?"

"That's me. And you're Maryanne?"

"Mary Ellen," she corrects me.

I snap my fingers. "Sorry. Mary. Ellen." Guess I better play nice. We are being taped, after all. "Where are you from? I can tell it's not from here." I offer a slight giggle.

She replies with a giggle of her own. Although it sounds more like a whinny. "No. I'm from Dallas."

Of course she is—she's Bo's partner. He is attractive in a sort of hay bale-y way. His arms sure are built, and I bet he has washboard abs to match. I wonder how these two came to be partners. Bet their brothers didn't set them up like Theo and Xander did to me. "You're here with Bo, correct? How did you two meet?" I pat myself on my back for asking such a delicate question.

She tosses her hair. "He's my ex."

Now that's a response I didn't expect. They're polar opposites to each other—she seems to be a demure Southern chick while he's more akin to a wild stallion.

I'm about to ask her another question, but Quinn appears in the doorway. "You'll have time to finish unpacking in a little while, but I'd like to meet up with everybody in the living room to finish giving you the tour and laying out what's expected of you over the next six weeks." As a group, we turn toward the door, but I resolve to learn more about this odd "ex situation" soon. Quinn adds, "Please bring your cell phones."

I pat my pocket to confirm I have my cell and stride away from my new sleeping quarters. *Away from my parents.* While Mary Sue—or whatever her name is—stops to get her phone, Nancy bumps my shoulder. "Can you believe we're here? Actually getting ready for a brand new show on Renovation TV? It's unbelievable to me! I keep asking Dan to pinch me, thinking that this can't be real. Isn't it so exciting?"

Seems pretty darn exciting to her. For me, it's a respite from the hell of my house. For that reason alone, I want to stay in this competition so I don't have to return there anytime soon. I give Nancy a brief nod. Taking my nonverbal reaction as encouragement to continue babbling, she does. Thankfully, it's a short walk to the living room.

Quinn takes charge of the group, showing us the rest of the apartment, which includes a half bath, an exercise room, and a game room. When we return to the living room, Quinn says, "Please take a seat next to your partner, and I'll go over the details of what to expect over the next six weeks."

The man I've been avoiding all day sits next to me on the long sofa. His dark washed jeans fit him to perfection, and his long-sleeved button down—rolled up to expose defined forearms—brings out the flecks of green in his eyes. *Not that I'm noticing any of that.* "Hey."

"Hi."

His tenor rumble conveys so much in a simple two-letter word. Happiness we're here, determination to win this competition, and a slight nervousness at what's to come. Why does he have to be so darn cute?

Bo and my bunkmate walk over to us, and he sits so our thighs brush. His light blue ripped jeans are in stark contrast to those of my partner's. He taps his shoulder against mine, passing me a bottle of fruit infused water. The flavor I told him in the lobby is my favorite. "Are you ready for this?"

I open the bottle and tip it to my lips. "Born ready."

Quinn starts talking, explaining what we should expect over the next six weeks, in terms of filming, wardrobe, makeup, and assignments. She tells us nothing is scripted, and not to hold back when we're interacting because of the cameras, as anything questionable surely will be edited out of the episode. With the ground rules set, she passes out keys.

"Now let's go visit the apartments you're going to be renovating as part of *NYC Views!*"

Jesse and I glance at each other, and a nervous thrill races through my body. I'm sure it's about the apartment. He leans over and whispers in my ear, "Shit just got real."

His puff of hot breath in my ear causes my skin to tingle. I give him a tight smile, while rubbing the affected area. Yes, Jesse is hot in an objective sort of way, but that's the extent of the boxes he checks for me. This is the third time I'm meeting the man, and he's yet to do anything on my checklist. Yet Bo's already given me infused water, and we only met an hour ago.

As a unit, we file out of the ViewPad, and each go to the ones indicated on our key chains. When we stand outside number 1626, I take a deep breath. Jesse inserts the key into the lock. "Ready for our castle?"

I square my shoulders. "As ready as I'll ever be."

The door swings open, and we're greeted with what can only be described as a disaster. He allows me to enter first, and we walk in on floors covered in a thin, worn, blue wall-to-wall carpet. A soot-laden red brick fireplace stands against one interior wall. Behind a dividing wall, I see a kitchen that's missing a couple of cabinet doors. Crossing the expanse of threadbare blue rug, I enter the kitchen where the island sports the same tops as the rest of the counters—Formica. Dragging my fingers over the top that's practically begging to be returned to the 1950s, I turn and am greeted with massive, floor-to-ceiling dirty windows running the length of the apartment, overlooking the Hudson River. Immediately, my mind pictures them, clean, letting in the brilliant sunshine and gorgeous views. No curtains or any sort of soft coverings needed.

"Quinn wasn't kidding when she said these are blank slates." Jesse bangs on the mantle. "But it's solid."

"And ugly."

"It's your job to make it beautiful. C'mon, let's check out the rest of this place."

I follow him to a door, which opens to a massive full bath. Total gut job. We move on to two bedrooms, followed by the primary suite. I suppose it can be called a primary suite, since a bathroom's attached, but I can't even imagine the obnoxious lime green tile ever being in style.

We return to the living room and stand next to the fireplace, facing the wall of windows. He rocks his right foot. "Well, shit."

Jesse's assessment is on point. "Yeah."

A knock on the door sounds, and I trudge across the room to answer it. Quinn walks in. "How are you liking your new digs?"

I lick my lips. "Is each apartment similar?"

"Oh, yes." She glances at her feet. "Some have different colored rugs and cabinets and such, but they're alike."

My heel scuffs across the shabby carpet—minus the "chic" part. "Joy."

Jesse comes up next to me and puts his arm around my shoulder, causing my head to whip to him. Ignoring my reaction, he says, "When do we get started?"

Quinn smiles. "Right now." Quinn opens her oversized floral Vera Bradley tote bag and hands us each a stapled document. "We start filming Monday, so I would use these days to plan what you intend to do for each room, in general terms."

She turns on her heel. "Oh, and before I go, please pull up one contact number on each of your phones."

I step away from my partner's weird embrace and retrieve my cell. They probably need an emergency contact, although I thought they already asked for them. Opening her tote again, she hands us each a phone.

"These will be yours during the shoot. You don't have to check, Wi-Fi is not enabled and photos cannot be sent out. My number has been pre-programmed, as have all the other contestants' numbers. Of course, when someone's eliminated from the show, their number will no longer be operational. There's space for you to enter one more number, but you won't be able to change it once you press 'Save,' so choose wisely. Oh, these numbers are for outbound calls only, not texts."

What the hell? Assuming these will be prop phones for the set, I choose Chloe's number and press "Save." I sneak a peek at Jesse, whose contact reads "Mr. Hooper, High School Teacher Extraordinaire." I wonder who that is.

When he finishes tapping his screen, Quinn says, "Great. Now turn off your personal phones and give them to me."

What does she want with them? Jesse shuts his down and hands it over like a good little boy, but I'm not such a rule follower. I hold my light blue case up. "Why do you need them?"

Quinn's gaze travels my full length, as if she's trying to see into my soul. Nah. I must be imagining things. She's probably trying to figure out if Jesse and I are together, considering she's eating him up with her eyes. "You're about to film a reality show, and we need to ensure you're not getting help from the outside world."

Makes sense, in a Draconian sort of way. Still. "As you probably know, there are things going on with my family, and I need to be able to keep in contact with them."

"We're aware. Don't worry. We'll be keeping tabs on what's happening with your dad and will tell you right away if something new breaks. Besides, I assume you programmed him into the new phone."

It's odd she focused on Father rather than VOW-cubed as a whole, but her response gives me comfort that I'll be kept up to date about the legal mess without actually having to do it myself. Besides, I did input Chloe's info. Not correcting her misguided idea I would've preprogrammed Father's number, I place my cell in her palm. Her fingers close around both phones for a minute, then she drops them into her tote. "Thank you. Now, I'll leave you to go over the paperwork and get to it. See you later."

Quinn leaves and takes all the air with her. My mind whirls—I'm adrift without my phone. My eyes flit to all the corners of the apartment. What on earth can be done to make this dump look habitable? Forget television-worthy.

Unflappable, Jesse flips through the papers. "Here's the schedule and a materials order list." He holds up the latter document. "I think we should take photos of each room and then go back to the

ViewPad, where we can at least sit on chairs, to strategize. We only have a week to get everything in order."

"I'm not sure a lifetime would be enough time to right this place."

Jesse focuses on me with a laser stare. "Hey. You rehabbed the house you flipped. Don't be put off by the exterior in here. The bones are fantastic." He tilts his head up. "Check out these high ceilings. What can you do to them to make them look even taller?"

I look up. Jesse's right, they're pretty high. How could I make them look even higher? A vaulted ceiling comes to mind, but such construction would be impossible in an apartment. However, we could put in some moldings.

I shift my weight between my feet. "I suppose we could make it look like it's a tray ceiling." I take a step backward and cross my arms across my chest.

Jesse claps. "What a brilliant idea. I could create squares out of molding and install them on the ceiling after painting it white. That definitely would give the illusion of depth and make the room feel cozy while expansive at the same time. Impressive."

His praise washes over me but I flick it away. He's only being nice. I'm his partner for the show, and he wants to have a good working relationship—and win. Besides, I never paint a ceiling white.

He rolls up the papers Quinn gave him and slaps them against his thigh. "Let's take those photos and get back to the ViewPad, where we can kick around our ideas in comfort."

"Sure thing."

I open the camera app on my new phone and take shots of the bedrooms and bathrooms while Jesse deals with the remainder of the apartment. Finished, I wonder whether anything new has broken about Father in the news, so I look for the internet browser app on the phone. But there isn't one.

Entering the so-called living room, I ask, "How do you get onto the internet with these phones?"

"Huh?" Jesse finishes scribbling something down on the papers and gives me his full attention. "Didn't Quinn say there's no Wi-Fi on them?"

Oh my God, she did. I let out an exhale. "You're right." Holding up my new *camera* with a couple of telephone numbers programmed into it, I ask, "Ready to head back? I don't want to spend any more time in this depressing place than I have to." This has been a long enough day for me.

He chuckles. "In six weeks, this place is going to be on everyone's bucket list of places to live. You're going to do an amazing job, I know it."

While living away from my parents' house. After the lock clicks shut, I wonder if I bit off more than I can chew.

Somehow sensing my wobbly self-confidence, he says, "You can do this. I have faith in you. This apartment is smaller than the house you flipped, so that has to count for something."

"Yeah, less area to hide mistakes."

"No, that's not what I meant." His fist connects with the underside of my chin, chucking me gently like a coach might do. "I bet things will be clearer once we brainstorm ideas."

Since the alternative is returning to my parents' place, I pull up my big girl panties. "You're right. We're going to make 1626 the apartment everyone wants."

"Exactly." I follow him back to the ViewPad and we stake out a workplace in the dining area, since the sofas were both claimed. We spend the next several hours trying to figure out how best to tackle the first makeover, which is the living room.

Yawning, I say, "I think we should give this a rest. Tomorrow's a new day."

Jesse pulls out his cell. "It's only six. Don't you want to keep going?"

As an answer, I stretch. "No. I want to eat dinner, watch some television, and get a good night's sleep. We can start fresh in the morning." The chair screeches as I pull away from the table.

Not caring whether my way-too-intense partner follows me, I walk into the kitchen, admiring the white cabinets, none of which are missing doors. Opening the fridge, I pull out a massive tray, check beneath the foil, and read the card aloud. "Lasagna."

"Sounds good," Bo responds.

I jump, not having heard him enter. The dimple on his right side beguiles me. I want the scoop about him and Mary Elise, so I force myself to read the directions. "It says we need to preheat the oven to three-fifty and bake this for thirty minutes."

"Got you covered." He heads over to the stove.

We work together, putting together a salad and some garlic bread to accompany our meal, all the while chatting about the crazy-ass state of the apartments. Others trickle into the kitchen, probably brought in by the smells of the warming lasagna. I set the huge island with placemats while Marion opens a couple of bottles of red wine the network generously provided. This is going to be great. A much-needed break from the infighting and drama of my parents' house.

When Bo takes the main dish out of the oven, everyone "oohs" and "ahs." That is, all but Jesse. Where is he? Feeling responsible for my partner—although I don't know why—I excuse myself and head to the living room where he relocated after I left.

"Hey, dinner's ready."

Placing what appears to be a piece of wood onto the living edge coffee table, he gets to his feet. "I'll return this to my room and be right there. Thanks."

Curious, I ask, "What were you doing?"

His ears turn pink. "Thinking. I find whittling helps me center my thoughts."

I try to check out what he was working on, but he shoves the wood behind his back. Whatever. "Make me a mermaid while you're thinking one of these times." I love mermaids.

He grimaces. "Don't ask for something easy, do you?" When I don't respond, he says, "We'll see," and disappears down the hall.

Having completed my mission, I return to the kitchen and pick up a plate next to Bo. "I thought I was going to have to send a search party out for you." His dimple softens his words.

"I wanted to be sure my partner knew dinner was ready."

"Very kind of you. I'm surprised your boyfriend didn't ask you to bring his grub to him, so he could keep working."

I pause in putting a large slice of the lasagna onto my plate. "Jesse? He's many things, but my boyfriend isn't one of them."

A full-blown, toothy smile takes over Bo's face. "This whole shebang just got a lot more interesting."

7

Jesse

After a delicious dinner, we pile into the living room and turn on the television. Not surprisingly, the channels are limited to the umbrella of stations related to Renovation TV. Nancy chooses a cooking competition show, and we settle in to watch. Instead of focusing on the TV, my attention strays to my partner. She's sitting on the floor, cross-legged, laughing with the rest of our competitors. Bo joins her on the floor.

She's my little sister. Thanks, Theo.

Not interested in either show—on the television or the floor—I duck out of the room. In the bedroom, I grab a pair of pajama bottoms and turn on the hot water for a shower. As the water runs down my body, I replay the day. Excitement has morphed into annoyance at the chatterbox, and something akin to dislike for my bunkmate—who is hitting on my off-limits partner. At least she had an interesting idea for a ceiling treatment. *Eyes on the prize.*

Ten minutes later, I towel off my wet head and slip into the bunk. Perhaps tomorrow will be better.

It isn't.

Neither is the rest of the week.

Paige and I discuss our plans for every room and submit our

requests to Quinn on the form she provided. Our preliminary designs are solid, but not extraordinary. We need to up our game if we're going to win this.

I'm sitting on the couch, whittling a car, when Paige plops down next to me. "Hey, so I've been meaning to ask you a question."

With my blood pounding through my body, I put my still unformed block of wood onto the coffee table and flip my knife between my hands. Given her expression, I'm pretty sure I'm not going to like whatever she's about to say. She better not want to quit. "What's up?"

She tucks her short hair behind her ear. "So, filming starts on Monday, right?"

"Yeah."

"Well, my cousins—they're actually twins, Chloe and Gabrielle —graduated from college last weekend. Since their father, Uncle Ward, is involved with the whole VOW-cubed mess, the family wasn't able to throw them a party like we've always done."

"I understand." Where is she going with this?

She rubs her arm. "I sort of invited my family over to 1626 for a little shindig to celebrate."

My eyebrows raise. "There's no furniture. No place for people to sit or anything."

She shrugs. "I know. I told them that, so people will bring folding chairs. I checked, and the fridge is working for drinks and stuff. Plus, someone with a real phone can put their music on a speaker."

She has thought of this from every angle. I can sympathize with wanting to celebrate her cousins' graduation, especially since she was here, thanks to me, and not able to attend the ceremony. "How many people are we talking here?"

"Not that many. Nine kids are in the family, but my brothers Kiefer and Ryder can't make it. When you add in Amelia and Madison, that's only nine guests. Plus whoever the twins invite. Oh, and the whole cast of *NYC Views*, of course."

"Of course." I repeat. Here I was thinking I'd be escaping them.

"What do you think?"

Isn't she a little late to be asking? "Haven't you already invited them?"

"Well, yeah. But I wanted to make sure I had your buy-in."

What harm can a simple graduation party do to the wreck that is the dismal apartment? I tap her shoulder with my fist. "When you put it like that, you make me feel special."

"You are special, Jesse."

She's buttering me up, but still those words coming out of her mouth sound dirty. *Mind out of the gutter.* "You're not going to think so when I give you my one condition." She tilts her head, so I continue, "On Sunday, 1626 has to be in the same condition as before the party started. The cameras can't pick up anything about the party. Got it?"

She nods. "Sure thing. Although I can't imagine how we could do anything to ruin the ambiance of the place." She laughs.

Because I agree, I join her. "You're probably right, but I don't want to see any wine or beer bottles strewn around."

She holds up three fingers. "You got it."

My partner leans over and kisses my cheek, then scampers away toward Bo. These are going to be the longest six weeks on record.

Music fills the air, together with the smell of beer and pizza. In the apartment, people bump into the other, celebrating the college graduation of two girls I've met for about five minutes total. If not for Xander, Madison, Theo, and Amelia, I would've bailed on this party hours ago.

At least the balcony is sturdy and provides a more comfortable setting than inside. After Amelia yawns for the third time, her fiancé takes pity on her. Kissing her hand, he addresses the rest of us. "I think we're going to congratulate the twins again and head home." He looks at me, a twinkle in his eyes. "Your new place has potential." His broad grin conveys his real thoughts about it.

"I think it's going to be amazing when Paige and I get through with it." I shake his hand and give Amelia a peck on the cheek.

Xander takes Madison's proffered cup. "We'll walk out with you guys."

I give my business school friends hugs. Madison whispers, "I have faith in you two. You're going to clean this place up and everyone will want to buy it." She motions toward the river. "With views like these, you're going to be on every real estate agent's short list."

"Let us know if we can be of any help." Xander slaps me on the back, then follows his fiancée into the living room to say their good-byes.

Alone on the balcony, I let my mind drift to how we can make this place spectacular. Ideas swirl to enhance the plans we submitted. A feature wall with millwork would boost the dead space near the door. My thoughts are interrupted when Nancy comes out onto the balcony.

I stifle a sigh. "Hi, Nancy. Enjoying the party?"

"Yes. Paige sure has some good-looking brothers. Not that they hold a candle to my Dan, of course, but neither one of them was hard on the eyes."

I don't bother to correct her about Xander's being Paige's pseudo-cousin. Not worth it. Since I have nothing to add to her observation, I ask, "Was Quinn right? Does your apartment look like this one?"

Nancy turns toward the living room. "Yeah. Ours is very similar only the bedrooms are on the opposite side of yours." She rubs her hands together. "I can't wait to start in on the living room Monday. My mind's swirling about how to make it pop." She bats her eyelashes. "I'm sure yours is as well."

Not about to spill any tea with her, I give her a noncommittal shrug. "We have some ideas, yes."

"Dan can't wait to dive in. He says—and I agree—the views are what's going to sell this place." I bring my beer to my lips. It's not Guinness, but the dark ale does the trick. Before I can swallow, Nancy continues. "We're planning on showcasing them from every angle. Don't you think that's the way to go? I mean, some nice architectural details inside exist, like the fireplace, but these views." She fans her face. "Am I right?"

In desperation, I drain the last of my beer. I don't want to share any ideas with my competition, nor am I enthused to be talking with her. Seems like her boyfriend isn't, either, considering she's out here alone.

Deciding to poke the bear, I ask, "Where's your partner in crime?" I pretend to peer into the apartment. "Haven't seen him lately."

She points toward the kitchen area. "Last I saw, he was in the kitchen chatting with Robbie and Frank. Or maybe the sisters. Definitely not that Bo, though." She leans toward me. "Don't you think he's kinda slick, in a cowboy sort of way?"

Alerts buzz from every corner of my being. Not only is Nancy a gossip, she's also judgmental. *Doesn't matter that I share her opinion of my bunkmate.* I flip my empty beer bottle so it points toward the patio floor—which needs to be resurfaced. "I think I'm going to join Dan in the kitchen. Need a refill."

Not waiting for her response, I simply plant one foot in front of the other and vacate her orbit. Inside the main area of the apartment, I'm put right back on high alert. Instead of dwindling, this party seems to be picking up steam. What I envisioned as about twenty or so people getting together has grown to fifty. People sit in folding chairs around the rooms, talking and clinking red plastic cups. Music blares from a speaker on the island. At least the cops won't be called, since no one's living in the building yet.

It's after one. Filming starts the day after tomorrow, and this place has to be clean. Or, as clean as it was before this party started.

Chloe and Gabrielle are surrounded by their friends and seem to be having a grand old time. They're great girls and deserve to enjoy themselves, but this party should be winding down. Paige needs to handle this.

I check around the public areas, but my partner's nowhere to be found. Maybe she's in the bathroom? I cross the room to the fireplace and rest my forearm against the mantle to wait.

Five minutes pass.

Five more.

Where is she?

Pushing away from the masonry, I walk down the hallway to the bedrooms—the only rooms I haven't checked. It doesn't take me long to locate my missing teammate. And she's with … Bo.

My stomach cramps. Seriously? How long have they been chatting it up? *They can't be hooking up, can they?* At least they're both still fully dressed. Except for his hat on the floor.

Memories of his ex-wife's description of their sex life comes to the fore—she's the only person to beg off tonight. So what? Paige can sleep with whomever she wants, so long as it doesn't affect our chance to win. My jaw throbs, causing me to unclench my teeth. *She's off limits.*

The duo stands at the oversized window, gesticulating with their Solo cups. Paige brings hers to her mouth, laughing while her teeth close around the plastic lip. Bo's free hand reaches out and strokes her arm, moving up and down.

Ready to knock his hand away from her person, I charge into the bedroom. Four eyes register my appearance. With a smirk, Bo's hand covers Paige's and he tries to interlace their fingers but she steps forward, effectively thwarting his overture.

Somewhat mollified, I address Paige. "It's getting late. You should let people know it's last call. Cleaning up in here's not going to be fun."

Bo pulls out his phone. "Dude. It's only one. Chill."

If he wants this party to move to his apartment, he's free to do so. Since it's being held under *my* roof, he has no right to give his hillbilly opinion. "The graduates have had several hours to party with their family and friends." My eyes skewer Bo. "Plus our television castmates." I turn to Paige. "The place has to be back in the condition it was before it started, and the longer the party drags on, the harder this chore is going to be."

"One more hour can't hurt anything." Paige tucks her hair behind her ear, a tic I've noticed she uses when she's thinking.

Going for a controlled tone, I reply, "Fine. Promise me you'll wrap things up and usher your last guests out in sixty minutes."

"I will."

I glance between the two of them, spin on my heel, and vacate the bedroom. One minute longer in there, with Bo making googley-eyes at my partner, and I might have decked him. Wouldn't the cameras have loved that?

Three steps out of the room and their laughter reaches my ears, causing me to pause. My spine straightens. If Paige thinks I'm going to help her clean this mess up, she has another think coming. This is all on her.

Resuming my path back to the kitchen, I give myself a pep talk with every step. Paige brought this on herself. She and *Bo* can clean this shit up. I resist the urge to throw empty, and half-empty, cups into a garbage bag.

Marion and Peyton stand off to one corner, by the cabinets that have seen better decades. "Hey, ladies. Enjoying yourselves?"

"We are." Marion raises her red cup to me. For her part, Peyton tips her glass against her lips.

"That's great."

"I'm not sure I'd have agreed to host a party in the apartment so close to filming. You're much braver than I am," Peyton says.

"Wasn't my idea." A shout of "Shots!" rings throughout the apartment. "Clearly."

Marion smirks. "I wouldn't want to have to clean this place up. Although, I have to say, I'm happy that's on you. Maybe that'll give us a leg up."

"Don't bet on it," I retort. "We'll be ready when Monday rolls around." If it kills Paige.

Marion holds up her cell. "What do you think of using these rather than our own phones? I wish I could've saved some photos."

"Of Hugo and Sally?" her sister asks, causing Marion to narrow her eyes.

Must be her kids. I'm about to ask their ages when Marion tugs on her pink hair. "My cats are beautiful. Haters gonna hate."

Their sibling banter tugs a chord in me. What would Diana think about the show? In my heart, I hang onto the belief she would've been excited for me. Hell, getting selected by the network was a big deal. No way would she want me to continue in a career I didn't like. Despite the fact it was the one she had chosen for herself.

I tune back into the siblings' conversation. "Don't look now," Peyton says, lowering her voice. "Nancy's in the living room." She knocks back whatever's in her red cup.

Marion responds, "Oh crap. I don't want to be stuck here with her. It's bad enough she's in our bedroom. Maybe we could pull a Janice on her." The two start cackling.

Intrigued when they don't explain, I ask, "What's a Janice?"

Peyton opens her mouth, but Marion forestalls her. "She went to high school with us. The girl never shut up. Drove the teachers bonkers."

When Marion takes a breath, Peyton jumps in. "My sister and I were only one year apart in school. One day, at lunch, we were sitting together when Janice came up to our table and made a rude comment about my outfit." Peyton gestures toward her body. "Anyway, my big sister here wasn't having any of that. She said—"

"'You and your mouth are not welcome here. No one wants to hear your whiny voice.'"

"She did have a whiny voice."

"Totally," Marion replies. "Anyway, Janice went away after that. Quieter than a church mouse."

My eyebrows pull together. She had to have omitted something. "There's more to this story." I focus on the ringleader. "What did you say to her, Marion?"

A devious smile extends across Marion's face. "I told her if she didn't mind her own business, I would expose the lie she told to reel in her boyfriend. You see, I knew she had claimed to be pregnant, which made him her lapdog. Worked for about six months until she failed to show, and he dumped her sorry ass."

I process her story. "So you think that's how Nancy got Dan? Faked being pregnant?"

Peyton purses her lips. "We're not sure, but why else would a good-looking guy like that, with obvious skills, willingly be with her? She. Never. Shuts. Up."

Shifting my weight to my left foot, I rock my right ankle. "You may have a point about Dan. I've already been cornered into one too many conversations with Nancy. How about we all make a pact? If we see any of us talking with her, we agree to extricate them."

"By any means necessary," Marion amends.

Peyton thrusts her hand forward. "I'm in." Marion and I place our hands on top of hers to seal the deal.

Yawning, Peyton says, "Okay, I'm beat. Thanks for throwing this great party, Jesse. We'll see you at the ViewPad later." The siblings toss their cups into a trash bag and depart.

While I was talking, Paige and Bo reentered the public area of the apartment and are now talking with the ladies of the hour, her cousins. Gabrielle told me she plans on making it in the music industry as a songwriter. Chloe is more traditionally inclined, with a degree in human resources and is looking for a job. I hope they both find their successes, but nothing's going to happen here. Especially at this hour. I hope my partner is telling them it's time to leave.

Frank and Robbie and Dan and Nancy approach me. Great. Why did the sisters have to leave before we were able to put the pact into effect? Forcing a neutral expression, I greet my fellow cast members. "Heading out?"

"Yeah. We want to get some sleep to be ready for Monday's show," Frank answers for the group.

I yawn. "I'll see you back there soon."

For once, Nancy leaves without running her mouth. Must be the hour. I walk about the kitchen into what's supposed to be the laundry room. Quite a large space. Hmmm. I get lost in my thoughts about possibly relocating the washer and dryer to a different area of the apartment, only brought out of my head when the front door closes. Shaking my head to clear it, I confirm most of the remaining guests have left. I give the twins another round of congratulatory hugs, ignoring their blatant interest in me. They're way too young. Besides, essentially being Xander's and Theo's cousins, I'm sure their hands-off warning extends to them as well.

Shortly, only Paige, Bo, and I remain. He's begun to help her collect empty cups and bottles, and they exchange soft laughter and stupid smiles.

Time for me to go. Lifting my chin to the pair, I say, "I'm going back to the ViewPad. Make sure everything's cleaned up by tomorrow afternoon. We don't want to earn demerits before the show begins."

Not waiting for a response, I walk out the door and pull it shut. *Give me strength.*

8

Jesse

The next morning, I shove the blankets down my naked torso and stare at the back of the bunk above me. Where Bo sleeps. He came in around four in the morning and woke all of us up—me, in particular, since we're sharing connected beds. After he climbed up the ladder, he fell asleep in short order, as verified by his loud snores. Which continue.

Used to my privacy since I was fourteen, sharing a room with four other dudes is a distinctive challenge. However, considering a show on Renovation TV is the prize, it's a minor inconvenience with which I'm willing to deal.

Sliding my legs free, I roll off the bed and land with a light thump on the floor six inches below me. Bunk beds were not designed for grown adults.

After brushing my teeth, I throw on my workout shorts and go to the exercise room. Skill is important for the show, obviously, but so is being camera-ready. I'm not about to leave anything to chance.

Even though I'm the first one in the gym, I'm soon joined by Mary Ellen, who's wearing a skintight pair of shorts and matching sports bra with blue flowers. Damn. She's smoking hot.

"Hi, Jesse," she says while setting up the elliptical in front of me.

"Thought I'd be the only one of us in here this morning. How was the party last night?"

"It was fun, although it ran long." I remember Paige and Mary Ellen's ex-husband in the bedroom and turn up the incline on the treadmill.

Mary Ellen's long arms move in time with her feet in a graceful manner. I increase the speed on my machine.

"Are you ready for today? Living room and patio in a week is going to be a challenge."

Wiping the sweat dripping down my forehead, I reply in the affirmative while mentally revisiting our plans to transform the room and outside area. I still want to do something more with the fireplace than what Paige suggested, but an idea is out of reach.

"We're going ultra-modern with the whole place. Have you decided on a theme?" Her blonde ponytail flicks behind her with every movement.

No matter how attractive she is, she's still my competitor. My rival for a new show on Renovation TV—and freedom from the staid banking world. Not going to give up any of our plans. "We're not sure yet." I may add an extra pant to convey my exertion.

"We always start with a theme. But I know everyone's process is different." Her ass sways with each movement, which appears more sensual than effective.

Tuning her out, I increase the incline and force my body into beast mode. Tomorrow's arm day but today's all about cardio. And I intend to get the most out of my workout. Before our first day of filming, whatever that might bring.

Wearing a bank t-shirt, I stand in the middle of the living room—have to hand it to my partner, the place doesn't show any additional wear and tear from the party. I don't share that praise with her, though, as she seems to *expect* kudos. Like cleaning up after her party is something to be celebrated.

Getting to work, we remove the ugly carpet and survey the

space. Paige focuses on the windows and furniture layout we created, while I stare at the ugly brick fireplace. We have to replace everything about it, but thanks to Renovation TV, we know it's structurally sound.

I walk over to Paige. Time for the rubber to hit the road, as Mr. Hooper would say. "What are you thinking?"

Her chocolatey eyes bounce around the empty room, an unsure glint in them. She points to her paper. "I guess we should go with what we discussed. Sofa there." She points in front of the fireplace. "Two chairs facing each other flanking it, coffee table in the middle, all anchored by a rug." She turns her back. "On the patio, a grill would be nice."

I follow her directions. "These are solid ideas, if a bit . . ." How should I say this? Uninspired? Boring? "Traditional. I thought we were going with pre-war with a modern twist? I'm only hearing pre-war with your concept."

Her eyes narrow. "I'm trying here! What brilliant ideas do you have, hammer boy?"

My eyebrows raise. On a deep inhale, I swipe the paper from her hands and reply to her acerbic question with calm. "I understand the need for a sofa facing the fireplace. How about we do back-to-back sofas?" Using a pencil, I sketch my idea.

"One facing the fireplace and another the kitchen, once we remove that God-awful wall?"

I smile at her apt description. "Might be cool."

She grabs my pencil and taps her bottom lip. *Distracting.* "I don't like the idea of two sofas, though. How about we play around with the back? And make the seating part serpentine and extra wide? Like this." She draws an image to explain her vision.

Very cool. "I could make that, no problem. I haven't seen anything like it before. Well done." I place my palm on top of her shoulder, which she leans into for a moment.

As if she realized our connection, she steps back. "As for the chairs, they could be something funky too. Maybe swivel chairs with arms that are uneven somehow?" The pencil taps her lip again.

Her creativity is sparking mine. "For the fireplace, I want it to be grand. Make it the focal point of the entire apartment. Especially since it'll be across from the kitchen."

She pauses from her drawing. "A covering going from the floor to the ceiling. With a television." At my expression, she says, "I know, I know. TVs aren't attractive, but they're a necessity in the real world. I bet you can create something to hide it when it's not in use, so it isn't a big, black square."

An idea takes shape. "I might be able to box it in as part of the entire design. We could put a piece of artwork over top of it that slides up hydraulically when you want to turn on the television."

She claps. "Oooh, I like that!" Approaching the fireplace, she turns toward me. "But our budget. Where are we going to get a piece of artwork that big and stay within it?"

Seems like a no-brainer. "You could do it yourself."

Shock crosses her face. "Are you kidding? Me? I'm no artist."

I point to her perfectly proportioned room layout. "Seems to me you're pretty good. I'm sure you could create something nice on canvas."

Her head shakes from side to side. "No. I can do layouts, interior design stuff. Not something this big. No way."

Why is she freaking out? It's not like I asked her to create the Mona Lisa, only something generic to give the illusion of artwork. "The network gave us access to painters only for the walls, remember? I'm going to be busy creating the sofa and chairs, not to mention the fireplace. Looks like it's on you, Paige."

After a moment, her shoulders slump. "Yeah. Alright. I guess."

She looks so dejected that I almost suggest we hit up the prop room, filled with items Quinn and her team scoured from all over the city. But we can't—between pillows, throw blankets, and the rug, we're banging against the budget. "I have faith in you."

She kicks the floor.

Which makes me realize we haven't discussed how we're going to tackle them. "Now that's settled, what about the floors?"

Her foot taps the subfloor, her mouth twisting to the side. "We have to use the same flooring throughout the entire space, from here through the kitchen and into the bedrooms. I want to give the appearance of an enormous space."

As she talks, she comes into her element. More secure. More assertive. More energetic. *Sexy*. I tamp my thoughts down.

"What do you think of dark hardwoods? I know lighter woods can make the room feel airy, but dark is bold and makes a statement."

I tilt my head. "I've never thought of them before. Don't most apartments have lighter-colored wood?"

She walks in a full circle. "They do. But dark could anchor the place. Then we can do lighter paint on the ceilings and walls in contrast. Sort of like the view. During the day, it's sunny and bright, but at night the water appears dark and moody."

She clamps her mouth shut as if expecting me to mock her. No way. "Good points. Reflect our surroundings." Because she looks like she needs it, I add, "Great job."

Her bright smile rivals the sunlight outside. "For the patio, in addition to a grill, we should have plenty of seating so people can relax and enjoy the view. And tables. I hate it when I'm outside and the only place to put my stuff is on the ground."

"I can make tables. What flooring out there do you think?"

She pauses for a moment. "Tile. Perfect in any weather. Obviously, we can put an indoor-outdoor rug over top of it to soften it up."

"Tile could be great. Maybe the same as you choose for the kitchen backsplash, to add continuity?"

She bumps my shoulder. "Here I thought I was the designer of the team."

With our final ideas in place, we begin working.

Before we know it, the week's up and we're standing in the middle of our completed living room and patio. Pride in our work zings throughout my body. While not avant-garde, it's novel. My gaze steals over to the fireplace and our most innovative idea, the painting concealing the television.

Paige came through on this big time. After several tries, she executed an artistic rendering of the furniture layout for the living room. It looks fantastic. I've told her this several times, but each time she bites her lip and looks at the floor. She has nothing to be insecure about.

Me? My furniture is well built, and the chairs, which were a bitch to create, fit in with the curves we tried to add in to soften the room. However, as expected, the fireplace is the focal point. While it's a thousand times better than it was before, it's still a little dated in my opinion. We ended up covering it in shiplap, which looks nice and is a nod toward the twist part of our theme. Yet, it isn't exactly cutting edge.

Quinn ushers in three people we've never met before, who are introduced as the industry experts who will be our judges throughout the show. She asks Paige to describe our living room and patio.

My partner straightens her shoulders and tucks her short hair behind her ear. Knowing she's nervous, I want to reach out and comfort her. Or take over the presentation. But she was asked, so I remain silent, hoping my teammate steps up.

After a few stumbles and mumbles, she looks to me for . . . guidance? Support? I give her a slow blink and dip my chin. *You've got this.* My life depends on it.

As if reading my mind, Paige restarts her presentation. Using hand motions, she describes how we came up with the idea for the flooring and seating arrangement. She picks up the remote control.

One of the judges asks, "Where did you get this glorious piece of artwork? It mirrors your room."

Paige lowers her hand holding the remote. "I, actually, well—"

Unable to hold back any longer, I jump in to rescue her. "Paige painted it herself. She wanted to reinforce the strategic layout of the pieces we brought into the room."

Paige turns her head toward mine, then returns to focus on the judges when the one who asked the question replies, "You did a nice job."

My heart sings. Her compliment has to count for something. I track the camera crew as they capture every moment.

Paige doesn't dwell on the flattery, though. "I appreciate your kind words. But there's a more strategic reason for the artwork. Watch." She presses the button, and the painting rises, exposing the television.

The judges let out an audible gasp.

Score!

"You see, we wanted to have a TV in here to accommodate today's lifestyle, but didn't want to see a big, black box when it isn't in use. So we designed this special track around the fireplace to conceal it when not in use."

The judges murmur amongst themselves, with the word "brilliant" clear as day. We're going to make it to the next round. I sneak a glance at Paige, who's sporting a secretive smile, and know she feels the same way.

We give the judges a tour of the rest of the furniture I built, plus the tiled patio, and then they leave the apartment. Remaining behind, Quinn says, "Nice job, Jesse and Paige. I think your artwork was the highlight of the room. I'll be back soon to pick you up for the elimination round. Ta!" She flips her long, brown hair and leaves us with a swirl of her brash perfume of raspberries and gardenias.

Paige sprawls across the sofa I built. "That went well, don'tcha think?" She crosses her ankle over her knee.

"I guess so. Depends on how the other teams did."

Her foot moves in circles. "This place isn't so cavernous anymore. When we do the kitchen and dining area"—she uses her foot to point in their direction—"it'll be opened up and spacious. The choice to use the dark floors will make more sense then."

Knowing she's stinging from one judge's comment about the "interesting" floor choice, I bolster her confidence. "I'm sure of it."

Paige sits up. "What do you think is going to happen at the elimination ceremony? I mean, we're not getting roses. Think they'll give a hammer out to the team getting kicked off?" She starts laughing at her rather ingenious quip.

Chuckling, I admit, "I have no clue. But if they want to reward contestants who did a good job, I would think they'd choose a nail."

She stops laughing. "Nailed it! Oh my God, that's better than mine."

She holds up her fist, which I bump. It's nice not being at each other's throats.

Someone knocks on the front door. "I'll get it." Treading across the newly stained dark wood floors, I turn the lever on the black doorknob I installed. "Quinn."

"We're ready for you guys now. Leave all your things here and come to the ViewPad. First elimination round starts in thirty." She swirls out over the threshold.

I catch Paige fiddling with her hair. "Let's get this over with. Remember, the judges loved your artwork and seemed impressed with the sofa we created."

Her hand flicks across the sofa's back. "I only designed it. You built it."

She needs a lot of confidence boosting. *I can do that.* "Wouldn't have had anything to build but for your brilliant design."

Her hand forms a fist, and she knocks on the sofa's back. "Let's do this. I'm rooting for Nancy to get kicked off. She never shuts up." She walks over to the window area and picks up her tote bag.

"Can't argue with you there. Although, this is a television show. They may want her to stick around for ratings."

"Ugh. I hope not."

"Me, too."

I allow Paige to precede me and lock up. In the ViewPad, we join the rest of our competitors to wait for the elimination round. Bo paces across the room, alternatingly flipping his hat and running his fingers through his hair. Paige ducks into her room to get rid of her tote bag, then reappears sucking on a lollipop. Where did she get that? *Why does her sucking a candy have to be so erotic?* I adjust my stance and indicate she should stand next to me.

Quinn, trailed by a couple of cameras, enters the apartment, which decreases in size as if they used a shrink wrap machine on it. I shake my arms in a failed attempt to expand the room. Paige taps me with her lollipop stick and leans over. "I overheard Marion apologizing to Peyton about not finishing something in their room. I bet they go home."

I find solace for myself in her words, although I like the sisters. "Wish it was Nancy you overheard," I whisper.

"I hear you."

Quinn gets our attention and describes how the elimination rounds will work. The show's host, Miss Antonia Banks—a famed designer who has several shows on the network—is escorted in and runs through her lines. Turns out, neither hammers nor nails are given out. The losing team—this time, Marion and Peyton for the reasons Paige shared—are simply asked to pack their tools.

After we've said our goodbyes and they've left the ViewPad, Quinn says, "Get a good night's sleep. Round two starts in the morning!"

Down to eight, we wander into the kitchen. Nancy, of course, breaks the ice. "Well, that sucked. But we're still here. This calls for a celebration." She dives into the fridge and pulls out a bottle of sparkling wine and holds it up high. Dan provides glasses and we each take ours.

Nancy lifts her flute. "To making it to Round Two!" Glasses clink to exclamations of "Hell, yes!"

Realizing I lost my "Nancy Buffer" when the sisters left, I withdraw from the group and retrieve my whittling block and knife. I'm ready to start a new project, so I flip the wood in my hand several times. Paige asked for a mermaid, but I'm not up for such a challenge—on any level. I decide on a housecat, in a more subtle nod to my partner—skittish yet fierce when the need arises. Wandering into the main area, I take a seat on the sofa and focus on what's in my hands rather than the actual fact that two of us are gone.

Mary Ellen sits next to me. "Hey. What are you doing?"

"Relaxing." I hold up the beginnings of a cat.

"Dope."

She stretches and I try not to notice how her shirt pulls against her rack. But I am human, so it takes me a minute to focus on my whittling.

In her sensual drawl, she asks, "What did the judges say in your room?"

"Not too much. They liked a couple of things we did in the living room. It wasn't as horrible as I feared."

"Yeah. Same. I was happy they didn't turn this into a spectacle on top of a competition."

"I'm with you."

Across the way, Bo approaches Paige and my fingers tighten around my tool. My whittling knife, that is.

I watch the flirty interactions between the pair for a moment. Glancing at his ex-wife, I see pain register for a moment before she covers it up. I hope the hidden cameras didn't capture her unvarnished reaction. No one's business but hers.

Tossing my whittling to the side, I stand and hold out my hand to Mary Ellen. When she's standing beside me, I raise my voice. "Who wants pizza?"

9

Paige

The next morning, I put my design items into my tote and grab a yogurt from the fridge. Everyone else had a big breakfast of eggs and bacon, but I was much happier sleeping in and missing all their excited chatter about starting the kitchen, dining, and laundry rooms today.

Selecting a spoon, I dip into my strawberry banana yogurt while mentally reviewing our notes for the rooms. White cabinets, including on the oversized island, will look fabulous against the dark wood floors. Quartz countertops are a must nowadays, and I prefer the look of a waterfall edge. Plus a farmhouse sink. Those things are huge. I don't care if they fit within the pre-war modern look we're going for—I'm not giving on this.

In today's design world, though, two-toned cabinets are the rage. If we go ahead with my plan, will it appear as if we're out-of-touch? Will black hardware and faucets appease the powers that be?

I'm mulling over these aesthetics when Bo wanders into the kitchen wearing just a pair of running shorts and sneakers, wiping a towel around his neck. His upper body is toned to perfection as I surmised, although a tad too muscular for my taste. Still.

"Hi." I greet him.

His eyes light up then travel my full length. "Well, well, well. You're a welcome vision this morning, Paige."

"As are you, Bo. Although I took the lazy way out and didn't do anything but take a shower this morning."

He flexes, his bicep bulging. *Impressive.* "I worked out enough for both of us."

"And I'm grateful." I point at the coffeemaker, the only appliance with which I'm familiar. "Want some coffee? I was about to make a new pot."

"Sounds good to me." He opens the pantry door and retrieves the Vitamix, then opens the refrigerator door. "Want me to make you a smoothie?"

"Nah. Yogurt's good for me."

We work together as if our actions were choreographed, the scent of freshly brewing coffee filling the air. I'm leaning across Bo to obtain the sugar bowl in the cabinet above his head when Jesse's voice freezes me in place. "Good morning."

Why did I react to my partner's tenor voice like he's accusing me of something untoward? Forcing my eyebrows to remain neutral, I reply, "Hey, Jesse." I turn toward him.

Like Bo, he's wearing a pair of workout shorts and sneakers, sans shirt. Unlike Bo, however, Jesse's well-defined upper body is more to my taste. Each of Jesse's muscles has a use and doesn't show off. My fingers tighten around the sugar bowl.

"Don't let me bother you. I need some protein and saw a drawer filled with different cheeses in the fridge last night." He walks to the other side of the kitchen.

I point to the coffee pot. "Want some?"

Jesse checks the counter where our mugs await the liquid gold and shakes his head. "Nah. I'll stick to water."

"You really should have a protein shake to go along with your cheese, buddy."

My partner's cheek indents. "I'm good."

Shrugging, Bo replies, "Suit yourself." He presses a button to turn on the blender. Over the whirring, he yells, "Shit. I forgot the chia seeds. Could you get me the bag? It's over there." He uses his chin as a pointer.

Even though Jesse's next to the cabinet Bo indicated, he doesn't move to respond. Of course he doesn't. *He's a cave dweller.* To be fair, he's been pretty considerate since we've been here, hitting several items on my checklist. Still, he's not hitting them today. *Certainly not boyfriend material.* I walk over to the cabinet, take out the bag, then stomp back to the island and hand it to Bo. "Here you go."

He shuts off the blender. "Thanks, doll." He grabs the chia from my hand, twists the lid, and plants a tiny kiss on my cheek. This is our first sexual contact. I wait a beat for a zap of energy to ring through my body . . . but it doesn't. Must've been too brief an encounter.

"I'll leave you two be." With that pronouncement, Jesse strides out of the kitchen.

"That guy's a real winner, Paige. How'd you get teamed up with him? He doesn't seem your type."

Like yourself? Actually, Bo's a good fit for me. Tall and good-looking with manners in spades that tick off the items on my check-list, like putting a package of flavored water in the fridge for me. Hell, he even stayed late to help me clean up the apartment after the graduation party. Jesse sure didn't.

"He's friends with my brother and cousin." I respond. "My older brother and even older cousin," I clarify.

"Ah. Now it makes sense." He pours the green shake into a glass. "Are you excited to start in on the kitchen area today?"

"I am." My automatic response is punctuated with the buzz in my body that was missing from his kiss. "I really am."

"Yeah. Kitchens are my favorite rooms in the house. They allow for so much creativity."

"True. Although, I'm a primary bedroom suite type of gal myself." I can't wait to get my hands on this debacle in our apartment, assuming we make it to the finale. Oddly, after one round, I now *want* to make it to the end of this contest and not only as a way to stay out of my parents' house. This is actually fun.

After Bo rinses the blender, I hand him his mug of coffee. "It's black. Didn't know how you like it."

His eyebrows wiggle. "I'll take it however you want to give it to me."

Heat rises up my neck. "I meant the coffee."

"I didn't."

With that, Bo turns and walks out of the kitchen, leaving me breathless. Taking a few minutes to calm down and finish my yogurt, I place my spoon in the dishwasher and sit on the stool to drink my coffee.

Frank and Robbie walk into the kitchen. "Hi there. How's it going?"

"Good. You?"

"Great," Robbie replies for the pair. "While this isn't Miami, the weather's still good and we took a long walk on the High Line after breakfast. Love the sculptures."

I sip my coffee, listening to the men discussing the various things they saw during their walk. They make a cute couple. Hope this isn't only for show, though. My parents seem to be the perfect couple out in public but at home, it's a different story. Remembering the vases breaking, I amend. A *very* different story.

"So, are you guys ready to tackle this week's assignment?"

"Sure are," Frank says. "We felt badly that the sisters were kicked off, but we understand they didn't finish their moldings. Can't expect to win this if you don't finish."

I place my empty mug down onto the counter. "Yeah. Too bad, though. Considering—"

Nancy's voice in the living room carries.

Frank answers for all three of us. "We *all* know." Everyone chuckles.

I check the time on the microwave. "Guess we should start our days. Good luck, guys."

"You, too."

Picking up my tote bag, I walk into the living room and spot Jesse sitting on the sofa talking with Mary Anna. For a split second, my entire body freezes. Shaking my head, I yell, "Hey, Jesse. Ready?"

The perfect length of his sandy brown hair swishes when he reacts to my question. *Why did I notice that?* He places his hands on his thighs and stands. "Let me get my notes and tools and I'll be right out." He disappears toward the bedrooms.

Mary Beth asks, "Excited for today?"

I don a practiced smile. "I love kitchens. They allow for some great creativity. How about you?"

"Same. Bo's super talented with all things cabinetry."

I bet. He seems quite talented in many arenas, something I might be persuaded to sample if he asks. Yet I wouldn't be working with Jesse if he were my ex-boyfriend, let alone ex-husband. I gathered that much intel from talking with Bo as he helped me clean up 1626 after the party—which Jesse ordered me to do. And *he* didn't help. I force my fists to open. I need to work with this man today.

My partner reenters the room and glances at the sofa. "Good luck today," he offers our competition.

The blonde waves. "You too."

Nice. Not. "Let's get going."

Jesse's eyebrows raise, but for once, he keeps his mouth shut and follows me out of the ViewPad. While we wait for the elevator, I pull out a lollipop from my bag and unwrap it. If I don't shove something into my mouth, I worry what might come out of it.

When we reach the sixteenth floor, Jesse allows me to precede him out of the elevator. First sign of manners I've seen out of him all day.

Using my lollipop stick, I point to the door, which he unlocks. When the door swings open, I check to make sure he wants me to enter first, then do. Two gentlemanly things in five minutes. Better check his temperature.

Dropping my tote onto the sofa Jesse made, I first focus my attention on the kitchen. Our preliminary plan calls for a six-foot island, but I'm thinking we could go bigger. I return to my tote for a measuring tape while Jesse opens and closes the cabinet doors, then walks behind them.

"Are you aware," he calls from the back wall. "We have a lot of space back here. This area was used as a laundry room, judging from the hook-ups. We do need laundry in the apartment, but I'm not sure this is the best place for it."

Using my lollipop stick, I tap on my bottom lip while I process what he's said. Joining him, I check out the large area available to us if we moved the laundry. "Where could we put it? It shouldn't be in any of the public areas."

"I agree." His eyes light up. "Come with me."

He races out of the kitchen, toward the bedrooms. Perhaps we could turn one of the bedrooms into a laundry area? But losing a bedroom is never a good idea.

Jesse passes the two extra bedrooms and enters the primary suite. It's large, but not big enough to move it in here. He checks every corner of the room, then his face falls. "Guess it won't work." He passes by me as he returns to the kitchen.

Why did he give up so easily? I'd love to add a pantry to the kitchen, so there has to be somewhere else we can hide the washer-dryer. I repeat Jesse's actions and come to the same conclusion about this bedroom and follow him back to the kitchen. *En route*, I pass by the utilities closet and stop. I open the door. We could use this and steal a pinch from the primary bathroom. With stackable machines rather than side-by-sides, this could work. Not perfect, for sure, but it would open up the kitchen tremendously.

"Jesse!" I wait for him to come. Finally, he appears. "Took you long enough," I mutter.

Ignoring my snark, he asks, "What?"

"We could move it in here." I swing the door to the utilities closet wider.

His eyes widen, then return to their normal size. "Too small." He turns on his heel.

"Not if we stole extra square footage from the primary bathroom and used stackables."

Returning to face the utilities closet, he assesses the space from where he stands. "Who would want to do laundry in a closet? Using stackable machines? Side-by-sides are prerequisites at this price point." He takes a step away.

"Not for me."

He cocks his head. "What do you mean?"

"I, uhm, I've never used a laundry machine. Neither have Mum and Father. Our maid does our laundry, so it wouldn't be a deal breaker to us."

His face registers shock. "You don't do your own laundry?"

I shake my head. "Don't you see? Stackables would solve the laundry issue in case someone wanted to do it. Or if their maid did it for them."

"I can't believe you've never washed any of your clothes."

Why is he so hung up on such an insignificant thing? "I can always buy more." However, with Father's assets being frozen, perhaps I should rethink my way of life? I suppose most normal people don't buy new underwear on the weekly. But this isn't about me. "What do you think?"

"It's not a perfect solution."

"No. But it's good enough. It'll allow the kitchen to have a massive pantry. Bonus!"

"What if the judges don't agree with you?"

I cross my hands over my chest. "What if they do?" His scowl spurs me on to add, "This competition won't be won with small ideas. And this one was yours, might I remind you."

"I don't know."

Hearing him waver, I jump in. "Great! We'll move the laundry in here. Since we're using a part of the bathroom, hook-ups won't be a problem."

"That's true."

"Settled. I'll do the paperwork about it for Quinn. Let's go back to the kitchen to figure out how we're going to transform the added space into a pantry." Everyone wants a pantry to store their stuff, especially with all the gadgets people use today. Bo and the Vitamix make an appearance in my mind. This is a good idea.

I brush past Jesse and, with a pep I didn't feel earlier, rush into the newfound square footage. My mind pictures a pantry the entire length of the kitchen, filled with shelves. I race to my tote bag and pick up my design notebook. Within minutes, the pantry takes shape on the page.

My next question—how to get in here? I suppose we could put in a door on either end, but that's expected. I want the wow factor. "Jesse?"

He doesn't answer.

I walk out from the new pantry area and find him sitting on the sofa, staring at my painting of the living room's layout. "Hey. I thought you were working on kitchen ideas."

He points. "Upper and lower cabinets, big island. Use the tile from the patio. Stools of some sort." His shoulders raise and lower.

What's going on with him? He's usually the upbeat one. I take a seat next to him. "Hey. Those are good thoughts. I bet your stools will make the entire room."

"What do you have?"

I show him my design, holding my breath. I think it's good, but what if I'm wrong? I'm basically pulling this stuff out of my ass.

He returns it back to me. With a warmth in his tone that was missing before, he says, "This looks great. Could sell a buyer on the entire apartment."

My lungs expand to their fullest. I beam at my partner. "High praise."

"It's the truth."

Not allowing his words to sink in, I plow ahead. "Only problem is how to enter? Doors on either end seem so, I don't know, boring."

Jesse snatches the drawing from my hands, his fingers tracing the shelving while his eyes bounce to the kitchen. "What if we expanded the kitchen all the way to the windows and push the dining area toward the living room a smidge. That would gain us another four feet of cabinetry, right?"

I guesstimate the measurement. "I think that's about right." What is he getting at? "It'll be a huge kitchen."

"May I see your design notebook? I have an idea."

"Sure. Here you go." I hand him the notebook.

He opens his palm, and I place my pencil in it, then he starts to draw. He's remarkably talented. The kitchen takes shape, as does a door that he places next to the refrigerator—but concealed by paneling that mimics the rest of the cabinets.

My mouth drops open. "A hidden door?"

He smiles. "Could work, don't you think?"

"Hell yes!" I throw my arms into the air and give my brilliant partner a hug. After a second, his arms close around me, and the zap missing from my contact with Bo this morning materializes. Vaulting back, I stare at his design. Once I can focus on it, I say, "I love this idea, Jesse. When someone finds the hidden pantry, they'll be super excited."

He clears his throat. "I've always been fascinated with surprise entrances. My sister—" He stops talking, then continues. "When we were kids, she always wanted to play hide-and-go-seek in the house. She found the best places to hide. I remember her telling me, 'Jesse, not everything is what it appears. Look deeper.'"

His voice modulates into a much higher pitch when he imitates her. So cute. "That's a good philosophy to have for life too." He doesn't talk about his family much. "What does your sister do?"

He swallows. In a low voice, he murmurs, "She died when she was seventeen."

Oh. My. God. "Jesse. I'm so sorry."

Before I can process this news—let alone ask a follow-up question, he says, "It's a lifetime ago. I was only fourteen at the time. Hmm, I've lived as long without her as with her." He gets to his feet. "C'mon, we have a lot of work to do."

I stand and we begin demolishing the kitchen before we can rebuild it with a pre-war era modern flair.

Days later, we're in the elimination round at the ViewPad. Our design was met with approval from the judges. They loved our relocated laundry room and the hidden pantry. They did note, with disapproval, that we didn't use two-toned cabinets, but I'm still optimistic we'll continue in the competition.

While we wait for Quinn to get the camera angles correct, Nancy pipes up about her design and how the judges *loved* the spacious laundry room. Good for her. Robbie adds that the judges were positive about their kitchen, too, especially their backsplash. Neither Jesse nor I share anything, although Mary Margaret comments that Bo did a phenomenal job with their bar stools.

Jesse created cool-looking ones, too, but I keep my mouth shut. Bet our laundry room blew anything they did away. Jesse's folding ironing board attached to the interior of the door was a surprise hit. Who knew people still used those things?

Quinn hushes us and gives final notes about blocking before Miss Antonia breezes in. I want her job. No work, walk in and read lines, then disappear. Collect a nice paycheck too, I bet. Although, I've seen her work on other shows, and she seems to have earned this cushy role. Maybe my effort here will do the same for me. I flick my hair away from my eyes.

The host reads the judges' comments about each of our kitchens, dining, and laundry rooms. Our washer-dryer combo received the highest marks, as we were the only ones to have relocated it. I shoot Jesse a sideways glance. He offers a slight nod, then returns his attention to Miss Antonia.

As for the kitchens themselves, Bo gets high praise for his stools, like Mary Alice said. Good for them. Frank and Robbie's backsplash and counter combination are noted, while Nancy and Dan's choice of flooring was deemed "unusual." Finally our pantry is given high marks for creativity and function.

Please, oh please, kick off the chatterbox.

My prayer soon is answered—Nancy and Dan are told to pack their tools. I give Dan a big hug and wish him luck. He'll need it with her. Bet they don't make it to the airport, although who knows? He could like the sound of her voice as much as she does.

After they leave to pack their stuff, Quinn suggests we rest up, because the second half of the show is going to be even more difficult—we're moving to the private spaces.

When she, plus the ousted contestants leave, the six of us start chattering about our experiences thus far. They congratulate us for relocating the laundry room. Jesse praises me for designing it, so I'm compelled to explain it was his idea to move it in the first place.

"Stackables, huh?" Frank says. "Not on my bingo card. Good job." He pats me on the back.

"Thanks. Guess it's good not to have a history with laundry." My chuckle earns guffaws from the group.

When it gets close to dinner time, Robbie and Frank, led by Mary Barbara, drift into the kitchen to see what meal was left in the fridge. I turn to join them with Jesse at my heels.

Bo slides in next to me, putting his arm around my shoulders. "Hey. Want to blow this popsicle stand? I want to try some of the vaunted food here in New York City, and I bet you're acquainted with all the best places to go."

Startled, I stop in my tracks. In my peripheral vision, I see Jesse's jaw twitching. What does that mean? I find my voice while my partner continues moving forward. "Oh, I don't know. Aren't we supposed to stay in?"

Bo kisses my cheek, whispering in my ear. "I think you're a bad girl, Paige. When have you ever done what you were supposed to do?"

He does have a point. If it suits me, I'll go with it. Since Jesse's now in the kitchen, I guess he doesn't give a damn what I do.

Turning, I give the man with his arm around me a carefree smile. "You have a point. Put on something black and we'll hit the city." On his dime.

10

Jesse

I can't believe she agreed to go out with that hillbilly hack. What does she see in his insipid Southern drawl anyway? Pushing away from the table, I bring my half-eaten plate to the garbage and dump the perfectly good mac and cheese into it.

"Right, Jesse?"

It's not like I could even ask her out if I want to keep my balls attached to my body, thank you Theo and Xander, but still. Why would she agree to go out with my bunkmate?

"Hey, Jesse. Do you agree?"

My *snoring* bunkmate, I amend. With dumb cowboy boots. Who wears them in New York anyway?

Someone touches my arm. "Hey, there. You ignoring us or is your mind elsewhere?"

It takes me a moment, but I focus on blonde hair first, then the shapely woman it belongs to. "Oh, sorry, Mary Ellen. Did you ask me something?"

She places her wineglass onto the counter, which prompts me to pick up the bottle. "White, right?"

"Please." I pour her beverage while she continues, "Frank asked you how you came up with the stackable idea."

"Oh." I place the bottle down. "Wasn't my idea."

Mary Ellen pauses in taking a sip. "Sucks that they're out together, doesn't it?"

Preach, sister. I keep my mouth zipped shut, knowing she's probably hurting worse than I am. After all, she was *married* to the southern un-charmer. I pour myself a cup of coffee, even though I'm well-aware caffeine won't do me any favors later.

When I don't respond, she continues, "Don't worry. He'll tire of her soon. That's his M.O."

Swallowing the hot beverage, I reply, "Paige and I aren't dating. She's my best friend's little sister, who also happens to be an interior designer. That's all." More accurately, she's my best friend's little cousin and friend's little sister, but details shmetails.

She sets her wine glass down with a clink. "Really? You might want to rethink that, given the look on your face when Bo asked her out."

"You've misread the situation." I cuddle my coffee against my chest.

"If you say so." She runs the pad of her finger around the lip of her wine glass. "Want to join us? We're going to play a game of backgammon."

"I've never played."

"I'll teach you. Although, I suspect the guys are sharks." She whinny-laughs.

The distraction from dwelling on whatever Paige and Bo are doing sounds nice. Not that I've caught any feelings for my teammate. *None. At. All.* Homer's warning surges to the forefront, reminding me never to mix business with pleasure—and always place my career first. I have to get out of my head. "Sure. Sounds like it could be fun."

She leads me back into the living room, where Robbie explains the rules of the game. Even though they sound complicated, I decide to push forward. What else do I have to do?

Rounds of the game pass, during which I start to get a handle on it. I surprise myself by executing a tricky play, receiving congratulations from everyone. While I lose badly, I have to admit it was fun. Robbie is a good sport about winning, which makes it even better.

After Mary Ellen and I pack up the game as our penance for coming in the bottom two, everyone yawns.

"It's been a long day," Frank says. "Congrats on making it to the next round, everyone. We're proud to be in this with both of your teams."

"As are we," I reply. An idea for the third bedroom came to me during the game, and I want to sketch it before I forget. Standing, I address Mary Ellen. "Mind if I go into your room to get Paige's design book? I need to draw something."

"Sure thing." I take a step toward the girls' bedroom when her voice reaches me. "Be warned, though. You might not find what you're looking for on the first try."

What does she mean? I wave my hand and continue to the hallway. When I enter the ladies' bedroom, I understand her warning. The room is identical to ours, with three bunkbeds. One is stripped of all linens, which had to have been Marion and Peyton's. One is tidy, with the top bunk stripped—guess that was Nancy's. The other looks like a tornado hit. Well, only half a tornado. The lower level's pristine while the upper-level sports twisted bedsheets and even a pillow curled into a ball. At the foot, next to the dresser, are two opened Louis Vuitton suitcases with clothes and accessories spilling from them.

Adorable.

What?

With a huff, I rummage through Paige's things and retrieve her sketch pad, plus a couple of pencils, underneath the pants she wore today. Despite my best efforts not to, I grab her pillow and fluff it, then toss the sheets and comforter over her bed. There. At least it appears less chaotic than when I walked in here.

Shaking my head, I return to the living area and hold up my prize. "Got it."

Mary Ellen glances at the oversized clock hung above the entry to the kitchen. "It only took you fifteen minutes. I'm impressed." She gives me a thumbs up.

Tucking the pad between my arm and torso, I say, "It's a gift. Well, I'm going to work on my design so have a good night."

Without a backward glance, I choose to go into the game room, where I can spread out. I spend the next half-hour drawing my idea for a desk that'll transform the bedroom into an office. Satisfied, mostly, with my design, I make a couple of additional tweaks then drop Paige's pencil. I'll run this by her in the morning. She'll probably have several ways to improve it, but at least I got my thoughts down on paper.

She's still out. What are she and Bo doing now?

Don't go there, Jesse.

Grabbing Paige's things, I rush to my feet and walk to the bedroom. When I enter, Frank pulls away from Robbie. They're both in their pajama bottoms and breathing hard. *Shit.*

"Sorry, guys." I point to the door. "I'll let you be."

Frank rubs the back of his palm against his lips. "No. Don't. It's fine."

"Not like we could've gone much further in this place anyway," Robbie grumbles, then collapses against the top bunk with a loud sigh.

Frank chuckles, which causes a ripple effect throughout the room. Helpless, I say, "This is so fucked up."

"Or not," Robbie responds.

Another round of chuckles.

Shaking my head, I toss the sketch pad on the floor, retrieve my pajama bottoms, and walk into the bathroom. After brushing my teeth, I knock on the bathroom door to announce my return. Don't need to interrupt another make-out session.

"We're in our *separate* bunks," Frank calls.

Whew. Opening the door, I cross the bedroom, turn off the lights, and slip into mine, trying to ignore Bo's empty bunk. Which, thankfully, is no longer above mine since he moved over to Dan's.

I'm about to say good night, when Robbie breaches the silence. "So. Bo, huh?"

My gut twists. Needing to play this off like it's no big deal—because it isn't—I reply, "Looks that way."

"Sucks."

Robbie's on point, but I don't want to engage. Paige isn't with me in any other sense than she's my teammate for this competition. "We're not dating or anything. She's free to go out with whomever she chooses." There. Sounds reasonable. Because I'm a reasonable sort of guy.

"I don't know, man," Frank replies. "If I were straight and was paired up with that knockout, I don't think I'd be able to let her get away from me so easily."

"But you're not." The bed crinkles as Robbie leans over the bunk.

"No," Frank replies to his partner. "I'm only saying if I were Jesse, I wouldn't be so blasé about it, you know?"

"I'm fine, guys. Let's go to sleep."

The room plunges into an uneasy quiet. Soon, their breathing indicates they're falling into slumber. At least no one's snoring like old jawbones Bo. In my mind's eye, I picture him with my partner sharing a meal or even drinks. They've been out for hours, so they're way past the dinner stage of the evening. Maybe she took him to a club. *Maybe he took her to a hotel.*

Paige needs to come into her own. She has a sharp decorating mind but lacks drive. And confidence in herself. For someone who portrays such a tomboy appearance, she's remarkably insecure. I can't wait to see her blossom. *But not with Bo.*

Beneath my hand, the sheets crumple as I make a fist. Theo and Xander warned me off her. For as long as I can remember, Homer railed against love before getting set into a career. No. Paige can do whatever she wants with whomever. It doesn't affect me. I slam my eyes shut and count sheep.

The next morning, the ViewPad's abuzz with excitement for the new project. Not to mention, we're down to the final two rounds, and sans Nancy. At least Paige and Bo didn't say a word about their date last night, so I can pretend it didn't happen. Time to focus.

With Paige at my side, I open the door to 1626, and my breath whooshes. The public areas look amazing. The dark floors anchor the space, as Paige promised they would. When we're inside, I give her props. "Your idea to make these floors dark was a stroke of genius. I went along with them because you were convinced, but you've made me a true believer."

Her cheeks flush, and she glances at the floors. "Thanks. I knew they'd provide the perfect backdrop in here." Her liquid chocolate gaze meets mine. "Let's get going on the two bedrooms and bathroom for this week." She opens her tote bag and starts digging.

I hold up her sketch pad and couple of pencils that I snagged last night. "Looking for these? I borrowed them last night and started drawing an idea I had for a desk."

"Oh." Her cheeks inflate. "Great. Let's see what you drew."

Her chirpy tone grates on my ears, but I ignore it. Not my business what Bo did to put it there. I show her my sketch, to which she cocks her head from side to side. Tucking her hair behind her ear, she grabs a pencil from me and adds some of her fantastic flourishes to it.

"There. I think this will be awesome. Great job!"

I accept her peppy assessment with a simple "thank you." We walk down the hallway, stopping outside the first bedroom. "I was thinking of using this as the office. It's the closest room to the public areas."

"True." She taps her bottom lip with the pencil. "But I'd rather have this one as a bedroom, considering no one wants their primary to be close to another sleeping quarters."

"You have a point. Okay, bedroom it is. We'll dress the other as the office. And since they both have closets, the next owners would be able to use them however they need."

"Yeah. Although, what do you think of turning it into a nursery? The next owners might have kids."

For a split second, the picture of a baby girl with sandy brown hair and large, milk chocolate eyes pops into my mind. Clearing my throat, I reply, "They might. But I do think this apartment screams uptown chic, so perhaps their child would be older?"

She taps my forearm. "I think you're right. We'll make this bedroom for an upscale kid." She claps. "Done." For the first time, Paige hums while she works. *Guess that's what a delightful date does to her.*

I tune her out and focus on my work. Considering I've been tasked with creating the bedframe, dresser, and side tables for the bedroom as well as the desk I designed and a credenza for the office, not to mention the enormous amount of knickknacks and doodads to complete the looks, I've got plenty on my plate.

I'm working on the desk when Paige stops by the large work area set up by Renovation TV in an empty apartment for all of us to use when creating larger pieces after we finished our public spaces. "This is looking great."

"Thanks."

She walks about the piece, studying it from every angle. "I heard Bo mention something about creating a secret drawer in a desk he did for a client in Texas. What do you think about adding in something like that? It'd be unexpected."

I drop my tools onto the floor. I'm not about to take design advice from a cowboy with a hammer. "I wouldn't want to steal someone else's idea."

"You're not stealing it. Who knows if he's even thinking about doing it in here?"

Despite my best efforts, I can't keep the snark at bay. "I'd rather do something bigger than a stupid drawer," I snap.

Paige takes a step backward. "I was only making a suggestion."

I inhale and hold my breath for five seconds. After exhaling, I reply, "I know you were." I cast about for a different idea to get us out of this current mess. "What do you think about a cutting-edge shelving design above the credenza?"

"That could work. I guess."

The disappointment on her face makes me want to throw my ever-present tape measure across the room. Bo's idea can go to hell, for all I care. Shoving my tape measure into my back pocket, I hold my hands up against the wall. "Picture it. I could make large X's to hold things like staplers, tape, and paper clip holders." I know I'm reaching, but I need to do whatever I can to get her mind away from a trivial hidden drawer.

She steps closer to me, her citrus and woodsy blend wafting into my nose. Placing her hand high on the wall, she says, "Not X's. I think if you take shelves and put a design over them, it would be more useful." As she talks, she becomes more animated. She grabs her sketch pad and slashes her pencil across it. "Like this."

Taking the pad from her, I review her design. It's distinctive. "I've never seen anything like this before. I bet the judges will love it."

She takes the paper from me, tapping her pencil against it. "You like this? Really?"

"I do. You're super talented."

"I think this design is fantastic, if I do say so myself." She claps. "Let's do it!"

Her eagerness propels me forward and, without my voluntary direction, my arms steal around her body. Closing them, I squeeze her for a hug, taking the moment to revel in her body plastered against mine like she was made for me. As soon as this thought enters my mind, I disengage.

Stepping back, I salute her. "On it, boss."

An hour later, she pops back into the work area. "Oh, wow. This looks even better than on paper. You're a fantastic carpenter, Jesse. What on earth are you doing in banking?"

A question I ask myself on the regular.

Not ready to give her the unvarnished truth, I explain, "My father's a chief compliance officer at a bank. I always found it fascinating to make sure all the 'i's' are dotted and 't's' crossed. Working with the regulators to ensure the bank's doing everything right provides me satisfaction."

"I guess that can be challenging."

"You have no idea." I launch into my oft-repeated story about how I did research that uncovered a tangle of shell companies serving as a front for a drug cartel and worked with the government to bring them all down. "Many branches of the bank were involved, but I was proud of my part to expose them."

"Oh." She bites her lip. "I wonder if that's how my father—" She trails off.

Shit. When I've told this story to my other friends, they all were impressed. Should've known Paige would be different. *She's* different.

"VOW-cubed didn't have any accounts at my bank." I checked when the news broke, but don't need to fill her in. I force a smile. "We're here not to think about real world stuff, but to create amazingly beautiful spaces that will make life easier. Your designs are fantastic, so I have every confidence we're going to move on to the next round."

After a minute, her face morphs into a sunny expression rivaling the rays outside. "'Every confidence,' huh?" She hip-checks me.

I pull her into a side hug. "Yup." *Dude, what are you doing?* I let her go and crack my knuckles. "I better get back to the credenza. It's not going to build itself."

"For what it's worth, banking's lucky to have you." Her words linger as I saw and square and sand.

When the judges walk through our spaces, my chest expands. I'm proud of what we achieved in these rooms. When they stop in front of the shelving unit, my breath stutters to a stop. The most critical of the trio walks over to it and checks it out from a variety of angles.

"I like this." She points at me. "Did you do this?"

Swallowing, I reply, "Paige and I came up with the design together, and I executed it." I shove my hands behind my back to prevent myself from wringing them together.

"Excellent job. This unit exhibits the most creativity I've seen since this competition began."

Out of her eyesight, my fingers dance. "Thank you."

As soon as the judges walk out, Paige grabs my hand. She mouths, "Good job." Not trusting my voice, I simply nod in response. After a moment to allow the judge's praise to sink in, she whispers, "Let's follow them."

We trail the judges into the hall bathroom, where their praise is lukewarm. They're critical of the vanity, saying it's not contemporary enough. They're wrong, but I keep my mouth shut.

After they leave, Paige and I collapse onto the sofa. "The shelving unit was our crowning achievement this time," she notes.

"Your designs were fantastic, even for the bathroom—I don't care what they said."

She tucks her hair behind her ear. "Maybe it wasn't as innovative as the rest of our apartment, but it's a bathroom. Geez. What did they want? Someone to magically appear and wipe their ass?"

Paige sure has a way with words. Grinning, I reply, "I'd pay money for that."

She crumples up a piece of paper and throws it at me. "Cave Dweller."

I deflect the battery and refuse to allow my mind to wander to any inappropriate thoughts of a naked Paige.

When our cell phones blare the arrival of a new text, we both scramble to open them. I read, "From Quinn. Time to check out how your competitors did. Everyone meet at Jesse and Paige's apartment and we'll tour the spaces. Then it's on to the elimination round."

"That's new," she remarks.

"Yeah. Guess since we're halfway done, they wanted to spice things up."

For some reason, I'm confident that we'll make it to the finals, based on absolutely nothing other than my belief in Paige's design and our product. Paige stands and fluffs the pillows on the sofa, even though this room isn't the one we're showing today.

"I have a good feeling, Jesse."

"Me too. Let's show them how the bedrooms and bathroom were supposed to be done." I walk to the front door and open it. Soon, Bo and Mary Ellen plus Robbie and Frank join us. Followed by Quinn and the camera crew.

We take the group on a tour of our spaces, pointing out what we believe to be the highlights of each room. Paige explains our thought process for why we staged the second bedroom as an office, and I describe how I made the shelving unit. They all make noises of being impressed.

When we go to Bo and Mary Ellen's apartment, I note there's no hidden drawer in the desk but keep this detail to myself. Their second bedroom is set up as a nursery, done in pastels. Nice, in a generic way, but I'm happier we did an office.

Robbie and Frank, on the other hand, created two bedrooms,

both of which appear to be more run-of-the-mill. Even their window coverings seem uninspired. The two men stand tall, proud of their work, so I shake their hands and keep my mouth shut.

This competition is hard. The fact we all completed the three rooms in only six days should be applauded. When we reassemble in the ViewPad's living room, I allow Paige to select her spot before standing next to her. Of course, Bo is on her other side.

Quinn walks in. "Congratulations, teams. You all did amazing work in the bedrooms and the hall bathroom, and I'll be sad to see one team depart. Know the network's thrilled with your work and the cameras love all of you. Bravo." She claps at us. Everybody joins in, causing me to follow suit, with Bo jumping in last. Why am I not surprised?

The show's host walks in and gets a touch-up on her makeup. At least I didn't have to wear any of that shit on my face. I suppose, if we win—*when*—this fact will have to be revisited.

Miss Antonia begins reading off the teleprompter, explaining about our designs for the audience who will watch the show. When she comes up to the elimination, her eyes skim over each one of us.

"The team that, unfortunately, will be leaving us this week is—" Following a dramatic pause, she says, "Frank and Robbie. It's time for you to pack your tools."

All the air rushes out of my body. We did it! We're going to the finale! With . . . Bo. Ugh. Returning to earth, I give Paige a hug, then offer my heartfelt best wishes to the guys.

Shaking my hand, Frank leans in and whispers, "I want you to beat some cowboy butt, you know?"

Smirking, I nod. "I'm down with that." Turning to Robbie, I extend my hand. "Great job in there. Very sorry to see you go."

He grasps my hand. "Thanks, man. I was hoping to face-off with you and Paige in the finals." Robbie places his hand on my shoulder. "If you want to start something with her, don't let anyone keep you apart."

Knowing he's referring to Paige, Bo, and me, I don't reply. Quinn instructs the guys to gather their things and turns to the remaining four of us. "Congratulations. You made it to the last round, which is the primary bedroom suite. Filming starts up in three days, so review these notes and enjoy the break!" She places some envelopes onto the table and leaves, trailed by the camera crew. Soon the losing team wheels their luggage out the door.

"And then there were four." Mary Ellen's comment sounds more ominous than jubilant. I'm with her.

Bo claps. "Damn straight." Extending his arm toward Paige, he bites his upper lip. "Let's go out and celebrate."

My body tenses. I want to scream she's my partner, not his. I want to toss the cowboy back to his Dallas roots. I want to plant a kiss on Paige and stake my claim. Instead, I clench my teeth and watch as she accepts his offer.

But not without looking in my direction first.

The pair go to their rooms to change, leaving Mary Ellen and me in the living room. I have no desire to ask her out, or even leave this oppressive apartment. Instead, I give Bo's ex a curt nod and walk to the exercise room.

To clear my head.

And perhaps pummel a punching bag.

11

Paige

Bo chews his apple pie, like he has every course, with his mouth open. Squirming in my seat at the disgusting noise, I place my fork onto the dish with a half-eaten cheesecake. I let Bo select tonight's restaurant considering I chose our last one. So, here we sit in the iconic, touristy venue, being jostled by other diners and servers.

"I think Frank and Robbie missed the mark by doing two bedrooms, right?"

"I suppose so."

"What's there to suppose? They did the same room twice. Mine was a sleeping quarter for an infant, which is different."

"You have a point." Something inside me argues that if Robbie and Frank had executed a more challenging design, they might've been left in the competition. After all, a nursery done in pastels isn't too cutting-edge.

"I'm always right." He squirms in his chair. "These seats aren't comfortable."

Shocked at the jump in our conversation—although I shouldn't be, because this is at least the fifth one of the night—Bo continues,

"I should offer to remake them. Bet a place like this would pay a pretty penny."

Having no idea whether the restaurant is even looking to replace their seating, I shrug.

"I'm sure they would." He leans over and whips out his wallet, pulling out a business card. Holding it up for me to see, he says, "Never leave home without them."

I'm tired of his conversation jumps. His self-promotion is exhausting. He doesn't have Jesse's wit or sense of humor, for sure. While he's nice to look at, he's all looks and little substance. Plus, a disgusting eater.

My mind replays some of the stimulating conversations Jesse and I have had throughout the competition. He's a fantastic conversationalist, and not only about home remodeling. There's a time and place for that, sure, but I'd like to discuss something other than design flaws in the restaurant. Even if the seats are hard.

When the server drops off our check, I pull out my purse in a half-hearted attempt to pay for my half. As expected, Bo scoops up the bill and pulls out a credit card, making a big show of using a blue card. Keeping my family's black one tucked safely inside my wallet, I murmur, "Thank you."

His head swivels until he locks in on our server, then he snaps his fingers. Mortified, I slump down in my uncomfortable chair. Maybe this is how he does things in Texas, but here, that shit doesn't fly.

The server, wide-eyed, appears at our table and Bo practically shoves the folio into her stomach. I offer her an "I'm sorry" look, then she disappears.

"So hard to find good help. I thought it would be different here in the big city, but I guess I was wrong."

If you treat people with respect, they'll return the favor. Mum's words pop into my mind. Keeping my own counsel, I reply, "She's been busy. I think she had at least ten tables tonight."

"Doesn't matter to me so long as I get the service I deserve." His hand snakes out toward mine and closes around it. "Only the best for my filly."

My eyes slam shut. So much is wrong with his statement, I don't know where to begin. Well, maybe I do. I'm not anyone's "filly," for starters. Not to mention the fact he thinks he *deserves* good service is plain old wrong. Mum's taught me to use the golden rule to bring out the best in people, which works well for me. Bo should try it.

I reopen my eyelids, realizing we're out in the open. Prying eyes from any source could be watching. "It's been a long day," I note. "I'd like to go back to the ViewPad and get some sleep before everything starts all over again."

"You heard Quinn. She said we have three whole days off. No need to rush back to that cramped apartment." His mouth twists in disdain.

"I know, but I'm beat. If I'm going to be of any use at all tomorrow, I'd like to get some rest."

His hand slides up my forearm, and he yanks, pulling me half across the table. "I know a better way to get the juices flowing."

My eyes zoom around the dining room. I used to not care about any sort of public displays, but now with everything going on around VOW-cubed, I've become much more sensitive. Especially after what the media did to my brother. And Xander.

I pull my arm away and sit properly in my chair. "Cameras can be anywhere," I warn.

A broad smile covers his face. "Let them take photos. They'll only be jealous I'm the one here with you."

I retreat farther into my chair. The server chooses this moment to reappear with Bo's credit card payment, and I use this opportunity to leap up. Slinging my purse cross-body, I thank her for her time and wait for Bo to stand.

"I'd like to return to the apartment, if you don't mind."

"Fine," he mumbles. Then he turns, gives me a broad smile, and plants a kiss on my mouth. Before I can react, he trails kisses to my ear. "Are you sure? This seems like a more pleasurable way to pass the time, if you ask me."

I place my palm on his chest. "I'm sure."

He snatches my hand and intertwines our fingers. "Alright." His voice raises. "Let's go home."

Knowing I can't do anything to change the course of this

derailing train, I go along with his outrageous behavior. Once we get into the taxi, I allow him to put his arm around my shoulders. We'll be back at the apartment soon. I can confront him in private, like I've been taught all my life.

When we walk into the ViewPad, it's dark save for a single light illuminating Jesse, who's sitting on the leather chair in the living room. *Shit.*

Seeing him, Bo slings his arm around me and kisses my forehead. In a booming voice, he announces, "I had a great time tonight. So good, in fact, I don't want it to end." He pulls me into his body and kisses me again.

Not wanting to make a scene in front of even just one person, I allow the kiss. For a short time. Pulling away from Bo, I'm about to tell him that the date's over when Jesse's tenor booms.

"You better get caught up. I don't want to deal with a slacker partner, not at this stage." An envelope flies at me and lands at my feet.

Even though I've been annoyed at Bo all night—comparing him unfavorably with Jesse—my partner's performance is way too high handed.

Bending down, I pick up the envelope. "Who the hell do you think you are? Father? I'll look at this shit when I'm good and ready." I throw it back at my partner. "I wish I'd been paired up with Bo!" With this final proclamation, I turn to my erstwhile date and plant a kiss on him, registering Jesse's expression of disbelief and something much darker. Turning on my heel, I race into my bedroom. Let them figure it out.

Slamming the door behind me, I let out a frustrated sigh. What a shitshow.

A voice comes from a bunk across the way. "Everything alright?"

Mary Eileen is the last person on earth I want to see right now. I almost wish Nancy's team had remained here. *Almost.*

"Fine."

I breeze past her and go into the bathroom. After I've washed my face and brushed my teeth, some of the anger about what happened tonight dissipates. When I return to the main bedroom area, hoping she'll be asleep, I'm rewarded with her sitting up in what used to be Nancy's bed looking over some paperwork. Probably what Jesse wanted me to review. *Fuck.*

"Want to talk about it?"

While my suitcase serves as my closet, I use the actual dresser for my unmentionables and sleepwear. I open the drawer, pull out my nightshirt, and toss it onto my bed.

Seeing as I have no one else to talk with about this, I walk over to Mary Linda and stand with my fists on my hips. "It's been a long day."

"And night," she supplies.

"True." Knowing she was married to Bo, I can't stop the question from leaving my mouth. "How do you do it?"

"I'm assuming you mean work with my ex-husband?"

My arms drop. "Yeah." Good as a place as any to start.

"He's very talented and brings it out in me. I tried to go it alone for a while but fell flat on my face. When I re-teamed up with him, clients reappeared. I suppose we work on some level, but it's not easy, to be sure." She pauses. "We broke up because he couldn't keep it in his pants."

Can't say as I'm surprised. "Sucks."

"Truth." She pauses. "I was surprised to see you come back tonight, actually."

Remembering Bo's inviting me to spend the night with him in a hotel, a spurt of compassion for this woman overcomes me. "Do you still love him?"

She plays with the blanket on her bed. "We're divorced."

That's not an answer, which is all the verification I need. "I'm not going to go out with him again." I stand straighter.

"Oh, no. Don't break up with him because of me."

"Well, I didn't feel the chemistry between us tonight. Knowing you and he have some unfinished business—"

"We're finished. Got the divorce decree to prove it."

"That's only paperwork. My parents are still married and all they do is fight." I stop short. All my life, I've only witnessed their example of love as being a perfect couple in public and bickering behind closed doors. Theo's showing a different side of that with Amelia. Xander and Madison don't seem to fight either.

I'm brought out of my head when she says, "If not you, there will be some other woman. And I like you."

"Thanks. I like you enough to stay away from your husband."

"Ex."

"Him too."

We giggle and I go to my bunk. After changing into my night-shirt, I lie awake under the covers for way too long. My roommate's breathing deepens into sleep, yet I can't shut off.

Is it because of how I acted with Bo in front of Jesse?

Is it because of my childish reaction to Jesse's throwing paper-work at me?

Is it because I don't want to be with Bo?

Maybe all three.

On a sigh, I shove the blankets down my torso and slip out of the bunk. I know what I need to do. Grabbing my sketch book and a pencil from my tote bag—once I locate it—I pad into the dark living room. Turning on the flashlight on my cell phone, I find the envelope with my name on it lying on a side table. It's the instructions for the final challenge in the primary suite.

When I plop onto the couch, my hip hits something hard and I swivel to retrieve the offending item. Which turns out to be a block of wood that Jesse uses in his whittling. Turning it over in my palm, I can see several cuts have been made to it, but nothing's formed.

Bringing the wood to my nose, I inhale the scent of jasmine and lemon which comprise the basswood he uses. This triggers an idea for the bedroom. I place the wood onto the table and begin to sketch.

12

Jesse

For the hundredth time, I check the screen on my phone. When the clock finally reads six, I give up the pretense of sleeping and get out of the bunk. Rather, roll out of it. Damn thing was made for midgets.

Rooting around the drawer, I pull out a pair of workout shorts and get dressed in the bathroom. Not sure why. The only other person left in here is Bo, and he's sawing logs on the bed that once upon a time belonged to Dan.

Splashing water on my face, I try to ignore the red dancing around my pupils. My eyes always get bloodshot when I don't get enough sleep. Diana used to tease me about it, especially since I was barely into my teen years, and she couldn't understand what would keep me awake. Even back then, I was restless. School was okay but I had yet to find anything that held my interest. After she was killed, I dedicated myself to being her replacement since she had everything so together. For the umpteenth time, I wonder why she was taken instead of me. At least she had a purpose—she was going to take up business in college and work for a bank. Follow in Homer's footsteps and become a bank's chief compliance officer.

Hence my chosen profession.

Trudging through the darkened hallway, I replay a scenario that happened way too often growing up. Diana would slip into my bedroom well after curfew and rail against whatever was bothering her at the time. Usually some restriction my parents had put on her. More often than not, she'd devolve into complaining about Homer. A smile plays around my lips as I remember the first time she called him that. It was after we watched an episode of the television show where his daughter was being reprimanded. Diana took her side. When our father came where we were playing, Diana swore he looked like the character's father. The name stuck.

Paige's yelling at me that I was worse than her father has to be what kicked me down this memory lane. I wasn't waiting up for them to get back. Well, maybe I was hoping they'd return while I was reviewing the notes.

Perhaps I harbored a bigger hope their date would've been a big fail.

But when they came in, all lovey-dovey, I couldn't handle it. I should've taken Mary Ellen's cue and gone to bed when she did. Instead, I allowed myself to get all riled up over the fact they're now dating and threw the show notes at her.

It's not like I want to date her anyway. She's a free agent—allowed to go out with anyone she wants. But seeing her like that with *him*, of all people, rubbed me the wrong way. So I acted like a sulky teen instead of a grown-ass adult.

Shit. She was right to call me out.

I better figure out a way to handle their relationship, even though the thought of them having one makes me want to hurt someone. Entering the gym, I take my frustrations out on the punching bag.

An hour or so later, I chug some water and toss a towel around my sweaty neck. This is what I needed to clear my head. Ready to tackle whatever the day holds, I saunter into the main space of the ViewPad. On my way across the room, I pass by the sofa and notice Paige sleeping underneath some papers. Shocked I didn't notice her before, I approach and clear my throat. When she doesn't move, I touch her shoulder.

Sleepy eyes meet mine. Lowering to one knee, I whisper, "Sleepyhead. What are you doing out here?"

She yawns. "Must've fallen asleep."

She struggles to sitting. I want to assist her, but don't trust myself not to do something foolish like pull her into my body, so I allow her to get her bearings. When she's upright, I sit on the sofa and help gather her notes.

I whisper, "Why don't you try to get some real shut-eye? It's still early."

"I think I will." She hands me her notes. "Please take a look at what I was drawing. We can discuss them once I'm awake."

"Sounds like a plan." She stands and I try not to notice her long, bare legs. Or how she's not wearing a bra underneath her sleepshirt.

After she leaves the room, Mary Ellen strides into the kitchen. "Paige fell asleep working out here." *Why did I feel the need to explain?* I pull out a mug and pour some coffee into it. "How are you doing this morning?"

"I'm alright. Talked with Paige last night, which helped and didn't."

Not going there. "Try to lean on the helping part." Wanting to change the subject, I ask, "Have you reviewed the notes for the primary suite yet?"

She points to the documentation strewn at one end of the island. "I'm going over it now. It'll be hard to be creative in such a defined space."

I didn't consider it like that. I'm itching to look at what Paige handed me but focus on the woman in front of me instead. "Well, many different options are available. Paint or wallpaper. The type of bed. Other furniture. Plus, the bathroom is a wide-open canvas."

"That's a good way to look at it. Thanks." She raises her coffee mug.

Lifting my arm, I reply, "Don't mention it." I catch my smell. "I better go take a shower before I stink up the whole place." I cringe at her horsey laugh but cover it up with a smirk.

"I wasn't going to say anything."

I drain my mug and return to the bedroom, where my roommate continues to snore from his top bunk. Choosing a comfortable outfit of sweats and a bank T-shirt, I take a shower. I can't get this one question out of my mind: What does it mean that Paige was up in the middle of the night working on the design for our next rooms?

Still unable to answer the question, I stroll into the bedroom. My roommate raises to his forearm. "Clear?"

"All yours."

The bunk creaks under his weight as he throws his legs over the side and hops to the floor. Above his boxers, he scratches his stomach. "Some partner you've got there—a real spitfire. She's got gumption." He elbows me in the stomach as he passes.

I don't want to talk about Paige, especially not with him. "Like you and Mary Ellen, we're not a couple."

"Ah. But we used to be."

I don't want to talk with Bo, but I'd rather discuss his failed relationship than delve into his new one. "What went wrong with Mary Ellen, anyway?"

He opens the dresser drawer. "Seemed like the right choice at the time to get married. It wasn't." He shrugs. "Not much more to it."

Yeah, right. I'm not a gossip, and this is none of my business, so I refrain from asking the myriad of follow-up questions begging to come out. Bending down, I pick up my casual sneakers and a pair of socks and walk toward the door. Raising one of my shoes, I say, "Well, I'll let you get ready in peace." Turning, I open the door and return to the living area.

All alone, I choose a chair in the dining room and allow myself to pull out Paige's notes. Her ideas explode off the page. Mary Ellen's assessment of the space fails. Boring? Certainly not with these drawings. I'm studying Paige's bedframe design when my partner reappears, rubbing a towel across her short, wet hair.

"Hey."

Her head turns in all directions until she spots me. "Oh, there you are."

She walks over to me, her shapely, long legs exposed in her

denim shorts. *Stop thinking about her like that. She's Bo's.* I hold up her sketches. "These are fantastic."

Pink crawls up from her neck to her cheeks. How can she be embarrassed at her talent? She waves her hand. "They were some ideas I drew. No biggie."

I pat the chair next to me. "I think they're innovative." Pointing to her creative use of the high ceilings, I note, "Not many people would think to go vertical."

She settles into the chair I indicated. "When the space is taller than wide, it seems a natural fit."

I place the papers on the dining table. Time to get to the bottom of her insecurity. "Paige, I think you're very talented. Your ideas are always fresh, and they spur me on to think outside the box. I don't understand why you try to hide your gifts."

She toys with the towel. "You must not know too many designers. I'm more run-of-the-mill." She half-laughs. "Hell, my degree wasn't even in interior design. And I only took one art class in college."

"What was your major?" She opens her mouth, but I don't let her speak. "Wait. Let me guess." I size up my partner for a minute then snap my fingers. "English."

"Wrong!"

I frown. "Don't tell me."

"I won't. I bet yours was business."

"Guess I'm pretty transparent."

"Only because I know you work in a bank. But I'm thinking you took some woodworking classes on the side."

My lips lift upward. "At a Vo-Tech nearby. My college didn't offer them." I can hear Homer's disparaging voice deride *because they're too blue collar,* and my lips return to normal.

"Very industrious of you. I couldn't imagine leaving campus to go to another school for more classes." She shakes her head. "By the way, my degree was Spanish. We have a place down in Cabo, so it seemed a natural fit."

"Did you want to teach?"

"Oh, hell no." She chuckles. "Consider me more of a liberal

arts person." She folds the towel on her lap. "So, what do you want to do today? Work on our designs?"

"Seems like the thing to do."

"I need some fresh air. How about we walk the High Line before getting down to it?"

I tilt my head. "I haven't gotten out of this building since we started filming. And we do have tomorrow free too." My hands land on my thighs. "Let's go."

She pops up. "Great. Let me get my sneakers."

She pads, barefoot, down the hallway and I decide to change into shorts considering it's over eighty outside. In the bedroom, Bo's putting on his workout clothes. I don't say anything to him, simply pull out a pair of shorts that will match my shirt. *If Paige wanted him to join us, she could ask him.* We return into the main area together.

When he sees Paige standing next to Mary Ellen, Bo lets out a whistle. "Lookin' good, cowgirl."

He used the singular so I'm sure he wasn't directing his rather uncouth comment to his ex-wife. My thought is affirmed when he continues, "Hi, Mary Ellen."

I have nothing to say, so I keep my mouth shut. Mary Ellen's eyes narrow, but she keeps her mouth closed too. For her part, Paige offers him a sunny smile. The one I thought was reserved for me. Evidence I'm not special to her shouldn't cause my gut to tighten.

Paige addresses Bo. "Going to work out?"

"Yup. These guns don't prime themselves." He makes a fist and raises his arm, exposing his biceps.

Probably steroids pump them, I think, but keep my comment to myself. Mary Ellen covers up what I suspect was a snort by coughing, drawing Paige's attention. "Let me get you some water."

Bo's ex accepts the glass from Paige, and I walk over to the women and touch Paige's shoulder. "Ready?"

She looks from Mary Ellen to Bo, then turns her attention to me and gives me a swift nod. To the group, she says, "Jesse and I are going to walk the High Line to clear our heads." She looks at Mary Ellen. "Want to join us?"

"No, thanks. I want to work on these designs."

Paige nods and turns to Bo. "Enjoy your workout."

Inordinately proud she didn't ask him to join us, I extend my palm toward the door. She precedes me into the hall and before I close the door, I can't keep from looking at my roommate. Bo's scowl could stretch from the ViewPad across the Hudson River. I close the door behind me.

"What brought on that smirk?"

Not about to confess to my partner, I reply, "I'm looking forward to getting fresh air, that's all."

We leave the apartment building via the High Line exit and are inundated with others doing the same exact thing. The old railroad tracks are filled in with lush vegetation. Statues are placed in random spots. Paige walks over to one installation called "Walking on Moonbeams," which depicts a child hopping across silver waves.

"This is fantastic!" Aloud, she reads the placard about the artist and the statue and takes out her phone for a photo. After showing me, she tries to email it to herself only to remember our phones don't have internet. "Shit. I can't keep it."

"We'll just have to come back here after we get our phones back and take another." *Whoa*. What's this "we'll" shit?

She reads from the placard again. "Says this sculpture will only be here through the end of the month."

Filming ends next week, which is the start of next month. Her face falls. To cheer her up, I say, "I bet there are tons of photos of it on the internet."

"Yeah." She kicks an unseen pebble.

She seems so forlorn, I wrap my arm around her shoulder and tug her close. "Let's see what other stuff we can uncover out here that we'll never memorialize. Like him." Letting her go, I point to a random guy with a cat on his head.

She giggles.

"Or her."

A woman hawks huge, ugly jewelry and yells at people who pass her by without purchasing.

Her giggles intensify.

We manage to get by the woman by hiding behind an unsuspecting group. "Or I could buy you an ice cream." I point to a vendor selling cones.

"Only if they have strawberry."

"Let's go check." We approach the booth and her eyes light up when they have her favorite flavor, so I buy two—vanilla for me and strawberry for her. Using my cone to point to a rare empty park bench, we hustle across the walkway and take a seat facing the Hudson River.

Her pink tongue catches the melting ice cream, and I focus on the water. No need to imagine what that tongue could do to any part of my anatomy. *She's with Bo.*

"Thank you. This is a perfect day."

My hand snakes down to touch her thigh, but I retract it at the last second. "Agreed."

Holding her cone upright, she lets her head fall backward. Too bad her expressive eyes are hidden behind sunglasses. *Maybe that's a good thing.* "I'm happy we came out here." She continues lapping at her cone.

"I am too. We needed a break from the ViewPad and the competition. Being out here reminded me to enjoy the gifts we have."

She swallows. "Some of them are even free, like taking a walk. People watching." She pauses. "Checking out amazing art."

Flute music starts up behind us. I add, "Listening to buskers."

"Feeds the soul, doesn't it?"

With the lyrical notes floating around us, and the bright blue sky overhead, warmth in my body comes from within rather than the sun. Growing up, Homer always put down the arts in favor of anything that would make money. Marge, on the other hand, supported the performing arts like plays, musicals, ballet, and symphony. Homer only agreed to them because it was a way to attend something and get credit for it in the business world. Neither thought much about furniture other than to hire decorators every five years to redo our home.

But this, here, makes me want to shout out to the universe *I belong!* I'm exactly where I should be. I finish my ice cream and the buzzing from inside my body has nothing to do with the coldness from the sweet. I've never felt this way about work. Or college. No, when I think about those things, a weight settles over me. But now, here, Paige has lifted it. The only other time I feel this free is when I'm in my workshop.

I turn my head and take in the beauty before me, and not only the High Line. "You have no idea how right you are." She takes her final bite of her cone and wipes her hands on the white paper napkin. Looking at me, she reaches over and wipes my cheek. Her simple, thoughtful touch scrambles my brain. Impulsively, I grab my phone and hold it up in front of us. "Selfie?"

"Of course!"

She tilts her head toward mine and I snap a photo from above. Lowering my cell, I glance at her and catch her staring at me, her eyes begging for me. To what? Kiss her? I've been warned off her by Theo and Xander. Besides, Bo. And Homer. Not a good idea to let our lips do the talking—despite how right it seems.

After a prolonged moment, I pull myself to standing. Not trusting myself to do more, I don't offer her my hand to help her up.

My soul may be feeling light, but my heart's dropping in the opposite direction.

13

Paige

Ever since we returned from our walk on the High Line, my mood's soared—which sparked my creativity. Over the past few hours, I've come up with a window dressing installation unlike anything I've ever seen before. It takes advantage of the primary bedroom's high ceilings, while also acknowledging the need for total blackness at night.

I glance over at Jesse, who's designing the bed. Last I looked, it was amazing. I poke my nose over at his drawing.

"That looks great. Although, what if you added some of your infamous whittling to the headboard?"

His head rears back. "You can't whittle something this big."

I flick my wrist. "Then carve it."

"Carve? Are you crazy? For one, it would take forever. Not to mention I've never carved anything larger than a breadbox."

"Ah-ha! But you *have* done carving before?"

"Well, yes. But as I said." He holds up his index finger. "Too much time." He adds his middle finger. "Never this size."

I tackle the only thing that matters. "How much time do you think it would take to carve the headboard?"

"I don't know. Three, maybe four days."

"And we have five. Problem solved." I offer him my biggest grin. He can do this. Show off his amazing skills.

"Paige," he stares at me. "I've never done anything to this scale. I don't want to—"

When he trails off, I dive in. "Don't you see? This would be an excellent place to showcase your skills. Besides the dresser and two end tables, what other pieces do you have to do for the primary suite? The closet organizer will be installed by the crew, and it's boring anyway. The bathroom doesn't have anything major for us to do, either. That's mainly on the plumber and electricians."

"I'll have to handle the framing for it."

"Half day. Max."

His right foot rocks on the floor. "Too much. I can't get all of this done in five days."

"I'll do the easy stuff. You can do the bathroom framing, bed, and dresser. I'll take over the side tables."

He flips through his sketches until he reaches the matching side tables. He stares at them for a while. "They are relatively basic. I wanted to dress them up, though."

"If they stay basic, I'm sure I can pull it off. Don't forget, I have done light carpentry before."

He gives me a skeptical look. "I don't know."

"I'll also handle the window coverings. Check them out!"

I thrust my design at him and his eyes double in size. "I've honestly never seen anything quite like this before. They're breathtaking."

Not even Father could wipe my smile from my face. "Thank you. I think our trip today inspired me."

"I'd say."

"So, think we can do it? Make our primary bedroom one for the history books?"

He's silent. His foot rocks several times as he contemplates my ask. His khaki eyes meet mine. "We could lose the show because of this."

"Or we could win big," I counter.

Arguing from across the apartment reaches our ears. "Seems like Mary Ellen and Bo are having a difference of opinion."

I giggle. "At least we're discussing our differences like adults." It hits me then that we *are* having an adult conversation. Jesse treats me like a full-fledged adult. Which makes me want to be one. I straighten my shoulders. I *am* one. An adult who has a goal to win this competition.

"True." Jesse's gaze returns to the sketches, and he flips through them. "Do you think you're up for building the side tables?"

My head bobs. I made tables in the house I flipped, so I know what I'm doing with their basic structure. I flip the pages in my hands to the ornate bed Jesse sketched. We have to do this. "I am."

"Call me crazy—"

"Crazy!"

He extends his hand. "Alright. Let's do this."

I reach over and we shake. Excitement bounces in my body. Finished with our drawings and unable to begin anything until the morning, I stand. "I feel like a big meal to celebrate. This will be the last night we're together under this roof before the final round starts."

Jesse joins me and we walk to the kitchen. He opens the fridge, "What's in here?"

"No idea." I'm not in the mood for another casserole. "How about we get takeout?"

"I could go for that. Something fancy as a way to end this on a bang. How about French?"

"Sounds good." I pull out the box of menus Renovation TV left for us, considering we don't have internet. What a pain! Although Jesse made it fun this afternoon. "Pick a place while I ask Bo and Mary Ellen if they'd like to join us."

I pat myself on the back for finally learning Bo's ex-wife's name, and since she usually takes charge of our meals, I'm sure she'd appreciate the night off. Especially after their fight, which finally died down.

I enter the exercise room, which they've appropriated for themselves. Mary Ellen's sitting on the weight bench while Bo's pacing next to the punching bag. "Hi guys. Jesse and I are thinking about ordering dinner in tonight as a way to kick off the final round. Would you like to join us?"

Bo steps forward. "I'm in."

Mary Ellen rises. "Sounds good."

"Come into the kitchen and pick your poison," I laugh. "Jesse's selecting the menu."

We cross the apartment and surround the island. Once we make our selections, Jesse calls Quinn to place our orders since our phones won't allow an outgoing call to the restaurant.

While we wait, the two guys go over to the sofas and turn on the TV. I remain in the kitchen with Mary Ellen, who takes a bottle of prosecco out of the fridge. "Everything okay with you guys? We heard you yelling at each other."

The sparkling wine pops and she rushes over to the sink to catch the overflow. I pull four flutes out of the cabinet. "This is how we design. We've almost finished all the details now." She pours the bubbly into the first glass.

But for them being divorced, and Bo taking me out on a couple of dates, I would think they were still in love. Fight when they're alone and appear happy in public, like my parents. Although, they don't have the happiness in public part down.

"Then I'm happy for you."

She pours the next glass. "I suppose we work on some level."

Her comment makes me wonder about her feelings for him— not for the first time. I hold up the third glass. This time I decide not to hold back. "Do you want to get back together with him?"

She sucks her bottom lip into her mouth and shakes her head. "No. I'm done with him. He cheated on me during our marriage all the time."

"For what it's worth, I agree with your decision. You deserve to be with someone who values you above every other woman. Bo is not that guy." *Other women* deserve this. Me? I'm only in the market for someone who checks off all my boxes—whom I haven't met yet.

Jesse calls, "Need any help in there?"

My pulse skips at the sound of his voice, but I remind myself he's failed miserably with my checklist: he's never responded to my hints, nor has he ever brought me a present, let alone every day. The ice cream doesn't count. So what if he passes the threshold one of being tall and good-looking? Men like that abound in this city.

I reply, "Be right there!"

Mary Ellen places the flutes onto a tray, and I follow her into the living room. When we each have our glass, Bo raises his. "To a great competition! May tomorrow's challenge be met by both of our teams, and may the best one of us win."

Before we can raise our glasses, he adds, "Meaning Mary Ellen and I will be helping you pack!" He swallows his flute in one gulp while the rest of us stare at him.

Jesse takes over. "To the end of an era!" We all drink to Jesse's toast.

I'm about a quarter of the way through my drink when Mary Ellen jumps up. "Oh. We didn't set the dining room table. Paige, help me?"

Surprised she asked, but knowing this is a task I'm well equipped to handle, I take one more quick sip of my drink. "Sure thing."

I go to the drawer where the placemats are kept and pull them out while she clicks the silverware together. In the dining area, she apologizes for Bo's terrible toast.

"Don't worry about it. You're not responsible for him." I bring the napkins into the dining area and together we put forks and knives at each of the settings.

She sighs. "I appreciate that. He was out of line."

Much of what her ex-husband says and does crosses it. With thoughts like these, I'm more convinced than ever that I'm through with him. It doesn't matter that he left me a cute note on my pillow when I returned from the High Line.

The intercom buzzes and we hear Bo allowing the delivery person up. Looking forward to my Quiche Lorraine, we join everyone at the island to divvy up the food. When our plates are full, we bring our meals into the dining area. Jesse dims the lighting.

"Nice job," Bo compliments him.

I agree but keep my thoughts to myself. The ambiance in here is amazing, especially overlooking the water. He pulls out my chair and motions for me to sit. The sound of Bo's chewing cuts through my serenity, though, and I return my fork to the napkin.

"Music!" I leap to my feet. "We need music in here."

Jesse wipes his lips. "Let me get my phone." He remains seated. "Okay. That's not going to work." He casts his face toward mine. "Sorry, Paige. I think we're SOL on this one."

"Yeah, no can do, Little Cowgirl." Bo points at me with his fork.

I smile and try to enjoy a little of my meal, which is tasty despite Bo's unappetizing soundtrack. "Oh, I forgot wine. Anyone want any with your French cuisine?"

"I'm good," Mary Ellen replies. Bo nods in agreement.

"I'd like some," Jesse says.

"I'll get it."

"Thanks."

I duck into the kitchen, open a bottle of red Zinfandel, and pour it through an aerator into two glasses. I remain in here for a couple of minutes to get the sound of Bo's chewing out of my mind before returning to the dining room.

Bo finishes his plate and chomps on some bread while we finish. Talk, naturally, turns toward tomorrow and the beginning of our last challenge.

"We're psyched," Bo says. "We finally figured out how we're going to dress these special rooms. We can be creative under pressure, right Mary Ellen?"

"I'm happy with our design." She looks at me. "Are you?"

I'm beyond proud Jesse agreed to do the carved headboard. His one-of-a-kind piece will make the biggest statement in the room by far. Although, my curtains will be awesome too. "We're excited. Our design is taking us away from our comfort zones."

Jesse swallows his beef bourguignon. "Paige can be persuasive. I can't believe I agreed to let you create the side tables," he chuckles.

"What?" Bo's yelled exclamation takes us all by surprise.

Studying Bo, I reply, "I offered to do the side tables for Jesse while his time is being taken up by other elements of the room." I word my response carefully so as not to give away any secrets. "No big deal."

"But you're an interior designer."

The hairs on the back of my neck bristle. "Your point being?"

"You're a girl. You design stuff and do crafts." He taps his chest. "I'm a man. A carpenter. I create things like side tables for you to pretty up."

I smack my palm on the side of my head as if learning a brand new secret. "Excuse me? I know how to use a miter saw and a caulk gun as well as a glue gun."

Bo turns his ire on Jesse. "And you. You call yourself a man? I'd never foist my work on Mary Ellen—"

My blood pressure rises. Cutting him off, I interject, "Jesse didn't *make* me do anything. I had to convince him to let me do it."

Jesse wipes his mouth with his napkin. "Paige is more than capable." He lays the white cloth onto the table. "You're being a sexist pig."

Instead of placating me, Jesse's coming to my defense ratchets up my ire. "Both of you shut up! I am a capable woman, like Mary Ellen here, and we won't be talked about as if we weren't sitting next to you." I shove my chair back. Mary Ellen does the same.

Stomping behind Bo, I bellow, "I don't want anything to do with you anymore. I don't need a keeper—if I wanted that, I would've stayed home with Father."

"You're as frigid as Mary Ellen! You belong with your cesspool of a father and his partners."

My breathing halts, then returns with a rush. "I'll never go on a date with you ever again. Have a nice life." At the threshold, I turn, "Hope your chewing keeps you company at night." I rush to my bedroom.

14

Jesse

Shocked silence supplants Paige's fiery outpouring. Not wanting to spend another minute in the room with Bo, I get to my feet and pick up my dirty dishes, then walk over to Paige's. Addressing my comment to Mary Ellen, I say, "I'll clean these up."

Bo's knife clatters to his plate and he pushes back from the table. "Take care of that, Mary Ellen." He storms out.

My eyes bug out of my head. I can't believe what I just heard. Placing the two plates down next to my roommate's, I shovel the remnants onto one plate and stack them. Walking behind Mary Ellen, I lower my voice. "Want me to take your plate?" I lift the three I'm carrying.

"What?" She turns her trembling chin toward me, causing my heart to lurch. Pain is written across her face as if someone wrote it with a Sharpie.

I glance at her mostly uneaten dinner. "Do you want to finish in peace, or should I take it away for you?"

"Would you mind?"

"Of course not. I'll set the dishwasher and put everything away. Don't give it a second thought."

As I'm scraping her plate, she says, "How did I not see how chauvinistic he is?"

"I'm sure he hid it from you. Maybe he's warming up to it now?"

She fingers her empty champagne glass. "Yeah." Her eyes close. "I'm going out to the patio. Join me?"

The ViewPad offers few places without cameras, with the patio being a safe haven. She doesn't need an audience—neither mine nor the one who will watch this episode when it airs. "I'll let you wrestle with your demons alone."

She gives a nod of acknowledgment and drifts away. As I load the dishwasher, anger at the dim-witted hick grows. How could he say such things to his ex-wife? To Paige? My partner's a capable adult who can handle herself. If she says she can make a side table, I have every faith she can.

Probably because I'm sure she's able to do a lot more and refuses to believe it of herself.

Once the garbage is thrown out and the placemats are put away, I go to the exercise room in search of peace. When I see it's dark, I know I've found my own haven. Closing the door behind me, I call my lifeline. "Hey, Mr. Hooper."

"Jesse, my man! How are you doing? Still going strong on the show, I hope?"

Loaded question. "We're starting up the final round tomorrow."

"Congratulations. I knew you were going to take that network by storm."

I wish I had his confidence. "I'm trying, Mr. Hooper. I never expected the emotional rollercoaster, that's for sure. Things got pretty tense here tonight."

"I'm assuming it's down to you and your partner and one other pair, right?"

"Yes, Paige is my partner," I remind him. "And the other team is a divorced couple, Mary Ellen and Bo." Even saying his name makes me want to rinse my mouth out with soap.

"I'm sure tensions are running high, but don't let it mess with your head. What do you have coming up for the final round?"

I fill him in on our design for the primary suite. He chuckles. "You don't do anything halfway, do you? A carved headboard?"

"I don't know. Am I biting off more than I can chew?"

"Have you ever done anything like it before? I mean, in my class you did carve legs to a dining room table, right?"

"Yeah. And that was ten years ago. I've done a little bit of carving since, but nothing to this scale. I'm more of a whittler."

He laughs. "I remember introducing you to that. Took to it like a duck to water."

Wishing I had a block of wood and my trusty knife in here, I wiggle my fingers. "It centers me. Always has."

"No matter what, know I'm proud of you, Jesse. You made it all the way to the final round. That's amazing."

"Thanks." Since I'm still in shorts from the High Line, I strip off my shirt and walk around the gym. Even though I already did my workout for the day, another round will take the edge off. While I talk with Mr. Hooper, I hop on the elliptical and tell him about tonight's dinner explosion.

"Hot doggie. That Bo sure has some backwards thinking. Paige was right to call him out."

"I know. But where's the quiet part of carpentry? I don't want to be involved with all this drama."

"You *are* on a reality television show. Stuff like that happens all the time. Wouldn't be surprised if the producers put him up to it."

Would Quinn do that? Somehow, I doubt it. I kick the bottom of the elliptical. "Sucks."

"Not for ratings."

He has a point. Changing the subject to focus on what I need to do once filming starts again, he gives me some wonderful pointers and time-saving strategies for carving. My confidence boosted—along with my faith his health is on track since he didn't cough once during our conversation—I give my high school teacher a big thanks, toss the phone onto a table, and hop on the rower.

An hour later, I get off the machine. Sweaty, tired, and not wanting to sleep in the same room as the snoring wonder, I decide to shower and take the couch. At least it'll be quieter. I enter the bedroom, where Bo pounces. "Your partner is fucking nuts."

I inhale a deep breath. With a level voice, I reply, "She's not the crazy one."

He steps into my face. "What's that supposed to mean, Daisy?"

Not about to let him get away with anything, I drop my shirt and get up in his grill like he's in mine. "It means you were spouting stupid shit and Paige called you out on it. What the hell were you thinking? You basically told her a woman couldn't be a carpenter."

"Haven't met one yet."

"Marion. Peyton," I counter.

"Kicked off in the first round." He shoves his palms against my bare chest.

I don't move a muscle. "Don't touch me, jackass."

"What? Like this?" He shoves me again.

This time, I've had enough. With a roar, I duck my head and rush him. He stumbles back toward the bunks, halting before making contact.

He counters by throwing a punch into my gut that makes me bend over for a second. Hands on my knees, I look up at him and yell, "You asked for this!" I race toward him and throw my weight against his abdomen, sending him flying into the side table. The lamp crashes to the floor.

Not a second later, he jumps at me, throwing me into the wall with a thud. One of the nondescript paintings flies to the floor.

We roll around, each grappling for the upper hand. Bo lands particularly hard hits to my stomach and upper pecs. I counter with a hook to his jaw. With energy mustered from deep within me, I toss him off my body. He whacks the dresser with a satisfying thump.

Standing, he shakes his head, howls, and charges me. I'm ready for him this time and sidestep his bulk at the last second, causing him to plow into the side of the nearby bunk bed. He bounces off the frame and grabs my waistband.

The door flies open. "What are you two doing?" Mary Ellen's voice cuts through our grunting. "Bo! Jesse! Stop it this minute."

Panting, both of us turn angry gazes to her. "I repeat. What the hell are you doing?"

Dropping his hold on my shorts, Bo singsongs, "Ooh. She cursed. She must be mad."

For my part, I pick up the shirt I threw on the floor when Bo first approached me. Like a child, I add, "He started it."

"I bet he did." Mary Ellen approaches her ex-husband and tweaks his ear, causing him to bend at the waist. "What is wrong with you?"

"How about what's wrong with *you*? You never were this assertive when we were married."

She shoves him away so they're as far apart as the room allows. "I should've been."

"Never would've married you if I thought you were like this."

"I would've been much better off."

While the pair trades insults, I gather my pajamas and go into the bathroom, locking the door behind me. I walk to the mirror where I see red marks on my chest. Asshole. I strip and take a shower, trying to erase the dinner and this fight. When I've toweled off, I put on my pajama bottoms and take a deep breath.

Putting my ear on the doorway, I don't hear anything, so I hope it's all clear. Unlocking the door, I notice the painting has been rehung and the side table righted, with the lamp off to the side by the garbage can. Bo's leaning against the bunk, alone.

Reminding myself of Mr. Hooper's advice not to let all this drama mess with my head, I dump my dirty clothes into the bag serving as my hamper, rip the sheets off my bed, and walk out of the bedroom. He can do whatever he wants in here. I enter the public area and am alone. Thank God. I don't need to deal with Mary Ellen or Paige.

In the kitchen, I grab a bottle of beer out of the fridge and stalk to the living room. Choosing one of the three sofas, I begin to set up my bed for the night. Forgot my pillow, but one of these toss ones will have to do. Sitting down, I down my beer and pray that tomorrow's a better day. Picturing my sister standing next to me, I absorb some of her positivity—which mirrors Paige's. Before all hell broke loose at dinner.

Settling into my makeshift bed, I try to expel the images of Paige from my mind. Even if she's no longer with the cowboy, she's still off limits per Xander and Theo. Besides, Homer taught me well that business comes before pleasure, and this show is all business.

I shut my eyes but open them minutes later when someone enters the room.

15

Paige

When Mary Ellen returns to the bedroom after breaking up the fight next door, it's as if something has shifted between us. She stepped into the fray when the mere sounds paralyzed me, catapulting me back to my parents' apartment. Not to mention, we've both suffered Bo—she for far longer and to this day on the show. I open my arms and embrace my roomie. We're both in tight spots, and we need to stick together.

After she yawns, adrenaline clearly crashing, I leave her to get ready for bed and cross the room to my bunk. I'm still too pumped over Bo's disgusting behavior to sleep, so I grab my notes and design notebook and hold them up. "I don't want to bother you. I'm going to take this outside."

I enter the public area, and all's quiet. Seems the guys hugged it out like Mary Ellen and I did. The mental picture this conjures is incongruous. I snort. Can't imagine Jesse doing that.

"Paige?"

A familiar tenor voice drifts from the sofa area. "Jesse?"

His sandy brown head pops up from behind the sofa back and he waves. "Hey. What are you doing out here?"

Leaving my paperwork on the island, I cross the room. "The

better question is what are *you* doing out here?" I survey his makeshift bed. "Sleeping?"

"Couldn't share a bedroom with that jerk any longer."

"I heard your fight. Are you okay?"

"Yeah. No permanent scars." He smiles. "I'm fine, really." When he becomes upright, the sheet falls to his lap and a large red patch on his chest reveals itself.

"Geez." I point. "That might not leave a scar, but it has to hurt. Here, let me get you an ice pack."

His large hand covers most of the mark. "It's fine. I'll be fine."

I hustle to the kitchen, take out a baggie, fill it with ice, and cover it in a towel. "Everyone on earth knows that when a woman says she's 'fine' it means anything but. I'm assuming it works the same way for men." I approach my partner. Moving his hand, I place the ice on his chest, causing his entire torso to constrict. Damn, that's sexy.

WHAT???

"It's cold," he complains.

"It's ice, silly. It's supposed to be cold." I move his palm so he's holding the pack on his chest. His well-defined, naked chest. Not that I'm looking or anything.

"I know you didn't come out here to check on me. Did you want a glass of water or something?"

"No. I knew I couldn't sleep and I didn't want to bother Mary Ellen, so I was going to work on our designs a little bit. Something's been bothering me about the bathroom all day, and I wanted to see if I could figure it out."

"Can I help?"

"You're injured."

"Only my pride." He moves the ice pack, causing me to arch my brow. With a sigh, he returns it to his chest. "I want you to know I gave as good as I got. Plus, I didn't start it."

"I believe you." I can imagine Bo throwing the first punch. Probably sucker-punched Jesse, although his face seems clear. At least that's good. Now's not a good time to remind him about the hidden cameras around the ViewPad.

He prompts again. "So, what can I do to help?"

"It's stupid, really. I'm sure the bathroom won't be a big deal."

He moves the ice pack off his chest again, offering me a clear view to his tight, little nipples. Replacing it before I have time to react, he says, "Everyone wants a spa-like retreat in their primary suite nowadays. I thought that's what you were delivering?"

He picked up a sense of serenity from my drawing? I settle into the sofa next to him. "You're right. But the bathroom is the same old thing." I hold up my right hand and use my left one to point to my fingers. "Toilet, double vanity, shower, tub." I wave my palm in front of my face and pretend yawn. "I think it needs something else."

"Like what?"

"I don't know." This is the point where he should give me a good idea. He remains silent. I open and close my mouth several times, but get nothing.

"You've given the main components of any bathroom. What would make it stand out?"

"A clothes closet? A linen closet? Not enough room in there for a separate water closet, though. I measured in every possible direction."

"Too bad. WC's are always welcome."

"I know." I flip through my two closet ideas, but nothing calls out to me. In my mind's eye, I walk through the bathroom and use it as an owner would. The space, while not small, isn't overly large either, since we stole square footage for the laundry room.

Sighing, I say, "I guess a linen closet makes the most sense." My fist bounces off my thigh.

Jesse's gaze lands on my fist and I don't move my bare leg. His chest is on display, so my legs can be as well. He licks his lips. "You're unhappy with this decision."

"It's so—expected. The judges always harp on creativity, so that's what I want to give them."

He tosses the ice pack onto the coffee table. "Don't try to force your creativity. It'll strike when you're least expecting it."

Since I have no other option, I agree. Flipping through our

designs, we discuss the primary bedroom and make some more decisions about the furniture I'll be making for it. Because I'm not as skilled as Jesse, we decide to pare down the legs on the side tables. Curved legs require a step more experience than I have. Other than that, we're good.

I place my design notebook next to his ice pack and turn to face him. His chest begs for my attention. Above his head, the oversized clock reads two. "I guess we should turn in. We have a big day ahead of us tomorrow."

"Sounds like a plan." His full lips curve upward. "Who knows? You may dream up the bathroom solution."

"Maybe." I drop my hand onto his forearm. "In case I didn't say it before, thank you for standing up for me with Bo earlier. I can't believe what he said."

"Even I was shocked. I mean, I knew he was a jerk, but not a full-on asshole like that. I don't know how Mary Ellen can deal with him."

I allow my hand to slide up and down his arm. "I've talked with her. My guess is she won't for much longer."

His head drops down, following my hand on his body. He swallows. "Good."

"I want you to know that I'll never accept a date from him again. I had decided this before his disgusting performance at dinner. And we never did anything more than the kiss you witnessed." I look down. "It was wrong. We were all wrong."

The air charges.

I've never taken the lead in any sort of sexual encounter in my life. Men always do that. Right now, though, I have the sense Jesse isn't going to make a move on me. Is it because of Bo? Unlike with the uncivilized cowboy, I have felt a spark between my partner and me since the beginning, regardless of what I denied to Mary Ellen.

I wet my lips. "I had a great time with you today on the High Line. Thank you for that."

He shifts in his seat. "You're welcome. It was fun."

My hand drifts higher on his chest, my fingers tracing the red mark Bo put there. Looking into his hazel eyes, which appear more khaki than green right now, I ask, "Does it hurt?"

His head shakes. "No."

"That's good." With our gazes locked, I lean forward and place a light kiss on the red mark. His body shudders at my contact.

"Paige?"

We're alone. No cameras are around—unless I count the "hidden" ones. Right this second, I don't care about them. Shifting closer to his body, I lean into his face. "Jesse."

"We shouldn't."

My palms slip to his shoulders. "Why not?"

He doesn't move. "Your brother and Xander—"

I don't want to be talking about my family right now. No, our mouths should be doing more important things. "What do Theo and my cousin have to do with us?"

He swallows, his throat capturing my attention for a moment before I return to his eyes. They're so expressive, I can almost read him like a book. A very interesting, complicated romance. Maybe involving a billionaire and a nurse. I digress.

"They told me to stay away from their baby sister."

His words land like a flame. What business do they have interfering with my love life? It's not like I warned Madison or Amelia against them. I stick my chin upward. "Is that how you see me? As a baby?" I shift my hips, causing his eyes to flare. I'm sure of his response but want to hear it anyway.

"No."

"Are they here now?" I place both of my palms on his cheeks.

"No."

I pause for a moment, giving him one last opportunity to bow out. When he doesn't, I close the gap between our lips. His are as soft as I imagined. Full, but not too much. I slide my hands around his neck and fuse our bodies together.

After a second, he joins me in a kiss so explosive, it's like I've never been kissed before. Our lips meld, over and over. I trace the seam between his lips, and he opens for me. Sliding inside, I thrill at the touch of his tongue on mine.

Lifting my leg, I slip it over his lap and sit on his thighs all the while rubbing my chest into his. I've never been the aggressor before, and can't for the life of me figure out why. This is like pure heaven. I grind on his growing erection, savoring the way he hits me in exactly the right place.

"Paige," he moans.

Between kisses, I reply, "Right there with you."

His hands cover mine. I reach for his lips again, but he pulls his head back a fraction. "No. Paige. Stop." His words don't compute. He cups my cheeks and prevents me from moving forward. "We have to stop."

I stare into his khaki eyes. His pupils have dilated to take over more than half of the iris. "Why? No one's here."

He closes me out by shutting his eyelids. "They're in the next rooms."

I grasp his hands and tug them off my face. "They're not here. And I don't care." I fuse our lips together again.

Beneath me, Jesse's legs move and his hands drop to my waist. When I pull back, he says, "I can't."

With a deliberate movement, he lifts me off his lap and stands. Turning on his bare feet, he leaves me in the living room.

Alone.

16

Jesse

Lying in Frank's stripped bunk—because my sheets remain in the living room—tonight's unexpected events replay.

The way Paige kissed me.

The way our tongues tangled.

The way she rubbed her body against mine.

"Get your career in order before you look for love." Homer's words repeat. I couldn't be further from being settled in my career, despite his wishes. True, I did follow in his footsteps like Diana was going to do. Also true, my boss told me the promotion was mine next month. But when I think about what I've accomplished here over the past weeks, all I want to do is more of this.

Which means I have no idea where my professional life is going. How can I take on a woman like Paige now? Especially since I have a sinking feeling she's more than my usual random hook ups.

Her creativity is intoxicating. Even though she doesn't recognize her talent, I do. The fact she came out to the living room to work on our show notes proves my point. She's fantastic. She's about to shine in front of the entire world.

Plus, her wrapping doesn't suck. Tall and lanky, with legs that go on forever. While I usually prefer long hair, her pixie cut rocks. And those eyes. Damn. I want to get lost in them for days.

The fact she's Theo's little sister, which makes her Xander's little "cousin," is one more stumbling block. I have to respect their wishes. Although, this has the potential of being much more than a fling.

If I let it.

Which I won't.

My erection throbs between my legs, but I refuse to go into the shower and jack off. Thinking about awful things like the last Mets game loss or an old sewer break causes it to deflate somewhat. Bo's snores finish the job. No. I'm not ready for Paige.

I manage to fall asleep, only to be awakened by the shower turning on. Guess it's time to get up. Our last first day of shooting. I manage to pick out my clothes—I can't bring myself to choose another bank t-shirt—and take a shower after Bo exits. Neither of us acknowledges the other, which suits me fine.

We're all in the kitchen, trying our best to ignore one another, when Quinn arrives. "Are you ready for your final challenge?"

We all mumble versions of yes, causing her to frown. "Everyone okay? Aren't you excited to find out who's going to win?"

"I am." Bo volunteers.

The three of us glance at each other, then try to make more of an effort to respond to the director. "Slightly better." She claps. "Let's see how you do with the primary suite challenge. The camera crews are in your apartments so go get 'em."

Grabbing my tools, I follow everyone down the hallway to the elevators. In silence, we shuffle into the cab and go down, down, down. Bo and Mary Ellen get off on seventeen and I wish *her* well. As does Paige.

When the elevator dings at our floor, I allow Paige to precede me to the front door, where she stands waiting for me to open it for her. Reaching into my pocket, I produce my key and open it. "After you."

She walks in without a word and goes straight to the primary suite. This is going to be a long week. As I follow her, I decide we're going to have to talk this out. On a sigh, I enter the bedroom, which has a couple of cameras set up. Great. No talking in here.

I join Paige in the bathroom. Since no cameras are in here yet, I jump on this opportunity to clear the air between us. As much as I can. "About last night—"

She rubs her arm. "Yes?"

I need to come clean. "I was shocked and honored you wanted to do that with me." When she doesn't respond, I add, "I liked it. A lot."

She throws her arms akimbo. "Then why did you stop us?"

"Remember, I was warned away from you by your brother and cousin."

"So what? They're not here."

"I can see why they stressed the word 'baby' when referencing you."

Oops. Wrong observation to make. "I am twenty-three fucking years old. I've had several sexual partners. I'm no baby." She twirls on her heel and faces the wall where the vanity will go.

"I didn't mean it that way." Now I have to process the fact she's been with another man. Several. Keeping my voice low, I continue, "The problem is that I like you. Too much."

She turns to me again, her fingers on her lips. "Really?"

Damn. I didn't mean to confess this part. She'll never understand why I have to keep her at arm's length if I like her. Yet, I can't lie. "I do."

A huge smile covers her face. "Let's stop here. After we finish filming in a few hours, know this conversation is *not* over." She leaves me alone in the bathroom. *Shit. This didn't go as planned.*

The camera crew files in to set up. Since this is the first room I'm going to tackle today, I lay out my tools and go into the living room to get the lumber I need for the framing. Since she didn't give me any changes, I'm going to assume we're using the bathroom design we agreed on the other night.

"Oh no!"

Paige's scream brings me into the bedroom in a flash. Nothing seems to be amiss. "What's wrong?"

"I forgot my belt." She pauses. "My *lucky* belt," she clarifies.

My eyebrows furrow. "Oh."

Shaking my head, I turn toward the door but stop when she asks, "Can you get it for me? You're all set up and I'm still getting my stuff ready in here."

I have way too much on my plate to get an inane piece of clothing for her. She looks perfectly fine. If she wants it that badly, she can take herself back to the ViewPad and get it. "No can do. I'm up to my neck with the bathroom remodel." I take one step and turn. Ignoring the purple blotches on her face, I ask, "Confirming you want to go forward with the design we discussed, and don't have any changes?"

"No changes," she huffs.

Seriously? All this over a belt? "Okay." I leave her, twisted as a knotty pine, and return to the bathroom.

I hear her tell the camera crew she's going back for her belt, and then the front door slams. Chuckling under my breath, I start hammering the required framing.

"And cut! Great job today, guys."

The camera crew packs up their things while I review the items we knocked off our to-do list for the day. The bathroom's done from my end, and I've made a huge dent in the dresser. Despite the tiff over her belt in the morning, Paige worked hard today. Her window coverings are coming along great.

I pick them up to examine her craftsmanship. "This is fantastic, Paige."

"You think so?"

I run my finger over the edge, which she smoothed like a pro. "I do. I've never seen anything like these. They are so creative."

She tucks her hair behind her ear. "Thank you." She links her arm in mine, causing a zing to race through my body. Which I tamp down. "Let's get out of these rooms. I need a break."

I escort her onto the patio and inhale the fresh air—or as fresh as city air gets. "This is a great area." I glance down at the floor. "You did a fantastic job with the tiles."

"I appreciate your kind words. I'm trying to keep up with your talent, that's all."

A few minutes pass in silence. "I was surprised you sanded out the edges so well on the window treatments. That's not easy to do."

"Tell me about it. I was going to ask you for advice, but you were busy working on the dresser and I didn't want to bother you. So I figured it out."

"Now I'm doubly impressed. Working with a sander can get tricky."

She blows on her fingers. "What can I say? I'm trickier."

Adorable. Red danger signs go off in my head. I need to put more space between us. "Want to return to the ViewPad for dinner?"

"No way. The less time I spend there, the better."

While I'm digesting her statement, the camera crew enters the living room. "You can stay in this apartment for however long you like, but you can't do any more work in the primary suite until the morning."

Paige salutes them. "Got it, captain."

We all chuckle at her words, then they leave us. In this apartment. *Alone.* Stepping away from her and into the living room, I continue our conversation. "How about we get a pizza?"

She closes the French doors we installed when we did this room. "Sounds good."

I walk into the living room to look for the box of menus, only to realize it's in the ViewPad. "Shit. No menus here." Her glorious face falls. "How about I go out and get us the pizza while you set up the dining area?" This will be good. Get out *alone* and clear my head of all things Paige. When I return, I'll be more able to ward off her advances.

"Great idea. Teamwork." She walks to me and wraps her long arms around my neck. A breath away from my mouth, she whispers, "Mushrooms and extra cheese."

I still. One movement and my lips will cover hers. Of their own volition, my hands close around her hips. *Don't pull her in.*

All my hard-fought inaction is quashed when she presses

forward and kisses me. With a groan of defeat, I pull her hips to mine and take what's being offered. Her lips are like the best epoxy —strong but sinking in everywhere. Leaving no part of me untouched.

My hand slides up to the back of her head and tugs her tighter. Her moan of acceptance short-circuits my brain and my tongue delves into her mouth. Hers dances with mine in an erotic tango.

Her stomach gurgles in protest.

Returning to reality, I release her from my bold grip and step backward.

Her hand flies over her midsection. "Sorry!"

"I'll get the pizza."

Without turning back, I cross the living room and am out of the apartment in under a minute. When the door snicks shut, I open my mouth and exhale a long breath. *This cannot happen again.*

Throughout my trip to the nearest pizza place a block away, my mental running commentary exhorts me to put more space between Paige and me. After I place our order, I sit. The television tucked into the side catches my attention. Because I haven't watched anything other than Renovation TV channels since filming started, I soak in NewsTime like it's a novelty.

A story about the decreasing crime rate in the city is praised, the upcoming crowning of a new beauty queen hyped, and mention of the plight of the VOW-cubed executives is mentioned before Theo's bestseller is reviewed. *Good for him.* I'm happy he found his happiness with writing. And he found his girl afterward. I smile, recalling the change Amelia caused in him. Which is replaced with a frown when I remember he met Amelia before he changed jobs.

At least Xander was set in his career long before he met Madison. Although after going to work for Madison, he's not in his original field either . . .

Discarding these anomalies from the world view Homer instilled in me, one additional reason to steer clear of the designing beauty pops into my mind—she's a New York City princess dealing with her father's alleged crimes. Who needs the paparazzi stalking them?

I could protect her.

What?

No.

When my order is called, I add a six-pack of Guinness and bottle of red, take the box, and return to the building. Before I open the door to 1626, I give myself one last slap upside my head—figuratively—and enter.

The lighting in the room is dimmed. She somehow found candles to adorn the cozy dining room. And she's wearing a breezy dress rather than her paint-splattered jeans and the belt that caused this morning's uproar.

I'm so fucked.

17

Jesse

"Hi." Her sultry voice wafts across the room and lures me inside.

"Hey." I hold up the box. "Pizza's here."

"Great." Her hand sweeps toward the dining area. "I'm ready."

As if adding its agreement, her stomach emits a loud noise, causing us both to laugh. Placing the box on the island, I say, "Better get you fed before that thing tries to eat me." As soon as the words leave my mouth, I realize my mistake.

"Save that for later, stud."

My eyes close. "I deserved that." Opening them, I choose to move on. I grab my pizza and take my seat at the table. On a chair the judges liked.

She devours her first slice faster than me. *Impressive.* Picking up her next one, she curls the two sides in to face each other but holds it away from her mouth. Swallowing my last bite, I remark, "This is good."

She places her pizza down on her plate and wipes her hands. "All pizza in the city is varying degrees of great, in my opinion. We don't live in some Podunk town."

"You're right there. Although, I'm sure the fine citizens of Podunk might take issue."

Shrugging, her talented hands bring her wine to her lips. Even though I prefer draft, I'll take a canned Guinness over any other label, any day. As our meal continues, we talk about mundane things such as the weather and sports teams. Safe topics. I can't help myself, though. I want to know more about my intriguing partner. "I already know your brother and Xander, obviously. I think you have two other brothers, right?"

Her empty wine glass lands on the table. "You're right. Kiefer's the oldest of us. I'm proud of him," she pours herself another glass of wine. "He got his medical license about a year ago and has started his own plastic surgery practice."

Theo's mentioned him a few times. "I heard. It's a hard slog, but he seems to be starting out well." I stand. "Excuse me. I need another beer. Do you want me to get you anything?"

"No. I'm good." I pick up the pizza box, together with our plates, and go toward the kitchen. "Thanks for cleaning up," she calls.

"Don't mention it." Why did her expression of gratitude sound like a sultry siren song? The mermaid she asked me to whittle for her seems appropriate. *Stop it, Jesse.* Keep things platonic.

I place the empty pizza box into the recycle bin and grab another beer. When I return to the table and crack it open, Paige continues, "Then there's Ryder. He's just nine months older than me, but light years ahead in terms of his career path. He's the catcher for the NY Aces."

I sit back. "Let me see if I got this right. Your parents are raising a plastic surgeon—"

"Dr. Kiefer."

"A best-selling author—"

"Theo."

"A baseball phenom—"

"Ryder." Before I can continue, she says, "And a house flipper." She snaps her fingers. "Which one of us doesn't belong?"

"I was going to say, 'and a fabulous interior designer.'"

She rolls her eyes.

The need to end her self-doubt rolls into me like a ball on an unlevel floor. I suppose being lumped in with a doctor, an author, and a pro-ball player can seem intimidating, but she has a special gift. "You are very good at what you do. Who else would've thought of designing unique window dressings for the bedroom, and then could actually create them with such attention to detail?" When she doesn't respond, I say, "I know the answer to that. No one but you."

"Whatever." She waves her hand. "It's not like I'm changing someone's fucked up nose or telling the world about an unsung hero." She pauses. "Or even winning a pennant for the city."

"True. Your brothers all have their own gifts. But don't belittle yours because it's different. Your designs can change people's lives. Enhance the beauty around them. Inspire them to dream bigger. These are worthy goals, different from what your brothers do, but as important."

She brings her wineglass to her mouth. "I've never considered it like that before."

"You should." Standing, I say, "Let's go to the living room. It's more comfortable in there."

"What? I didn't make this room inviting enough?"

I smile at her petulant tone. "It's wonderful in here. I should've said let's get a change in scenery." Reality is, I need to have more distance between us. Not about to admit that, though. Grabbing my beer, I stride over to the sofa we designed, facing what should be a real television. Too bad it's only a prop.

Taking off my shoes, I stretch my legs and let my feet rest on the coffee table I built. I raise and lower my heel on it. Sturdy. When she finally enters the room, I say, "See. This is strong. Like the woman who designed it."

"More like the man who built it." She takes a seat next to me. As in, right next to me. Cuddled up against my body next to me.

"What are we doing, Paige?" A dalliance, I can do. Been there many times. Anything more? My life isn't set up for that.

"I'm having a wonderful time with you." She adds, "Talking."

We don't need to nearly be in each other's laps to talk. I shift my body to put some distance between us.

She places her hand over my heart. "That about covers my family. Tell me about yours. I remember you had a sister who died when you were fourteen."

"Diana. She was seventeen, all set to go to Fordham in the fall and major in business."

She sips her red wine. "Do you have any other siblings?"

"No."

"Where did you go to college?"

My lips twist. "Fordham. Majored in business."

"Oh wow. I can see you two were close since you followed in her footsteps. Her death must've been hard."

I never talk about Diana to other people, preferring to keep her bottled inside myself. My therapist said I could tell everyone or no one, my choice. I've never been tempted to share. Paige doesn't pry but somehow compels me to divulge details about my vivacious sister. "She was a lot like you. Outgoing. Friendly. Wicked sense of humor."

Her hand strokes my cheek. "I bet I would've liked her."

"I think so."

"Did she have," she swallows. "Cancer?"

"No." I pull away from her touch. I *never* discuss this with anyone. Sure, I make donations to MADD every opportunity I can, but I don't advertise this fact.

"Oh. A car accident then?"

How is this woman so perceptive? I suppose these are the two leading causes of death among young people, besides gun violence. And if she were a victim of a mass shooting, Paige probably would've heard her name. I stand. "Yes," I croak. Tipping my head back, I finish my beer and go to the kitchen to get rid of the can. Conversation closed.

From the sofa, she says, "That's awful."

Apparently, I was wrong. I toss my empty can into the recycle bin beside the pizza box. "It was a long time ago."

"I can see it still affects you. I'm a good listener."

I march back to the living room and sit in a chair this time. She can't crowd me here. I purse my lips and stare at her artwork covering the fake television.

"Was she handy, like you?"

When I don't respond, she asks, "Did she have a keen eye for design?"

Still without my participation she barrels forward. "I bet she made you go to tea parties when you were a toddler." She chuckles. "I always wanted a little brother to do that to." After a pause, she adds, "Or a sister."

Her last comment forces me to reply. "She tried when I was six. She passed me the teacup and it was empty. I remember flipping it upside down and yelling she drank my tea. Marge came in and had to console me."

"Did your mother give you any tea?"

"Yup. With extra ice, the way I liked it." I smile at the memory she unlocked. "Still do."

"Note to self. Make sure to have enough ice cubes for Jesse's iced tea."

Another fun memory about Diana resurfaces. And another. I don't stop to think about it, but simply share the good times I had with her. All the laughter. She was a great big sister, and we had so many adventures.

Wiping a tear off her cheek after a particularly funny story about how my sister insisted on dressing up our German shepherd like Max from "The Grinch" one holiday season, Paige says, "You're good at this. You should talk with Theo. I bet he could write a great book about Diana so people learn about her wonderful, although too short, life."

Perhaps it's all the happy stories. Or it's the innocent laughter still echoing off the walls. Maybe it's the newness of telling her things I hadn't thought of in a long time. Whatever the reason, I choose to come clean to Paige.

"She was hit by a drunk driver."

Her hand covers her mouth. "Oh my."

Because the floodgates are open, I can't stop the story from pouring out of me. "She was walking home from the convenience store with a loaf of bread for Homer's lunch. She was on the sidewalk. A guy in his early twenties roared up the road and plowed right into her. The coroner said she didn't know what happened, and she didn't suffer. One second she was walking back to our house, and the next. Poof."

"Jesse, I am so sorry." Paige gets up and races into the bathroom —the one we completed—and returns with a box of tissues. Pulling one out, she doesn't use it on herself, rather wipes my cheeks.

I was crying?

She perches on the arm of the chair, urging me to continue. "It was a beautiful ceremony. There were so many flowers, the church smelled like a garden center. And the people! What I remember the most was the entire high school came out, or so it felt. She was a senior."

"And you were a freshman when it happened?"

I nod. "Yeah." I don't want to return to that time. I don't want to remember what happened next. How my parents fell apart. Marge blamed herself for asking Diana to get the bread. Homer's guilt was worse. She was getting the bread for his lunch. Plus, she had him wrapped around her finger. After all, she was following his footsteps into banking compliance.

Then there was me. Aimless. Adrift. Alone.

Paige prods. "Did you have to go for counseling?"

I snort. "You bet your sweet ass. My parents threw me into therapy with a vengeance. They hovered over me, not letting me do anything that might be considered 'dangerous.' High school turned into a nightmare."

"I'm sorry you had to go through this." Her brows furrow, as if trying to remember something. "Your contact, Mr. Hooper. Did you meet him in high school?"

"How do you know Mr. Hooper?"

She tucks her hair behind her ear. "I might have caught a glimpse of his name when Quinn asked us to put in a contact on our new phones. You had written high school something by his name."

My shoulders slide downward. "He was my high school wood-working teacher."

"I'm happy you had him on your side when your family was imploding."

My lips curl upward. "I loved his class. It was the first time I was able to use my hands to create something functional. It was like magic."

"And then you took all of his classes and started learning more about carpentry." She pauses. I can see her working out my professional choices. "Oh shit."

Sad eyes meet mine. "It was more important for me to live out my sister's dream than follow my own, which I didn't have at the time. Homer wanted a protégé in the industry, and since he lost Diana, I stepped into her shoes. For the first time ever, he was proud to have me as his son. Someone to carry on his legacy."

"But didn't he want you to be happy?"

"It was a fucked-up time. I did what I did to try to help them. Honestly, I didn't give my love for woodworking too much of a second thought back then." Without realizing it, I'm holding her body in my lap. Somehow, she slid down the arm of the chair during my "confession."

She cups my cheek. "What did your parents say when you told them about this show?"

I glance away. "They told me to get this out of my system and take the promotion I've been offered at the bank."

"You're too good to, quote, get this out of your system." Paige squirms in my lap. "My parents were much more up in my business before the FBI—"

It's her turn to stop talking. "How has it been for you since the indictments?" I've heard from both Xander and Theo, who had already established themselves in the professional world before everything went down. Paige is still struggling to find her way. When she doesn't reply, I turn her trick on her by cupping her smooth cheek.

She sighs. It's not an audible noise, rather a movement deep within her chest. "Honestly, it's been hell. My parents fight all the time. All our staff except our maid and personal chef were let go. When things get too bad, I stay with Theo. But since he's found Amelia, I feel like a third wheel there." She bites her thumb.

"This show was a respite for you, huh?"

Her gaze drops. "Kinda."

I know something about running away from problems. Hell, I fled to Fordham and didn't return home, even during breaks, by making up excuses. "I get it. College was that for me. Although, I got four years out of that deal. You're only away for six weeks."

"Despite the shit that went down with Bo last night, this has been like heaven for me." Like me earlier, it seems as though her dam has burst. "I used to love our place. We have views of Central Park. It's magical and serene. Rather, it used to be. Now it's filled with breaking glass and screaming."

I hug her. "Sounds awful."

She rests her cheek against my pecs. "It has been. I mean, don't get me wrong. Growing up, my parents always fought when we were at home. But it was more like bickering. Now, it's become a full-fledged war."

"Your parents were always portrayed by the media as the perfect couple."

"In public, they were."

"Wow. Yet they managed to produce four amazing kids. A doctor, a writer, a baseball player," I tick off her description of her siblings. "And a wonderful interior designer."

At my final addition, I score a small smile. "House flipper," she corrects.

"I'm sure they're proud of you. They're just preoccupied right now."

She snorts, then tries to cover it up by coughing. *Adorable.* "Want some water?"

She snuggles into my body, her fingers tracing the spot where Bo hit me yesterday. "No, I'm good."

We sit in silence for a while. Until her hand stops moving. And her breathing smooths out into slumber. Only when I'm sure she's asleep do I kiss her cheek. Knowing this position won't allow me to get any shut eye, I hook my arms behind her back and under her legs and stand.

Despite her height, she's light as a feather.

I carry her down the hallway into the one completed bedroom in the apartment. I pull the duvet down and lay her on the sheet. While sleeping in her clothes isn't the most comfortable, I can't imagine undressing her. Instead, I slip off her shoes and tuck her in.

After watching her sleep for a few minutes, I go into the bathroom and splash some cold water on my face. I'm tired, but I can't force myself to leave her in this apartment all alone. We both opened wounds tonight, and I want some comfort. Against my better judgment, I return to the bedroom and slip into the bed, making sure to leave space between our bodies.

Lying here, my mind churns from the truths I shared with her earlier. Memories I haven't thought about in years, and facts I never reveal. She shared some deep secrets with me, too. I want to wrap her in my arms and tell her everything will be alright. I don't move.

I close my eyes and pray for a reprieve.

Sometime later, my eyes spring open. Something's pressing against my morning wood. I take in my surroundings and realize what it is. Rather, who. I'm spooning Paige, whose ass is plastered against my lower half—because my arm is pulling her tight. I release the pressure against her abdomen.

"Don't."

Her sleepy murmur almost makes me return my arm. Almost.

I try to put distance between us, but she turns over. Face to face, she stares into my eyes, which I'm sure are rimmed with red.

"The red in your eyes brings out the green in them."

Her words mimic Diana's from years ago. "Go back to sleep. It's early." I have no idea what time it is.

She pushes against my front. "I'm not tired anymore."

Your cue to make a graceful exit, Jesse. "I can make you coffee. I know the decorator here included one of those machines." I force a smile, however, all I want to do is enjoy her as my breakfast.

She shakes her head. "I don't want coffee either."

Heaven help me, I know what she wants. I want it too. After

sharing so many secrets last night, it's as if the universe wants us together. And I'm tired of fighting against everything I want.

"How about this?"

I bring my face closer to hers, receiving a beautiful smile. My hands cup her cheeks and I pull us together. Her soft lips are like a gift. One I want to unwrap forever. The kiss turns carnal in two seconds flat, with our tongues stroking each other's and hands sliding up and down our exposed bodies.

Which are covered by too many clothes.

My fingers unzip her dress. She tosses my T-shirt over my head. Her tongue laves the mark left by Bo on my upper chest, making my stomach contract. Not with pain—rather, desire.

Before I turn her onto her back, I tug her dress over her head, followed by her lacy bra. When she stares at me with big, brown eyes, I refuse to hold back any longer. My palms cover her boobs while I babble about how much I want to be with her.

Paige's fingers tangle in my hair. Dragging her lips away from mine, she replies to my nonsense with her own. "You're not like anyone I've ever known. You're sweet," she kisses my left eyelid. "And sexy." She kisses the right one. "And funny." Her lips find my nose.

She pulls back. "But most of all, you've been through hell and are ready to live your best life. Show the world—and your father—that your talent matters."

Before she can make contact with my mouth, I affirm, "Like you're doing. You're not only a house flipper, Paige. You have a keen eye for design. Don't ever dim that." I push forward, and all talking ceases.

Her little moans drive me wild. God, I want to hear this woman come undone for me. For longer than a day, a week, or even a month. My soul screams she's mine for keeps.

A voice in Homer's tone says, "You're still not settled in your career." I shut him down. I don't want to hear any nonsense now. I only want to be with Paige.

Skimming my hand down her torso, my hand lands on the top of her panties. Instead of diving beneath them, I slide over them, covering her pussy. Her hips buck into my hand, her back undulating on the soft bed.

She breathes. "God. Yes, Jesse."

"You like that?"

"Yes," she moans.

Her sound undoes me. I slip beneath the material, inside her folds. My breath sputters at how wet she is. For me. Because of me.

I circle her clit, not touching the nub even though I know that's where she wants me to be.

"Yes. Please. Right there." Beneath me, she wriggles to entice my finger to give her what she wants. As if it's been denied her in the past.

I pull my hand away and bring my finger to my mouth. And lick. She tastes divine. "Paige. You're sweet, inside and out."

"I need you," she wails. Her legs bang against the bed, and her eyes bore into mine.

How can I refuse this woman anything? I return my hand to her pussy as our mouths meet in a kiss filled with need and promises. "You feel so good."

"For. You." Her breathing comes in shorter pants, wanting what I'm about to deliver.

Offering her my tongue, I sweep inside her mouth at the same time my finger caresses her clit. Locked from head to toe, both of us still partly dressed, I massage her.

The front door opens and bangs against the wall. In a panic, I jolt out of the bed, trying to process who might be entering our space.

"Who's that?" Paige, on her elbows, squeaks from the bed.

I'm about to say I don't know when chatter reaches my ears. *Fuck.*

18

Paige

Wearing yesterday's breezy dress, I walk out of the bedroom to confront the cockblockers, otherwise known as *NYC Views*'s camera crew. Could they have any worse timing?

"Hey," I muster. Poor Jesse's still in the bedroom trying to tame the beast we unleashed. It was the least I could do to get out here and stall for time.

The guys in the crew give me a double take, then they wave in greeting.

Better take this bull by the horns. "Jesse and I were working late last night—not doing actual changes but discussing our ideas. We fell asleep here. Sorry."

The crew smirks, and I know they're not buying what I'm selling. Oh well. I tried. Besides, who's reputation am I trying to salvage? Not to mention this place is wired, so they might have been watching us. Although Quinn did say they would be turning off the cameras in the rooms once we filmed their episodes. I hope so. I don't want our private business ending up in someone's spank bank.

The leader of the pack replies, "Not a problem. We're setting up for today's shoot. Why don't you go back to the ViewPad and put on a more appropriate work outfit? For filming, of course." He snickers.

"Hey guys," Jesse emerges from the back hallway. I wonder how he got himself under control in such a short time. On second thought, I don't want to know.

They respond with a rousing, "Good morning," and the guy closest to Jesse holds up his palm for a high five. With cheeks stained a light shade of pink, he connects with his own, then shakes his head.

"You can go about your business. Pretend like we're not even here."

Yeah, we'll be right on that. I turn to Jesse. "I'm going up to the ViewPad to take a shower and get ready to face today's challenge."

"Go ahead. I'll meet you there soon. I want to take one last look at the, uh, thing back there." His thumb points toward the bedrooms.

Because I don't know which "thing" he's referencing, I give him a noncommittal nod. When I close the front door, I sag against it for a second, fanning my cheeks. While mortifying, the stuff that happened before was damn hot. Remembering Jesse's hands all over my body, I take frustrated steps toward the elevator. My first orgasm with a man was so close.

Hope helps me sail into my bedroom in the ViewPad, where Mary Ellen's working on her manicure. No wonder it always looks amazing.

"There you are."

I flip open my luggage and toss through the assortment of clothes. More like the couple things I still have that are clean. If I had my phone, I could call our service to make a run. Maybe I should go shopping?

"Earth to Paige."

"Excuse me." I glance at my roommate. "Did you say something?"

She returns the brush into the nail polish container. "Have a good night?" Her eyebrow raises.

I control my need to crow about Jesse and me. "It was good." Noncommittal enough?

Screwing shut the nail polish, she urges, "Do tell."

Not about to spill *all* the details, I have to share a few. Those moments were too delicious. "Jesse and I worked late last night. Well, not actually worked. Talked. Yeah, that's a good way to put it. We talked." About my deepest fear that I'll never live up to the examples of my brothers. About his sister, and the aftermath of her death. A sadness fills my soul until I remember this morning. I force my body upright.

"And by talking, you mean your lips were moving but no words were said?"

I bite my bottom lip. "Something like that."

"I knew it! Didn't I tell you there was something brewing between the two of you?"

"I don't know if this qualifies as a thing. More like an," I search for the right word. "Exploration."

"So tell me. Was this a Lewis and Clark type of expedition, or an Amelia Earhart crash and burn?"

How Jesse turned on my body with only his fingers answers her question. "Definitely an American tale." I giggle and she joins in.

Her lips turn downward. "At least one of us is getting some."

Her statement returns me to earth. "There are a ton of men out there. Much better than Bo." It's as if I spit out his name.

She taps her fingernail against the dresser's surface. "Yeah."

Selecting one of my remaining clean pieces of clothing, I walk over to her. "Leave him in the dust where he belongs. Think of it this way—be grateful you didn't have kids with the jerk."

Her hand covers her stomach. "True. A small blessing."

"See. There's always a silver lining." I take a step away, then turn back around. "Your man is out there, waiting to meet you. Or getting himself ready. I know it."

Walking into the bathroom, I place my clean clothes on the counter and check my reflection. Do I look any different? I've had several sexual encounters with men, which they enjoyed, but I'm sure Jesse was about to give me a taste of what I've been missing. Damn camera crew.

I'm aware sex is a physical act, but I was getting worried something was wrong with my plumbing since I never felt anything close to the bliss I feel when I touch myself. From the way Jesse handled me this morning, it's a good bet he's going to break the frustrating streak.

I turn on the shower and step inside, letting the water roll over my body. I imagine Jesse in here with me, his hands running all over my body. Dipping into my pussy, like he did this morning. I mimic what Jesse did earlier, before the camera crew came in and ruined everything. I touch the special place he worked into such a frenzy, and excitement springs to life. Angling my body in the right way, the shower spray adds to my pleasure, and I fly off the cliff. Panting, I reach out to the white marble tiled walls for support.

If only Jesse could do this to me. *I know he can.*

Allowing myself a few moments of grace to get my breathing back under control, I pick up the shampoo and wash my short locks. I wonder if he prefers longer hair? Rinsing off, I decide I don't care. I'm not changing for anyone and I like my cut. It's easy. Not complicated. Perfect for me.

I turn off the water and step into the bathroom, drying my body with a plush, soft white towel. As I run it over my legs, I picture Jesse's muscular ones. While I have a small chest, his pecs and abs are defined. Not like Bo's over-the-top muscles, but his six-pack suits him. I'd like to run my tongue over it to confirm. Laughing, I put on my clothes, leave the bathroom, and enter the empty bedroom.

While I've become friends of a sort with Mary Ellen, I'm happy to have this place to myself for a few. Allows me to moon over my partner a little while longer. At eight-thirty, I saunter into the public area for a cup of coffee before filming begins, only to hear low rumbles and growls. Should've stayed in the bedroom.

Bo announces, "It's a stupid idea."

"I think it would be good," Mary Ellen counters.

The two continue arguing, and I tune them out in favor of searching the area for a much more pleasurable sight. When Jesse comes into focus sitting on the sofa holding a coffee, I drink him in. He looks edible. I'm not thinking this because I'm hungry, either, although I do need to find some fuel.

Walking over to him, I whisper, "How long have they been going at it?"

"Longer than I've been out here." Knowing how miserable Mary Ellen is with her partner, my heart goes out to her. When Jesse adds, "I brought some cinnamon buns from the bakery across the street," I focus on the good.

Glancing around to ensure no one's watching, I kiss his cheek. "You're the best. Want me to bring you one?"

He points to a plate sporting crumbs on the coffee table. "Couldn't wait."

I leave my man and go into the kitchen where the box of deliciousness sits on the middle of the island, not even slightly annoyed he ate without me—a definite no-no on my checklist. Pouring a mug of coffee, I select the largest bun in the bunch and drop it onto my plate. Snagging a napkin, I return to the sofas thrilled I can no longer hear Bo and Mary Ellen's "discussion."

Plopping down next to Jesse, I hold up the pastry. "Thanks."

He moves his coffee mug away from his talented lips. "Enjoy."

I take a bite and moan. Swallowing, I exclaim, "This is fantastic!"

"Better watch it, or Bo will think you're doing something other than eating breakfast." He tucks my short hair behind my ear. "Besides, I want to be the only one to elicit such a noise from your pretty little mouth."

I'm down with that.

Quinn chooses this moment to enter the ViewPad, a clipboard in her hands. "Good morning! I trust you had a good night's sleep and are ready to get back to work at the apartments?"

I swear she shoots Jesse and me an approving glance, but I must have imagined it. Mary Ellen and Bo join us in the living room.

"I wanted to tell you the network's excited for the show. I've shown some of the execs the footage so far, and they're impressed with your skills and how well everything's coming across on the small screen. Well done!"

Everyone chimes in with variations of "Thank you."

Her praise shoots through me. We have a fifty-fifty chance of winning this. Given all Jesse confessed to me last night, I want to win it now more than ever. He's repressed his desire to be a carpenter in favor of keeping his sister's dream alive, and to honor his father. I understand the inclination to follow in your father's footsteps, although I brushed mine off while Jesse's taken it to the opposite extreme. If he enjoyed banking it would be another thing—but he doesn't. He was built for this. Anticipating a victory, my hands rub together.

Sitting across from Bo, whose mouth isn't running for once, I study his features. He is classically handsome. Well-proportioned with symmetrical features. His muscular frame is bulky in a meathead way. His dark brown hair is the right length of shaggy.

I angle my head toward Jesse, and my heart leaps. His short sandy brown hair is styled in an effortless manner. His body has the right amount of muscles. But his eyes are what steal the show. The hazel—with flecks of khaki and green and amber tell the true story. Of intelligence and devotion. A girl could get lost in them for days. *I want to get lost in them for years.*

Trying to control my thoughts about my sexy partner, I lean against the sofa and force myself to be impartial. If I were an executive, which of these two men would I want representing the network on their own show? A cowboy persona could garner ratings. An earnest carpenter could draw people in as well. I'd choose the real-life man over a caricature any day. *Twice on Sundays.*

While Quinn keeps talking, I turn my attention to Mary Ellen. Now there's a beautiful woman. The cameras must eat up her gorgeous body, long, blonde hair, and perfect nails. As I watch her, she frowns and pulls her mouth into a slight grimace. I can't imagine the network would want that representing them, but expressions are an easy fix. Compared with her, I'm essentially a tomboy with my short hair and crappy nails. It hits me. I'm the one bringing our team down. Sitting straighter, I vow to do better.

Quinn asks, "Ready?"

Might as well try to start winning them over now. I don a cheery smile and yell, "Heck yeah!"

My response garners chuckles from the rest of the people in the room, and an "are you okay?" glance from the man sitting next to me. *Trying to pull my weight, Jesse.*

I stand. Since we left everything in 1626 this morning, we wait while Mary Ellen and Bo gather their stuff. As a group, we enter the elevator, Quinn offering pieces of advice which I don't hear. Instead, I keep formulating ways to earn points and help us win.

When we're inside our apartment, I take a second to enjoy all we've already accomplished in here. I'm most proud of the hidden pantry, while I know Jesse's partial to the hydraulic lift above the fireplace that moves the artwork over the television. That was a feat, to be sure. Doesn't compare with his using cabinets to conceal the pantry doorway, in my opinion.

"Ready?"

For more things than one. Even though the cameras are stationed inside the primary suite, out here we're alone. I kiss his cheek. "Let's do this."

In the bedroom, I put the finishing touches on the curtain holders and figure out how I'm going to attach the material to them. Needing a breather, I lay the long pieces of timber on the floor and go to the work area where Jesse's working on the bed. "The frame looks great."

He glances at me. "Whatever. That was the easy part." He taps the butt of the handle of the knife he's using to carve the head-board. "I don't think this is going to work."

Since he's blocking my view of his work, I place my hands on his shoulders and move him to one side. Blowing on the wood, I uncover the work he's done so far. It's . . . minimal. "Can I see your sketch again?"

He flips a piece of paper at me like a petulant little boy. I hold it up against the massive wood he's laid out on the bed. "Looks like you're starting off strong." I purse my lips, trying to figure out the best way to offer him advice. "You may want to draw your sketch directly on the board. It might make it easier for you." I hand him my pencil. "You can use this. It gave me luck with the window covering frame."

He snatches the graphite out of my hand. "Thanks," he grumbles, dropping it onto the bed.

Irked at his reaction, I toss, "Just trying to help." I give him my back. "I'll return to my assignments and get out of your hair."

"You do that."

Jerk. How can a man who was so tender this morning revert into such a rude cave dweller on a dime? Vowing not to engage him again, I pull out my sketches for the side tables and assemble the materials.

Focused on sawing the wood needed for the tables, I jump when someone taps me on the back—luckily, I had finished the cut. Spinning around, I scream, "What!"

Jesse stands before me, hands in his pockets, looking at the functional concrete floor. "Didn't mean to scare you."

My heart continues pounding. "Well, you did." This is the first contact we've had in hours. Jutting my chin, I ask, "Can I help you?" Still not over the earlier fiasco.

"Guess I deserved that." His foot rocks. As if being forced out of his soul, he asks, "Can you take a look at what I've been doing?" When I don't react, he adds, "Please."

Knowing it took a lot out of him to come to me, and wanting to present a united front for the cameras that have now appeared, I force my expression to soften. "Of course."

I follow him, stopping in front of the headboard he's carving. His hand runs over it, removing sawdust. "It's much harder than whittling. What do you think?"

Glancing from the headboard to him, I take in his dejected air and let go of my anger from before. He was frustrated and lashed out, and I happened to be the lucky recipient. "Let me see." I study what he drew and the carving he's started. He followed my advice and sketched the drawing onto the wood, which is good. His carving, however, is tentative at best. Already a day and a half of this challenge have gone by, and he's barely made headway on this project.

Best to start with the positive. "I like your sketch. I think you accurately drew it. Good job."

He shoves his hands into his back pockets. "Thanks."

"As for the carving, it feels, I don't know, timid. This design calls for big, bold strokes of your knife, but these"—I run my finger over a small groove—"are too light. Do you understand what I'm trying to convey?"

His hand slashes through his hair. "Bolder, got it."

"Yeah, and maybe try to angle the blade more. You also might want to consider deleting some of these lines," I point to them on the headboard. At the rate he's going, he'll be lucky to finish the larger outlines. Picking up the pencil, I start erasing some lines. Stepping back, I examine my handiwork.

Grumpy Jesse comes out to play. "Fine. I got it."

"Only trying to help." I take a step backward. "You asked me, remember?" He wanted help and that was what I was giving him. Guidance. He doesn't have to be sulky about it. If he's like this now, what would he be like in a relationship?

Relationship? Just because I have high hopes he'll be the first man to give me an orgasm doesn't mean we're in one. From his demeanor, it looks like he doesn't remember this morning at all. I stomp back and resume working on the side tables. Which I'm creating for him so he can carve the headboard. He's frustrated, not mad at me. *Let it go, Paige.*

The end of the day arrives faster than I thought possible. I got both side tables done today, plus the window coverings are ready to be hung. Tomorrow, I need to turn my attention to the other elements of the bedroom before spending the final day on the bathroom. I checked and the tilers did a great job, so there is that.

Quinn breezes into the work room. "Thanks for all your hard work today, guys." Her eyes linger on me a tad too long. *What's that about?* The director announces, "Day Two is in the history books. Like before, you're allowed to stay in the apartment as long as you would like, but you can't do any more work in there."

"Great," I offer as Jesse responds, "Okay."

We return to the apartment to gather our things. "How are you two feeling? Excited for the competition to be coming to a close?

Wanting more time to execute your vision for the suite? Enjoying this process?"

Why is she being so chummy? Considering my choices are talk with her or my downtrodden partner, I choose her. "This has been a fantastic opportunity. Thank you for choosing us, Quinn."

She smiles. "Have to admit, I championed your application the moment it crossed my desk. I love the zing you two have. Also, since neither one of you has been in the industry before, your ideas are fresh. That's a plus."

"Thanks."

"Paige, I want to put your mind at ease." Our gazes meet. "No new news has broken about your father."

Why is she so focused on Father? She's probably simply trying to relieve my mind. I bring my lips upward. "I appreciate your letting me know."

While Quinn's talking, Jesse has moved himself into the kitchen and took one of his beers out of the fridge. More-or-less day drinking. Oh joy.

Quinn watches my partner for a minute, then claps. "I'm going to visit with Bo and Mary Ellen. Do either of you have any questions for me?" When we both answer in the negative, she and the camera crew leave.

The room falls silent.

Wanting to pull Jesse out of his funk, but not in a particular hurry to be the butt of his snarls again, I pick up my design book. "I think we did a lot today."

He tips the can to his mouth. "I guess."

"Got the side tables done and I've started working on the millwork design."

"That's great. Good job."

At least I earned a pat on the back. "What are your thoughts about dinner?"

His shoulder rises. "I'm not hungry. You can get what you want."

Annoyed, I snip. "How about I want to rewind this day and start over in bed with you?"

His response is fast. "Not going to happen again. That was a mistake."

My fists ball at my hips. "I didn't think so."

19

Jesse

The stricken look on Paige's face almost makes me recant my statement. But Homer's mental assaults all day keep my lips locked.

You're not good enough.

You're going to make a laughingstock of yourself in front of the whole world.

You're too smart for this.

And then the kicker. *Career before love.*

Turning my back on the beauty with fire in her eyes, I finish my Guinness and crumple the can. "I'm going back to the ViewPad." She can follow me or not. I start toward the front door.

When my hand lands on the knob, she says, "You're better than this."

Slamming my eyes shut, I take a deep breath through my nose. Bowing my head, I admit defeat. "No. I'm not, Paige. I don't know how to carve a headboard. I'm going to lose this competition for us."

A touch on the back of my shoulders makes my shoulder blades bunch. Her fingers play at the bottom of my hair. "You're doing your best. So am I. Don't give up now."

I open my eyes but remain staring at the dark stained hardwood.

"I'm not—I'm only admitting reality. If you were paired with Bo, I'm sure the room would be in much better shape by now."

"Maybe." She runs her fingertip down the center of my spine. I try not to react to her touch but can't help leaning into it. "But I'd be miserable dealing with his chauvinistic comments. Plus remember—he didn't think I could handle the side tables."

He did say that during our awful last dinner together. "You did a great job with them." She cheated a little on the corners, but overall, it was a strong effort. I'm sure the judges won't give us too many demerits for her work. No. That honor belongs solely to me.

"Your work on the bed is going to be much better."

I want to fling her away from my body so I can breathe. Race into the hallway and onto the sidewalk. Drown the voices in my head with Guinness on draught rather than these cans. Since I'm stuck here at this moment, I settle for, "We'll see."

She tugs at my hand, and I have a choice. I can return with her into the apartment or pull away and live out my destructive fantasy.

"Come here," she half-commands, half-begs.

It's now or never. Return or go? No choice, really. "I need fresh air." Without waiting for her, I open the door and walk down the gloomy hallway. Need some lighting in here. Change up the carpet. Add some bright artwork on the walls.

When I reach the elevator, I press the call button, banging my fist against my thigh. In short order, the doors open and I walk in, only hesitating when I hear Paige yell my name from the apartment. Ignoring her, I press the button for the lobby and smash the "close door" button.

The entire descent, I battle with myself over whether I should return to Paige or unleash my demons. The doors open and standing in the lobby is Quinn with her camera crew. Bo's there, too.

I can't. I just can't.

Instead of getting out, I press sixteen and return to "our" apartment. This time, when the door opens, Paige is crumpled in front of the doors, her head on her knees with her hands in her hair.

I exit the elevator and creep over to her dejected form. Touching her shoulder, I say, "Hey."

She raises her face toward me, her light brown eyes awash in unshed tears. "You came back."

"I did." I slide down the wall and join her on the floor. Guilt bubbles that it wasn't her who made me return, but I squash it. The fact I returned has to be enough. "I'm sorry I was a jackass to you in there. I wasn't lashing out at you, but at myself."

"Figured. You're like how Theo was before Amelia." Her arm drops to the floor. "I only wanted to help." She flicks the rust-colored carpet. "Talk to me." When I remain silent, she adds, "I'm not a baby. I want to make this better for you."

Theo and Xander see her as the baby of the family. To me, though, she's a fully formed, capable adult. With keen observations. Plus a sharp wit and an excellent eye. Banging the back of my head against the wall, I admit, "I kept hearing him all day. Saying I couldn't do it."

She absorbs what I've said. "Your father?"

I nod.

"Why would he say that? You were trying to accomplish something you've never done before."

My voice lowers. "Because it's not a worthy endeavor."

She tilts her head. "What makes it unworthy?"

There is only one answer. "Money." I pause. "And prestige."

Paige drops her chin onto her knees. "My family has money, tons of it. Well, until the government freezes it all." Her nose wrinkles. "Guess what it taught me? It could buy fancy stuff but not happiness. You could afford to go on vacation, but misery went with you, too. Money's not what's important."

Her words land like an arrow to my heart. "My father's bank account didn't save my sister from the drunk driver, either."

"And who's to say there's no money in carpentry? When we win, you'll get a television show, which has to come with a nice paycheck."

I let her answer soak in. Ignoring her blatant optimism, I reply, "You're right. But it's still an elevated blue-collar job. Not white collar, following in Homer's footsteps and becoming the chief compliance officer like my sister dreamed."

"Father's white collar. Look where that landed him."

The pain in her voice pulls me out of my own misery. She's going through as much pain as I am, if not more, considering her family's currently in the middle of it. I drop my hand on top of hers. "I'm being selfish. I know what you're dealing with right now is awful."

"Yeah." She turns to face me. "We make some pair, huh? Morose and depressed, at your service."

A grin forms. "Which one am I?"

"Morose." A brilliant smile crosses her face. "We're both resilient, too."

I squeeze her hand. "You certainly are." Her quick wit and positive attitude are like a salve on my gaping open wounds. With clarity, I realize she's what's been missing from my life. For years. Slapping my hands on top of my knees, I say, "Let's move out of the hallway, shall we?"

I scramble to my feet and offer my hand to help her up. She places hers inside mine and I pull her to standing. I must've overestimated my strength because she lands against my body. Closing my arms around her, I whisper, "I got you."

She doesn't move. "Promise?"

In that instant, I allow myself a piece of paradise and close my arms around her body. Holding this brilliant woman next to me, all the voices in my head flee, leaving an intense need to spend more time with her. Alone.

Stepping back, I sling my arm around her shoulders. "Let's go."

Inside 1626, we go about collecting our things. Since we're not allowed inside the primary bedroom, I pick up my sketch for the headboard and collapse onto the sofa. I can't figure out what's holding me back from working on it.

Paige comes up next to me. "Want to talk about it?"

I do and I don't. After a brief internal debate, I toss the sketch next to me. "Nah. I think I need to take a break from it for a while. Want to get dinner?"

"Sure. Someplace quiet, though. I don't want to be around a ton of people. And I *definitely* don't want to deal with Bo."

Her mentioning the rival carpenter reminds me of what I witnessed in the lobby, and I relay it to my partner. After a moment, she says, "That is weird, right? She didn't want to talk with us outside of this apartment. What do you think they were discussing?"

"I don't know. I didn't hear anything. And Mary Ellen wasn't there either."

Her eyebrows rise. "Do you think Quinn was talking some sense into him? Telling him his brand of assholery doesn't play well on television?"

Her description of Bo makes me chuckle. "You didn't seem to mind at the beginning." Why did I say that? I sound like a jealous boyfriend. Which I'm not. Jealous. Or a boyfriend. *Whoa.*

Her eyes bounce to the wall of windows, then she focuses on me. "At first, I liked him because he was paying attention to me. He brought me flavored water, my favorite. He got overbearing fast, though. He eats with his mouth open." She grimaces. "Then, at our dinner, he was awful to our server."

"He never came across as anything other than a jerk to me." I pause. "And he snores."

Her fingertips rub my chest over the mark he left during our fight. "Let's not talk about him anymore. We'll find out what they were talking about, or not. None of our business right now."

Can't argue with her logic. "What do you think about Japanese? I remember hearing about a good sushi place near the High Line. Want to try it?"

"Let me wash up and we can go." She disappears down the hall to the completed bathroom.

Alone, I enjoy the sound of silence. For once, Homer isn't criticizing me. I'm aware I need to come clean to my parents about the changes I want to make to my life, but this can wait until after the results of the show are made. If we win, I'll be able to celebrate with them and hopefully gain their approval. If I lose, no harm, no foul. I never told them about Handmade by JD and my Etsy shop. I can close them down and they'd never be the wiser.

I scan the room, sitting taller. We did a damn good job in here. Our plans for the primary suite are creative, too. I hope they're enough to win this competition.

I hope *I'm* enough.

Before I can go down that road again, Paige re-enters the room. "I'm ready. Let's get out of here."

We go to the Japanese restaurant and sample a few different rolls. My favorite is the "Dynamite Roll," basically tempura shrimp with a delicious sauce, while Paige favors the eel.

Blowing on the hot green tea, she says, "I'm not ready to return to the apartment building. Want to do something fun?"

I stare into her silky brown eyes and am lost. "What do you have in mind?"

"A club."

I blink. I like clubbing as much as the next guy, but this isn't what I expected to hear from her now. Especially since she said she didn't want to be around a bunch of people. Yet, I can't deny her anything. "I'm game."

She whips out her phone, then drops it onto the table. "Shoot. I was going to call Jimmy, but I don't have his number memorized."

My stomach hardens. "Who's Jimmy?"

"Our vehicle concierge."

I understand the three words she said by themselves, but not as a phrase. "A what?"

"Jimmy's in charge of all our family's vehicles. If we need a ride somewhere, we call him and he sends a car to us."

Okay. When she said she had money, she wasn't kidding. I've long known that Xander and Theo are rich, but never considered the implications. "Most of us call an Uber."

"Can't do that now either. No internet, remember?"

"Taxi? Subway?" I pause. "We can always walk."

She scratches the back of her head. "You can hail us a taxi."

I motion for our check, then tease my partner. "Is My Lady too good to ride the subway?"

She crosses her arms across her chest. "I'm not royalty."

I chuckle. "A subway ride will do you good." I pay the bill and escort the brooding woman next to me down the stairs into the subway station. The typical unpleasant odors assault our senses.

She fans her face. "It smells horrible down here."

I buy us one MetroCard with two rides on it. We can share it to take us to the club, as I'm sure we'll take a taxi back to the apartment. I inhale deeply. "Nothing like the scent of dank garbage on a late summer's evening to get the senses rolling."

She hits me and I laugh. Grabbing her hand, I lead her toward the middle of the train, which comes within five minutes. Enough for her to get an eyeful of the buskers and others milling around.

We walk into the rather full car, where one seat's available in between two large men. She shakes her head and stands in place. Unlike her, I grab the pole before we move but the sudden lurch throws her off balance. Because I was watching her, I prevent a potentially embarrassing fall into the two men and guide her hand onto the pole.

Not a single word was spoken between us. Her eyes, though, convey thanks. Among other things.

We arrive at our destination seven stops later and she's the first person off the train. Following the sway of her hips, she leads us toward the exit. I don't bother to tell her that the other exit would take us closer to our destination, enjoying experiencing the subway with her for the first time.

When we reach street-level again, she whirls on me. "Do you seriously travel like that through New York City?"

"I do."

"It's dirty."

"It's fast. And cheap. Two good things, from my point of view." Although usually without the gorgeous decoration she provides.

Paige tucks her hair behind her ear, the dark brown locks glinting in the moonlight. "Perhaps," she allows. "Let's get to Club Cielo and dance off the subway." Looking at the street sign, she points, "This way."

We arrive ten minutes later, and Paige gives the bouncer a hug. While she's never taken the subway before today, she's connected with all the right people. We're inside the crowded club, drinks in hand, before I would've made it to the middle of the line cued outside.

A new song by The Light Rail echoes throughout the club. "I love TLR! C'mon, let's dance."

I hold up my beer. While I enjoy dancing, I much prefer savoring my Guinness in peace. She shrugs and chugs her entire Mexican mule, then flips over her copper mug in triumph. She leans forward and screams, "Your turn!"

I shake my head. It's heresy to do what she asks.

Hands planted on her hips, she stares into my eyes. "I rode the subway. You can chug." She adds, "Or leave it."

Not an option. Offering a prayer I'm not struck by lightning, I bring my glass to my mouth and let the dark stout slide down. Finished, I hold the glass in front of me, mourning the swift loss of the Irish ale.

Paige claps, then grabs my hand and drags me onto the dance floor where she proceeds to shake her ass in all sorts of illicit ways. I have rhythm but can't compare with her moves. She doesn't notice. When the music changes to a Hunte anthem, we both jump high in the air pumping our fists.

And laughing.

So much laughter.

Then there's the kissing.

So much kissing.

When "This Can't Happen Again," the anthem Cole Manchester wrote for the Concert for the Children of Ukraine that debuted at the worldwide event held in July, the place goes bonkers. We end up singing the final chorus, arm in arm with a bunch of people we've never met. After it comes to an end, Paige runs her palm over her forehead and points to the bar. Slinging my arm over this spitfire, I lead us toward rehydration.

Standing in line to get the bartender's attention, I kiss her cheek. "This is exactly what I needed. Thank you."

"Agreed." She raises her hand and the bartender points to her, so she gives him our orders.

"You're amazing. I'd probably still be waiting outside to get in if not for you. I'd definitely be dying of thirst."

Her fingertips bounce off my stomach. "Stick with me, kid."

This is sounding like a better idea by the second.

When the bartender returns with our drinks, I pay him while she chats him up. He seems interested in her. I place my hand on her ass and give him an innocent smile. The guy takes the hint and moves on. *Smart.*

We scope out the tables and are crossing the room when I spot Quinn. Pointing, I yell in Paige's ear, "Quinn's here."

She follows the direction of my finger and takes a step, then stops. "Shit! Look who she's with."

A sinking feeling overcomes me. It better not be who I think it is. I check out Quinn's companion and sure enough—Bo sits across from her, drinking a pale lager out of a bottle. Heathen.

I grab Paige's hand. "Let them be."

She lowers her voice, "Do you think they're dating? Why are they here together? Will this fuck up our chances in the competition?"

All good questions. For which I have no answers. "I don't know. But she isn't a judge, so hopefully not. Let's go over there." I indicate an area across from them, separated by a multitude of club goers. We beat a hasty retreat.

Sipping our drinks, Paige moves on from our work colleagues to giving me the dirt on the other people at the club. I try to ignore Quinn and Bo together here, but it's hard. When an upbeat tune by Untamed Coaster rings out, I debate returning to the dance floor but decide I'd rather vacate the premises altogether. The sighting has ruined the club for me.

I finish my Guinness too fast for my sensibilities and place the glass onto a countertop. Leaning in, I ask, "Want to get out of here?"

She holds up her mug and uses the other hand to point to the ceiling with her index finger. A second later she shows me an empty copper container. "Thought you'd never ask. Although," she hands me her mug which I place on the counter next to my empty glass, "We're taking a taxi this time."

"At this hour of the night, that's a given."

We slink out of the club without causing a stir, and I hail a yellow cab, which returns us to the High Line after several traffic snarls. After I pay the hefty fee, she remarks, "I get the subway now. Traffic like that sucks."

Holding the building's door open for her, I agree. When we approach the elevators, I cock my eyebrow. "Which floor?"

"Sixteen."

Since I don't want to return to the ViewPad either, I press the button and soon we're inside the apartment we're renovating. She looks adorably disheveled after having drunk, danced, and delighted in the night.

With me.

She giggles. "Alexa! Turn on my sexy playlist."

Silence.

Curious as to what's on her "sexy playlist," I swivel my hips. "Is this a Spanish song by Ozzy Martinez?"

"Nope. It's 'Love Rules.'" She shakes her body to an imaginary beat. "Good choice, though." Twirling around my body, she sings some of Hunte's lyrics in a surprisingly melodious manner. Then she changes to "Let Me Give You a Sweet" by TLR. She shimmies in front of me in the most seductive of ways. "Then, there's—"

I silence her with a passionate kiss. Like the ones we shared in the bed in the other room, not the tamer ones from the dance floor. Here, no one's watching.

I pull back. Cameras roll twenty-four-seven in the ViewPad, but not in here. Right? My brows pull together.

Her fingers trace my eyebrows. "None of that now." She smiles. "Not when the music's playing and we're the only two people around."

I kiss the tip of her nose and grab one of her hands. "Let's move our party."

Her hand squeezes around mine and all my synapses fire at once. I'm eager to finish what was interrupted this morning, knowing we'll be able to see it through until the end. Which I don't expect will be until the very wee hours of the morning. As we walk down the hall, I pull out my cell and tap the screen. "There."

She pokes her nose toward my phone. "What did you do?"

"I set an alarm for seven, so we have enough time to return to the ViewPad, shower, and get ready for the shoot without the camera crew as witnesses."

She wraps her arms around my neck. "I knew I was with you for a reason."

Her lips meet mine and I kick the bedroom door shut. Even though we're alone, I don't want any stray camera angles picking up X-rated material.

Standing, we kiss and explore each other's mouths for a long time, molding and reshaping our lips, our tongues replaying our dance moves from the club. I pull her shirt up and over her head and kiss each boob through her flimsy white bra, nibbling on her taut nipples. Her hands go behind her back and soon she's bare from the waist up. I allow myself a moment to revel in her form.

"You're gorgeous."

She cups her boobs. "An A-cup does not gorgeous make."

I kiss the back of each palm and then her small endowments. "You're gorgeous to me."

"I'll take that. I also will take your shirt, please." Her fingers land on the material covering my torso, which she tugs out from my waistband.

Taking over, I rip it over my head. Breathing hard, she examines my chest, then leans over and kisses the mark Bo left behind. Neither one of us comments about it, and she undoes my belt buckle. Theo's and Xander's warning about staying away from their "baby sister" flits through my mind, and I dismiss it. She's clearly no baby.

My belt clatters to the floor, then the telltale zipping noise indicates my fly's down. I glance down and she's eye level with my erection, which is at about ninety percent. She latches onto the top of my jeans and boxer briefs and I take over, kicking the remaining clothes and shoes off. Before everything hits the floor, I grab my wallet and toss it onto the bed.

"You're glorious."

"I'm defined, but your brother and cousin make me look like a fifty-pound weakling." I'm satisfied with my body but I know my limitations. Time to guide her down to the bed.

She amends, "You're glorious to me." She steps forward and kisses the center of my chest, then trails kisses down, down, down. On her knees, my erection grows to its full length as she stares at it. Extending her tongue, she licks the pre-cum off my tip.

The top of my head explodes. Because I want our first time to be more memorable than a blow job, I grab her arms and pull her to standing. "I want more than that with you now. Kick off your shoes."

After she complies, I pull her pants down her amazingly long legs leaving us both naked. "Last chance. If you don't want this, now's your chance to duck out."

Her face twists and I can't read her expression. Shuttering whatever thought passed through her mind, her lips turn into a sultry smile. "I'm all in."

I expel the breath that caught in my throat when I feared she might turn me down, then wrap her in my arms. "Tonight's about you and me. Not the designer and the carpenter. Not the reality television wannabes. Just us, Paige and Jesse."

"And you giving me screaming orgasms." Her tone holds a note of hope.

"Them too."

My finger traces her lips, drops to her chin and over her pronounced collarbones. It slides down her sinewy arms and joins with its partner around her waist. This sexy tomboy is all mine tonight.

Our lips clash again as my hands drop to her ass and squeeze. She doesn't have too much junk in the trunk, which works for me. For her part, she kisses her way down my torso and licks my abs. *Thank you, sit-ups.* Time to relocate this party.

"Bed."

Instead of turning her, I nibble on her ear and blow while maneuvering us toward my goal. When the back of her legs hit the furniture, she sits. Liking her placement, I drop to my knees and push her thighs wider. Her musky scent tickles my nose and makes my mouth water. I can't wait to make her squeal.

Without hesitation, I run my fingers over her thighs, which tremble at my touch. Dropping kisses on the inside of her right one, I jump over her pussy and give the other the same treatment. Her scent intensifies.

Since she's already wet, I toss both of her legs over my shoulders and lean forward to lick her like her beloved lollipops. Beneath me, her hips lever forward, and I guide her back to the bed with my hands. Keeping her wide open for me, my tongue encircles her clit, eliciting a low moan.

I want more. Louder. Tell the world who's getting her off.

I refocus on her core, swirling around, around, around. She pulses into my mouth, demanding more, which I give. Her legs tighten around my head, and I use my finger to enter her wet channel. She writhes, bringing her palms upward, and I watch as she pinches her nipples. My own erection demands in on the action. I ignore him for as long as I can, but the noises she's making—combined with the way she's thrashing against the bed—are my undoing.

Pulling my face away from her pussy, I admit defeat. "I can't wait any longer. I have to be inside you."

Paige's chest expands on an inhale, then she nods and pulls away from me, arranging herself on her back with her head on the pillows. Like a present. Or a smorgasbord laid out for my pleasure.

On my way up the bed, I grab my wallet and remove a condom. Tossing the wallet onto the side table and dropping the condom on the pillow, I get on top of this amazing woman and rest my weight on my forearms. I wish I'd gotten her off already, but that'll have to wait for another time. I'm beyond the point of caring. All that matters is coming together with this woman and making us both scream.

Retrieving the condom on the pillow, I rip it open and roll it over my straining erection. Latching onto her nipple, I slide into her body—her warm pussy welcomes me home.

Definitely not a baby.

I allow her a few moments to accept my cock deep inside her. With a bite to each nipple, I move up to her mouth and give her a carnal kiss. Filled with teeth and lips and tongue. She rocks her hips and I pull back before surging forward, eliciting a long moan from her.

She's more responsive than any other woman I've been with. Makes me want to hear this sound again, so I repeat the move.

"You feel amazing, Paige."

On an exhale, she utters, "You, too."

Increasing the speed, my hips move in and out of her, faster and faster. She tenses and I think she's going to go over, but she doesn't. What's holding her back? I'm almost at the end of my restraint.

Without thought, I fall to my side and bring her with me. My hand steals between our bodies, and I stroke her clit in an imitation of what my tongue was doing prior.

"Oh my. Jesse!"

Thank fuck. I can hold off a few more strokes. Especially in this new position. Although, the way she's squeezing me into her body blows my mind.

Continuing my assault on her pussy, I nip her ear and glide over to her mouth. Connected on every level, I don't stop. It's like something's holding her back. "Let go, Paige."

That's all it takes. Her scream continues for maybe forever, and the ripples inside her body trigger my climax. Over and over, I pump into her body with a guttural roar.

Panting, I collapse onto the bed. We're a sweaty mess.

I've never come that hard. Ever.

When I'm able to move my limbs, I pull out of Paige's body and remove the spent condom. Wrapping it in a tissue, I toss it into the garbage can beneath the side table. Smart design. Thank you, Paige.

Returning to focus on my partner, I lean over her still cooling body and kiss her. "That was amazing."

Her hand caresses the back of my head. "I've always wondered."

"What?"

"Why all the fuss. Now I know."

Her words don't compute. "Excuse me?"

"Sex being mind-blowing."

My eyes pop open and I struggle to my elbow. Running my hand down her naked arm, I wonder about all her prior lovers. "It hasn't been before?"

"I've never orgasmed with a partner. Until you."

20

Paige

Oh my God. What just popped out of my mouth? By the look of shock on Jesse's face, I can safely guess I said my confession out loud.

I set my chin. I refuse to be humiliated by the truth. Besides, he should be proud of himself—it was his sexual prowess that got me off.

I open my mouth but Jesse beats me to it. "You've never climaxed with a man before me?" His tone indicates he doesn't believe me.

I would think any red-blooded man would be excited to learn his skills are second to none. "Nope."

"How many have you tried it with?"

I tap my open palm on his muscular chest. "Five."

He clears his throat. "None of them brought you home?"

Now this conversation's getting weird. I mimic his posture. "Should I not have told you?"

"No. I mean, yes. I'm honored to have been your first." He leans over and kisses me and all my worries evaporate.

I stare into his mesmerizing eyes. "Can we do it again?"

He kisses me again. "I've unleashed a monster, haven't I?"

"If by monster, you mean awakened your sexual slave, sign me up." I trail my hand down his torso. "You're really good at it."

He grabs my hand and kisses it. "I like the sound of that." He yawns, sparking me to do so as well. "But for now, you wore me out, woman. I think we should rest."

He strokes my arm in a rhythmic pattern and despite wanting another round with this amazing man, I succumb to sleep.

An alarm wakes us up, causing Jesse to get out of bed and pull his cell phone out of his jeans pocket. Naked, he sits on the bed next to me. "We have to get back to the ViewPad unless we want a repeat of yesterday."

Shoving the duvet off my body, I note, "If nothing else, your crazy just-fucked hair would give us away." I run my fingers through it, but only succeed in making it look more disheveled.

He leans forward as if to kiss me, then pulls away and stands. "No more of this. We have to get cleaned up. Day three awaits."

We dress quickly and, grabbing my design book, leave 1626 for the elevators and enter the ViewPad holding hands. Bo's sitting at the island, alone. He gives us the once-over and sneers, "Well, well, well. Isn't this cozy? I can see you gave it up to him. Was she as cold as her kisses led me to believe? You must've worked hard to get any response out of such a dead fish."

Jesse tries to let my hand go, but I won't let him. Not even this asshole can ruin my glow. I don't want Jesse to get another mark on his body because of me. Unless it's *from* me.

Looking at my partner, I say, "Let's get ready for another full day. Thankfully, we work together."

Jesse's jaw clenches but he gives me a quick nod and we enter the hallway toward the bedrooms without saying a word to the Texas carpenter. How could I have thought he was good-looking?

When we reach the doors to the bedrooms, Jesse says, "Thanks for back there. He's not worth either of our time. Let's shower and get ready. I'll see you out here in twenty."

I pout. "I want to have shower sex."

He grins. "Soon. But not here, with—" His eyes travel down the hallway.

I sigh. He's right, dammit. I tap the center of his chest. "I'll hold you to that." After a brief hug, I duck into my bedroom.

Mary Ellen comes out of the bathroom as I'm trying to figure out what to wear. Rather, what's still clean. I dig out a pair of underwear and a bra. My shirt with ladybugs on it will have to do. I'm leaning over at an awkward angle to sort through my jeans when my roommate says, "Have a good night?"

Memories of the amazing time I had with Jesse replay and I smile. "The best." Losing my balance, I land on my butt.

She laughs. "I can see." Toweling off her wet head, she remarks, "At least one of us got busy last night. I was all alone in here. Which, given my only other option for company, was a good thing."

Should I tell her that we saw Bo with Quinn? They're divorced, but still partners. Perhaps she knows what that was all about? Standing, I dive headfirst into the deep end. "Jesse and I went out to Club Cielo last night." When she doesn't react, I explain, "It's a popular club on the Upper East side. You can get to it from here by taking an express subway." I'm proud to have gathered this knowledge, no matter how trivial it is.

"I've been warned off the subways in New York City. My friends made me swear I wouldn't get on one."

"I understand. I've never been in one until last night. Aside from the smell and the tons of people packed on them, they're an efficient way to get around the city."

"Duly noted."

She doesn't look convinced. I get it. "Anyway, when we were there, we happened to see Quinn. She was with Bo."

If Mary Ellen knew what was going on between those two, she's an excellent poker player. I doubt this sweet Southern girl plays. "He didn't mention anything to me."

"Well, we didn't intrude on their evening, so I have no idea what they were discussing."

She picks at her nail polish. "That's." She walks over to her dresser. "Odd."

"I take it they didn't know each other before the show?"

"No. I wonder what they were talking about?"

I scoop up my clothes and walk toward the bathroom. "I'm sure if it was something big, he'll tell you today."

She picks at her nail polish again.

In the shower, I let the warm water run over my body, wishing Jesse were here to wash my back. I giggle. More than my back. While pleasant memories flood my system, they're mixed with questioning what Bo's up to. Does he think he'll score brownie points with Quinn and win this competition? As Jesse said, she's not the judge.

Only the director.

My guess is he was schmoozing her to sway the decision. *Not on my watch!* I'm going to make sure our primary suite is beyond reproach so the judges have no other option than to choose us.

New course of action selected, I scrub my skin and finish my shower, then throw my clothes onto my body. When I get out of the bathroom, Mary Ellen's blowing on her redone nails. I don't linger, but drop my dirty clothes next to my suitcase and wish her well. After all, it's not her trying to rig the system.

In the kitchen, I join Jesse by the coffeemaker. He hands me a mug with my coffee already doctored. "Thanks." I kiss his cheek to the sounds of gagging noises coming from the living room area. Bo can suck it.

Jesse touches my cheek. "You're beautiful."

I soak in his compliment. We can do this. Make our rooms shine as well as our relationship. He's wearing another pair of dark blue jeans and a T-shirt, this time in blue—without a bank logo. "You look handsome yourself."

Someone knocks on the door and then breezes in. Quinn. I can't help it, but my eyes steal over to Bo, who's standing with his toothy smile. What are they up to?

After Mary Ellen joins us, Quinn begins, "So nice to see *all* of you here this morning. We've reviewed the footage from yesterday and the day before, and you're all doing great. Bo, Mary Ellen, we like how you've decided to work in the different rooms. Makes it easy on your camera crews to capture all of your hard work. Keep it up."

She turns toward us. "Jesse, Paige. Interesting choice to go big in the bedroom, and we find it fascinating how you haven't divided up the tasks. We think the audience will as well."

Somewhat mollified, I swing my gaze toward our rivals. Bo's still wearing the same shit-eating grin. My gaze travels to my partner and my heart stops. He stands tall and proud, absorbing everything going on around him. Probably why he's excelling in the banking industry—nothing gets by him.

I return my focus to Quinn, who's moved on to giving a little pep talk. She concludes, "Now, go to your apartments and continue doing what you've been doing. Good luck!"

With our marching orders, I precede Jesse out of the View-Pad. The ride down on the elevator is quiet, although a tension bubbles between Mary Ellen and Bo. Can't say as I blame her. Perhaps she'll figure out what her ex-husband and Quinn are up to.

Jesse opens the door and the normal camera chaos reigns. The crew wanders throughout the rooms chatting with each other, and not paying us any attention. I drag my partner into the dining room and slam him against the wall. Okay, slam might be an exaggeration. Gently throw him against . . .

"Oof!"

I giggle. Maybe slam was the right adjective after all. Getting up close and personal with my talented carpenter, I kiss him. "I'd much rather be doing this than that." My eyes swivel toward the primary suite.

He chuckles. "I can tell." His hands land on my ass and he pulls our bodies together, stealing another kiss. Then he drops his hands. "But that's not how this game is played. Let's get to work. More of this later."

Playing with his intriguing earlobe, I whisper, "Promise?"

He grabs my wrists. "What have I unlocked?" His lips find mine once again, then his hands land on my shoulders and he moves me backward.

"Fine. We both know this is a hell of a lot more fun than carving a headboard." When his expression morphs from silly to unsettled, I know the moment is over. Injecting excitement into my voice, I say, "I can't wait to see what you do with it today!"

"Yeah." He pushes away from the wall and trudges down the hallway.

"I have faith in you."

He throws his arm in the air. "I'll make it good." In a much lower tone, he mutters, "Hope that's enough."

Because I have no experience with carving, I keep my mouth shut. From his demeanor, I can tell he's not open to hearing me anyway. It's not like I don't have my own work to complete. I organize my tasks for the day, deciding to check in on the bathroom first. Perhaps having the bedroom all to himself will help him think.

When I walk into the bathroom, the guys are working on the tile. Due to budget constraints, I couldn't put in the double shower heads I wanted, but this still looks nice. Although, the outline for the niche seems . . . off.

I point. "Why is the niche so small?"

The tile worker glances from me to it and shrugs. "We had to make it that small because of the framing."

I designed the niche to be a long, rectangular shape spanning much of the accent wall. "This is too dinky." My mind scrambles to come up with options and after about an hour, we've relocated the niche to the inside of the half-wall tile surround. Even though it won't be visible unless the person's using the shower, it will be much larger, ergo more functional. Bet the judges will eat it up.

This problem solved, I turn my attention to the various accessories we'll need to complete the room. Making a list, I detour to the work area.

When I enter, Jesse's back is to me. His T-shirt is riding up from his jeans—yet his jeans aren't low enough on his hips to give the dreaded plumber's crack. Wouldn't want to tantalize the viewers with his backside anyway. I walk up behind him, aware of the cameras, so I don't do anything crazy like pinch his delectable behind. *It's a close call.*

"I solved an issue for us in the bathroom and made a list of décor we need."

"Good," he grunts.

I crane my neck. "How's it coming along?"

He blows on the wood, sending sawdust swirling. "Alright."

Since he doesn't move, I walk around and check out his handiwork. Today's attempt is much better than yesterday's. The carving, while meticulous, also shows bold strokes. The only problem? He's done maybe a foot by a foot, and the headboard is for a king-size bed. Perhaps he'll speed up as the day progresses? "Wow. This is looking good."

"Thanks. This is much harder than I anticipated."

I study the drawing he's carving. "Think you could scale back even more?"

His mouth purses. "I have."

Sensing anything more I would say would not be well received, I hold my hands up. "Well, you're doing good work. Keep it up. I'm off shopping for the items I need to complete this suite." I pat myself on the back for remembering not to say "prop room." Quinn told us they want the viewers to believe I actually went shopping. His response is to resume carving.

Throughout my "shopping spree," I think about how Jesse can complete the headboard by the deadline. Because of where he started on the wood, he can't limit his work to a well-placed rectangle. Unless . . . I head to the fabric section and find batting as well as some plush cottons and linens. Selecting a couple of colors that will complement the window coverings, I grab them all and rush back to the work area.

Jesse's going to go blind if he continues to stare down the headboard like this. Ignoring the cameras, I rub his back. "Hey."

He stands, and my hand slips off his body. "What's up?"

I hold up my finds from the prop room. "Look what I saw when I was shopping for the bathroom."

"Looks nice."

His eyes stray back to the headboard, and I can tell he's clueless about my idea. "What do you think about upholstering the bottom part of the headboard and leave a carved strip up top?" This is the perfect solution. He can showcase his work and not be so stressed.

His expression turns stormy. "Don't think I can hack it?"

"What? No. It's not like that." My breathing speeds up. "I can see you're struggling, and thought this was the perfect solution."

The carving knife flips between his hands. "By covering it up?" His tone is low. Deadly.

I hide the material behind my back. "I only thought you could carve out a small slice instead of the entire headboard."

"I got it, Paige." He turns away from me and raises his knife.

Chastised, I hold my head high and leave the work area. In the prop area, I return the batting and fabric, explaining we changed our minds. Wandering around, I listlessly pluck at some fake plants. I need to get away and clear my head—the cameras can focus on Jesse and his carving. Exiting the building, I enter the High Line. Because it's a weekday, it's not as crowded, although tons of people still mill around. I pass the ice cream vendor, ignoring the call of strawberry, and bounce from one statue to the next. Stopping in front of one called, "Stormy Tides," I stare at the harsh lines, imagining I'm being sucked into the storm. Not much of a leap.

Needing someone to talk with, I pull out my phone and call the only person I have access to. My lifeline. Chloe picks up on the third ring. "How's it going? The competition must be winding down, right?"

"We're on Day Three of five in the final round."

"You must be excited. Tell me all about what you're doing." I describe the bathroom and then the bedroom, skimming over Jesse's issue with the headboard. "Sounds amazing. I'm happy for you. Want to know what else?"

I can tell she's bursting. "What?"

"I don't want to jinx anything, but Madison referred me to her friend Stephanie, who's a headhunter at Elite Placement Agency. Well, I met with Stephanie and she thinks I'd be a good fit for some positions she's trying to fill. She's going to recommend me. Isn't that awesome?"

I inject excitement into my voice. "Super!" Hope that sounded positive enough. I *am* happy for her.

She rambles for a while, then stops. "Alright. I can tell you're humoring me. What's eating at you?"

Too much. "It's Jesse. He's carving the headboard—"

"You mentioned that earlier. You said he was doing a good job with it."

"I might have been a bit optimistic. He's meticulous with each stroke. Which makes him slow. I don't know if he'll finish on time, and he won't get to any other items on his to-do list, that's for sure."

"What else does he have to do?" I list out the things he has to finish. "And you? What's on your plate?" I give her my list. "Can you take on any more of his work?"

"I think so. He's built the pieces, but they need to be painted or stained and such. I can do that." A jolt runs through me. Instead of focusing on the headboard, I should leave that item to Jesse. His work in the bedroom has been stellar, if not slow. "Stellar" may be overstating things a little. Still. If I take over the rest of his work, his burden will be eased. "I'm not as good as he is, but I've done it before."

"See. Easy peasy. Now we're both on track." She pauses. "No checklist required."

Ignoring my cousin's teasing, we hang up and I notice the sky is bluer than before. Even "Stormy Tides" seems less intimidating. I can do this. *I hope.*

When I get back into the work area, a couple of guys on the camera crew are eating lunch. I pass Jesse a cup of vanilla ice cream. "Present. Thought you'd like something sweet."

He blinks, but doesn't make a move toward his dessert. "I apologize about before. This is overwhelming, and I want to do a good job."

"I understand." I shake the cup, and he takes it from my hand. "I talked with Chloe and came up with another solution."

He pauses in bringing his spoon to his mouth. "Dare I ask?"

I square my shoulders. "I can take over your to do's, leaving you with the headboard only."

"I don't know, Paige." His right foot rocks from side to side. "All of the furniture needs finishing work. Think you're up for it?"

He didn't discard my idea as stupid or treat me like a child, as everyone else does. He's asking me a question, not overriding my suggestion. Standing taller, I reply, "I can do it." *I hope.*

"Then I'm up for it. I'll get more than half of the headboard carved today."

I glance from the clock on my cell to the headboard, which boasts maybe about one-quarter done now with four more hours to go today. He can do it. "And I'll start to work on the dresser." This is the largest piece, which will make the rest seem easy.

The day speeds by. We work together like we were born for this. Were we? As I paint the top of the dresser, I wonder if this is what fate feels like. I glance over at Jesse, who's concentrating on his woodwork, his tongue sticking out of his mouth. What a talented tongue it is! I can't wait for tonight.

No sooner does this thought cross my mind then the lead cameraman says, "Alright, guys. Day's over. Why don't you get cleaned up and return to 1626 for some final video."

Placing my paintbrush down, I examine the dresser with a critical eye. It's not perfect, but it's a good effort, if I do say so myself. I want to get different drawer pulls in the prop room tomorrow. I think they'll enhance the beauty of the piece more so than the current ones.

I get to my feet and walk over to Jesse, hoping he's at least halfway done. Standing behind him, I appreciate his body before moving over to peruse the headboard. Well, he's not quite at fifty percent. More like forty. Still, he has all day tomorrow and then he can finish up on the final day. I'll need his attention on the last day, though, as I can't hang the window coverings by myself. Among all the final details.

"Looks good, Jesse."

His fingers swipe the excess sawdust away and he drops the knife onto a table. "Thank you. This is more involved than I thought it would be."

I wrap my hand around his arm, enjoying the feel of his biceps. "Let's get out of here. Clear our heads." Meaning—go into the finished bedroom in 1626 and get lost in each other.

"If you don't mind, I need to make a call. I want to discuss this project with Mr. Hooper."

My body falls. Guess I'm the only one who wants to have sex? Yet, I can't prevent him from seeking advice from his woodworking teacher. Maybe he'll offer some tips about how to go faster. "Sure thing. I'll go to the ViewPad and get cleaned up."

I turn away, but Jesse stops me. "Hey."

"Yes?"

"You're amazing. Once I get this straightened out, I want to straighten you out." He grabs me around the waist and pulls me into his body.

"I like the sound of that." I lead him into 1626 where the cameras capture us doing some "fake decorating tasks" to use in the show.

We're kissing when Quinn saunters into the room.

21

Jesse

"Oh, sorry. Didn't mean to interrupt." Quinn looks around the room, surveying what we've done.

I disengage from my beguiling partner and focus my attention on the show's director. "Quinn. What can we do for you?"

"I understand you're switching up the game." Her foot taps.

"What do you mean? We haven't broken any rules."

"True. But you're both now doing carpentry work. Paige here spent the afternoon working on the dresser you built."

In order to give me some breathing room for the headboard. I open my mouth, but Paige beats me to it. "We have a lot of things to finish, and they're more along the lines of carpentry. I offered to help Jesse out. I'm still handling all the design elements."

"Don't you think the viewers will be confused by this switch? How do you expect me to portray this to an audience?"

"Didn't Marion and Peyton do both design and execution? How did you handle it then?"

Paige has a point. I focus on Quinn, who fiddles with her necklace. "Their roles were made clear from the start. You're switching it up midstream."

It's time for me to come clean. "The headboard project is larger than I expected. Paige offered to do some finishing work on the pieces I built previously. She's essentially decorating them, so can't you put that spin on it?"

Quinn's eyes narrow. "I suppose that's a good explanation. I'd like to do a side interview with you both to add to the footage. Separately."

We exchange glances while Quinn instructs the camera crew to set up in the corner. Someone brings one of the barstools into the room and places it, moving it a few times until Quinn's satisfied.

"Jesse, you can go first. Off-camera, I'll ask you questions for you to answer." She turns to Paige. "I'd like for you to wait outside so we can get your unvarnished take during your interview." Behind her back, my partner blows me a kiss and exits the room.

Once I'm seated, Quinn asks me to repeat why we decided to mix up the duties for this final round. She seems satisfied with my responses. I'm about to stand when she asks one more question. "How does having a burgeoning relationship with your partner influence your work?"

What? This is none of her business, and certainly doesn't belong in the public domain. I don't care too much about myself, but Paige doesn't deserve to be drug through the mud. Although, given my partner's family's situation, I bet Quinn was waiting to be able to exploit the situation.

I choose my words carefully. "Paige is a consummate professional. Her work product speaks for itself. She offered to finish up a few pieces to allow me some more time to work on the focal point of the room, the headboard."

Quinn's finger goes around like a tornado. "That's a wrap. Thanks, Jesse. Please send Paige in for her interview."

Unsure if my responses were what she wanted or not, I take my time getting to my feet. Since she's talking with the camera guys, I let myself out, closing the door behind me.

Paige pounces. "How did it go? What did she ask?"

"She basically asked about why we split up the duties like we did." Her final question bugs me. "She also asked me how being in a relationship with you influenced our work."

Her hand covers her mouth, fingernails smudged with paint. "That's so rude."

"That's a word for it."

Quinn opens the door. "Paige?" My partner gives me a questioning look, then follows the director.

What was that all about? Why would Quinn care so much about our relationship status? I would think filming Paige doing what is traditionally thought of as "carpentry" would make for good television. After all, she doesn't know exactly what to do so her take on it has to be a bit unorthodox. I smile. Like the rest of her.

All alone in the living room, memories from last night replay. When she admitted she never orgasmed with a man before, I almost lost it. A feeling of responsibility settles over me. Paige clearly wants to explore her sexuality—with me. I sit taller as excitement buzzes throughout my body.

No sooner do I picture her riding me, but the door opens and Paige herself pops out, scowling. She hugs her design book to her chest. "Let's get out of here."

Resisting the urge to ask her what happened, I follow her out of the apartment, onto the elevator, and out on the street. Horns blare around us as we walk up Eleventh Avenue, then turn toward Tenth. I point out a coffee shop and we duck inside.

Sitting at a table while our coffees brew, I broach the subject. "What happened back there?"

She leans back into the chair. "Quinn asked me questions about why I'm taking on more carpentry projects. No biggie. Then she noted the bathroom lacks some of my usual flair and asked if sleeping with you has impacted my interior design capabilities." Her fist contacts the table, making the napkin holder jump. "Can you believe that shit? What business is this of hers? Or the public's?"

"Hey," I grab her hand. "I'm sorry you had to go through that. She didn't go that far with me. I wonder why she did with you? It's not like the network will let her use this footage." I stroke the back of her palm with my thumb.

"Well, I didn't take it sitting down. I looked right into her eyes and asked what she's doing going out with Bo when the cameras aren't rolling."

My thumb stops moving. "You did not!"

"Did too."

I shake my head. "You're a force of nature." I resume stroking the back of her palm. "What was her answer?"

She gives me a self-satisfied smirk. "She didn't reply, but the look on her face was priceless. She's guilty of something, I'm just not sure what. At the very least, it got her thinking of something other than my love life." She beams at me. "I have a love life. With you."

Quashing my natural desire to know what's going on between Quinn and Bo, I return Paige's smile. "I'm the lucky one."

She laughs. "No. That honor goes to me because I'm getting lucky. Finally."

My name comes over the loudspeaker, and I collect our drinks. After we finish them, I say, "Ready to go back?"

As we pass yet another decorating store, our conversation turns to how to finish up 1626. We agree we need to add flair to the rooms, but we're at odds about how to do it. Returning to our apartment, she picks up her drawings and we toy with some ideas.

With nothing new decided, Paige tosses the sketchbook onto the floor and wraps her arms around my neck. "I'm done with work. I want orgasms, please." She bats her eyes.

"When you put it that way." I kiss her lips, enjoying how responsive she is. Soon, we're horizontal on the sofa and she's naked beneath me.

"Not fair," she pouts. "You're still wearing all your clothes."

Lying over her body, I push her hair off her face. "But you're not." My lips travel down her chest and take her small nipple in my mouth while plumping her other boob with my hand. Her head thrashes at my contact, and her legs move under mine. I expel her nipple from my mouth with a loud pop.

"You really want to see me?"

She gives me an earnest affirmative head shake.

Sitting up, I grab the hem of my shirt and peel it off my body.

Balling it up, I toss it to the end of the sofa and the green light facing me reminds me we're not alone. "Fuck."

Giggling, Paige replies, "I hope so."

Focusing on her body—on display thanks to yours truly—I collapse on top of her and reach for my discarded shirt since her clothes are all over the floor.

"What are you doing?"

When my fingers wrap around the material of my shirt, I snatch it and thrust it at her. "Here. Put this on."

"Uhm. Isn't the idea to do the opposite?" Her fingers reach for my belt.

"Not when there are cameras in here." I drag my shirt over her head and pull downward.

Her short hair pops out of the material first, and she shoves her arms through the holes. "I forgot."

"So did I." Once I'm convinced she's covered, I pull myself upright She adjusts her legs, which look even longer only wearing my shirt. Looks damn good on her.

In my brain, Homer clears his throat and I shut him down. I refuse to give in to old fears. Paige is smart and sassy and she doesn't take any shit—as witnessed by the question she had the audacity to ask Quinn onscreen.

When she sits up, I scoop her into my arms and carry her into the completed bedroom. Where the cameras don't travel. Paige's fingers toy with the bottom of my hair as I set her down onto the duvet and plant my ass right next to her.

"My hero," she mimics a Southern accent. Then frowns. "Screw that. I'm no shrinking violet. But I am polite. Thanks, Jesse, for bringing me in here and away from the cameras." Her hands move to my T-shirt covering her body, which she whips off. "There. I'm naked. Your turn."

Can't argue her logic. Within moments, I kick off my shoes and get rid of my jeans. As bare as her, I stand in front of the bed, allowing her to give me a good once over. I know she's been with men before, and has seen them naked, but something in her eyes conveys a sense of wonderment.

"Like what you see?"

"I do. Very much." Her hand reaches out and she cups my erection, which had grown to almost full mast under her perusal. "I'm good at giving blow jobs."

Okay. Not the type of comment I expected to hear. Or wanted to, for that matter. "I bet you are."

Her hand moves lower, and she contacts my balls, giving them a little squeeze, which causes my body to stiffen. "You like?"

Need zips through me. "I do." But tonight's not about my wants, rather satisfying hers. I step back. "Perhaps another time. I want to make you scream again." I crook my finger toward her.

She stands, and much like she did, I run my gaze over her every dip and follow up with my tongue. As I'm laving her belly button, I decide I want her first orgasm to be in my mouth. "I'm going to lie down and I want you to sit on my face." *Crass, much?*

I glance at Paige, who's nearly jumping out of her body. Guess she didn't think I went too far. Both of her hands push against my chest, knocking me down onto the bed. Chuckling, I inch upward, delighting when her knee reaches my shoulders.

Grabbing her one leg, I make her straddle my chest. Her musky scent tells me how turned on she is. Which is good, since my erection has become as hard as quartz.

She bends down and kisses me. "I think I'm going to like this."

We indulge in a few more kisses before my hands land on her ass and I guide her forward. She grips the headboard—one I made before the idea of carving one in the primary bedroom came to be —and I'm enveloped in the wonderful world of Paige's pussy. Holding it in the right place, I lick and swirl and don't let up my assault until she says, "Oh my God, Jesse. Yes!"

Then I redouble my efforts.

When she clenches around me, I continue stroking her core until her screams die and her body falls limp. I guide her to the side, then join her. My body screams for release, but not until she's come down enough to be brought back up.

Reaching for the condom I left on the side table, I kiss her. "I want you to ride me. Take everything you want from me."

She snags the condom out of my hand. "Starting with this." She rolls it on me like the expert I thought her to be, then stares down at her handiwork, which jumps at her attention. Bending over, she kisses my tip. "I like you too."

"Enough talking and more action."

She giggles. "I'll be right on it. You. I mean, I'll be right on you." She swings her leg over my body again and gives me a wide-eyed glance.

"Here, let me help." I lift her slightly so her body's aligned with mine, then lower her down. Her sliding over me makes stars flash behind my eyeballs.

"You feel amazing. You're so deep." Her purr echoes my thoughts.

She rocks into me, and I allow her to find a rhythm she prefers, since every movement is like heaven to me. Reaching up, I move her hips, guiding her to hit my pelvic bone with each thrust.

Her boobs bounce with her exertion, which only hardens me further. Reaching out, I flick her nipple, and she moans. She rides me faster and faster and faster until she tosses her head back and screams, "Jesse!"

Contracting around me, she propels me to the point of no return and I still. Followed by an unbelievable release.

She collapses onto my chest, her hair tickling my cheek. I wrap my arms around her and pull her to me, drinking in the serenity of the moment. No assignments. No carving. No voices in my head. Only Paige.

After a few moments, she rests her chin on the center of my chest. "You're amazing."

I chuckle. "You did all the work. I was only there for the ride." I smooth her hair. "What a ride it was."

I blow on the headboard, now attached to the bed in 1626. Stepping back, I assess my work so far. I'm about five-eighths of the way done, which is good because today's the final day.

"Are you finished yet?"

"Getting there."

Paige's constant questions sink into my bones. I know she's not nagging me, but her constant monologue about my work strikes the wrong note. Since the cameras are rolling, she can't even lighten things up with a kiss. Not that I want to kiss her right now anyway.

As if she realizes the cameras are rolling, she modulates her irritated tone and says, "It's looking good."

"Thanks." My mumble will have to suffice. I *know* I have to finish this up, help secure her window coverings above the two windows, and make sure the two rooms are ready for the judges. Don't need her flitting around to remind me.

"How's this?"

From the corner of my eye I can see she's holding something up. Taking time away from my carving, I face her. "I like it."

"Good. What do you think if I put it—"

She continues talking, but I tune her out. I don't have time to deal with her insecurities. Why she has them is still a mystery. I've watched her make decisions on the fly rivaling most seasoned veteran's choices. Her skill with the carpentry pieces she volunteered to handle also shows she's more than a beginner.

"Huh, Jesse?"

Her use of my name pulls me out of my own head. "What?"

She rubs her arm. "I was asking how much longer before we can get to these? I think it'll take us a good three or four hours to complete this room and I don't want to scramble against the clock."

"Give me an hour."

"Alright."

She leaves me in peace. Thank fuck. Sixty minutes later she reappears. "Done?"

I smooth my hand over the carved headboard. It's a fantastic piece, if I do say so myself. Some of the edges are rough, and we need to stain it, but I'm proud I agreed to undertake this task. I step aside for her perusal.

"It looks great!" Her eyes squint and she walks closer. Her finger traces some of the carving, then she pulls it back. "Well, we need to sand it. And maybe try to hide these imperfections with paint." She points to some of my missteps.

Homer's voice agrees with her and takes it one step farther by mocking me as a blue-collar laborer. Against the floor, my right foot rocks. "Wood this beautiful should be stained."

"Usually, I would agree. But we're down to the final hours, and it would be faster to paint it. Plus, paint would hide some of the defects."

Defects. Did she call me defective? I cross my arms. "It should be stained."

She tilts her head. "Black. I think a nice black paint would complement the colors in here and cover over things like this." She runs the pad of her finger over a particularly challenging spot.

I'm not one to disagree for the sake of arguing, but to paint this piece would be a sacrilege. "I can't imagine the judges' reactions if we were to paint this. It has to be stained. A nice, dark cherry."

"Oh my, no way. Those deep reds are so last century. If we were to stain it, I would choose a light color. Another reason for paint because instead of concealing things, a more natural stain would highlight them."

My jaw clenches. I agreed to do this damned piece because she begged. How dare she criticize me now? "It should be stained."

"Painted."

As our discussion becomes louder and louder, the cameras swirl around us, making sure to capture every second. Paige checks out the cameras and offers an olive branch. "I know you worked hard on this all week, Jesse. I couldn't be prouder of what you've accomplished. The time constraints made creating the perfect headboard impossible for anyone to handle. As the interior designer of the group, I'm only trying to put our best face forward."

Now she has to try to sound all reasonable. Sensing I lost this argument before I even opened my mouth, I give in. "Fine. We'll do it your way." Doesn't mean I'm on board.

The day drags on with Paige and I bickering about every last detail. This pillow or that one? By the end, I can't care.

Quinn walks into the room and I breathe a sigh of relief.

"Alright, folks, contest is over!" The camera crew claps and we join in. Despite everything, we made it through. We survived. Our rooms look damn good.

Paige turns to me and opens her arms wide for a hug. In spite of my misgivings, I give her what she wants, allowing myself to enjoy the feel of her body pressed against mine. Aware of the cameras, I kiss her cheek instead of giving her the inappropriate kiss I know she'd prefer.

Maybe it's better this way?

22

Paige

I savor how Jesse's body molds to mine. His sweet kiss warms me from the inside out. We did it! The primary suite is completed and I'm proud of what we did in here.

So what if the bathroom doesn't have a double shower head? Or the headboard is painted rather than stained? At least we completed everything. My lungs expand as I take pride in what we accomplished. I bet Bo and Mary Ellen's suite doesn't look this good.

My eyes scan our room, landing on slight missteps. Perhaps the judges won't think too much about them. My gaze swings toward my partner, standing tall and proud. I know exactly how sexy this man is. I want more.

"Congratulations on finishing the primary suite! Why don't you gather your stuff in the living room and go tour what Bo and Mary Ellen did while they check yours out?"

Heeding her advice—rather, direction—I grab my design notebook with my assorted pens and colored pencils while Jesse gets his tools together. I follow Quinn into the living room. "Nice job, Paige."

Shocked at the compliment, especially after our last exchange about her and Bo, I reply, "Thanks."

"I think you two were the best teams on the show, by far. I'm glad you were in the finals. The audience is going to eat you two up, considering your fledgling relationship. As for Bo and Mary Ellen, who doesn't love exes working together? Yes, the network's very happy with this final round."

"Does Renovation TV have a preference as to which one of us will take home the title?"

She slants me a glance. "No. The judges, who are all respected in the industry, will make the decision without our input."

I hope she's not lying, but having grown up around VOW-cubed, I'm aware of how things can be manipulated. While I'd love to win and start a career on television, I know Jesse *needs* this with his whole being. He doesn't want to return to banking, and I believe in him. In his skills, both in and out of the bedroom.

Jesse joins us, depositing his tools on the floor. I want to rub myself all over him, but that'll have to wait until our tour is complete.

Quinn says, "Go to Bo and Mary Ellen's apartment. The camera guys will follow you and get your unvarnished reaction."

"Sure thing."

I allow Jesse's response to suffice for the both of us. With one final glance around, I precede Jesse out of 1626, and take the elevator to our rival's floor. Before we can open the door, it swings wide and Bo exits. Tipping his hat at us, he offers, "Check out the winning digs." His chuckle follows him out of the apartment.

"Please don't go anywhere until we're all set up, okay?"

"Sure thing," Jesse responds to the camerawoman.

Standing in the middle of the living room, I check out what they did. Since we haven't been in here for a week, it's good to get a refresher on their entire design aesthetic. I reach for Jesse's hand, which, after a brief pause, closes around mine. Leaning over, I whisper, "I like ours better."

"Yeah." He lifts our joined hands and kisses mine, then releases me. Inane cameras.

Once we're given the go-ahead to start touring their primary suite, I nod and begin walking. I point to where we relocated our laundry room, stealing square footage from the primary bathroom. Stopping outside the bedroom door, I glance at the floor then at Jesse.

"Ready?"

His warm tenor sends a ripple down my spine. *For more things than touring this stupid room.* "Let's do this."

He opens the door and allows me to enter first, like the gentleman I didn't think he was. The walls are painted a royal blue, the bed has an upholstered cream headboard. A bench is placed in front of the footboard. Shit. Benches are a good accessory for a bedroom.

We go our separate ways, and I examine the window coverings, which are cream plus a darker shade of blue than the walls. They're nice, but don't have the same heft as ours. Underneath the bed, a wool patterned rug in varying shades of blue anchors the room. Mismatched side tables sit on either side of the king-sized bed. Placed over the light blue duvet and cream sheets, a wooden tray with an empty coffee mug and a book completes the vignette.

Jesse and I trade places, and I check out the dresser plus a niche they created for a television. This is a good idea. *One I should've thought of.* A divan fills out the corner in front of an old-style screen. Not carved. Painted, with a scene of birds in a Western motif. Makes sense, considering from where they hale.

I meet my partner in front of the bench. Knowing we're expected to give our appraisal of the room for the cameras, I begin with a compliment like Quinn taught. "I like the color scheme of blues. It's calming."

"Agreed. Blues and cream are a classic combination. In fact, this whole room is an ode to the Golden Age of Hollywood, with the dramatic window coverings and divan plus the screen in the corner."

Now's the time to move onto the harder assessment. "I think their side tables are unusual, but don't exactly go with the theme of the Golden Age, do you think?"

"I see what you mean," my partner agrees. Twisting his mouth, he adds, "At least the closet, which is as large as ours, has been tweaked with that vintage feel."

Because the upholstered headboard is such a focal point of the room, I run my fingers over it. "They went with a headboard along the lines of what we were discussing before you took on the carving project. It fits with their theme and is executed well."

Next to me, Jesse swallows. "It is." He walks to the other side of the headboard and examines it from a variety of angles. "This is well done, I have to hand it to them. The tufts are spaced evenly apart, and the nail heads accent it perfectly." His right foot rocks.

I want to comfort him. I want to put my arms around him, but the cameras are rolling, so I don't. Our damn headboard was a bone of contention this whole week—Bo and Mary Ellen sidestepped a more challenging choice, in my opinion. Trying to maintain a unified front, I word my question with care. "I wonder how ours would've turned out if we had upholstered it?"

His cheek indents. "We'll never know."

This truth ends our assessment of their bedroom. We turn toward the attached bathroom, which they expanded to include double doors. Eschewing the rule to say something positive first, I allow my initial thought to pop out. "Kind of pretentious, don't you think?"

Possibly still raw over my headboard comment, he shrugs. "Goes with their theme."

He has a point. I slam my lips shut and enter the radiant-heated marble master bathroom, complete with a two-person, double headed shower and a graceful soaking tub. The toilet has been tucked into its own water closet—where our laundry room now sits. A large double vanity graces the wall. Looking at the ceiling, a chandelier hangs above the tub, giving off a distinct Hollywood vibe. I revert to the compliment-first requirement. "Mary Ellen did a fantastic job of carrying their theme throughout this space."

"She sure did. Did you see the niches in the shower?"

He points to a long, rectangular niche accessorized with shampoos, conditioners, razors, and liquid soap. It's the size of the one I wanted in our bathroom, but the framing prevented it. I step up to the oversized sheets of marble they used around the tub and shower and examine the niche. With the back tiled in the same blue glass tiles as on the shower floor, it looks fantastic. Still, ours keeps with the theme of the entire apartment, while their entire primary suite took off on a different direction.

I tap the marble. "This is nice. For me, though, it loses a coherence from the public spaces to here."

His face turns toward mine. "I understand what you're saying. It's as if they made a change for this part of the apartment. Maybe that was their goal."

Perhaps Quinn tipped Bo off as to what the judges were looking for. I keep this thought to myself. Not going to say something dumb on national television. When we're alone tonight, though, I'll bring it up with Jesse. In a noncommittal tone, I reply, "I suppose."

Finished with our inspection, the cameras' green lights shut off. All the air inside my body wooshes out. We'll soon find out which one of us will get their own show on Renovation TV. *Please let it be us.*

Jesse needs this in his life.

I need him.

We *can't* lose.

Quinn finds us inside the luxurious spa-like bath. "Bo and Mary Ellen did an incredible job with their space."

Unwilling to address her, given my current thought regarding the change of direction they took here, I allow Jesse to respond. "I liked this Hollywood Glamor theme they chose to take. So different from the rest of the apartment."

He can say that again.

"I liked how you did your primary suite as well. Good job." Quinn consults her clipboard. "We have to get out of here so our judges can tour both apartments and choose a winner. Go on back to the ViewPad, get changed for the finale, and we'll be up when a decision has been made." She claps. "Good luck."

As we leave Bo and Mary Ellen's apartment, I stick my nose into the kitchen one final time. The laundry room's location makes it much less open than ours. Has to count for something.

Back in the ViewPad, Jesse hooks his thumb toward his bedroom. "Gonna grab a shower and get ready to hear the judge's decision."

I wiggle my eyebrows. We still haven't tried shower sex. "Want any company?"

"Better go it alone. You never know who might walk in at any moment."

His reference to Bo makes my shoulders sag. After today, though, he won't be an issue. We'll win this competition and start our new lives. Together. "Damn. I'm sorry I won't be able to wash your back."

He leaves me and I enter my bedroom. I did it! I made it through the entire competition. Father and Mum have to give me props for doing this. It's been wonderful not hearing them fight all the time or having to duck flying vases.

From my suitcase, I pick out the designer dress I had selected if we made the final show and take a quick shower. Next time, Jesse's going to give me another orgasm in one of these. When I walk into the bunk area, Mary Ellen breezes into the room.

"Hi! Sorry I'm so late. We loved your apartment. Great job!"

Why is she extra-perky? "Oh, uhm, thanks. Yours was good, too."

She looks up from her dresser drawer. "I can't believe it's over. We made it to the bitter end and one of us is going to walk away with a television show. Incredible."

"I know. Mind blowing, huh?"

"Right." She holds up a royal blue dress—one that matches the walls of their primary bedroom. "I'm going to take a quick shower. I'll be faster than a one-legged man in a butt-kickin' competition."

While the water runs in her "butt-kickin'" competition, I put on lotion and slip into my Vera Wang dress. I bet Jesse's going to want to rip it off my body as soon as he sees it. For this reason alone, I dawdle. Deciding to make a perfect entrance, I futz around until Mary Ellen's ready. After sharing a hug for good luck, we stroll into the living room arm-in-arm.

"Took you long enough."

Bo's opening salvo strikes his mark, as Mary Ellen flinches and steps away from me. Annoyed the cowboy carpenter still has any sway over his ex-wife, I defend her. "We're not late. Quinn isn't even here yet."

"Whatever." He addresses his partner. "I wanted to coordinate my tie with your dress. I'll get my blue one."

Bo strides out of the living room and I inhale a cleansing breath. Mary Ellen looks as if she's about to burst into tears, so I dive into verbal diarrhea. "We won't be in the ViewPad after tonight. Isn't that great? No more hidden cameras stalking our every move. I, for one, will be happy to get rid of them. How about you, Mary Ellen? What are you happy to be leaving?"

Using her palm, she straightens her long blonde hair. "With any luck? Him." She points toward the hallway her partner took.

"Can't blame you." If they win, she'll be stuck with him for at least one more season—more, if the show's a hit. All the work we put into our primary suite can't be for naught, though. I pray Jesse and I will be crowned the winners and Mary Ellen can get her life back. Correction. A new life.

I walk over to Jesse and do a twirl. "Do I look ready for my close-up, Mr. Dimon?"

He smiles. "You're always ready."

I accept his compliment. As they go, his is tame, but still a vote of confidence from him. I run my palm over his torso. "You're looking mighty handsome yourself. I like the way this button-down hugs your arms and chest."

He tugs on the untucked, beige checked shirt. "I bought this hoping we'd be in the finals."

"Like your sense of positivity, partner." Because of the cameras, I don't give him the kiss I'm dying to share with him.

"You don't have to pretend to be so lovey-dovey. The cameras aren't rolling."

Jesse's comment catches me off-guard. "Way too much is wrong with your statement. First, just because the camera crew isn't filming doesn't mean that the hidden cameras aren't rolling. Second, I'm not pretending anything."

He grabs my hands. "That was a moronic thing for me to say. Must be nerves." He kisses the back of my palm. "Forgive me?"

When his khaki eyes meet mine, I'd forgive him anything. "Don't let it happen again, Mr. Carpenter Extraordinaire."

We share a chuckle as Bo reenters the room, now wearing a blue skinny tie. "I'm ready to start working on the name for my own television show." He elbows Jesse. "Didn't do it sooner because I thought it was in bad taste."

I slap my hand over my wrist to keep it at my side. Next to me, Jesse straightens to his full height. "I think I can safely say for all of us we're happy to see this contest come to a close."

"Here, here!" Mary Ellen gets into the mix.

The front door opens, and Quinn walks in, trailed by the host of the show and the three judges. Since she already has our attention, Quinn starts talking. "It all comes down to this. Well done, Bo and Mary Ellen," she directs her attention toward our rival team. "And Paige and Jesse." Her head swivels in our direction. "Let's get set up for this last part of the show, the final elimination round."

We got this. We worked hard on our rooms, and I'm proud of what we produced. So what if we had a few minor flaws here and there? Our aesthetic complimented the whole apartment. I'm sure anyone would want to move into ours. Hell, *I'd* love to move into 1626.

After we're all situated and the lighting has been set, Miss Antonia takes over explaining what's about to go down. First, she'll give her assessment of the apartments, followed by each of the judges. When the show airs, though, the judges' reviews will be done by overdubbing a taped walkthrough of the primary suites.

I smooth my dress. Even though I'm in black and white and Jesse's wearing a cream shirt, I prefer our look to the matchy-matchy of Bo and Mary Ellen. Kind of a metaphor for our apartments. And our relationships.

"Rolling!"

The green lights flick on over the cameras, and the host begins. "Since you've enjoyed a recap of the apartments our teams did to date, let's take a deep dive into what they accomplished in the primary suites. Jesse and Paige continued with their pre-war with a modern twist feel, while Bo and Mary Ellen went in a different direction for this round with an Old Hollywood theme."

After a brief pause, during which I presume they'll splice in clips from our completed rooms, Miss Antonia continues, "I toured both of these suites, and have to admit I'm impressed with all of your work."

I tuck my hair behind my ear. Our first real-time assessment of our work from a revered show host. I can't wait to hear her review. I steal a glance at my boyfriend, and his face has lost all color. Poor guy. Can't imagine why he's so nervous, though. He did a fantastic job. Must be his overriding desire to get out of banking, and impending discussion with his parents about his new television show.

In front of us, the host turns to the other team. "I really loved the colors you selected. The blues are an excellent choice to relax, and your bedroom invited me in from the start. Your bed beckoned, and the divan was a great touch."

Bo smirks. "Thank you, Miss Antonia."

Take all the credit much?

"I adored the transformation to the bathroom, starting with the double doors and the chandelier you selected. It felt to me like a getaway from the rest of the apartment in the most gorgeous way."

She smiles at the cowboy carpenter, and a hint of dread enters my being. Was this rigged from the start? Was the network looking for a Southern couple to do the next show? *Stop.* No. I have to be overthinking this. Besides, Miss Antonia hasn't given her thoughts about our rooms yet.

The host adds, "However, to me, the juxtaposition of Old Hollywood glam with the rest of the apartment was a bit jarring. But, overall, very well done."

She turns to us. Here goes. "I thought your choices were right on point with the vibe of the rest of the apartment. The headboard, while not without its flaws, was a masterpiece and deserved to be the focal point of the bedroom. I liked the black paint you put on it, although some might call that blasphemy."

Jesse's eyes dart to me. We knew this was a risk, but the flaws would've been more pronounced with the stain, I'm sure of it.

"Your bathroom was nice as well. I loved your tile choices, although by having relocated the laundry room into the back corner, you weren't able to include a separate room for the toilet, which was a pity. I also felt the rooms lacked a sense of cohesion to themselves —like you were putting expected pieces into the bed and bath, but didn't pull them together. Overall, though, I liked your design very much and think it showcases your talents perfectly."

When she finishes speaking, a smile blooms on my face. She thought we did a fantastic job, like I knew she would. So what if she and our competitors are both from the South. Us northern folks got it going on, too.

Miss Antonia turns to the judges. "But my assessment of these apartments isn't what matters here. It's your take on which of these two teams created and executed the best spaces that does." She stares into the camera. "Allow me to re-introduce you to our judges." She rattles off their names and bona fides, and they start their reactions to our spaces.

The first one compliments Bo and Mary Ellen on their perfect execution of the Old Hollywood theme. He notes it's more feminine than he would like, but a great space. As for ours, he was impressed with my curtains and Jesse's headboard, but felt the bathroom was an afterthought. I purse my lips.

The second one agrees with the first, expanding upon her love for the divan and the bench at the foot of the bed. She also notes their spa-like bathroom retreat was done to perfection. Turning to us, she gives kudos to Jesse for his headboard, although thinks it should've been stained rather than painted. She also didn't care for my bathroom design. I bite the inside of my lip.

The final judge starts with our rooms first, applauding Jesse's bed as well as my curtains as "inspired." My chin raises. She criticizes flaws in his carving, though, but is more critical of what she called the "pedestrian" bathroom. She turns to Bo and Mary Ellen and says they did a good job but wished they'd chosen a more unique color combination.

Maybe we got this?

Then Miss Antonia holds up an index card. "I have the winning team's name right here." She pauses and the camera does a close-up on each one of us, then Quinn cues her to continue.

Before she opens her mouth again, my stomach does a flip and I grab Jesse's hand, cameras be damned. He squeezes mine back. *We had to have won.*

"And the winners are," she holds up the index card. "Bo and Mary Ellen!"

I blink several times, trying to understand what just happened. Reading the card five times, it sinks in that we lost.

Lost.

Lost.

As in did not win.

Came in second place.

Across from us, Bo pulls Mary Ellen into a bear hug, which almost makes me gag. I turn my body toward Jesse, who has disappointment written across his face. Maybe if he'd listened to me about carving only a rectangle of the headboard and upholstering the rest, we would've won?

I was hoping this would be my permanent ticket out of my parents' house. And Jesse would get a much-needed new life.

Quinn interrupts my pity party. "That's a wrap, folks. Congratulations, Bo and Mary Ellen! Well done. Jesse and Paige, you put up a valiant effort—thank you so much for your time." She gives us quick hugs and walks over to the winners to lavish them with attention.

I turn to Jesse. The judges were critical of his headboard. The flaws in his carving. Lack of finesse with the design he chose. The paint used. They weren't excited about the pieces I chose to include in the bedroom, either, especially noting that it was too much one-note. This axe falls heavily on Jesse, considering he created the furniture pieces and I only finished them when he was focusing on the carving.

We stand in silence next to each other, not touching, working through our loss. Quinn approaches. "Hey, great job you two. Please don't be disappointed with the result. You should be proud of all you accomplished."

Jesse offers a dejected, "Yeah."

"Plus, if I'm being truthful, your chemistry didn't crackle like Bo and Mary Ellen's. Our viewers want to relate and engage with our show hosts, and they exuded a certain type of appeal you two didn't."

I snort. "They're divorced. They hate each other."

She shrugs. "Two sides of the same coin."

Here I thought falling in love would've given us an edge in that department. *Love?*

Jesse extends his hand. "Thank you, Quinn, for this opportunity. I'll never forget it."

She shakes both of our hands, then returns to the winner's celebration. I face my partner. "Great job."

"Thanks. You, too."

We stand in awkward silence.

This doesn't have to be the end of the line for us. Just because the show didn't pick us doesn't mean we can't move forward as a team. Jesse can't give up on his carpentry dream. He's too talented for that. Working with him made me a better designer. We can do this together. I want this.

"We can start a business together, you and me." My palm paints a rainbow. "PJ's Designs." I giggle. "Wow. That sounds like we're making sleepwear. How about JP's on Fifth? I love the sound of that."

His sandy brown hair shakes. "I don't think so."

23

Jesse

J *P's on Fifth.* Is she on drugs? We just lost this competition, and she wants to open up a new business?

I shake my head. "I don't think so."

She tucks her hair behind her ear. "I'm sure we can come up with a different name that we'll both like."

Needing a breather, I say, "Excuse me. I have to use the restroom." I leave her in the living room and walk down the hallway, into the exercise room. My father jumps all over the silence:

Don't try something so beneath you.

You're white collar—stay in your lane.

Plus my personal favorite, *I told you business always comes before pleasure.*

Truth is, I tried as hard as I could during this competition to showcase my work. Even though Paige talked me into doing the carved headboard, it was a project I was eager to take on to prove myself. Guess what? I proved I'm not worthy.

Bo enters the room. Great. "Tough break."

Shoring up my strength, I reply, "Congrats, man. Bet you're on top of the world."

"Rather be on top of your partner, if you get my drift." He glances toward the door, a disgusting gleam in his eye.

Fists form at my side. Didn't the asshole call her frigid? The need to stick up for her fights its way out. No matter Homer's been proven right and I'm clearly not cut out to be a carpenter, I'm not about to let him spew against Paige. She's still accomplished in her own right and deserves to be treated with respect. "She's an extraordinarily talented designer."

"Bet she is more so in the bedroom." He slants me a glance, stepping back as I advance. The cowboy continues, "Although, if I had bedded her during this competition, her ideas would've flowed more freely." He throws his head back and laughs. "I mean, I'm sure you tried your best. Too bad it wasn't good enough."

Disgusted by his crude comments, I slap him on the back. Hard. Before another fistfight erupts, I vacate the room and bump into his partner in the living room. Shoving my angry feelings about her partner down into the pit of my stomach, I offer, "I'm happy for you."

"Thanks!"

Mary Ellen wraps me in a hug, which she holds a couple of beats too long. The zing that rips through my body when I hold Paige doesn't materialize. Guess this competition sunk more than my nascent carpenter career. "Congrats on getting your own television show."

"I can't believe it." She runs her hand through her hair, causing her blonde bangs to bounce. "Wish I didn't have to share the spotlight with my ex, though."

"I understand. Perhaps he'll change when you settle into your show?" Doubt it.

Her expression indicates she doesn't think so either. "We'll see. What are you going to do next? What's on your design horizon?"

I'm going back to banking. Accepting the promotion my boss promised me. Work my way into becoming a chief compliance officer somewhere like Homer. Keep following Diana's dream. At least I'm rewarded at the bank. *Should tell me something.*

Not about to reveal my thoughts, I reply, "Oh, I don't know what the future holds."

She taps my shoulder. "I'm sure something awesome will come up."

One of the judges calls Mary Ellen over, and Quinn approaches me. "Sorry how things turned out for you guys. I was impressed with your work."

Not a ringing endorsement. "Appreciate that."

It's as if the air around me encircles my neck and pulls. I need out. To flee this building. Find fresh air. "Do I have to sign anything, or am I free to go?"

My question pulls Quinn upright. "Of course, of course. You already signed everything, so you can pack your things whenever you're ready."

"Great."

"Oh, and I have something belonging to you." She fishes into her multi-colored tote bag and hands me my cell. On impulse, I do a quick photo transfer and return the one she issued to me. "There's a town car outside that will take you to wherever you want to go."

With a nod, I stride into the bedroom filled with the three bunk beds. Opening my suitcase, I dump all of my clothes into it, then go into the bathroom and clear out my toiletries. Less than half an hour later, I zip my luggage and wheel into the public area of the apartment, where people still linger.

Of its own volition, my gaze lands on Paige. She's across the room laughing with a couple of the camera crew. Pain at what could have been slashes through every pore, confirming my decision to leave and not look back. She's a living, breathing reminder of what I'll never have—a career in carpentry, days spent creating fantastic pieces with my hands, and dare I even think this, love. Or what approaches love. I make my way to her and whisper in her ear. "Bye."

Seeing my luggage, she tilts her head. "You're leaving?"

My gruff voice replies, "Yes."

"Wait. I'll get my stuff and we can go together."

I shake my head. "No. Stay here where you belong. Goodbye, Paige."

Forever.

Her eyes widen, understanding dawning that this is our final interaction. Not wanting to drag out our breakup, I walk away from this amazing woman. My hand lands on the doorknob and I give one final glimpse into the place that holds so many memories. Soon, I'm down the hallway and ramming the elevator button.

So many scenes flit through my mind. Six weeks of my life. With nothing to show for it.

The elevator cab dings and I slip inside. Crossing the lobby, I wave to the receptionists and hop into the car, which takes me to my apartment on the Upper East Side.

Everything is as I remember it, only with a coating of dust. My fridge only has water and lonely crackers are on the shelves. Ignoring the kitchen, I walk into my bedroom and pull out my phone. My real one. With Wi-Fi and all my contacts.

I have only one person I want to talk with, and he was on the network's phone as well. I press "Send."

"Jesse. How'd it go? Am I talking with the next Renovation TV star?" His voice picks up with excitement.

I sit on the bed. "Sorry, but no. We lost."

My statement hangs for a moment. "I'm sorry, Jesse. Don't get discouraged, though. This was your first attempt at doing anything with your skills, so I guess you can't expect to take the world by storm."

"It's over for me." I drop my head. "I tried to carve a headboard and got dinged by the judges for it. Plus, I agreed to paint the wood."

"In an effort to mask some missteps?"

"Yeah." I half-smile. "Didn't work. They pointed out it was a smart design move to hide my flaws, which reflected well on my partner." I quash the annoying twinge stealing across my heart. No more time for that.

"I'm sure you did a good job on it. You love whittling, and carving is along those lines."

I'm done with that too. "Well, those days are over for me. I'm returning to my job in banking. I only called to say thank you for all your help and support. I wish I had better news to share."

"Don't quit because one set of stupid judges couldn't see the value you bring. You're a great carpenter. The world needs your talent. Remember, a man can be destroyed but not defeated." When I don't respond, he adds, "At least keep on whittling. Can you do that for me?"

My heart sinks. I'm not sure I can go cold turkey on all things having to do with carpentry, so maybe this little hobby will be enough. "Sure." After a few more platitudes, we hang up.

In the silence, it's as if all my dreams have evaporated, yet my life is set. Return to the office, take the promotion, and continue on as before. Forget my foolish idea of making a go of it with my carpentry. It was all a pipe dream anyway.

Since it's only three o'clock in the afternoon, I decide it's time to clean up from the competition. I drag my ass over to my desk and boot up my computer, then enter the Etsy shop interface. Twenty orders came in while I was filming. Inhaling, I respond back that I won't be able to fulfill their orders. When I'm done, I delete my shop and close the account.

There.

Handmade by JD is no longer.

Pain slashes through my heart, but I ignore it. No more dwelling on what could have been.

I only have one last task to complete. Since it's a weekday, my parents will be in their city apartment rather than their weekend house in Connecticut. After Diana was killed, Homer decided to move us into the city, but Marge wanted to be able to go out with her friends, so he bought them a "weekend" house there. None of us wanted to remain in the family residence after the accident.

Following a quick shower, during which I refuse to dwell on my former partner's interest in having sex in one, I put on some clean clothes and head over to my parents'. I arrive a little before six, and stare at their doorway a full five minutes before I'm able to knock.

Marge answers. "Jesse? You look great. Come on in. Your father got home about ten minutes ago." She sweeps the door open, and I enter.

Guess my face and body language aren't betraying how I feel. Or my mother isn't all that observant. I kiss her cheek. "Hi, Marge."

My father makes his appearance. "Jesse?" He shakes my hand.

"We were going to order dinner from a Thai place we like. Want to join us?"

Marge used to be one of the top cooks in the neighborhood. All the kids would bang down our doors when she made a pie or cookies. Another casualty of the drunk driver's actions.

Her question makes me realize I haven't eaten since yesterday. "Sounds good. Thanks." She hands me the menu and I circle what I want, although "want" might be too strong a word.

Once the order is placed, Homer leads us into their living room. It has a good view, although not as nice as the ViewPad or even 1626. I'm sure Paige could make this place sing.

"So, what brings you by?"

Of course he didn't mention the show. I decide to give them the news they most want to hear first. "My promotion starts next week."

Homer's smile could stretch from here to our weekend house. "A real chip off the old block."

Marge adds, "We're so proud of you." She addresses my father. "We should've gone out somewhere special to celebrate."

The word "celebrate" together with my job at the bank is discordant. "Nah, this will be fine."

"Executive director at only twenty-eight. This is fantastic, son. You're a shooting star."

His phrase reminds me of Paige with the "Walking on Moonbeams" statue on the High Line. I semi-successfully stifle a sigh. "Yeah, the youngest in the bank's history." So exciting. *Not.*

Screwing up my courage, I say, "There's one more thing I need to tell you."

Our conversation is interrupted by the intercom. Marge raises her finger. "Hold that thought. Dinner's here." She scampers to pick up her purse and goes to the door.

Ignoring my previous statement, Homer peppers me with questions about the bank and my impending promotion. I try to sound upbeat, like I know he wants, yet it's difficult. Guess my time on the show helped with my acting skills, as he never questions my lack of enthusiasm. Or doesn't care to notice.

Another thing the drunk driver killed. Our family's communication.

Seated around the dining room table, eating my pad Thai, I wait for a lull in the conversation. "The Renovation TV show wrapped today. My team made it to the final round—the primary suite." Why did I tell them which room? Not like it matters. Shrugging, I stare at my full plate. "We lost."

Marge plays with her wine glass. "That's too bad, honey."

"Now you can focus on banking." Leave it to Homer to stick true to his career.

I wipe my hands on my napkin. Everyone's quiet for a few minutes until Marge asks, "Is this something you'd like to pursue? Carpentry?"

"He's on his way to becoming a chief compliance officer, for goodness sakes. Of course he isn't interested in going any deeper into the trade."

Homer's use of the word "trade" is exactly what I expected. Not the white-collar profession of banking like him.

"We only want you to be happy."

"Which he'll be with his new promotion," Homer completes her thought. And mine.

24

Paige

A couple of months have passed since we lost the competition, and I haven't heard from Jesse. He hasn't responded to any of my texts or messages or emails. The fact he ghosted me after the last taping, as if I meant nothing to him, still stings. Especially when he meant *everything* to me.

After the taping ended, no way was I going to return to my parents', so I stayed with Theo and Amelia for a few weeks, until their happy-happy-joy-joy gnawed my insides raw. Luckily, Chloe was able to put me up in her sister's room. Uncle Ward doesn't seem to mind the extra person in his space, considering he generally stays in his wing anyway.

Chloe brings a huge bowl of popcorn into the media room and sits next to me. Tonight's the finale of *NYC Views*, which I didn't want to see, but Chloe insisted. Not only that, but she invited all my brothers and cousins plus the two fiancées to join the watch party. I was able to stop her from inviting any non-family members, but it was touch-and-go for a while.

A buffet table has been set up on the side, complete with various snack foods. The three rows of leather seats have been laid out with their own bowls of popcorn and glasses, so people can choose their beverages at the wet bar.

"I don't see why we need a viewing party," I grumble.

"Because we're celebrating the fact you made it all the way to the finals. This was a huge accomplishment, even if you didn't win." Chloe puts a metal straw into her glass of root beer.

Not interested in any of the alcoholic drinks, I choose a water—cucumber flavor—which I drink from the bottle.

The intercom buzzes and Chloe flits out of the room to greet our guests. I'm not excited for tonight's show at all. Watching Jesse fall on his face, no matter the fact he's ignoring me, isn't my idea of fun. Yet, here I am. Getting to my feet, I prepare for the onslaught.

Theo's the first through the door, and he gives me one of his bear hugs. His fiancée Amelia comes in next, and Xander, plus his fiancée Madison all file in and each give me a warm welcome. When everyone's settled into their seats, Xander says, "I invited Jesse to come over and watch with us." He spears me with his blue eyes, causing my eyebrows to shoot to the ceiling. "He turned me down. Flat."

Not a shock. The only surprise is they're still talking. I shovel popcorn into my mouth rather than ask about the man who doesn't want me. No one except for Chloe knows we were involved. Even she has the abridged version.

"You've done a great job this entire time, Paige," Amelia remarks. "I can't wait to see what you do with the primary suite. I know you didn't win, but your design has been great this whole time. Very creative."

"Thanks," I mumble around a piece of popcorn.

"Shhh, it's starting." Amelia's unneeded warning quiets the room.

Relieved no one else from my family was able to make it, I watch this episode with an analytical eye. They highlighted Jesse's challenges with the carving which, at least on television, looks pretty darn great. I can read the frustration on his face, but his finished product appears on point. The other furniture he made for the room is gorgeous. When I'm on screen, I force myself to pay attention. And cringe at my critical tone and perfectionist expectations. His work was fine. Mine, on the other hand, is where our team fell short.

Why did I insist on painting the headboard?

Why didn't I pay attention to all the little details in the bathroom?

Why did I ignore the harder design elements in favor of easier carpentry items?

It's almost as if I was sabotaging our chances at coming out victorious. I shove my body into the overstuffed recliner.

By contrast, the videos of Bo and Mary Ellen don't depict the couple I knew in the ViewPad. They worked well together, even if she let him take the lead most of the time. Yet, her ideas enhanced their room. All in all, their design wasn't better than ours, only different.

I was the reason we lost.

When the winner is announced, everyone in the room boos and yells at the screen. Theo's "You were robbed!" doesn't make me feel any better about my poor performance.

I hold up my hand. "Thanks, guys. Your support means the world to me." It also highlighted how much I owe Jesse.

Later, as I lie in my bed, I wish with my whole being Jesse were here with me. Not only did he give me a proper introduction to what sex can be, but he also was a damn fine partner. Much better than I was to him. *I* lost the competition for us, not him. *I* ruined his dream.

I pull out my phone and go on Etsy, looking for Handmade by JD. Nothing. What? I search again and get the same result. Pulling up Google, I do a search and the entry says "closed." Oh. My. God. He went full-on back to banking.

I forced him back into a job he doesn't like because I lost the competition for us. He told me it was his last shot at making a go at carpentry. Now he's pulled out. This can't stand.

The next morning, I steal the real estate section from Uncle Ward's newspaper and flip through the pages.

"What are you looking for?"

"I'm checking out what listings are out there, Uncle Ward."

After he swallows a spoonful of cereal, he asks, "Are you looking to buy another house to flip?"

I nod. "Yeah. Figure I might as well capitalize on the publicity the show brought." Not a lie. Not the full truth, either.

"Do you want any help? I could pull up some listings on the computer for you."

I need to do this on my own. For once. "Thanks, but I got it. Don't want to take away from your stuff with VOW-cubed."

He grimaces. "I'm available if you need me, okay?" When I smile, he stands and brings his bowl over to the dishwasher. Ever since his last girlfriend moved out, he's become more fastidious about keeping things clean. Can't imagine Father doing anything so domestic.

Alone, I flip through the listings but nothing seems interesting. Chloe enters the kitchen and pours herself a cup of coffee. "Want any?"

"Sure. Thanks."

She puts my mug down in front of me and cranes her neck. "What are you doing?"

I look up from the paper. "Checking the real estate listings. I'm looking for another house to flip."

"That's great. Find anything?" She blows on her coffee.

I sigh. "Not yet."

"I'm sure you'll find something amazing. Want some help? Doesn't seem like I have anything else to do." She traces an imaginary shape on the table.

Pulling myself out of my own misery, I focus on Chloe. "Give it time. You've only been out of college for a few months. You had your interview with Madison's friend at the placement agency not long ago."

"I know." Her finger encircles the lip of her coffee cup saying *HR Professional.*

My eyes skim the next page of the newspaper and I bounce upright. "Hey. This looks like it might be something. It's on the High Line. Want to come with me and check it out?"

Her grey eyes light up. "That sounds like fun. It'll get me out of the house and my own head."

Using the red pen Uncle Ward left behind, I circle the listing and rip out the page. "Let's get ready. I'll call the agent and we can meet her there."

Two hours later we stand outside the apartment building a couple of doors down from where I spent six weeks of my life working and falling in love. Despite the fact that Jesse's ignoring me, I refuse to take his silence as a final answer.

The agent, Lelah, greets us and ticks off the building's amenities. Rather, the amenities to come, considering the entire building is undergoing a renovation. There will be a pool, workout room, theater, and even a bowling alley by the time the developer is finished. However, the developer doesn't want to handle individual apartments, hence the listing.

We follow the woman, dressed in a designer pantsuit—Victoria Beckham if I'm not mistaken—up the elevator. When it dings on the tenth floor, energy zaps through my body. As if it's already agreed to purchase this place. Swallowing, I enter the apartment.

"Wow. This needs a lot of work."

Chloe's not wrong. The floors must be refinished, several walls need to be moved. Paint. Molding. Millwork. I walk over to the windows and run my hand over the casing. "Can these be changed, Lelah?"

"Not the size, but the sliding doors can be switched out to French doors, if you'd like."

I can use window coverings to make the windows appear taller. Like in 1626. I'll definitely take her up on her offer to change the sliding glass doors, though. Anything to open up the space. I slide the door and allow Chloe to walk out ahead of me.

"Wow. This is a huge balcony. Look, it spans the entire length of the apartment. I think there are a couple more sliding doors out here as well." She walks toward one end and yells, "Here's one." Passing me, she walks to the other end and skips back. "There's another one down there. Very cool."

"I agree." My voice is low, trembling with my desire to renovate this apartment. I re-enter the living room and examine the kitchen. The remainder of the tour goes about the same. When Lelah finishes showing us around, she gives us a few minutes to talk between ourselves. I'm ready to put in an offer, but Chloe's more cautious.

"I don't know, Paige. This is a shit-ton of work. You can't possibly do it on your own."

"Of course not. I'll be the general contractor, overseeing everyone." I know who has to go in with me on this project. Even if he's not taking my calls.

Chloe walks in a big circle around the primary bedroom, opening the small closet door. "You'll have to add in decent closet space. Not to mention changing out all the floors."

"All cosmetic stuff." Items Jesse could handle with one arm tied behind his back. So long as I'm not doing the tying, like I did on the show.

My cousin's face breaks into a huge smile. "When you're done, I want to buy it. It does have a spectacular view."

I raise my fist, which she bumps. Without a job and the freezing of our trust funds a definite possibility, I doubt she has the money this place will command once I'm done with it. I'm not going to dash her hopes, though. "We'll see. You might like a different one of my projects better."

Her mouth falls open. "You're planning on taking on more than one of these?"

With Jesse by my side, I'll be invincible. "I'm not sure yet. I'd like to. Let's go talk with Lelah."

We return into the living room, ideas forming about how to reorient the entire interior to take advantage of the breathtaking view. I've learned it's not a good idea to seem too anxious, so I tell the real estate agent I'll think about it and take her card. Printed on thick cardstock. I thought these things were a relic of the past, but boy does it make a positive impression.

When we exit the building onto the High Line, Chloe remarks, "I've lived in New York City all my life but haven't come here since this was built. Care to take a walk with me?"

The ice cream stand where Jesse and I shared a sweet treat is to our left. Calling to me. I link my arm with hers and point us right, joining the crowds on this sunny afternoon. When we reach "Stormy Tides," I stop. "Isn't this magnificent? It's one of my favorite statues here. I'm happy it hasn't been removed." I pause. "Walking on Moonbeams" was my favorite, but it's gone now. Like Jesse. I rub my arm.

My cousin takes in the glorious work of art and bites her bottom lip. "I don't need anything reminding me of possible problems ahead. I only want positive artwork."

She walks away, leaving me in front of the statue. "I think you're very uplifting. You're aware storms are ahead, but don't let them stop you. You're a winner." This work of art gives me hope that I'll win, too.

After we return home, Chloe dives back into scouring all the websites and working her LinkedIn profile searching for job openings. I, on the other hand, retreat into my bedroom, pick up my journal, and write down a list of points about why Jesse has to help me with the High Line apartment.

Figuring a text might be better received than a phone call, I decide to write him my pitch. This way, he can digest everything and not turn me down without all the facts. I open a new text:

> **Hi Jesse. Hope you're doing well. I'm writing because I have a proposition for you.**

"Proposition"? Sounds too sexual. Even though I'd love to proposition him again . . .

Getting my thoughts back on track, I erase the last four words and try again:

> **an opportunity I'd like you to consider. I toured an apartment on the High Line, a few doors down from where we filmed. It's in need of as much—if not more—renovation than the one we did on the show. I'm interested in buying**

it to flip, but only if you'd be willing to be the carpenter for it.

Now the harder part. I need to convince him he can do it even though he's returned to the banking world. Where his passion does not lie. I continue:

Before you say no, hear me out. You could work on this project during the weekends and after banking hours. I would coordinate all the other trades, once we've agreed on the best course of action.

I reread my text. It needs a close.

I watched the show. I am sorry for not listening to you, and putting my nose into places it didn't belong. I'm the reason we lost, and I can't live with myself knowing this. For this project, I promise to give you total control over all the carpentry items. There is no one I'd rather do this with than you. No one I WILL do this with. Please say yes.

I read the text once more, gasp, and press send.
Please respond, Jesse. With a yes.

25

Jesse

I read Paige's text for the millionth time. The ache of seeing her name settles low in my stomach. I have no intention of replying, but seeing her heart poured out about a new project gives me a sense of joy. For her, not for me. Never for me. I'll never take her up on her offer, never pick up another hammer. My whittling block and knife are as close to carpentry as I'll ever get again. The network proved my pipe dream belongs in the sewer, and that's where it's going to stay.

My new boss, Louis, stops by my desk, and I shove my phone into the drawer—my promotion came through last month. "Hey, Jesse. How are you settling into your new role? Getting a handle on everything?"

I tap my computer. "Been working up a spreadsheet so I can capture all the moving parts. It's a lot to wrap my head around, but I'm getting there."

He puts his hand on my shoulder. "Sounds good. Let me know if you need anything. We're all excited to have you onboard."

"Thanks."

He leaves and the bottom falls out of my stomach. I've thrown myself into my job ever since *NYC Views* wrapped. If I'm too tired and overworked, I can't look back. The ping of a text comes in and I pull my cell out of the drawer, dreading who it could be. Well, only dreading one person it might be.

Opening the messages, I'm relieved when Xander's name pops up as the culprit. Him, I can handle. He asks if I want to play racquetball after work. Letting off steam sounds good to me, so I reply with a heartfelt yes.

A few hours later, I'm in my workout gear and whacking a ball against the wall. It whizzes by Xander for the third time in a row and he signals he wants to take a break. Nodding, I join him by the water station.

"You're playing like the devil's on your shoulder." He slurps down a cup of water.

"More like two," I mumble. "Or twenty."

He slings back another cup. "What's up?"

"Trying to settle into my promotion. Need to get my head around the department." I crumple my cup and toss it into the bin.

"I have faith in you." He slaps my back, then takes a third cup of water.

Grabbing a towel, I wipe the sweat off my forehead. I'd rather get back to the game when I don't have the ability to think of anything outside of hitting the ball.

"That was half-hearted." *Busted.* "Isn't this the promotion you've been working toward? You're an executive director now, right?"

"You got it—excellent memory." I lower my shoulders. I try to ignore the long stretch of my career ahead.

He bounces the ball on the head of his racquet. "I watched the finale with Paige."

"I didn't bother. We lost."

"You did good, man. You're crazy talented. No way would I have even tried to carve a frickin' headboard, and you did it." His blue eyes leave the bouncing ball. "Good on you."

Fat lot of good it did me. It wasn't good enough to win. *I* wasn't good enough. I shrug. "Well, that's all behind me now. Got it out of my system." This has to be the biggest lie I've ever told.

Xander's eyebrow quirks up. "Really?"

"It was a stupid fantasy. Nothing more." A fantasy I built up in my head for years and finally got the guts to pursue. Failed. It's over now.

"How long have we known each other?"

I consider his unusual question for a moment. "Since business school. That's what? Eight, nine years ago."

"Sounds about right." Xander captures the ball in his hand and bounces it on the floor. "We've been through some crazy shit in classes, right?"

I remember some of the onerous projects we were assigned. I chuckle, which sounds a bit raspy to my ears. "Very true."

"We've also had some amazing times together. Mainly involving drinking and hanging out." His eyebrows wiggle. "And women."

Where is he going with this? "Also true."

"Guess what I saw when I watched your show?" Without notice, he tosses me the ball. My reflexes take over, and I catch it. When I don't respond, he says, "I saw a man I've never seen before. A man who was happy. Doing something he loved. Fighting for his concepts. Secure in his knowledge and skill."

My hand clenches around the ball. "Doesn't matter."

He pretends to hit an imaginary ball by swooshing his racquet in the air. "You've always gotten good grades and have been a worthy colleague. Never missed a deadline and were well prepared. I always had the feeling you were going through the motions, though." He lowers the racquet. "On the show, I saw a man on a mission because he was all in. Not simply doing what was expected."

I have nothing to add. Instead, I hold up the ball. "Ready?"

I give him exactly one second to get into position, then serve. The ball thwacks against the wall and speeds toward Xander, who returns. The game doesn't deter him, though.

"I think you're damn good at your job in banking. Others must agree, considering you've been promoted."

Focusing on the game, I hit the ball—harder this time. He returns.

"I also think you should be working with your hands and wood. Creating more of the gorgeous furniture you showcased on the show. Maybe even carving more pieces." He runs for the ball and makes the save. "How's the Etsy shop going? It must've blown up since the show aired."

My racquet doesn't make contact with the ball and it bounces off the back wall. Shit. Walking over, I scoop it up and take a moment to catch my breath. "Closed it down, man."

"What?" Xander's response is faster than our volleys.

Shaking my head, I admit, "I didn't see any reason to keep it open. My life is with the bank now."

"Your professional life maybe. Not your heart and soul. Not your passion."

"Enough." Xander looks at me. "I lost the fucking show for our team. I wasn't good enough. That's all I needed to know to get my head set back on straight. I'm now an executive director at the bank, on my way up to becoming chief compliance officer. Like Homer." Like Diana would've done. I bounce the ball, using my racquet instead of my hand.

"Dude. You're wrong. First, from what I saw, you weren't the one who lost the competition. If anything, Paige did. Love my cousin to death, but she took over projects that were over her pay grade and ignored items on her to do list she should've done."

"You're wrong. I let her do those things. I could've told her no."

Xander's head flies back in a loud guffaw. "Paige. We're talking about my cousin here. The one who's never heard the word 'no' in all her life."

I told her no. Several times. "She would've listened to me."

Xander's head tilts. "You think?"

"It happened several times."

He swings his racquet. "Well, this is a whole different game now, isn't it?"

I let the ball bounce itself to the floor. "I don't follow."

"We were only messing with you."

Now I'm all sorts of confused. "About what?"

"Theo and me." Xander snatches the ball from the floor and resumes bouncing it on the head of his racquet. "True, Paige is his little sister. We've been raised like cousins. But I can't imagine a better man for her than you."

I cringe, as if the ball smacked me in the stomach. Hard. "What are you talking about?"

"C'mon. We've established we've known each other for almost a decade. I can read you. Now this is all making sense to me. You fell for her, didn't you?"

My gaze follows the bouncing ball. "I don't know what you mean." My phone rings. Breaking game protocol—since we're clearly not playing a real game anyway—I pick up my phone and check to see who it is. Spam call. Great. I block the number.

I'm about to shut off my cell when Xander asks, "Can I see that?" I try to hide my phone from him, but he's too quick. "Thought so."

He twists his hand so my wallpaper faces me. Looking back at me is the cute selfie I took of Paige and me eating ice cream on the High Line that I managed to snag off the Renovation TV phone before I turned it in. *Busted.* "You fell for her."

Defeated, I rest against the back wall. "Sort of," I mumble.

He joins me in holding up the wall. "She broke up with you when the show ended?"

"Other way around."

"*You* broke up with *her*?"

"Don't sound so surprised." My racquet springs off the wall.

"I get it." Xander pushes away from the wall and positions himself in front of my face. "You're at the bottom of a bourbon bottle like when I thought things between Madison and me were over. Racquetball. Interesting choice."

I force my feet to hold my own weight. "You invited me, remember?"

He chuckles. "I would've said meet me at a bar had I known. Although, you'll thank me in the morning when you wake up without a hangover." He holds up his hand. "And a gauze wrap."

"I'm not wallowing like you were."

"Perhaps you should. You gave up on your dream to do carpentry. You pushed a good woman away. What's next? Sell your apartment and move into a youth hostel?"

"Are you fucking nuts?"

"Glad to see you still have standards. Fine. No hostel."

I pick up the ball and squeeze. In. Out. In. Out. In. Out. Xander's hand closes over mine. "It doesn't have to be like this."

I can't walk away from the bank now—my promotion is final. Plus, Homer's expecting this to be a stepping stone to banking glory. Paige? She's not an option, if she ever was one. I'm sure she'll find another guy to give her an orgasm. I squeeze the ball so tightly the veins on my forearm protrude.

Xander pries my fingers open and removes the ball. "Let's go to a bar."

"No." I don't want to be around crowds. In fact, I don't want to be with anyone, Xander included. I need to crawl back into my apartment and put my head on straight. Stop thinking impossible thoughts. The kind Xander's spouting.

I need to fulfill my sister's dream—the one that was cut off way too soon, courtesy of the drunk driver. I inhale. I will work my way up to chief compliance officer. I need to honor my promise to Homer.

Dropping my racquet onto the floor, I say, "I'm going home. Thanks for the game."

Not wanting to engage any farther, I don't look back. I simply walk out the door, grab my bag from the locker, and leave the building. Even though the air's fresh, I can't smell it. The sky is still light, but I don't notice its color. Everything's black and white. Has been since the day I lost the competition for us.

I walk the twenty blocks to my apartment. I'm among people but not with them. Existing. Metaphor for my life.

Inside, I take a shower to get rid of the racquetball stench, then dress in a pair of shorts and a NYU biz school shirt. Plopping down in front of the television, I reach for the block of wood I've been whittling for days. I promised Mr. Hooper I'd continue to do this, but my heart's not in it. Nothing is.

Needing a distraction, I turn on the television to NewsTime. Not

Renovation TV, that's for sure. They talk about another wildfire out west. Discuss the political races. Express concern over some trade imbalance. My mind clears.

The "breaking news" chime sounds and I focus on the anchor. "This just into the newsroom. It seems the partners at VOW-cubed are going their own ways. We have confirmed that Ogden Hansen, and Ward and Vince Turner each have retained their own, separate lawyers in the case against the trio who founded the media conglomerate."

She continues talking, but all I can think about is reaching out to Paige to see how she's handling this new development. She must be a wreck.

I drop the wood and reach for my cell to call her. When our smiling faces on the wallpaper greet me, I release it. Like I need to do with her.

26

Paige

"Thank you for your time, Mr. Laughlin." I disconnect the call and review my notes from the attorney who now only represents Uncle Vince. I've been so focused on my own business that I haven't had to deal with the VOW-cubed fallout—thankfully, my call was about my business and he was able to confirm ideas I learned on the internet, without charge. He also gave me the names of the two new lawyers representing Father and Chloe's dad.

Uncle Ward's been mum, so the only reason I know our fathers each retained separate counsel was through Theo. Not that I could do anything about it, but he wanted me to be aware. I told Chloe, who cried a little, but turned her energy inward. Getting a job is priority numbers one through fifty with her, especially since I also shared about the government's motion to freeze our trust funds. At least I have access to the funds from my earlier flip—Chloe doesn't have such luxury. I'll loan her some money if she needs it.

"Paige, I got some good news."

The lightness in her voice is welcome. "What's up?"

Chloe flips her long curly hair, the brown so shiny it glints in the light. "I got an interview with Benson Technologies! Stephanie finally came through."

"That's wonderful." I open my arms and she gives me a hug. "I knew the placement firm would come through for you."

"Thanks to Madison passing my resume along to her bestie."

"If there's anything I've learned, it's that your network is as important as schooling. If not more so."

"So true." She cranes her neck. "What are you working on?"

"Putting the finishing touches on my plan to buy that apartment we toured. I got all my financing in place and most contractors lined up. I need to iron out one final detail and then the deal can go through."

"Seems like we both have good news. Want me to break out the bubbly?"

The lure to toss all my work to the side and join my cousin in drinking the day away is strong. Especially considering how things have turned for the worse with our fathers. Yet, I have way too many loose ends to tie up. Beginning—rather ending—with getting a very recalcitrant carpenter onboard.

"I would love to, but I have a meeting in an hour. It's going to be a late night for me," hopefully. "Don't wait up. I promise a raincheck."

She holds up her pinky. "I'll hold you to that."

I lock my pinky around hers, and then grab my notebook plus the file I've been working on, and dash out. Can't be late. Double-checking the address, I enter Arch Pointe Furniture and go to their main office on the fortieth floor. I'm ushered into a conference room where I let my pen bang against my notebook until Ms. Kennedy appears.

Once formalities are exchanged, I get straight to the purpose of my meeting. "I appreciate your agreeing to meet with me. I know you saw *NYC Views* on Renovation TV, so you've already seen my partner's work."

"I have. I found it quite impressive, even if your team didn't win the competition."

I bow my head. *Because of me.* Gathering my wits, I continue, "The thing is, I've checked out your furniture line, and I believe

Jesse would make an excellent addition to your design team. You both specialize in creative wood furniture that enhances living spaces. I think he could create fantastic new prototypes for you to market." I hand her my proposal.

She takes her time flipping through every page. "This is a bold proposition. I agree that Jesse's talent would be a good synergy with Arch Pointe Furniture. We have a similar aesthetic."

"I agree."

"Unfortunately, I don't have the sole say over such decisions. I'll have to present this to our management committee. But, I can tell you, he has my vote." She frowns. "Why isn't he here?"

The moment I've been dreading arrives. Inhaling, I reply, "He got called into another meeting unexpectedly." Beneath my notepad, I cross my fingers.

"Pity. But there will be plenty of time to meet if the committee agrees."

Relief wells throughout my body. "Thank you. I appreciate your taking this up with them. I believe now's the best time to do this, since the publicity surrounding the show is still strong."

"I agree." She checks her watch. "As luck would have it, we're meeting in about an hour. So you'll get a response from me, either way, soon."

My nerves rush to the fore, which I shove down for the moment. "I look forward to hearing from you with a yes."

On the street, I debate what to do for a couple of hours. The High Line isn't far away, so I decide to take a stroll. Perhaps the sunshine will provide a balm while I send massive good vibes for my proposal to be accepted by Arch Pointe Furniture. And Jesse Dimon.

I pass the ice cream vendor and keep walking. Not even the lure of strawberry makes me tarry. I need to expend some energy, so I walk several blocks before realizing I'm standing in front of the building where *NYC Views* was taped.

So many memories are locked inside this building. About the show, the contestants, Jesse and me. I wonder who else started their stories inside these walls? The building's being renovated now, but what was it like ages ago? With no answers, I continue forward when the door opens and Quinn saunters out.

"Paige!"

Her yell stops me in place, planting a smile on my face. "Quinn."

We meet in the middle of the wide walkway and give each other a quick hug. Stepping back, she adjusts the strap of her Vera Bradley tote bag. "What have you been up to?"

Since my hands are full of paperwork, I can't deny I've been working. "I'm figuring out my next steps. Might have found a new place I want to flip."

"That's great. Do you have time for a coffee and to catch up?"

Quinn always was the all-business type, but maybe it was due to her role on set? A tad bit too interested in my family, but she didn't air anything about VOW-cubed on the show. Since I have time to kill before Ms. Kennedy gets back to me, I shrug. "Sounds good. Lead the way."

She brings us to a small café a couple of blocks away, where we order coffees and score a table next to the window. We get our drinks, and find a table where Quinn places our order number so the server can find us with our food.

After blowing on her cup, she asks, "I saw the news about your father getting separate counsel. How are you all holding up?"

She's only being chatty. "To be honest, I've kept out of it and focused on my own thing. I've been staying with my cousin and her dad doesn't talk about work at all, so I've been isolated."

"Oh." She takes a sip and pulls back, presumably because it's still too hot to drink. "Have you talked with your own father about it?"

"I called him when I first heard. He told me he was handling it and passed me to Mum. His way of avoiding having to answer too many questions." I tuck my hair behind my ear.

"Interesting."

"Excuse me?"

"Oh nothing. My mother does the same thing, that's all. If she doesn't want to talk about a subject, she's tighter than a clam."

"She should meet Father. Two peas in a pod."

She coughs, then raises her cup to her lips. "Renovation TV has received lots of fan mail for you and Jesse. People love you guys."

"Really? Thanks." What else can I say to that?

"Do you want me to forward them to you?"

I'm about to say no, when a thought occurs. "Please." I give her my personal email address so I'm sure to see the file when it arrives. My mind goes off in a million directions about how I can use this in my current quest.

"So tell me, what are the mysterious next steps you mentioned before?"

I play with the handle of my mug. Might as well tell her a limited truth. "I'm looking into new properties to flip."

"That's great. I think you have a good eye. Some of your choices were on par with what I was thinking. Moving the laundry room was a brilliant idea, for instance. Plus, I loved your hidden pantry."

"Thanks. I was proud of that as well." One of the only things for which I'm proud, and Jesse made each idea sing.

The server delivers our sandwiches, and we dig in. In between bites, she peppers me with questions about my life and family. Turns out, Quinn has a sister who works in the news business here, but I haven't heard of her.

Finishing her sandwich, she wipes her hands on at least five paper napkins. "And how's Jesse? Are you two still going strong?"

This is the one question I was dreading. Do I tell her the truth? —we broke up when we were kicked off the show. Or share my hopes of getting back together with him? I decide on a middle ground.

"He's good. Very busy, with lots of balls in the air."

"I'm happy to hear that. He's talented. You two make a cute couple."

Agreed. Heat rises up my neck, and I place my palm beneath my ear to hide the telltale pink. "Appreciate it." Needing to deflect, I turn the tables. "So, what about you? Any special man in your life?" A vision of her and Bo together at Club Cielo pops into my mind.

"No way. Too busy with work."

Might as well go for it. "What about Bo?"

She inhales. "We work together, nothing more."

I finish my wrap. "Oh, c'mon. I saw you two out together at a club when we were filming."

She shakes her head, her dark brown, chin-length hair swinging against her jawline. "Can you keep a secret?" I nod and she continues. "He hit on me and we went out on a date to a restaurant and to the club where you obviously saw us. But he ate with his mouth open, which turned me off."

I laugh, and she stares at me. "Oh, I know! He did the same thing with me. Disgusting."

She joins me in laughing. "Right? He's a good-looking guy, for sure. But please, keep your mouth closed."

"Oh my God. Believe me, though, it's better to listen to him chew than to let him talk. He has some seriously out-of-date ideas about women. I'm actually shocked he pursued you, considering you were his boss on the show."

Still chuckling, she replies, "Not really a boss. I didn't have any sway with the decision-making, which was left up to the judges one hundred percent."

Anxiety I didn't realize I was still carrying dissipates. Bo truly was barking up the wrong tree. "Good to know."

We continue to chit-chat until my phone rings. *Shit*. I'd almost forgotten about this call. I hold up my finger. "I need to take this."

Quinn nods and stands. "I'll run to the ladies' room."

She walks away from the table, and I answer my phone. "Ms. Kennedy?"

"Paige. I'm happy I caught you."

I swallow. Rather, gulp air since no moisture is left in my body. "I'm all ears." I slam my eyes shut, hoping for good news.

"I presented your proposal to the committee, and they were impressed. I pulled up tape from *NYC Views* so they could experience Jesse's work firsthand."

Blinking, I rub my hands together. I've never been this nervous. Not even when I turned over my flip to the real estate agent. "I hope they liked it."

"Very much. They want to meet Jesse and have him design his own line of furniture for Arch Pointe."

I sag in my chair. They accepted my proposal! I knew Jesse was destined for more than banking. Here's proof. "Thank you so much," I gush.

I open my mouth, but Ms. Kennedy leaps into the conversation. "However, we have one stipulation. The management committee enjoyed how you worked together as a team. We saw flashes of brilliance when you were collaborating, and we're positive the show didn't do your partnership justice. So, we want both of you as a team."

My mind blanks. I never considered this. "Well, I, ah." I shake my head. "Jesse is the carpenter of the group. It's his designs you want."

"We do. But your aesthetic added something special on top of his great designs. We want you both."

I bounce against the back of the seat. Not only do I somehow have to sell Jesse on this leap of faith, now I have to tell him I'm part of the package? "I'm shocked."

Quinn returns to the table and retakes her seat.

"We understand that your proposal was for Jesse alone, so let's all meet next week and hammer out a new pricing strategy. Say, next Wednesday. Is that good for you two?"

My head nods before my mouth engages. "Yes. We'll be there."

"Great."

I disconnect the call and stare at my phone. "What was that all about, if you don't mind me asking?" Quinn's soft voice intrudes on my silent freak out.

I force my eyes in her direction. Focusing on the woman in front of me, I flip my cell from head to tail, over and over.

Quinn snaps her fingers. "Earth to Paige."

I blink once more. "That was a furniture store. They want to hire us to design a new line for them."

She claps. "That's awesome. I'm not surprised. You make a great team."

"Yeah."

Now to convince Jesse of this.

27

Jesse

I review the memorandum I've been working on for my new boss, setting up new protocols. I think I've covered all the bases. Stifling a yawn, I perform one last spell check and press "save."

I'm good at banking—guess it's in my blood. Homer's over the moon at my promotion. My new subordinates kiss up to me, which is weird. The title "Executive Director" doesn't represent a big deal to me, however.

More money.

More problems.

More of the same, only with a shiny new title. Ho-hum.

Ready to go out for lunch, I leave my office—another perk of the promotion—when a noise in the front of the room catches my attention. The normally quiet open desk system has come alive with murmuring. What's going on? Maybe one of the muckety-mucks is making their monthly visit. Unfazed, I put on my suit's blazer and shove my cell into my pocket.

One of the guys stands and looks toward the front of the office. "Ho. Ly."

Interest piqued, I force my gaze in the same direction. "Fuck."

Paige Hansen has two escorts walking her into the office.

Toward me. Wearing a cream pantsuit with a pinkish blouse, she looks like her favorite ice cream cone. Bet she smells better. Her short brown hair appears to have been trimmed recently. The closer she gets, the higher my walls build. She can't scale them. Not even a fingerhold exists.

Since I never told her what bank I work for, I assume she's meeting with someone about an account. Maybe I can scoot backwards and not draw her attention? I don't need this shit in here. The show—which I lost, thank you very much—has never come up in conversation, so my co-workers have no idea we're acquainted. Intimately.

Echoes of her moans replay and I shut them down. Chest heaving, I slink down a side aisle.

One of her escorts points at me. "Aha! There he is."

Trapped.

Her other escort yells, "Jesse Dimon. You have a visitor."

Fuck, fuck, fuck.

One of the nearby guys complains, "You've been holding back on us."

Frowning, I reply, "She's my friend's little sister." With no other alternative, I mutter, "Excuse me," and walk toward the trio barreling down on my office. Pain about letting her down on the show and agony over Homer's mantra of putting career before pleasure battle for supremacy, with neither giving an inch. I can't look her in the eye.

Her first escort says, "Told you we'd bring you to him."

Her other escort agrees. "Safe and sound."

"Thanks so much, guys. You're the best." Her throaty giggle makes my cock stir and I rock my ankle to keep myself from jumping them. Or jumping *on* her.

Knowing how persuasive she can be, and determined to stay in my new job at all costs, my first words to her are curt. "Let's take this to a conference room."

She extends both of her hands. "Jesse. You look so business-y."

Shit happens when you work at a bank. Not acknowledging her

comment, I bark, "Follow me." Without waiting for a response, I storm toward an empty conference room.

As soon as I enter the room, I do the only sensible thing and press the button to frost all the windows. Don't need any curiosity seekers witnessing whatever the hell she has planned. Arms across my chest, I spin in her direction, still keeping my gaze averted from her form. This is Homer's world. "What the hell are you doing here, Paige? We have nothing to discuss."

She places a bunch of papers onto the table and stands taller. "You need a haircut."

Steam billows out of my ears. "I'm sure you have much better things to do than comment on my grooming."

Her chin raises. "You're right. I do." She opens a file folder and pulls out a stapled document. Approaching me, she says, "Actually, we have a lot to discuss."

Do not inhale. Do not look into her mesmerizing eyes. Confused, I snatch the papers out of her hand and skim the three-page document. It's a contract with Arch Pointe Furniture. "What the hell are you up to, Paige?"

She sighs. "Can we sit down and discuss this like normal people?" Without waiting for me to invite her—wise, because I wasn't about to—she drags the chair out from beneath the table and sits. When I don't move, she opens her tote bag and pulls out a pen and her cell phone wrapped in a light blue cover.

Sighing, I sit a few spaces down from her so as to make it the most difficult to look at each other.

She taps her pen against the tabletop. I think it's Mont Blanc. Pulling my bank's pen out of my blazer pocket, I click it open and shut. The noise is the only sound in the conference room for a full three minutes. At my wit's end, I blurt, "Why are you here?"

"Thought you'd never ask. I'm here to present an offer that came to me." I push away from the table. I'm not her business partner, advisor, or boyfriend. I'm about to tell her this when she continues, "It's for both of us."

Her statement hangs in the air, and I swivel my chair to her general vicinity, still not allowing myself to make eye contact. "Excuse me?"

"Yes." She inhales. "I approached Arch Pointe Furniture to ask if they'd let you create a line of furniture for them."

My hands land on the top the table. My voice booms. "What? Why on earth would you do that?"

She waves her hand. "As you can see from this contract," she points to the document in front of me. "Their offer is for both of us. They watched *NYC Views* and think we make a great team. Ms. Kennedy explained that we complement each other and together, we create a better piece of furniture than if we were working alone."

My head shakes. "I'm not interested."

"There's more." She passes me another stapled document. "I purchased another apartment on the High Line to renovate. It's similar to the one we did at 1626 but has its own idiosyncrasies. I have enough cash in the bank from my previous flip to purchase this one, but decided to finance it in order to purchase more apartments in the building."

This has nothing to do with me. "I'm very happy for you."

"I have only one problem. I need a carpenter to help me design some of the furniture pieces. Not all of them, only a few big ones like the sofa in the main living space and the bed. Plus, a couple of other odds and ends."

A pang of longing runs through me—I want to be this man for her. Yet I can't be and remain loyal to Homer. "Good luck finding someone."

"Jesse."

She caresses my name as if it were precious to her. I don't understand why. I lost the competition for us. I crossed the line between work and professional, one I'm never going to cross again. I clench my jaw.

"Xander told me about your promotion."

Damn my best friend. He caught me at a low point and blabbed our conversation to his cousin? He better not have said anything else

—I'll wring his neck the next time I see him. I give her a noncommittal shoulder shrug.

"Let it go."

Her direct order does what everything else so far has failed. Mouth agape, I stare at her. A tomboy appearance hiding a sensual woman beneath. Short hair framing a gorgeous face, complete with bee-stung lips. Which she knows how to use.

Shifting in my seat, I answer, "Too late."

As if I didn't negate her order, she continues, "I have one more document to share." She passes yet a third stapled document down the table to me. It has colored tabs. "Here is my business plan. Since you're a banker, I wanted to talk in language you converse with on the daily."

I'm not that type of banker. Biting my tongue to keep it in place, I flip through the twenty-page document, complete with marketing analysis and financial projections. Which show her company making more than five times my salary during its first year.

Returning to the beginning of the plan, I skip to the part about the owners of the company, which has been left blank. "Who are your partners, Paige?" A subheading about *NYC Views* catches my attention.

I'm engrossed reading snippets of our fan mail and jump when her hand lands on my shoulder.

"This is the final piece of the puzzle. I've worked my ass off pulling all of this information together. Met with execs and lawyers and real estate agents, contractors, and subs. Researched how to write this. I've done it all with one single guiding mantra."

Knowing I'm going to hate myself for asking, I whisper, "What is it?"

She removes her hand, and my shoulder runs cold.

"We do this together."

Together? She wants to work with me? After I lost us the competition? I flip to the financial section of the plan. Pointing to the projected net revenue, I ask, "This is your bottom line. Why would you want to share this with anyone, let alone me?"

She pulls out the chair next to me and sits, twisting my body to face hers. "Because we work great together. Even Arch Pointe Furniture recognizes this. You make me want to do better, be better. I'm so sorry I lost the competition for you. I only want to make it up—"

"Excuse me? You did what?"

"I cost us the show. It was because I followed my own selfish whims rather than work with you that the primary suite got away from us."

I resist the urge to smack the side of my head against my palm. I must have misheard. "What are you talking about? My inferior skills are why we lost. I wasn't good enough." I flip the pages of her plan. "I'm not good enough."

Paige grabs my hands and squeezes. "Are you crazy? If I hadn't insisted on doing the side tables and other pieces, I would've seen all the flaws with my bathroom design and made it much more of a showcase. Plus, I should've deferred to your knowledge about staining the headboard." She takes a breath. "You did a fine job carving it, by the way. I was hovering over you like a shrew."

"You have everything ass-backwards."

She places her other palm on top of my hand. "I don't."

"You're wrong."

Paige's smile could light up the entire city. "How about we call it a truce? We were both wrong. And both right."

In the face of such creativity, I can't hold my own smile back. "Seems like a smart white flag."

Releasing my hands, she leans forward, a distance still between us. "What do you think of the business plan? The apartment flips and partnership with Arch Pointe Furniture?"

Disappointment flows through me. "Sounds like you have a busy life ahead of you."

Her face falls. "I don't want to do any of it without you at my side, Jesse. We're a package deal—Arch Pointe says so."

I pick up their proposal and give it more than the short shrift from before. Their offer is substantial. In fact, it rivals my new salary. Still, no way to get around the fact that I can't let Homer down. I owe him. And Diana.

"I appreciate all you've done, Paige, but I belong here." I wave to the four corners of the drab conference room with its utilitarian furniture, beige walls, and generic artwork.

"You don't. I know the real Jesse Dimon." Her hand steals over my heart. "I know what makes your heart tick. It's not any of this."

She may be right, but Homer's mantra not to cross business with pleasure rings true. If I hadn't crossed the line on the show, we might have won the whole thing. I let my guard down. I can't do it again.

I allow myself to close my hand over hers. Enjoy this small, final contact. "You may be right, but this is how it has to be." I release my hand and shove backward. Standing, I say, "Congrats on all your hard work. I'm sure you'll be a big success."

She gives me a dirty look and collects her things, leaving my paperwork on the table. Holding the file against her chest, she says, "We have until Wednesday to give our answer to Arch Pointe. I'll be at Vinnie's Tuesday night at seven, waiting for you to come to your senses." She leaves, and a waft of citrus, woodsy scent lingers in the air. I breathe in my final memory of Paige Hansen.

Days go by in a blur, and I studiously refuse to study the paperwork in my drawer. Today, I meet with my new boss, Louis, for several hours, reviewing my mind-numbing proposed protocols. "These are great. Make the changes we discussed and send me the revised memorandum." His hand clamps onto my back. "Happy to have you here with us."

With his final words ringing in my ears, I return to my desk and pull up the memo on my computer. I look around my new office. It needs a paint job. Perhaps some millwork.

Shaking off those thoughts, I start in on my to-do list. When it's quitting time, I glance at the photos on my desk. All four of us on my thirteenth birthday when we went to the beach. Diana's holding a piece of saltwater taffy over my head and laughing while our parents kiss in the background. A different time. My gaze travels to graduation shots from both college and business school. The warmth of happier times swamp me.

Putting a few items I intend to work on over the weekend into my backpack, the drawer with Paige's documentation seems to grow larger, like something out of Alice in Wonderland. I turn my back and leave my office before doing something dumb like opening the drawer.

Saturday, I reorganize my closet to accommodate the new suits my parents bought me for my promotion. At seven, I meet up with Theo and Xander for a quick drink before they join their significant others to do a band tour for their joint wedding.

Sitting in a booth, they discuss the trials and tribulations of wedding planning. More than once, they complain about how drawn out it is. "But she's my sister. Can't stop Halle—she's a force of nature." Xander drinks his bourbon.

We laugh and enjoy our guy time before they have to turn in their man cards and leave for the dreaded music night. Lifting my Guinness in the air, I say, "I bet you'll be surprised. You might enjoy it."

Xander grumbles as he slings back the remainder of his drink, and Theo does the same with his Dark 'n' Stormy. Before they leave, Theo turns to me. "Congrats on your promotion at the bank. Paige was talking like you're going into business together, but I guess she was wrong."

My breath catches. I wish. Perhaps in an alternative universe, she and I would be conquering the design world. "Nah. It was a nice dream, but I'm out of the renovation business. I wish your sister well."

Xander rubs his goatee, an unholy twinkle in his eyes. "I don't know about this. I've seen your work, and heard you talk about Handmade by JD for years now. I can't believe you're giving up your dream so easily. So what if three people decided your stuff wasn't good enough? Who are they anyway?" He taps his Bourbon glass. "Plus, you and Paige popped off the screen. That's all I'm saying."

Theo knocks his empty glass onto the table. "You and Little Bit?"

Damn Xander. Thought we were in the clear, but no. He had to bring the big brother into this. And by "big," I'm not kidding. He's put on twenty pounds of muscle since he joined the ice hockey team at Chelsea Piers. I pick up my glass. "Nothing to tell."

Using his finger, he taps his chin. "I can see the two of you together. You'd balance each other out. Maybe that's why she's been more put together than I've ever seen her. Working and drawing up plans and such."

Which are burning a hole in my desk drawer in the office. "Don't worry, Theo. Xander's just being a dick." I slant him a dirty look.

Chuckling, Xander stands. "We have to go. Good seeing you again, Jesse."

Theo gives me one of his bear hugs. When Xander approaches, I punch his arm. "Douche."

"C'mon. What are best friends for?" He forces me into a bro hug, which I try not to reciprocate.

After finishing my Guinness, I make my way back to my apartment. My lifeless, empty apartment.

For a moment, I allow myself to picture Paige in here, making all sorts of design changes. Then I shut it down. Nothing good can come from this. I crawl into bed and let sleep take me away.

I spend the next day whittling a bunch of nonsensical mythological figurines. On Monday, I go to the bank and sit in my new office, studiously ignoring the drawer with Paige's business plan. Instead, I make comments on SlideShare decks. Work on pivot tables. Have several Zoom calls with people all over the globe. Not a chief compliance officer yet, but on my way.

Where's the creativity? The life? The excitement?

At home Monday night, I pull out the piece of wood I've been whittling and focus on it. Spend time on the eyes and the curve of the neck. The peace I've been missing since *NYC Views* wrapped blankets me. My soul needs this. *I need it.*

The next day, Tuesday, I go to work thinking things will be better. Conference calls lead to additional tasks to complete. More responsibilities. None of which excite me as much as my whittling project did last night. During lunch, I succumb to temptation and open the drawer with Paige's business plan. In St. Patrick's Basilica,

I sit and read it. I almost fall out of the pew when I see she included a monthly donation to MADD.

At six, I show up at the restaurant my parents insisted on taking me to for the delayed celebration of my promotion. Homer rambles on and on about how much power an executive director has and how to wield it effectively. As I listen to him, Paige's business plan counterbalances his words. Needing to shut her down once and for all, I do a reckless thing and pull it out of my backpack.

"What do you have there, honey?"

I glance at Marge before settling my focus on Homer. Clearing my throat, I begin, "I had this business plan presented to me last week."

Homer's eyes grow wide and I swear he grows in stature. "You're already having clients come to you? Amazing."

I flip through the pages and open it to where she's discussing how our fantasy business would work. Homer will take one look at this and tell me it's a foolish pipe dream. I hold my breath. On a rush, I explain, "It's actually a business plan for Paige Hansen—my partner on the Renovation TV show—and me to start our own carpentry and home flipping business."

Time stands still.

No one moves.

Marge finds her voice first. "Excuse me? It's what?"

"A business plan for Paige and I to go into business making furniture and renovating houses."

"Why on earth would you do something like this when your career is ahead of schedule?" Homer's fist pounds the table.

"Maybe because he likes working with his hands and creating beautiful pieces out of wood, like he did on *NYC Views*." Marge's response floors me. *She watched the show?*

With a growl, Homer snatches the business plan from my hands and flips through it. I steel for the derision I'm sure is coming. He points to one of Paige's tables. "Are these numbers for real?"

"I've reviewed them. They are."

"Holy shit. Who knew there was this much money to be made with this stuff?" He keeps flipping the pages.

Who are these people? Marge defended me and Homer's not outright snorting with laughter. It's her next questions that nearly put me on the floor. "You never talk about women with us. Did you fall for Paige? She's a beautiful girl. When can we meet her?"

"We're not together." Anymore.

"I can tell from your expression that you want to be, honey."

"I can't," I exclaim. "I can't put pleasure ahead of career." I turn and stare at my father. "That's what you always taught me, Homer. I'm not set in my career, so how can I get together with Paige?"

A confused look crosses his face. "Wait. You're not set in your career? But you were just promoted."

I throw my hands in the air. At least Homer doesn't disappoint.

Marge's hand lands on top of his. "I think what our son's trying to say is that his career doesn't lie in banking, but rather with construction and carpentry. He's very talented." She places her other hand on mine. "I also think you have to grab onto love whenever you find it. If Paige is your girl, don't let a ridiculous saying stop you from getting her. I scolded your father for parroting it." Her head turns toward Homer. "Don't forget, you were working in retail when we got married."

Retail?

In a voice barely above a whisper, he says, "I only told him that to make sure he would focus on his coursework." Homer clears his throat. "Jesse, if these figures are as accurate as you believe them to be, you'd be a fool to pass up this opportunity. You won't be making this sort of money in banking for a long time." He turns more pages. "Plus, you're going to have to apply your business degree to this Arch Pointe Furniture contract."

He points to something and shows Marge, who gasps. "A portion of your proceeds are being donated to MADD? Diana would be so proud of you." Tears stream down my mother's face, and I feel them welling up behind my eye sockets as well.

With a gruff voice, Homer adds, "I love having you in the same industry as me, I won't lie. According to this business plan, though, you'd be an idiot not to try this new business." He puts the plan onto the table. "And I know I didn't raise an idiot."

Maybe I've misjudged my parents this whole time?

Maybe they've always wanted me to follow my dreams?

Maybe Paige is healing our entire family, and not just my damaged heart?

Whatever the reason, I'm not going to dwell on this right now. I have a woman to meet. But not before making one quick pit stop at home.

28

Paige

I toy with the mug of my Mexican mule, the same one I've been nursing for over an hour. Got here at quarter to seven and told the hostess, Shelby, I'm meeting someone in the bar. Still no sign of Jesse. His heart is in designing furniture. If only he'd let himself.

A guy wearing a shirt proclaiming his love for the city approaches. "Hey there, Sweet Cheeks. Want some company?"

"Not really. I'm waiting for my girlfriend."

His eyes bug out and he stammers, then leaves. Men. So easy to redirect. Unfortunately, the next guy doesn't seem put off by my line —more like he's interested in watching or joining a threesome. My gaze keeps directing to the door, but still no Jesse. Now I've acquired a leech. Guess I'll have to use plan B.

"I need to use the restroom."

Leaving my drink so he thinks I'll return, I walk away and duck into the hallway before turning around and going to a different part of the bar with a pretty good view of the front door. I observe the guy as he waits for a good ten minutes before the lightbulb goes off that I ditched him, and he approaches another poor woman. Better her than me.

The server walks around, and I order another Mexican mule plus some nachos. Seems like I'm in for a long night.

The hours tick by.

I triple check my cell to confirm today is Tuesday.

Finishing the nachos, I use a piece of chip to scrape some guacamole off the bottom of the plate. *Could he not show?*

The bar fills, then most of the patrons leave. Only a smattering of folks remain at ten o'clock on a Tuesday night. *I can't believe he didn't come.*

Signaling the server, I get my check and pay up. With heavy limbs, I trudge into the bathroom and use it this time. I stare at my face in the mirror, my brown eyes paler than before. *He doesn't want me.*

I sling my purse over my shoulder and pull out my phone. Time to admit defeat and call Jimmy, our vehicle concierge, to pick me up. In the middle of the hallway, I stop. I told Chloe not to expect me tonight. I guess I could ask Theo if I can crash at his place. Or my parents. None of my options are how I expected this evening to end.

Entering the main area of the bar, I debate where I want to go tonight. The thought of being around the love at Theo's is too much for me to bear, so my parents win. At least their fighting won't affect me so much. I bring up Jimmy's contact info.

"She's about this tall, lanky, with the most beautiful brown pixie cut you've ever seen." The tenor voice assails me. My phone clatters to the floor.

Jesse turns.

The world stops spinning.

My pulse accelerates.

A heart-melting smile crosses his face.

He takes a step toward me. And another. And a third.

When he reaches me, I gulp for air, trying to assimilate the fact Jesse's here. He did come. He does want this. Me.

"Paige."

His warm palm covers my cheek, and is greeted by a tear. On a whisper, I murmur, "You're here."

"I am." His thumb captures the moisture, which is replenished.

Acting as windshield wipers, he clears my tears as fast as they fall. "I had to come."

"Why?"

"Because when you realize your life means nothing without the woman who breathed new life into a husk of a man, you have to follow her instructions."

My eyes meet his. His gorgeous, hazel ones present more khaki than green right now. Followed by his strong jaw, Roman nose, and imminently kissable lips. "You do?"

He nods. "Especially when she prepared a business plan, complete with color coded tabs and fantastic financial projections." He reaches inside his pocket and pulls out a piece of wood surrounded by a stapled document. "I'm sorry I didn't have time to wrap this properly."

"What is it?"

"Proof. That I want to be here, with you. That I'm all in. That you mean the world to me." He extends his hand toward me.

With his every statement, my breathing hitches. I remove the document from the figurine and stifle a gasp. He whittled a gorgeous swan. "Thank you. This is beautiful."

His gaze drops to the wood figurine still in my hand. "Your long neck reminded me of a swan. I thought it was a perfect representation of you. But it's not the real reason I'm here. Go ahead, read the paperwork."

I glance from him down to the stapled document. "You did this? For me?"

"For us," he corrects.

"'JP's on Fifth' is official. You incorporated it." I skim through the legal notice from the State of New York he printed off the web. "We're both partners." My eyes zoom in on the figures. "You gave me fifty-one percent?"

He shrugs. "Seemed only fair. You did the business plan."

His lips turn up into a delicious smile. I don't know how to process his amazing gift. I was going to go online and find out how to incorporate this once—if—Jesse agreed to be my business partner. Truth be told, I was hoping for more than a business partnership.

My brain freezes when he pulls me to his warm body and stares deep into my eyes. "I love you, Paige. All of you. Your excitement, your design, your ideas. The way you challenge me, expect me to do better." He leans closer. "How you come undone for me."

No amount of windshield wiper thumbs can staunch the tears free falling down my cheeks. It doesn't matter—his cheeks are equally wet.

All my dreams have come true. "I love you, too, Jesse."

His eyes close, as if savoring my words. Then he leans forward and our mouths meet. The fact we're in the middle of Vinnie's doesn't stop me. I wrap my arms around his neck and mold my body to his. The hard planes of his body provide a homecoming beyond anything I've ever experienced.

Clapping. Catcalls. Cheering. Banging of glasses on tables. The noise from outside our bubble pulls us apart, yet none of this matters because Jesse's back in my world, my arms, my life.

"How about," he leans down to my ear. "We take this to a more private location?"

Not trusting my voice, I simply nod.

Bending down, I pick up the phone at my feet and he takes my hand. With a wave to the others in the restaurant and a wink to Shelby, he leads me out of Vinnie's. He hails a cab and soon we're in his apartment, which is painted white. Sterile. Doesn't represent this vibrant man in front of me.

Redecorating will be for a different time. Right now, we're focused on shucking our clothes and kissing each other to within a last gasp. Recriminations from how I treated him during the final round of the show pop into my mind. "I'm so sorry," I say as he leads me into his bedroom. I take in his white walls and navy sheets —so like Bo and Mary Ellen's winning primary suite—and vow to change them.

"No, I'm the one who's sorry." Naked, he sits on the bed and opens a condom packet. "I shouldn't have shut you out after the show. The promise to my father to carry on Diana's legacy has been ingrained in me for fourteen years, not to mention his rule that my career must be set before love. Working through it all was tough."

I blow into his ear. "But you did it."

"Marge did."

My teeth close around the bottom of his lobe. "Come again?"

He smirks. "We will." His hands guide my equally bare body onto his lap so our bodies touch where they most need to, but not in the way I want. "She supported my dream of becoming a carpenter —even watched the show—and your business plan proved to Homer it's a lucrative option." His fingers run through my hair. "Besides, I promised to live out Diana's dream when I was a kid. Which I no longer am."

My fingers snake downward encircling his erection and I giggle. "You most certainly are not." I glide my hand up and down.

A moan tears from the back of his throat. "And neither are you. Now let's focus here." His powerful arms lift me and I guide him into my body, eliciting a soft mewl from me and a louder groan from him.

In this position, he hits my clit at the exact right angle to spiral me out of control with only a few thrusts. He stops for a minute to allow me to collect my wits, then stands up while we're still intimately connected. Holding my hips in place, he strides forward until my back connects with the wall. He pounds into my body.

With my legs wrapped around his torso, I can do little more than hold onto this amazing man. "Oh. My. God. Yes!"

With a sinfully sexy snicker, he says, "More to come."

He clamps down on my nipple, which zaps directly to my core, prompting a long moan from my soul. His thrusts continue. Face contorted with exertion and pleasure, he brings us both up the ladder toward our ultimate goal.

My body responds to his every movement as if he were in control of the orchestra buzzing inside me. Which he is. When he twists his hips, he grazes my clit and my head bangs against the wall. "Yes! Jesse, yes!"

He repeats his actions once more and a thrill only he can give explodes throughout my body. I clench around him, both inside my body and out, screaming his name in an everlasting torrent. As soon as I let go, he stills, then the chords on his neck become more pronounced as he empties himself inside me with a loud roar.

Sweat dripping down our bodies, we remain against the wall for as long as it takes for our breathing to even out. He kisses me. "You are amazing, Miss Hansen."

"You're not too shabby either, Mr. Dimon."

He takes a tentative step back and I unlock my ankles. When we're two separate beings again, he leads me to his bed. Where we repeat this act in so many different ways, all night long.

J esse helps me put the finishing touches on the staging of the first High Line apartment remodel we purchased five months ago. I smooth my Max Mara pantsuit. I chose this latte color to match his amazing eyes and wasn't disappointed this morning when he first saw me in it. He was careful when he removed it so as not to rip off any of the buttons, too.

With a fist to the final throw pillow on the sofa he designed as a prototype for our Arch Pointe Furniture partnership, I declare, "Done!"

"We did it!" He scoops me off the floor and twirls me in his strong arms. Our mouths fuse in a celebratory kiss.

Returning me to the floor, he says, "This looks fantastic. I bet buyers will be climbing over themselves to scoop it up."

I tuck my short hair behind my ear. "I hope so. I employed every trick I learned in my real estate course to drive up interest." I'm the proud owner of a brand-new real estate license.

"All your hard work will pay off today, I'm sure." He kisses my cheek. "Now, I'm going to leave you to your open house, while I review some designs for Arch Pointe. I'm sure you'll be amazing today. All I want is three offers by the time we meet up tonight, alright?"

I giggle at his optimism. "I'd love that, but let's be realistic here. It usually takes days, if not weeks, for a buyer to make an offer."

That's what my textbooks said. "I'll be happy if three couples even show up today."

He winks. "I have faith in you. Meet you at the wine bar in Hudson Yards when you're done here."

Alone in the apartment, I review each room to ensure it looks the best possible. The kitchen where we gutted everything and reorganized the workspace toward the windows. The dining room with a cozy fireplace. The family room with the amazing accent wall and millwork. Not to mention the faux-coffered ceilings. I enter the bedroom, and a blush prickles my cheek. Hope the new owners have as much fun in here as Jesse and I did. A smile plays around my lips.

Once I'm sure the apartment is ready, I put out the signs and balloons and return to the kitchen to take out the freshly baked cookies. These do double-duty—perfume the air as well as make a wonderful gift to people attending today's open house. Once I ensure all the lights are on, I spread out my brochures highlighting the apartment's many features. I'm ready.

Someone knocks on the door, I invite them in, and give them the spiel about the apartment. No sooner do I close the door, then someone else knocks. This scene repeats during the entire four hours. When the last potential buyer leaves, I collapse onto Jesse's sofa.

We did it! My first open house was a huge success. I lost track of how many people told me they were interested in the building and our apartment. Realizing I haven't been on my phone at all, I click on it and see twenty-two missed messages. I bet they're all from Jesse and my family. Smiling, I open the messenger app and I'm right. Jesse sent a couple, as did Theo and Xander—and their fiancées— plus Kiefer and Ryder. Chloe too.

As did seven people who came today.

I sit upright. *Holy shit.* Inhaling, I open each of the messages. Each one—EACH ONE!—put in a bid. Unable to contain myself, I leap up and do a jig. We can do this. My dream is turning into a reality. Given their bids, my financial projections were low. Way low.

Strapping my purse over my shoulder, I lock up and leave the building, turning left toward the Hudson Yards Shops. Inside the mall, I go up to the wine bar, where Jesse's sitting at the counter, two glasses in front of him. I slip onto the stool next to him. "Fancy meeting you here."

His broad smile warms my heart. He doesn't even know my good news yet. "Hello, gorgeous." He hands me my glass of bubbly. "Got us some champagne. We have a lot to celebrate."

More than he knows. "We do." Clinking our glasses, I allow the effervescence to bounce down my throat. "How'd your day go?"

"Great. I'm pleased with all the designs, and looking forward to meeting with Arch Pointe's marketing team to go over the finer points for the launch."

"I'm looking forward to it." I kiss his cheek.

"How about you? How was the open house?" His hand strokes my forearm.

The floodgates open. "Amazing. I have no idea how many people toured the apartment, but foot traffic never stopped. At least two, if not four or five groups were inside at all times. Plus," I pull out my cell. "We got some offers!"

"I knew you could do it. You can do anything you set your mind to." He pulls me in for a hug without even knowing how many or what they were.

Against his shoulder, I ask, "Don't you want to hear the bids?"

He chuckles. "Can't wait to hear how big your success was today."

"*Our* success. I couldn't have done this without you." We kiss and I almost forget why we're here.

He breaks the spell. "I can feel you vibrating."

I'm excited, but I doubt that's what he's talking about. I check my phone. "Got another text." I open and read it:

We loved your apartment today and want to put in an offer before anyone else does.

I slant a glance toward my partner. "Too late for that, sweetie. Seven others already beat you to it."

Jesse's mouth drops open. "Seven?"

I nod. "Yup."

He jumps off his stool and picks me up. "You're a one-woman wrecking ball!"

Laughing, I return to my stool and we go over the *eight* offers on our flip. Three even want it furnished. One remarked on the sofa, saying she's never seen anything like it before. After some debate, we select the all-cash, no inspection offer at twenty thousand over asking. Plus, an additional twenty for the living room set, bar stools, and bed. Jesse liked this offer because it didn't ask for any pieces he didn't design.

"I can't believe this." Jesse repeats. His index finger connects with my nose. "You're magic."

"Nope. I'm only someone who's doing what she loves with the man she loves. Who gave up his stable life in banking for an exciting challenge with me."

"I couldn't be happier." He squeezes me again. "Can't wait to share the good news with my parents. And Mr. Hooper."

I've met his parents several times, and they've welcomed me into the family. They're supportive of Jesse's new career, and his father even asked if he could invest in JP's on Fifth. Of course we turned him down, but the ask was a giant leap forward.

While we celebrate, someone sits at the stool next to me. Time to go home. "Home." For the first time in my life, I understand what this word means. I've added color and turned Jesse's bachelor pad into something reflecting both of our styles. The idea of buying our own place and making it our own has taken root in my mind, though. I have to figure out the best time to approach Jesse with this idea.

I'm about to suggest we relocate to our bedroom when I hear, "Paige?"

My head swivels and I recognize the person who sat next to me. "Quinn. I didn't see you there." We exchange quick hugs, as does Jesse with her.

She points to our drinks. "Celebrating something?"

I square my shoulders. "I held my first open house this afternoon, at the apartment we renovated." I point in the general direction of the building.

"I saw your announcement about becoming a real estate broker on social media a few weeks ago." She raises her wine glass toward me. "Congrats."

"Thanks. Our apartment got eight offers, and we just accepted one."

"Very impressive." I slip my arm into the crook of Jesse's. "I see you're together now?"

"We are," Jesse kisses my cheek.

Her question reminds me of what we had to overcome to get to this point. I wouldn't trade a second of it, despite the heartaches. Makes today seem even sweeter.

"That's great." She holds up her finger as she opens her purse. Pulling out a business card, she passes it to me. "You guys have been on my mind a lot lately. I have something I'd like to discuss with you. Think you could stop by tomorrow afternoon?"

Jesse and I exchange a shocked glance, and he shrugs. Flipping the card over in my hand, I reply, "Sure thing. How's two o'clock?"

"Perfect."

Jesse pulls away from the counter. "It was great catching up, Quinn. If you'll excuse us, though, I need to take this wonderful woman home for a private celebration."

He wiggles his eyebrows—he's gotten as bad as Theo. With a quick "sorry," I allow my boyfriend to lead me out of the wine bar and back home. Jesse jumps when the door closes.

"I swear, you've been as jumpy as a cat ever since we left the wine bar. What's going on?"

His right foot rocks. "Nothing." His eyes shoot in every direction.

I place my hand on his well-defined chest. "Talk to me."

He huffs out a laugh. At least I think it might be a laugh. It's a strangled sound, for sure. "I have something I want to give you."

Adrenaline rushes through my veins. Far from being the caveman I originally believed him to be, Jesse surprises me with little gifts on the regular. He's taught me what it means to be loved, and to love in return. I'm truly a lucky woman. "A present?" I clap and look all around. "Where is it?"

He leads me over to the sofa—another one of the prototypes Arch Pointe wants to produce—and pushes on the top of my shoulders. "Sit. I'll go get it."

I make myself comfortable while he slips out of the living room. I like this space, but a new one specifically for Jesse and me would be better. My parents are so embroiled with the whole VOW-cubed debacle I'm sure they don't care where I'm living. Father did mention he was relieved I got my ass in gear and am making my own money. His ominous comment is the only sign I've received things might not be going well for him and his partners. While I wish them luck, there's little I can do to help, so staying away has been the most prudent course of action.

My eyes stray over to the closet with a washer and dryer. Jesse tried to teach me how to do my own laundry but gave up when I turned all his underwear pink. Now, he cleans our clothes and I fold them. Good compromise, in my opinion.

Jesse finally reappears, holding something behind his back. He joins me on the sofa, and I crane my neck to see what he has. "What is it?"

He shakes his head. "Always so impatient."

I hold out my hands, palm up, wiggling my fingers. "Gimme."

His tongue wets his lips. His chest expands and he produces my present from behind his back.

My heart rate kicks up. "It's a mermaid! You whittled me a mermaid!"

I pluck the wooden figurine out of his hand and my eyes go wide. The mermaid's holding a wooden lollipop. Sporting the most glorious words ever written:

Will You Marry Me?

Epilogue - Jesse

Hands behind my head, I lie in bed while Paige gets up, naked, and heads for the bathroom. Well, she's naked except for the rock I put on her finger last night. A small smile plays around my lips as I relive the glorious moment.

The look of wonder on her face. Tears. Joy.

Her cry of, "Jesse, you've made me the happiest woman on earth!"

Then the hours of proving how much we love each other. It was a perfect night. Perfect morning, too.

A towel lands on my head. Her sultry voice asks, "Coming?"

Flicking the duvet off my bare body, I reply, "With you? Always."

I follow her into the bathroom, where the shower's already heating up. She steps inside. Remaining outside, I watch the water sluice over her slight curves. She may complain about her tomboy figure, but it's perfect for me. She opens the door and holds out a loofah. "Wash my back?"

"With pleasure, soon-to-be Mrs. Dimon." She giggles and I join her in the shower and delve into this very important task.

Which devolves into her washing my abs.

And then my cock, with her mouth. I've never been one for blowjobs in the past, but with her, it's like nirvana. She sucks me hard, which causes my hips to rock into her mouth. But I don't want to come like this now, in here. I find my voice. "Stand up, Paige."

Big brown eyes gaze up at me. She mumbles around my erection, "Now?"

God help me. I manage, "Yes."

With a pop, I spring free from her warm mouth. Once she's upright, I physically turn her body toward the bench and tap her lower back. Bending over, she places her hands on the bench and twerks. She's a quick study.

I reach inside the niche where we store condoms for this purpose. Once I'm sheathed, I ignore my screaming body and reach between her legs. Wet—not from the shower. Perfect. At the same time as I enter her body, I bring my finger around to her lips and tap. "Suck." She obeys, which almost sends me over the cliff.

Her lips and tongue caress me as deliciously as her pussy drives me insane. Using my free hand, I lower it and encircle her clit. She lets go of my finger and moans, "Yes! Jesse, please."

I drop my hand and pinch her erect nipple. Seems like this was the right move, as her next words are, "I'm coming," punctuated by her inner muscles clenching around me.

With no other alternative, I pound into her body a few more times. My balls tighten, and my own release surges. I climax with a loud roar and collapse onto her back.

We let the water run over our bodies before washing off and getting dressed. A little while later, we walk into the office of Renovation TV, hand in hand. Quinn leads us into a conference room.

Paige practically shoves her left hand under Quinn's nose, who grabs her fingers. "Oh, wow. Congratulations! Looks like I was interrupting a bigger celebration last night than simply selling your flip."

Sporting a huge smile, Paige describes how I proposed to her. "Jesse's wonderful, as you're well aware. He whittled a mermaid for me—he's amazing at it, by the way—and she's holding a lollipop with the words "Will You Marry Me?" on it. Of course, I said yes. Then, only wearing—"

I clamp my hand around my fiancée's mouth. "That's enough. I think Quinn gets the picture."

Smiling, our former director nods. "Yep. Understood. I'm happy for you both."

We find our seats and Quinn moves on to the purpose of our meeting. "We've been filming Bo and Mary Ellen's show for a few weeks now."

The reminder I lost us the competition makes my good mood plummet. Until I remember Paige's and my conversation when we agreed our loss was a team effort. I find my voice. "I'm sure you're happy to move on with a more scripted show, rather than the reality television version."

Quinn rakes her hand through her long hair. "Actually, that's why I wanted to talk with you." She offers us some water, which we both refuse, and opens one for herself. "You see, even though we've only filmed a little of their show, we see warning signs. More like flashing red lights going off all around them. No, not them. Bo."

I stifle a snort. Could've told them.

Paige asks, "What's he done?"

"He's come to the set drunk at least five times. That is, when he deigns to show up at all. To make matters worse, when he is on set, he constantly quarrels with Mary Ellen. Not the cute bickering they did on *NYC Views*. More along the lines of the director having to step in before things get totally out of hand."

"I can't believe it," I admit. "I mean, I knew he was an asshole, but I figured he'd pull it together once he got his own show."

Quinn nods. "I knew he was a bit . . . uncouth. I'm shocked at the reports coming in from the set. The higher ups aren't happy, to put it mildly."

Paige grabs my hand. "Sounds awful."

"I might as well get down to it. We'd like to offer you their show. We can put out a statement that they had an unavoidable conflict, and you're going to take their place." She stares at Paige. "With your family's notoriety as of late, I'm sure this opportunity is welcome."

Paige's grip on my hand becomes taut. Her family is a sore spot, not one to be blundered into like this. I've met her parents a couple of times and find it hard to believe they spawned my fiancée. Theo either. I don't know her other brothers too well, but I'm sure my observation holds.

I need to stop this train wreck before it gets even more out of control. Not wanting to burn any bridges, I reply, "Quinn, thanks for your offer, but we have a lot on our plates. House flipping, a furniture design contract, and planning our wedding is going to take all our attention for the near future."

"Yeah," Paige agrees. "Plus, we lost the competition. It would look weird if we got our own show."

The fact she used the "we" pronoun makes me squeeze her hand. We've come a long way since the end of filming.

"We've already thought of that." Quinn hands us each a document with an outline describing why we're hosting the show. Gotta hand it to Renovation TV, they really know their stuff. I'm almost convinced.

But we lost the show.

Paige turns to me, an inscrutable look on her face.

Taking matters in my own hands, I direct my question to Quinn. "Would you mind if we had a moment to discuss this?"

"Of course. I'll be in my office down the hall. Come and get me when you've decided to take us up on our offer."

Alone with my fiancée, I watch as she paces around the conference room. The show was my goal. My way to get out of the banking industry and show my parents this was a viable career choice. Things are different now.

I focus on Paige, who's now staring out the window. "What do you think? I guess it could work."

She turns toward me. "I know this was our goal all along. To win the competition and get a television show."

"It was."

"This feels wrong, though. We didn't win. We don't deserve this.

And you were right—we have our own flipping business and the Arch Pointe Furniture designs to do. Not to mention planning for this." She holds up her left hand.

I approach her. "We are busy. We're like this because we *lost* the show." I rub my palms up and down her arms. "The show's an old dream, which has been replaced with a better one." I kiss her. "A much better one."

Our kiss explodes.

Against my lips Paige murmurs, "Let's go turn down Quinn." She gives me a peck on the lips. "Then more of this."

We walk down the hall and I knock on the doorframe to Quinn's office. "Do you want to go back to the conference room?"

Paige answers her for the both of us. "No, we'll be quick. We want to thank you for your offer, but we're going to have to decline."

Quinn's brows come together. "This is what you signed up for when you went on *NYC Views*."

"It is. But things have changed. We've changed." I squeeze Paige's hand.

"Our lives are busier now than ever," my fiancée adds. "Thanks for the opportunity."

"This is what I get for working with my sister."

Every molecule in Paige's hand stiffens. "What did you say?" Each word out of Paige's mouth is clipped.

"I said," Quinn continues, "I should've known better than to cast my sister on this show."

Paige leaps forward, her hands landing on the desk. "You're delusional."

"No, you're deluded. Our father's been hiding me from his other family—yours—forever. He even moved us out of our house in New Jersey to Westchester, so my mother would be more convenient to him. Didn't you ever wonder about his so-called 'business trips'?"

She whips out her phone and shows us photos of Paige's father with his arm around her and an older woman, presumably her mother. The date is last year, before his arrest. *Shit.*

I place my hand on Paige's shoulder. To offer her comfort. To give her strength. Her whole body's coiled to spring, but I'm not sure at whom—Quinn or her father.

Paige turns tortured eyes to me. Stepping up, I say, "Our answer is no, Quinn. We're leaving." Slipping my arm around my fiancée, I rush us into the hallway and out to the street.

On a whisper, Paige says, "I need to see Father."

"I understand." I pull her into a hug, where she trembles in my arms. When she doesn't move, I ask, "Want me to join you?"

"No."

I rub her back. My brave girl. Still, she doesn't move. I ask her again, "Do you want me with you?"

She looks up at me, her eyes now watery. "Yes. I want to do this by myself, but I'm afraid Father won't believe me—rather, he'll try to blow me off. If you're with me, he won't be able to do that, since you heard what Quinn said." She sobs. "You heard her, right?"

"Yes, sweetheart, I did." I wish I could do more than hug this woman whose life is shattering, but I can be her support system. "I'll go with you."

She fumbles for her phone and places a text. "Car will be here in five minutes."

"I got you." I kiss her, imparting all my love and support.

Too soon, we're zipping through Manhattan. Too soon, we arrive at her parents' apartment building. Too soon, we get off the elevator into their living room, a luxury I once thought amazing.

Okay, still do.

Luna, their housekeeper, invites us to follow her into the solarium, where Paige's parents sit. I run my thumb over her diamond, trying to impart strength to the strongest woman I know. Before she leaves, Paige asks Luna to close the door.

After greetings are exchanged, I slide toward the back of the room. Standing with my legs open and arms behind my back, I observe the solarium. Considering bookcases filled with tomes line the walls, it could be called a library but for the baby grand off the to the side. Her mother sits on the sofa while her father's seated on a leather recliner. It would look homey, if it wasn't so contrived. Not to mention the windows overlook Central Park across the street.

My fiancée tosses her head over her shoulder, and we make eye contact. I bend my chin downward and she gives me a swift nod. She turns to face the wrath to come.

"We just came from an interesting meeting."

"Oh really. What was it about, Paige?"

Ignoring her mother's question, she focuses on her father. "We met with Quinn Walker. You remember her, right? The director for *NYC Views*?"

Her father doesn't betray any emotion, except for his jaw becomes squarer, if that were possible. Her mother, on the other hand, babbles, "How nice."

Paige plows forward. "It was a very enlightening meeting. She wants us to take over the show Bo and Mary Ellen won."

"That's wonderful," her uninformed mother exclaims. She focuses on me. "Did you agree to do this, Jesse?"

Why would her mother ask *me* whether we accepted Quinn's offer, when Paige was leading the conversation? More importantly, why hasn't her father uttered one word since the name Quinn Walker was brought up?

Paige answers for me. "Mum, we turned her down. We didn't win the competition and we have more than enough to keep us busy now." She shakes her head. "Have to admit, Quinn got quite angry at our response. The network wants a change, and we were the easy solution." She pauses. "Quinn isn't the type to be told 'no.'"

Like someone else in this room.

"I don't understand—"

Ignoring her mother, my fiancée focuses her attention on her father. "Then she said the most amazing thing. She said this was what she got for working with her *sister*. I'm paraphrasing, but that was her gist. Right, Jesse?"

"I think her words were more along the lines of being sorry she cast her sister on the show," I correct her. "You got the sentiment right, though."

All hell breaks loose.

Her mother grasps her heart. For his part, her father bounds to

his feet, his ankle monitor clanging against the recliner's metal acti-
vating mechanism. "This girl has no idea what she's talking about."

"So you didn't move her and her mother up to Westchester?
Install them close by so you could have access to her mother whenever you wanted? Pay for all her bills? You didn't do all that."

With each accusation, Paige walks closer to her father, ending up
right in front of him. He looks like he's about to blow, so I stop
studying her mother, who has turned an alarming shade of purple,
and cross the room—ready to intervene if need be.

I place my hands on Paige's shoulders, which have turned to
granite. My woman is the bravest person I've ever witnessed.

"She was lying to you to get you all riled up. Did she send a film
crew to follow you?"

"Renovation TV is not that kind of network."

He pulls his hand back, and I jump in front to prevent him from
striking Paige. As if sensing how stupid his move would be, or aware
of the repercussions should he succeed in hitting her, he drops his
arm. When I'm sure the danger has passed, I return to my spot
behind Paige.

"Quinn's older than me. You've been hiding a secret family all
my life."

"This is rubbish. You're only a spoiled child with a vivid imag-
ination."

"I saw the photos." Paige turns to me, lips drawn tight.

I answer her unspoken plea. "Mr. Hansen, I heard Quinn and
saw the pictures. My fiancée, your daughter, who I can assure you is
no child, is telling the truth." Prick.

The man visibly shrinks in front of me, then puffs back up. He's
not going down without a fight—personally or professionally.
"Alright. Fine. Quinn wasn't lying. I moved her, Petra, and Jackie to
Westchester so they'd be closer to me."

I knew Quinn wasn't lying but hearing him confirm it is surreal.
I've only met this man a handful of times before now. For Paige, her
world must be crashing around her shoulders.

My fiancée's mouth drops open. "Petra and Jackie?"

He shrugs. "Jackie's not mine."

"PETRA?!!" His wife's screech pierces my eardrums. "You promised me nothing was going on between you two! You lying, miserable, son of a bitch! Go rot in hell, asshole!" She grabs her purse and storms out of the room. The ding of the elevator is the only audible sound following her wake.

I grab Paige's hand. "Let's go." I tug but she resists me.

Giving in, she follows me for a step, then releases my hand. Turning on my heel, I watch her hands land on her hips. "I bet you deserve all the hell that's raining down on you from the FBI. But my guess is you'll be longing for the sweet arms of the feds when Mum's done with you." She stomps out of the room.

I take one final glance at her father who's staring out the window. For a man filled with such bluster and arrogance, he's all alone without anyone to control. He deserves to reap what he's sown. I leave him to his demons and meet up with my fiancée at the elevator.

Later that night, following many tears and phone calls to her brothers, I hold the woman I love in my arms. All the hateful words against her father and his secret family have been said.

She props her chin against my pec. "The weirdest thing is I like Quinn. She and I sort of bonded after filming."

"You don't have to cut her out of your life. She had nothing to do with her parentage."

"True." She traces a heart over my actual heart. "It's a lot to take in."

"I know." I kiss her forehead. "Why don't you call her in a few days, when you've had a chance to get everything sorted?"

She looks at me, love shining from her eyes. "You're right, I think I will. I owe her an apology."

"Quinn should've dropped her bombshell in a better way, but I'm sure she'll be happy to hear from you."

She giggles. "I can't believe I have a sister." She leans over and kisses me.

Before we get carried away, her cell rings and she checks the screen. "It's Chloe. I better take this."

Want to see how Paige truly becomes Jesse's Girl? Download this FREE Bonus Epilogue today ~ and enjoy!! https://BookHip.com/ FXZHCQC

Next up is Quinn Walker's story, SINFUL BEATS, which releases in early 2023. It's a crossover novella between the Sins of the Fathers series and a brand new rock star series, Untamed Coaster! Please pre-order it on Amazon at https://geni.us/UntamedCoaster1, and add it to your GoodReads TBR list https://geni.us/UntamedCoast er1GR.

A Note from Arell

Dear Fabulous Reader,

Thank you so much for reading IDLE, the fourth entry in the Sins of the Fathers series!

This is the story of the youngest child of Ogden Hansen, the "O" in VOW³ Media, Paige. She's led a charmed life, always being babied by her family and coasting through life. Even the events in Vice only affected her in a "life adjacent" way—temporarily needing to relocate out of her parents' house when their fighting became overwhelming. When things at home come to a boiling point, she realizes her days of being idle may be coming to an end. But she doesn't go willingly!

Jesse Dimon is fighting his own demons. The death of his sister half a lifetime ago still guides his life choices, as he stepped into her dreams of becoming a banking executive like their father. He's imminently qualified to do this, of course, but Jesse's heart lies in a totally different direction. When the opportunity to try out for a home renovation competition show presents itself, he jumps on it and finally finds his partner in Paige. Jesse's best friend's and his brother's warn him away from their "little sister," plus his father's mantra of getting set in his career before love, guide him ... until he can no longer deny his attraction for the tomboy. And the competition brings out much more than just his carpentry skills!

As usual, some of my own life experiences appear in IDLE ~

• Walking the High Line in New York City is a wonderful way to spend an afternoon! I recently took a tour of this approximate 1.5 mile elevated linear park created in 2009, and learned so much about the temporary installations and the area in general. Many apartment buildings dot this walkway, which is how the location for *NYC Views* was born.

• After my stroll on the High Line, my friend (author Sophia Henry) and I ducked into Milos Wine Bar in the Hudson Yards Shops. What a fantastic experience! I highly recommend it to all thirsty visitors to the Big Apple.

• Jesse finds his "Zen" at St. Patrick's Cathedral on Fifth Avenue in the middle of Manhattan. This is a gorgeous church that will instantly transport you to a different world, especially if you're in need of a mental reboot.

• The subways in New York City are NOT all that scary! I've taken them for years, ever since I lived in Brooklyn after college. They are a great and fast way to get around the city, even if the smells are less than ... perfumed!

Please stay in touch! Subscribe to my newsletter list at https://geni.us/SinsNewsletter ~ or join Arell's Angels, my reader group on Facebook at http://www.facebook. com/groups/arellsangels ~ or both!!

If you have any questions, feel free to email me at Arell@
ArellRivers.com. I love chatting with readers!

Thanks for devoting your precious time to IDLE. I hope Paige and
Jesse's story encourages you to follow your passion!

All my love,
 Arell

Gratitude

IDLE couldn't have happened without so many awesome people!

I'm blessed to be surrounded by so many supportive people! My husband, Big Mike, and my Mom both encourage me to continue writing, prop me up when I'm exhausted, make me laugh, supply missing words, and help with plotlines. Thank you!

Paige and Jesse's story wouldn't be here without my fantastic team. Theresa Leigh of Velvetfire Press reviewed my plot before I even typed Chapter 1, pointing out awesome ways to enhance the conflict. Trenda Lundin of It's Your Story Content Editing looked over my first draft, and poked numerous holes that I then filled. Nancy Smay of Evident Ink took a second developmental look as well as edited my words with flair. Angel Nyx, the Proofreading Bayou Queen, and Roxanne Blouin proofed the final product, catching all last-minute typpos. 😊 Then Jennifer of Romance Rehab crafted my intriguing blurb and Dar Albert of Wicked Smart Designs created this droolworthy cover! BIG THANKS to these amazing women!!

I can't express the love I feel for my ARC Team!! Each and every member of this Team gives me so much encouragement to create more wonderful and complex characters. Thank you for taking the time to read, review, and share Idle!!!

My Facebook reader's group, Arell's Angels, is my go-to place to hang out, check out hot photos, and simply just vent! Shout out to "Arell's Insiders" who post daily and keep the group rockin' with your wit and devotion. To all the Angels who participate in our Hotties of the Month, daily games, my crazy Facebook Lives, sneak peeks, collaborative stories, and author Takeover Sundays ~ you make this journey so worthwhile (even when Facebook tries to suppress our notifications)! Remember ~ there's always room for more angels!

I'm so lucky to have met, in person and virtually, many wonderful authors who generously give advice, support, and friendship. Taylor Delong, Libby Waterford, Mary E. Montgomery, Nicole Locke, Sophia Henry, Aviva Vaughn, Claire Marti, Lilly Wilde, Isabelle Peterson, Joslyn Westbrook, Jessa York, SH Pratt, Nancy Herkness, Stacey Wilk, JB Schroeder, Serena Bell, Brenda St. John Brown, Sylvie Stewart, and Hope Ellis simply are fantastic human beings.

And to everyone who picks up this book, *I hope Paige and Jesse invite you to follow your passion.* If you enjoyed IDLE, please share it with your friends and write a review.

Blessings,
　　Arell

About the Author

For as long as Arell Rivers can remember, she has been lost in a book. During her senior year in college, she picked up a romance novel … and instantly was hooked!

Arell started writing her first book because the characters were screaming at her to do so. The story came out in her dreams and attacked her in the shower, so she took to the computer to shut them up. But they kept talking.

Born and raised in New Jersey, Arell has what some may call a "checkered past." Prior to discovering her passion for writing romance, she practiced law, was a wedding and event planner and even dabbled in marketing. Arell lives with two adorable cats and a very supportive husband who doesn't care that the bed isn't made or dinner isn't on the table. When not in her writing cave, Arell is found cooking in the InstantPot, working out with Shaun T, or hitting the beach.

Want to keep up to date with Arell? Sign up for her newsletter at https://geni.us/SinsNewsletter. All new subscribers receive a special gift!

Connect with Arell

- Subscribe to Arell's newsletter - https://geni.us/SinsNewsletter
- Join Arell's Facebook Group, "Arell's Angels" - http://www.facebook.com/groups/ArellsAngels
- Like Arell's Facebook Page - http://www.Facebook.com/ArellRivers
- Follow Arell on Instagram - http://www.Instagram.com/AuthorArell
- Hang out with Arell on Amazon - https://geni.us/ArellRivers
- Check out Arell on Goodreads - https://geni.us/ARGoodReads
- Follow Arell on BookBub - https://geni.us/BookBubFollow
- Head over to Arell's website - http://www.ArellRivers.com
- Email Arell - Arell@ArellRivers.com

Other Books by Arell

Sins of the Fathers

A series about the children of 3 notorious businessmen

Book #1: VICE (short story, originally published as "Tinsel Bomb" in the 2021 anthology TINSEL AND TATAS) - http://geni.us/Sins1

Book #2: ANGER (Theo and Amelia) - http://geni.us/Sins2

Book #3: PRIDE (Xander and Madison) - http://geni.us/Sins3

Book #4: IDLE (Paige and Jesse)

Sinful Beats (Quinn's crossover novella introducing a brand new rock star series) (pre-order now!) - http://geni.us/UntamedCoaster1

The Hunte Family Series

A series about the dynasty created by rocker Braxon Hunte

Book #1: Out of the Red (Brax and Sara) - https://geni.us/OOTR

Book #2: Out of the Shadow (King and Angie) - https://geni.us/hunte2

Book #3: Out of the Gold (Melody and Chase) - https://geni.us/OOTG

Book #4: Out of the Blue (Trent and Cordelia) - https://geni.us/Hunte4

The Hold Series
A series about rock star Cole Manchester, his publicist Rose Morgan, and their friends

Book #1: No One to Hold (Cole and Rose trilogy, part 1) - https://geni.us/NOTH

Book #2: Hard to Hold (Cole and Rose trilogy, part 2) - https://geni.us/HtoH

Book #3: To Have and to Hold (Cole and Rose trilogy, part 3) - https://geni.us/THTH

Book #4: Hold On (series prequel novella) - https://geni.us/HoldOn

Book #5: Take Hold of Me (Wills and Emilie) - https://geni.us/THOM

Book #6: Hold Still (Ozzy and McKenna) - https://geni.us/GDwdlls

Book #7: Hold Me: A Rock Star Box Set (includes Books 1-4 plus a bonus novella) - https://geni.us/HoldMeBoxSet

PRIDE

Want to learn more about Xander and Madison?

Read on to enjoy the first chapter of Pride,
  Book #3 in the Sins of the Fathers Series!

Breaking News: NYC's Golden Boy Takes A Walk

This "Breaking News" about Xander Turner hardly deserves such a title. Then again, the mere mention of Xander's name has always made my ladybits tingle, no matter that he never gave me a second glance when we were in school. But when the news anchor announces he's out of the high-profile marketing position in his now-infamous family's business, my wayward thoughts shift to my struggling PR agency. I want him. Ahem, to save my firm.

Much to my shock, Xander accepts my job offer. Not only does his sexy face and business savvy bring in the clients, but he adds a layer of fun and creativity I hadn't expected. He even makes the transition from uptown shark to downtown employee seem effortless. Soon I come to realize that Xander's more than just his looks. A hell of a lot more.

When the paparazzi catch wind of our unlikely pairing, will their ruthless pursuit give my agency more exposure, or will NYC's dog-eat-dog media industry tear apart all we've built?

Pride
Sins of the Fathers Series, Book 3

Arell Rivers
©2022 Tarnished Halo Publishing LLC

Chapter 1 - Xander

If possible, my eyes would hurl daggers at my father. "How could you take money from such a little prick, Dad? Hudson acts like he *owns* us."

Standing behind his desk in his home office overlooking Central Park, my father fumes. "Look, I know he's an asshole, but Gold Fleet Capital's money is green, and we needed the infusion. But he had no right to fire you. Here I am trying to save VOW3 Media through the damn bankruptcy, and this weasel pulls a stupid stunt like this." He fixes stormy blue eyes on mine. No questioning my parentage. "And you fell for it, Xander. You should've made him file the damn lawsuit."

Patrick Hudson, head of VOW-cubed's creditor's committee in our company's bankruptcy, breezed into my office not thirty minutes ago, wielding a draft motion to reject my employment contract. Gave me the impossible option: quit or be fired, publicly, by the court. No choice really.

A frisson of fear runs up my spine. I am going to get my job back, right? "You'll have this straightened out soon, though? I mean, it's our family's company. I deserve to be there."

In an ugly tone, Dad replies, "I don't know, Xander. Don't you think I *deserve* to work at the place I built? And what about your uncles, Ward and Ogden? Do we *deserve* to be stuck in our respective homes, wearing stupid ankle monitors?" He lifts his pant leg to reveal the device slapped on him and my uncles by the government at their bail hearing.

"Dad, I—"

My father cuts me off. "Looks like you're going to have to do what the three of us have been doing since that goddamn Gala. Suck. It. Up."

I shift my weight between my feet. He can't leave me to hang in the wind. "You're filing a motion to dismiss soon, and then we'll all be back at our desks. Everything will return to normal."

"That's the idea. But nothing's going according to any damn plan." He moves some of the papers on his desk and holds up a daily. "If you had stayed with Darcey Abbott like I told you to do, the media would be happily reporting your upcoming nuptials and maybe Hudson would've been more circumspect." He taps on a photo of her with some guy. "Look. She's on some football player's arm now."

At my former fiancée's name, my stomach clenches. Swallowing to keep the bile from escaping my esophagus, I respond, "Good for her." I was fucking fired, and he's getting on my ass about her?

"Should've been you. Fuckin' gorgeous with a pedigree a mile long."

What is she? A thoroughbred? My reflexive defense of the woman dies when I remember her throwing my Tiffany ring at me after Dad and his partners were arrested at the Tinsel and Tatas Gala. Which she followed up with a venomous article in *Spill It Magazine*.

Dad flings the daily onto his desk as if it bit him. "I bet you could still get her back. All you'd have to do is grovel a little. Maybe buy her a car or something. Women like that shit. And the press would eat it up. Lord knows we need some good news reported about our families now, other than in our own magazines."

Her rejection seared me to the core. We *were* media darlings. Until that awful night five months ago. When everything came crashing down.

Dammit, I thought I was in love with her. Caught up in the heady whirlwind our combined lives brought. Dazzled by her beauty. Not to mention the sex.

It's been five months since I had any of that, too.

"Not. Going. To. Happen." My voice is laced with steel.

"Well," his head jerks back.

Dad's surprise at my standing up to him is evident in his posture, which turns rigid. I've always done what he told me to do, as proven by *almost* becoming the first Executive Vice President of VOW-cubed when I got engaged. If only the FBI hadn't come in and ruined my whole life—professionally as well as personally. To which Hudson just did a final swift kick.

Anger surges. I've run the company, mediating between my father and his partners, ever since the indictments. Hell, right before Hudson showed up, I sent them a PowerPoint deck outlining a new strategy about how to engage readers. Not once did any of them express their gratitude over my impossible situation. All my life I've followed Dad's advice to the letter, including getting engaged to his choice of my perfect wife—which *his* arrest dissolved. What have I gotten for my obedience? A broken engagement and no job.

And when did he ever say he was proud of me for all my compliance? I can count the times on one hand. At my acceptance into his *alma mater*. At my college graduation, for following in his footsteps and not because I made the Dean's List once. He even said the word when I graduated from NYU Business School five years ago because my degree enhanced VOW-cubed's resume. The last time? When Darcey accepted my wedding proposal. I snort. Seems like I only earned accolades from Dad when I followed his instructions.

My body tenses. "You know what? Nothing I do will ever make you proud of me, will it? I'm out of a job at *our* family business and all you have to say is suck it up and buy Darcey a car? This affects my entire life, and it all started with whatever you did to get arrested."

He growls, "I do not have to listen to this shit. Get. Out."

Assuming bravado I don't feel, I echo his pitch. "Gladly."

My heartbeat takes off into the stratosphere as I stalk out of his sanctuary. Unseeing, I pass a wall of windows framing the Park. When I cross into the family room, Mom greets me. "Everything okay, honey? I thought I heard raised voices." Her eyebrow shoots upward even as her arms open wide for me.

I enter her embrace—if palms hovering over each other's shoulders and air-kissing both cheeks counts. "No. It's not by a longshot."

"Oh." She pastes a smile on her face and steps away from me. "Well, I'm sure your father can fix it."

"We'll see." My body shakes with pent-up anger at the situation I'm in, fear at my unknown future, disappointment about Dad's reaction. My forehead crinkles. Make that fury at his suggestion I get back together with Darcey. Not wanting to share my feelings with Mom, I murmur, "I have things to do. I'll see you soon."

She offers a small wave. "Bye. Don't be a stranger."

After I smack the elevator's call button, their housekeeper appears at my side holding my coat. "Here you go, Mr. Xander."

Taking it from her, I reply, "Thanks, Luna."

Giving her a wan smile, I shove my arms into the sleeves and stride to the cab. As the doors close, I exhale. Shit. I need to return to the office and clean out my stuff before Hudson posts it on eBay. Exiting the grand marble lobby of my parents' apartment building, I hop into the family's SUV that I presciently asked to wait for me and instruct the driver to take me back to VOW-cubed.

Despite the fact she's been gone for nearly three decades, I picture Grandma Lucia giving me a hug like she used to do when I was a child. Can almost smell her lilac perfume. If only she were still with us, but breast cancer robbed the world of her presence when I was only five.

Now, at age thirty-three, I'm unemployed. Unmoored. Aimless.

Needing to talk with someone who can talk back, I reach for my phone and call my lifeline. "Theo. I need you."

"Be there as soon as I can, bro."

Theo's always been there for me, as I have for him. Son of Ogden Hansen, Dad's best friend and one of his partners at VOW-cubed, we were raised together like one big family. God bless a man who answers a distress signal without asking even a single question.

Returning into my office, my open palm sends the empty cardboard box Hudson "gave" me flying. A beat later, I deflate. What am I going to do?

I snake over to the windows, tracking the ants and toy cars below my fifty-second-floor view. I'm lost inside my mind when Theo enters the room. He picks up Hudson's cardboard box and places it on the low coffee table. "Talk to me." After a long moment, my brain kicks into gear and I lay out the day's gory details while collecting personal items from my office. "What did your dad say?"

"Basically told me to figure it out—his plate is full. Then he went off on how I should reconnect with Darcey as it would bring much-needed positive headlines."

"I hope you told him to get the fuck out of your love life."

"I did." My hand lands on a picture of Theo and me from the Tinsel and Tatas gala, which was snapped an hour before our lives fell apart. After showing it to him, I deposit it in the box of keepsakes. A ping from my cell phone catches my attention. Checking the screen, I roll my eyes.

"Who was that?"

"Not who. What. A stupid reminder about my b-school networking event tonight."

He holds up a framed certificate from the Chamber of Commerce to which I shake my head. Won't need it in the unemployment line. "I think you should go to the business school event."

I pause from adding another piece of memorabilia into the box. "Why? So I can be the poster boy for out-of-work losers?"

He approaches me. "No. Because you have to keep your chin up to show Hudson he doesn't faze you in the least. And you never know—you might get a lead on a job opportunity."

I turn my head away, my eyes landing on a sanitized piece of artwork, which is typical of VOW-cubed's decorating style. "Not how I want to spend my Thursday. Cold appetizers and watered-down drinks aren't on my agenda, especially after—"

He places his hand on my shoulder. "I understand. But what better way is there to show Hudson that he means nothing to you than attending this NYU thingy? Plus, shove it in your father's face, too."

Theo's words hang like a cloud bubble over my body. "News hasn't leaked about my leaving here, so I guess it would also be good to keep up appearances."

He checks his watch. "How long until the party starts?"

"Doors open at seven." Seems like I'm going to a party. I rub the back of my neck. "Can you help me pack first?"

"You got it."

* * *

My Rolex reads seven-thirty as I get out of the limo to attend the b-school's networking event at the trendy restaurant downtown. Despite Theo's best efforts, my mood is decidedly sour.

I cross the sidewalk and walk toward the front door, which is lined by reporters. Of course it is. With effort, I force my "pleasant face" mask into place and take a few steps. Offering a nod as I pass them, I stop to answer a couple of the more innocuous questions—and sideswipe the more probing ones.

"*Xander, how are your father and his partners holding up?*" I respond to this softball by putting the most positive spin on it as possible. "They're working hard to clear their names."

"*Xander, what's the atmosphere like at the office?*" I can take this one. "We're very busy keeping up with deadlines." Yup. My leaving VOW-cubed isn't public knowledge.

"*Xander, any truth to the rumors that the execs at VOW-cubed don't see eye-to-eye on whether to cut a deal with the Southern District of New York?*" What the fuck? I keep my smile schooled and focus on a different reporter who asks, "*Xander, do you feel your degree helped in your career, or did having the last name Turner do that all for you?*" Christ. I deflect with my response, "Education is always a positive enhancement. I was thrilled to earn my business degree from NYU and use the strategies I learned in class every day."

Okay, enough. I stride past the rest of the gauntlet and am gratified when I reach the door. Half-turning, I wave to the press and step into the sanctuary of the restaurant. Sans paps. Thank fuck.

I pause at the threshold to allow my vision to adjust to the dim, ambient lighting inside. A moment later, I approach the hostess. "Can you please direct me to the NYU Business School event?"

The woman, approximately five or six years my junior, glances up from the reservations book and her eyes glaze over. While I've been getting this reaction from women since I was a teenager, it's beyond annoying today. It's only a face. I have to keep playing the game, though. Not allowing my mask to falter, I force a smile.

The young hostess blinks, then her tongue swipes her plump lips. "It's, ah, in the Eastman Room." Her finger, complete with white nail polish with crystals on it, points off to the right.

I nod and take one step in that direction when her voice stops me. "Although, I could make it worth your while to skip that stuffy event."

Brazen. Never one of my turn-ons. And certainly not going to work now. "Thanks, but I've been looking forward to tonight for a long time. Have a good evening." I dip my chin while maintaining eye contact, then take measured steps toward the room she indicated. Drawing nearer to the entrance, I prepare for the crush of this networking event and dredge up my façade as an Assistant Vice President of Marketing. God, I hope Jesse is here. He said he was coming, although that was weeks ago.

I check in, donning a sticky name tag with Xander written in black Sharpie. Somehow, I doubt anyone will need to look at it.

The room is about three-quarters full when I enter. B-school alumni are a sociable lot, and tonight's similar to the other events I've attended—pre-indictment. As I travel deeper into the room, I ignore my classmate's whispers behind my back. I've gotten used to this treatment over the past couple of months, but it still stings. *I did nothing wrong.*

When I turn toward the bar, Madison Welch crosses my field of vision. The short, roundish woman wears a pair of black pants with a black shirt. Her blond hair's down, like usual. We never socialized when we were in school, but her rep as being scary smart intrigued me—especially since no one's ever accused me of the same. She started her own PR firm a few years ago, which I have to admit is cool. Being able to work with a wide variety of clients rather than being relegated to only VOW-cubed, always fascinated me. It never was an option.

Before.

Our paths have crossed over the years, but we're barely acquaintances. Saw her at the Tinsel and Tatas Gala before all hell broke loose. Even thought about reaching out to her agency to find out if they could help us out. *Not your problem anymore.*

"Glad to see you showed!" Jesse Dimon punches my shoulder.

I spin around and give my best friend from school a bro hug. My mood picks up—at least the evening's taken a turn for the better.

Even if my future is still unsettled.

Read the rest of Xander and Madison's story on Amazon now! http://geni.us/Sins3